PRAISE FOR RANDALL SILVIS AND *DOUBLY DEAD*!

"Randall Silvis is a masterful storyteller."
—*The New York Times Book Review*

"An extremely creepy thriller."
—*Booklist*

"Silvis laces his narrative with astute observations and hard truths."
—*Publishers Weekly*

A DANGEROUS PREY

The doctor leaned forward in his chair and spoke to Poe. "What kind of man, do you think, might be responsible for these crimes?"

A pause before Poe answered. "Brute," he said. "A savage brute."

Brunrichter nodded, then looked my way. "Would you agree?"

I was startled to be included like this, on an equal footing with these learned men. But I tried not to show my nervousness and to live up to the task. "Well, yes. An animal, to be sure. Who else could do such a thing?"

Again the doctor nodded, then leaned back in his chair. "Conceding that," he finally said, "by which I mean, conceding the brutish nature of the crimes, or at least the appearance of such, should we not also consider this brute a very clever fellow?"

I glanced at Poe, expecting his protest, but he merely sat there staring at the fire as before, his brow now furrowed.

Brunrichter continued, "To leave not a trace of evidence—I find that fact intriguing. No bodies, no buttons torn off and left behind, not so much as a single drop of blood to pinpoint exactly where one of the girls might have disappeared. The man must be a magician."

"This is what troubles me most," he said. "A dumb beast is easy to track. But one so guileful..."

DOUBLY DEAD

RANDALL SILVIS

LEISURE BOOKS  NEW YORK CITY

This book is for Rita and Bret and Nathan,
my respite and nepenthe,
evermore.

LEISURE BOOKS ®

December 2004

Published by

Dorchester Publishing Co., Inc.
200 Madison Avenue
New York, NY 10016

Originally published as *Disquiet Heart* by Thomas Dunne Books, an imprint of St. Martin's Press.

ISBN 0-8439-5477-9

Printed in the United States of America.

AUTHOR'S NOTE

Doubly Dead is a work of fiction. Although I have employed the names of real historical figures and actual places, and have made every effort to portray those people and places as accurately as possible, the descriptions in this book should not be construed as biography or fact. As is the case with all historical fiction, dates have been altered, personalities manipulated, realities reconfigured so as to best suit the narrative. As just one example, the real Dr. Brunrichter lived in Pittsburgh not in 1847, as depicted here, but around the turn of the twentieth cen-tury.

Few books are written by the author alone. This book certainly was not. As always, I thank my family for their succor and support, as I thank my agent, Peter Rubie, and my editors. Dr. Louis Boxer provided me with extensive information about the long-drop method of hanging as a means of execution and the possible consequences thereof. The Eccles-Lesher Library has cheerfully and unfailingly supplied, not only for this novel but for each of my previous books, numerous reference works and sources of information. My thanks to one and all.

DOUBLY DEAD

Come! Let the burial rite be read—the funeral song be sung!—
An anthem for the queenliest dead that ever died so young—
A dirge for her the doubly dead in that she died so young.

From "Lenore" by Edgar Allan Poe

Prologue

There exists a sketch of Poe that few have ever seen. It resides in a drawer in my library, and there it will remain until I hear the Grim One come scratching at my door, at which time I will consign that sketch, along with a few other more personal items, to the purity of the flames. I will do so not because the sketch would be, to the casual eye, repugnant or, for that matter, even provocative. It would no doubt be viewed as Poe intended it; a joke at his own expense, a lighthearted self-ridicule. But often men are not the best judges of themselves, not as keen-eyed or astute when gazing into the mirror as someone apart from them might be, especially someone who has already observed the man at his best and his worst, and who, for better or worse, has lived, if only briefly, inside that man's soul.

How do I view the sketch? you might ask. And also, if it is to be incinerated eventually, why not now?

Not now because it was rendered by Poe's own hand, and by retaining that yellowing piece of parchment I remain somehow connected to him even yet, more than half a century after the date of its composition. And even now I have a need for that connection. As to how I view the sketch: As the truest encapsulation of the journey we took together, that hoary fortnight spent between the confluence of two rivers, when each of us was looking for violence and found too much of it, and when each of us was challenging death to take us on, little realizing that we were already locked in its embrace.

It is a simple pencil sketch, drawn in the space of half an hour. Filling the foreground and both sides of the paper, stacked to a height representing a full ten feet and terraced like a wide staircase leading to empty sky, are four tiers of long wooden boxes made of pale, unpainted boards. Positioned in the center of this display, stretched out on the next to highest tier, is Poe. In a black linen suit he lies on his side, facing the viewer, right elbow on a wooden lid, head resting atop his hand, left knee bent and raised—as insouciant a position as if he were taking the sun on the Bowling Green, watching a Sunday parade of sails across the Hudson.

But he is on his way to Pittsburgh, and the boxes are coffins, all and more soon to be filled. At the bottom of the sketch, he titled it *The Conqueror Worm*.

He laughed when he handed the sketch over to me, when he gave it away so blithely, a half-hour's diversion, with the words, prophetic, "A little something to remember me by." I folded the paper in half and slipped it into a coat pocket, and then, fortuitously, forgot about it until many days later.

How that sketch came to be made, and how the two

of us, Poe and I, each came to a clearer understanding of what it might be like to lie not atop but inside one of those boxes, that is the story I am about to relate. Before my voice, too, is drowned out by the gnawing of the worms.

Chapter One

27 February 1847

My Dear Mr. Poe,

I write to you as no mere admirer of your work, but as one who has discerned in your essays and criticisms a singular honesty of intellect; and in your tales a willingness to plumb to the very depths, however rank, of human nature; and in your poetry a rare and penetrating acumen conjoined with an altogether unearthly music. I write to you, sir, as your devoted disciple. As such it is my hope and desire that you will consider an invitation to visit me here in Pittsburgh and thence to remain as a guest in my house for as long as you might choose to do so.

As incentive I offer you a speaking engagement before an enthusiastic audience, to be presented by the Quintillian Society, on whose board I am privileged to serve as president. As remuneration we will gladly provide your usual stipend and a more than usual attention to your every word. You may address us on the subject of your choice. We have in the past hosted to great success other writers whose names you will recognize, as for example Messrs. Dickens and Longfellow and Bulwer-Lytton, all of whom we lavished upon but a modicum of the enthusiasm with which you will be greeted.

Moreover, while a guest in my home you will want for nothing. I am a man of ample means, all of which I shall endeavor to employ in the furtherance of your comfort. You will not want for edifying company, sir, of either gender, for your admirers here are many. However, if solitude is what you crave, that, too, shall be yours.

I pray you will not consider it indelicate if I extend to you my condolences on the loss of your young wife in the early days of this year. I do so only to ensure you that I am well aware of a man's special needs in the wake of such misfortune, and to make it known to you that each and every one of those needs will be provided for here in Pittsburgh.

In closing, Mr. Poe, allow me to confess that though we have yet to meet vis-à-vis, I consider you my brother in spirit. Many among my acquaintances have remarked upon the striking similarity of countenance we share, while others have gone so far as to suspect your writings as my own, composed under the nom de plume of E. A. Poe. In my estimation these conjectures scarcely scratch the surface of the bond we share, for it is my belief, sir, that you and I are reflections of the same spirit. We are closer than brothers. More alike than twins. We are the same man in two bodies. We drink the same air of devastation.

You will not, I pray, be put off by this assumption of familiarity on my part. Only know that the kinship I feel for you, derived through the study of and esteem for your work, is both real and profound.

In my own line of work I have occasion to witness numerous variations of unnatural behavior. These, too, we might discuss and analyze during our time together, should you agree to accept my humble invitation. Such discussions will be to my edification, I am sure. Though perhaps it is not overly presumptive to suggest that one or two of my scientific investigations into the grayer realms of the disquiet heart might provide inspiration to your own endeavors. For I suspect that our labors, like our temperaments, are of a kind, sir, though conducted by different means. You employ the pen whereas I the scalpel. But we are nonetheless embarked upon the same journey, you and I. We can perhaps provide for one another not only pleasant company but some assistance along the way.

I await your response and the consummation of a brotherhood.

Yours most sincerely,
Alfred K. Brunrichter, M.D.

The sunlight of the late afternoon fell across my hand and across the single sheet of ivory parchment as I read this letter, fell upon the handwriting composed in a tight but elegant script, the lettering so precise as to seem almost feminine. Yet the soft yellow light did little to warm or brighten the dark chill in me.

"It isn't more bad news, I hope," said Mr. Longreve. "Edgar has had enough of that to last him a lifetime."

I did not answer for a while but stood there in Longreve's office, my shoulder near the window, as I stared at the letter and tried to fathom the sudden lassitude I felt. After a half minute or so I told myself that I was merely weary, a simple fatigue from the long journey that, I realized, was not yet over.

"No, no, in fact it is good news. An invitation for Poe to read. In Pittsburgh." Yet even as I refolded the letter, some backwater tug of gravity pulled at me, weakening my legs.

"But it tells you nothing of his whereabouts?"

I shook my head. "It does not."

Mr. Longreve, an editor for *Godey's Lady's Book*, stood with his back to the window, a hand to his cheek, rubbing up and down. The letter had been sent in care of his office, and he seemed more than a little relieved now to entrust it into my care. He told me that he had not spoken with Poe for the past several weeks. Poe's young wife, Virginia, had passed on January 30th. A few days later he had escorted the girl's mother back to the comfort of family and home in Richmond, Virginia, promising to return to Manhattan at the earliest possibility. It was now the third week of March, and Longreve's only word from him had been a telegram dated February 19th, in which Poe stated that he would be interrupting his return to New York City with a brief stopover in Philadelphia, for reasons he did not provide.

"May I take the letter with me?" I asked.

"Will you go to Philadelphia?"

"I don't know where else to look for him. It seems the logical choice."

"You might try the *Dollar Newspaper*," he said. "He's published there. They may have an address for him."

I nodded and slipped the letter into my coat pocket.

"I can only pray that no further misfortune has befallen him."

My knowledge of Poe, though now some seven years

old, suggested that if misfortune had waylaid him in Philadelphia, it was the misfortune of his own proclivities.

In the summer of 1840 I had lived with Poe awhile, for a few frantic but fecund days that had changed my life. I was then a ten-year-old street arab, a sticky-fingered liar and thief upon whom Serendipity shined one day by making me the only witness to a young woman's desperate leap into the Hudson. The attempted suicide brought numerous curious onlookers to the site, one of them a threadbare journalist in search of a story. Poe took a liking to me, and I to him, and the peculiar bond of kinship we felt for one another was strengthened further upon our mutual discovery of the pale and bloated body of a second young woman, Miss Mary Rogers, that had become lodged beneath the pier.

In any case, Poe had plucked me out of the gutter and invited me to his home on Bloomingdale Road, there to live temporarily with him and his lovely sweet Virginia and their bastion of steadfastness, Virginia's mother, Mrs. Clemm. Later he arranged for my placement on a farm in western Ohio. Over the next seven years, all three members of the Poe household had written to me regularly, Poe's letters more philosophical than intimate, subtly affectionate admonitions that I remain on the straight and narrow, that I keep my nose to the grindstone, that I do not fritter away life's opportunities for success. More often than not the letter was accompanied by a book he could ill afford, sent, he always wrote, "in the furtherance of your education." The more strident the admonitions contained in his letters, the more desperate, I somehow knew, was his own situation.

Virginia's letters, on the other hand, those sweet epistles from Sissie, were invariably bright if empty chronicles of the day's weather, which flowers or fruit trees were in bloom, or, in winter, the ones she most looked forward to seeing in bloom once again. There was little else for her to talk about; she seldom left the house; she seldom could.

It was Muddy, Mrs. Clemm, who kept me apprised of the family's true condition. She sent copies of the few stories and poems Poe managed to get published (this was how I learned that he had honored me by transforming the humble name of Augie Dubbins into C. Auguste Dupin, literature's first investigator of crime!). Muddy also kept me apprised of Sissie's slow decline, of how the tuberculosis in her lungs grew steadily stronger and she weaker, of Poe's occasional retreat into drink, the disorienting highs and lows of his manic optimism and his bottomless despair.

Muddy's letters were always long and intimate but never mournful. She seldom referred to herself or to her regimen of daily chores, the ceaseless ordeal of caring for the two individuals she loved most in all the world. I was, I'm sure, her only confidante. Yet not a word of complaint did she send my way. Every letter opened with the address, "My good and lovely boy," and closed with, "Until we meet again, dear Augie." Small wonder that my heart broke anew with every letter she wrote.

It did not cross my mind, not once in those hard seven years, nor in the years to follow, until too late, that I would never again behold this woman who had mothered me more truly in a few short days than any other woman ever had or would.

Her letters became a model for my own infrequent responses to the Poes. Because Poe had set me up in this position to divert me from a life of squalor and crime, I never wrote to complain about the grueling, endless work, the meager victuals, the friction, like grit rubbing grit, between me and Deidendorf, the brutish farmer to whom I was apprenticed. "Just because you come from New York City don't mean you know your ass from a hole in the ground" was one of his favorite endearments for me.

All this I kept to myself. If I wrote, "We put in three hundred bales of rye today," I hoped that Poe would somehow intuit my blisters and itch, the dead ache between my shoulderblades. If I wrote, "Deidendorf thinks I'm lazy, but I'm working as hard as I can," I prayed that Poe would close his eyes and envision the new bruises laid on my chest by Deidendorf's fist, or the blood dried on my scalp from when my employer had dragged me halfway across a field by my hair.

A part of me believed that by not giving voice to misery I was sparing Poe an extra concern, of which he had too many already. But another part of me filled every dispassionate letter with tears and silent pleas.

Then came Muddy's final letter to me, dated 4 February 1847:

My good and lovely boy,

Our beautiful songbird is gone at last. What a sweetness of voice she will add to the choir in Heaven. But it is hard on our Eddie, I'm afraid. He is at a loss to know what to do with himself. He could use a true companion now. As could we all.

Until me meet again, dear Augie,
My love is with you Always.
Your Muddy

The farm where I had been working, where I had been all but enslaved the past seven years, lay, like most northern farms in February, in a relative ease. There was as always livestock to be fed and tended, repairs on buildings to be made, equipment to be readied for spring, but the eight hundred acres of wheat and corn and potato fields slept under fifteen inches of hard-crusted snow. Still, Henry Deidendorf refused to grant me leave.

But I was seventeen that winter, or close to it. I was more than willing to grant myself leave. My old skills as grifter and pickpocket had not been abandoned completely when I became a farmer, and over the years I had managed to squirrel away a nice bit of traveling money. In truth, even before Muddy's letter arrived, I was itching to find a new home. All I had needed was some news of a wagoner heading south, for I had my heart set on Mexico and the conflict there. In May of the previous year President Polk had convinced Congress to declare war on Mexico, and with that declaration my own manifest destiny had been assigned a destination.

I was not a farmer, never had been, never would be, no matter how long and hard Deidendorf worked me. I had no love for neat rows of freshly turned soil. My spirit did not soar at the stench of fresh cow manure. I longed for dry ground beneath my feet, dry air in my lungs. After seven years I had had seven years too much of pig shit, horse shit, cow shit, and chicken shit, of defecation of any species, which I then had to shovel from stall to wheelbarrow to field, acre after unending acre of steaming manure shoveled and spread, scraped off my boots, picked from under my fingernails. I longed for the clean clash of steel, the sharp aridity of gunpowder.

Yes, I admit to a bloodthirst that year. My favorite days were those Sundays when Deidendorf sent me out with his small-bore shotgun to bring home a brace of pheasants, rabbits, or squirrels. I even enjoyed the act of gutting and skinning, of handling the still-warm corpses of bare meat. A lifetime of anger, I suppose, was boiling away inside me, seeking a vent.

Then came Muddy's final letter. It arrived weeks after its date of composition and had probably spent a good portion of that time crammed into a pigeonhole in Deidendorf's desk before he deigned to give it to me. I read the letter at the end of a workday, promptly requested leave from my employer, was refused with a laugh and a snort, and, at shortly after midnight that same night, cleaned out my trunk and began the long trek east.

For spite I stole Deidendorf's favorite saddle from the tack room, a black leather affair with red-and-tan inlays. But after a mile or so the stink of him imbedded in the leather was too nauseating to bear, so I tossed the saddle into an icy creek and strode away feeling very nearly weightless.

An hour after dawn, some fifteen miles or so east of my jailer, I flagged down a coach heading for Columbus and paid my fare. In this manner, walking when necessary, hailing a wagon or coach when I could, I covered the distance in thirteen days. Had I known that a new rail line ran from Pittsburgh to Philadelphia I might have veered south and shortened my trip considerably (only to learn, after landing in Gotham, that Poe was in fact somewhere back in the city of brotherly love!). As it was I kept to the north, across the uppermost forests of Pennsylvania, the midreaches of New Jersey, and finally into the state of New York. When I finally hit Manhattan in midday I went directly to Poe's last address there. I did my best to ignore the way the city sang to me, the welcome I felt in its clamor and chaos. I tried to ignore the way my mouth watered each time I caught a whiff from a corn brazier or a pastry shop. I felt like a soldier home from war, and I even began to wonder if maybe the fighting in Mexico could do without me.

But then I found another family living where I expected to find Poe and Mrs. Clemm. And my sense of homecoming turned cold.

That was when I turned to the downtown offices of *Godey's Lady's Book*, where Poe had published several pieces. The first editor I spoke to, the man named Longreve, recognized my name, said that Poe had spoken of me often. All this I found warming. Until the news that Poe had gone incommunicado somewhere between Philadelphia and New York.

"If you find him," was the last thing Longreve said to me, as he pressed a dollar into my hand, "send a wire immediately. If he has no intention of returning, or can't, well . . . the man's not indispensable. Tell him that for me."

But he was as worried about Poe as I; his eyes shone dark with concern.

I walked away, exhausted. *Poe alone in Philadelphia*—the implications were staggering. He was not a man cut out for the solitary life. Bereft of Virginia's adoration, devoid of Muddy's steadying solidity, the only place Poe could turn for succor was to his own mind. Unfortunately, that dark labyrinth concealed far fewer pleasures than pitfalls.

Chapter Two

Next morning I left for Philadelphia by rail and arrived in the city midday. Straightaway then to the address Longreve had supplied. An editor informed me that he had indeed spoken with Mr. Poe, who had come to inquire of the newspaper's interest in publishing "a longish piece" not yet composed.

The gist of the proposed composition, which Poe had described as a poetical essay, was not, the man told me, easy to grasp. "He claimed it to be an explanation of the universe in toto." The editor smiled and shook his head. "Only a man in Poe's condition would ever presume to conceive of such a work."

"His condition being what?" I asked.

His answer was to lower his chin so as to look at me over the rims of his spectacles.

"Are you saying that he was in his cups?"

"I am saying what I said."

I nodded. The man would say no more because even a drunken Poe inspired a degree of respect. I asked, "Did he happen to mention where he is making his residence while in Philadelphia?"

"He did not. But it could not have been far. I asked that he commit his plan for the composition to paper so that I might better understand it. He agreed to do the same that very evening. And, seeing as it was nearly dark already, I offered to convey him there in my carriage. He demurred. Said that he could be seated at his desk, writing, before I could summon a hack."

He turned in his chair then, facing the window, and pointed south. "The closest hotel is there across the street. But I would suggest that you try two blocks farther on. The rates, you know. More moderate. More . . . suitable to his means."

"And since that day a fortnight ago. You have not seen him since?"

He eyed me critically for a moment, as if trying to determine whether to speak freely or to hold his tongue. I think he read the worry in my eyes.

"You know Mr. Poe well, do you?"

"I think I know him as well as anyone can."

He wanted to smirk at that remark, that presumption from a stripling, but confined his mouth to all but a twitch at one corner. One of Poe's most endearing qualities is that every person he meets, whether in person or through his compositions, soon comes to believe that he or she, better than any other, has peered into the very heart of the man. In truth they have had only a fleeting glimpse into their own heart.

"I did see him one other time, yes. A few days after we spoke." Again he turned to the window. "He was right out there. Standing dead still in the middle of the street."

"He had paused in the middle of the street?"

"Paused? Yes, call it that if you will. He had paused in the middle of the street, at the busiest hour of the day. Horses and carts and carriages and omnibuses coming and going in both directions. Drivers and passengers alike giving him an earful. Yet there he stood, hands clasped behind his back. Coat unbuttoned. Hair uncombed. For all appearances, deaf to the world."

Something in the man's tone, some slight edge of ridicule, made me long to throttle him, to feel my fists against his face. Instead I asked, "And you did not go to him?"

Had he offered me any type of smug retort, I would have bashed him. I stood ready to do so. But he said nothing. He continued to stare out the window.

I turned on my heels and started for the door. He mumbled something, and I stopped.

"Pardon me?"

"I should have," he said, still not looking at me. "I wish that I had."

Pity and contempt, these were the emotions Poe so often aroused. Admiration and disdain.

I vacated the office without another word.

As for Poe, I found him two hours later. The Nevens Inn. A tavern and dining room on the first floor, "Sleeping Quarters for Travelling Gentlemen" on the second and third. It was not the most objectionable of such establishments in the city, but few could have bested its air of dishabille, its foot-worn, uneven hallway, the peeling flocked paper on its walls, the piebald ceilings brown-stained and sagging. Odors of fried fat and spilled ale accounted for at least half of the breathable atmosphere.

In the hallway of the uppermost floor I stood outside room 6, having been directed there by the barman downstairs, who, though he did not recognize Poe's name, recognized him by my description. Poe's was one of only two rooms on this truncated level, a level that was in fact an attic, now partitioned into a pair of tiny rooms. From behind the door of the adjoining room, two feet to my left, came the rasp of a phlegmy cough.

And I could not help thinking to myself that even in this city, the Athens of America, Poe had managed to ensconce himself in an external ambiance to match his inner one.

I rapped on the door, and was answered with silence.

I knocked a second time. "Mr. Poe, it's Augie Dubbins," I said. "I apologize for not getting here sooner, but I left Ohio the moment I received—"

Before I could finish the door flew open. And there stood Poe. He was dressed only in an old dun banyan, an overcoat, over cotton undergarments and stockings. How frail he looked, how pale and thin. He had the eyes of a ghost.

Yet as he stood there and scrutinized me, his hand still on the door but otherwise unmoving, as we took each other in, as we allowed the images of a seven-year-old memory to juxtapose themselves upon the realities there before us, his eyes began to glisten, as did my own. Neither of us moved for several moments. Until finally I smiled.

And then Poe did what I had never before seen him do, and never saw again. He began to tremble, to quiver head-to-toe with a frozen rigidity. And then to weep.

And then this man who had long ago offered me the first hand I had ever shaken, this man who had been the first to treat me as a human being, who in a few cherished days had lavished sufficient attention and affection on a cast-away boy to see him through another hard spell of abuse, this man held out his arms to me, he wept at the sight of me, and he staggered forward into my hungry embrace.

* * *

We needed little time to get reacquainted. Too many of the past seven years could be reduced to a few sentences. My time had consisted wholly of hard work, day in and day out. With each passing year, more work had been piled on. As for Poe, despite his sudden but nonetheless unremunerative success with "The Raven," he was still battling editors and publishers for every dime, still trying to stretch that dime the length of a dollar. He had worked for various magazines but always departed in a rush out the same dark door, the one sprung open by harsh words and accusations, intemperance and an inability to compromise. And, each time, he had straggled home to be faced with his wife's decline, to watch her soft pale face contort, those eyes of purest sweetness squeeze shut, every time she coughed up another piece of her lungs.

"The peculiar thing," he confided to me, huddled in his banyan on the edge of the narrow plank bed, having insisted that I take the only chair in the room, my back to the sooty window, "the peculiar thing is that it is all over now, all of that life, and I . . . I am at a loss as to know how to feel about it. The times I thought her dead, Augie, I could not count for you the times. I would look at her motionless on her bed, and put my hand to her cheek and feel only coldness. And I would grieve, I would keen like an old woman. Only to have her look at me again, and smile, and whisper hoarsely that she was merely resting for a while. Other times, for days at a time, she seemed on the very precipice of death. So many times I thought to myself, *She will not last the night*. But then, suddenly, a morning or two later, there was my Sissie back again, sitting up and asking for some tea."

He put both hands to his unshaven cheeks, and

rubbed hard, pulling the skin up and down as if he hoped to rub away his own countenance. "For years now, Augie, *years*, I have lived through her death every few months or so, every few weeks. And now that it has finally happened, can you imagine what I feel?"

"I cannot. Only what I feel."

"You feel loss," he said. "As do I. A bottomless, swirling loss that is trying its best to pull me in." He now leaned toward me, leaned forward and laid both hands atop my knees, gripped them hard, and spoke in a hiss of breath, with nothing but a sour contempt for himself and his words, "But I also feel . . . *relief*."

He read the look in my eyes. "It is shocking to myself as well," he said. "Shocking and loathsome. I have done all I can to exorcise the feeling, but sometimes, upon waking, when I first remember that she is gone, it rushes over me, this sudden ease, a sense of freedom, and then, just as suddenly, just as powerfully, comes the contempt I feel for having allowed myself such a thought. The certainty that I am a wholly detestable man."

"But surely, after such an ordeal . . . it isn't so unnatural a sentiment as you imagine. It is an honest sentiment. She no longer suffers. Her anguish is over. It is for Sissie that you are relieved."

He waved this away, chased it away with a fling of his hand. He did not wish to be absolved.

Then his hand dropped onto his own lap again and his body sagged. He closed his eyes as if expelling a last breath, and sat motionless, crumpled over. Half a minute later he lifted his head and looked at me anew, and tried hard for a smile.

"But enough of this for now. Tell me about yourself. I cannot believe how tall you've grown, a full three inches taller than me, if my eyes are not mistaken. With you, at least, it appears that I did something right. That my efforts were not misdirected."

If he needed to take some credit—or solace, compensation, whatever you wish to call it—for the fact that I was now a healthy young man nearly six feet tall, I was not about to deny him it. So I said nothing about the hatred I felt for the man and his wife in whose care I had been placed. Both were severe and coarse individuals. Together they possessed not a drop of human kindness, but measured out their days, and mine, in the number of bales stacked in their barn, the bushels of grain and corn and potatoes hauled off to market, the pounds of bloody meat slaughtered, the miles of intestines stuffed and strung up to dry. I had measured those same days in bloody blisters, broken fingernails, sunburn and thirst, headache, and hunger.

There had been three of us who worked the farm for Deidendorf, and I the youngest, the only hand under thirty, so all of his bullying had fallen upon me. His favorite motivational tool was his carbine, which he carried in a sling over his back wherever he went. When I was not moving quickly enough to suit him, or whenever he was bored, he liked to fire a shot at my feet, sending up dirt and splinters of rock to pelt my pant leg. The two other farmhands, Pike and Wiley, assured me over exhausted games of euchre that they had received similar treatment, but only as long as they had allowed it to continue.

"One of these days you'll have had enough," they told me. "Soon's you're at the right age for it. He'll be doing the same things he's always done, and you'll have had your fill of it all of a sudden for no other reason than that you're sick of yourself for taking it so long. And he'll see that look in your eyes when you turn and look at him. And he'll stop."

"What look?" I had asked.

"The one that says, 'You ever do that again and I'll take it as an invitation to break your goddamn neck.' "

"I'd like to do that already. To him and his ugly wife both."

"You'd like to, but you ain't ready to."

"I'm ready," I told them.

"Not yet. Won't be long though."

But instead of committing a double murder I slipped away in the middle of the night. I stole his favorite saddle and tossed it horn down in the middle of a creek. But I still wanted to kill him. I still dreamed of driving a pitchfork into his chest. And just last night, the night before I had located Poe, as I slept I'd heard that familiar gunshot exploding in my ear, felt the sting of dirt splattering my leg, and I had all but leapt out of my bed, blinded by rage.

None of this, of course, could I share with Poe, lest he assume that guilt on top of the burden he already shouldered.

I told him, "It was just as you promised. Do you remember what you used to tell me? Hard work and fresh air would stand me in good stead. Well, I had plenty of both."

He smiled and nodded. "I cannot tell you how pleased I am to hear of it. And you have kept up with your reading?"

"Thanks to you and Muddy and Sissie, I did. I only wish I could have brought all your books back with me."

"They are your books, not mine. Besides, you did indeed bring them all with you, did you not?" With a fingertip, he tapped the side of his head.

"Yes, and it is getting to be a crowded place in there. Aristotle, Plato, Thucydides. Dante, Homer, Hawthorne, Shakespeare . . . It's like one big literary salon in there, everybody talking at once."

This much, at least, was true. The sun-baked brown of my skin and the roughness of my hands, the hard musculature of my shoulders and back, all these marked me as a commoner, a laborer. But thanks to Poe I was a peasant with the mind of a professor. I could speak the idiom of a prim New England Bible-thumper as easily as the vernacular of the unwashed illiterate. Either one while, boiling away inside of me, beat the heart of a murderer.

"And what next for you?" he asked. "You cannot go back to the farm now, can you? It is time for you to move on, to move forward."

"Speaking of which, how about if you get dressed and we go out for a bite to eat." His room was dark and chill and stale, it stank of alcohol, it reeked of despair. I wanted both of us out of it.

"You go," he said. "I have no appetite."

"We'll take a walk first. You can show me the city."

He shook his head. "I have no strength for the kind of idle walking we used to do."

"It needn't be idle. Isn't this a city of museums, of art and science and all the nobler pursuits of man?"

"You would never know it by me," he said.

Whether he meant by this that he had not availed himself of those pleasures here, or if the nobler pursuits no longer existed in him, I did not know. But in either case I considered it imperative to get him moving again, despite the weariness of my own legs. Our best times together, the ones I most liked to recall, were of when he and I were on the march. Side by side we had traversed every acre of Manhattan. And now he had imprisoned himself in this one tiny cell.

"Take me to see the Liberty Bell," I said.

"Augie, I have no strength for it. The truth be told, I have no interest. It all smacks of futility to me. Futility and arrogance. Every puny endeavor of man."

"But I'm staying only a day or two. And then I'm off to Mexico."

At this his eyes brightened. I was more wary of than pleased by the sudden smolder in his eyes. "You intend to join the fray?" he asked.

"I do."

"I have considered the same myself. And why not? What holds me here?"

"You mean . . . you wish to fight?"

"You think me incapable? Too old? I can hold a carbine and wield a saber, I promise you that." His voice had risen with this declaration, grew adamant. But now he paused. His face softened. He smiled like a man imagining a restful sleep. "Not that I would have to do so for long, of course."

A shudder ran through me. "We need to get out of this room, sir. We need to find some good air and some good food."

"I have been following the dispatches," he said. "The accounts in the newspaper. Do you know how many West Point men are there already? A man named Lee, Robert Lee, the son of Light Horse Harry, he is there with General Scott. His chief engineer. He graduated from West Point one year before I entered. I could be there with them now had I kept my wits about me. I could have been with Taylor at Buena Vista. And I should have been, Augie. I realize that now. This other life I chose, this effete, cerebral life . . . What has it availed?"

"You are a writer, not a soldier."

"Not what I am but what I might have been!" he raged, his answer an explosion that set me back in my chair. "Had I not disgraced myself! Had I not frittered away every opportunity! Well, I have one opportunity left, and I mean to take advantage of it."

I had nothing to say. I sat there stunned by his outburst.

But just as quickly as the storm had raged, it now dissipated. His voice softened, and once again he leaned toward me and spoke in little more than a whisper, as if to plot a conspiracy. "Which of the men down there, do you think, will be best remembered?"

"Are you asking me for a name?"

"Not a name but a deed. Whom will posterity preserve and cherish in its memory? The many who march en masse—doing their duties as good soldiers, but only that duty and nothing more—dying, as soldiers often do, by the hundreds?"

I waited.

"Or those few who will lead the charge? Those few out front who drive the point of each attack?"

So this was what he had been thinking about through all his dark hours. This was the worm that had burrowed into his brain.

"I could win a commission, Augie, I am certain I could. An old West Point cadet—even one so disgraced. Who are they to turn me away? And my name—I am not unknown, Augie. I have a certain fame. A West Point man is a well-read man; they will have heard of me."

"Of course," I said, though I wanted to keep silent.

"And just think of the good that can be done for their cause by a famous man who has nothing to lose. A man with nothing to lose has nothing to fear, am I correct? And this is the quality, precisely the quality that renders a man a hero. Think of the glory to be attained! Imagine such a man bravely leading a charge, grinning, as it were, in the teeth of Death. Eventually he will be struck down, certainly. But until that moment he would appear immortal. And afterward . . . A man such as that would be remembered forever. No critic would ever dare castigate his name."

He sat smiling at me now, waiting for my collaboration, my acquiescence of his dreadful plan. His smile was black and his eyes were black and the air of that very room was black and thick with dreams of death.

I gave it consideration, I admit to that. But I had no intention of dying in Mexico. To be an agent of death, yes, of course. To slash and shoot until all the hatred had been expunged from me. But beyond that, all I could think of were the many pleasures of life I had not yet sampled, all the places and wonders not yet experienced, the sensual delights, the joys of the flesh. Cigars, thick steaks, fine wines, pastries dripping with icing. . . . My revenge, somehow, on Deidendorf.

And women. Women and revenge—the thought of either made me flush with desire. Even the battles I hoped awaited me in Mexico, even these I had thought of as pleasures to come.

As for Poe, I considered it best to placate him. He was in no state for disagreements.

"You make a good point," I told him. "And we must discuss it further. Lay out our plans. In the meantime, I have to eat, I'm starving. Come out with me. Or at the least, downstairs."

"No, no, I can't. There is too much light this time of day. My eyes are weak."

"You've been inside too long."

"Tomorrow perhaps. If the sun is not so bright."

I knew that he would not be moved. "I will bring something back for you."

"I have no appetite, Augie. Go tend to yourself. But come back, you must come back. The bed is yours. I am more comfortable in the chair."

It was how he had slept with Virginia all those years, in a chair pulled close to her bed. And now, to see him reduced like this, virtually wallowing in his mire of loss . . .

Not that I had ever succumbed to blind hero worship. Even as a boy I had been too clear-eyed and cynical for that. But his flaws as much as his virtues were what I had admired, his bullheadedness and arrogance, an uncompromising belief in himself. Yet he sat now thinking wistfully of death, of suicide at the hands of a Mexican soldier as his last chance for glory.

Those slow swirls of nausea in my stomach—they were not caused by hunger.

"So tell me," I said. "Since last I heard from you, what have you written?"

Poe laughed, sourly, something very like a snarl on his lips. "My own epitaph. 'Here lies Poe. Nobody saw him go.' "

"Seems to me," I began, then paused, searching for the right approach, the least accusative way to say this, and then finally gave up on circumlocution. "You might feel better if you were to go back to your writing. Didn't you tell me once that a man's work is his dignity?"

"If there is dignity to be had. Which there is not. Not in this business of writing. Publishers cheat you, editors coerce you, critics assail you, the public ignores you."

"Then perhaps you should find other work."

"I am not suited for other work. Augie, please, I do not wish to be angry with you. But you are attempting to discuss a subject of which you have no knowledge. Therefore it is a subject you should let drop."

But I could not. "Aren't you the man who wrote 'The Raven'? *Gordon Pym? The Masque of the Red Death?*" With every title mentioned, he flinched.

He said, "Dip your bucket all you wish, but the well is dry."

In the end, so as to avoid further argument, I went out. But not without qualms, as if, somehow, in the space of thirty minutes, I had become his keeper. It was a role I did not much relish, but who else remained? Virginia was gone, Muddy had returned to Richmond. And Poe was one of those unfortunate men who can never be complete when alone, who must always have a student, a reader, an editor, a mirror in whose eyes he can see himself reflected and therefore know himself to exist. He needed always another person in life to provide him ballast, lest he fall sideways off the world and slip away on his own gravity, engulfed in the blackness of his own bottomless pit.

An hour or so later I returned to his room, belly full and pockets crammed. A small sausage pie wrapped in brown paper. A half-loaf of pumpkin bread. And the letter from Dr. Brunrichter.

Initially I laid only the food atop the little table at the foot of his bed.

Poe, now seated in the chair I had earlier vacated, looked at the parcels with his head cocked, a hand to his cheek, his eyebrows raised as if he expected the food to do something other than just sit there.

I was pleased to see that he had washed his face in my absence and had run a brush through his hair. He had even put on a shirt beneath his banyan, though he had not bothered with a collar. Still, if my presence could precipitate even this much activity at first, then perhaps I could do him some good after all.

"You should taste the meat pie," I told him. "While it's still warm. I had two of them myself."

It took him awhile to stand and cross to the table. He put a finger and thumb to the pie's wrapping, then laid the paper back to expose the browned crust. "My stomach is uneasy," he said. "I appreciate your kindness, but . . ."

"Try a few bites at least."

He did not look at me when he asked, "Have you brought anything to wash it down with?"

"I think maybe you've washed down enough for a while."

He turned a harsh eye on me then, but found me smiling. And in a few moments he smiled in return. "As outspoken as ever in your advanced age, I see."

"Please eat," I told him. "I'm standing here stuffed to the gills, but you—you look as if you haven't had a meal in days. If you are hoping to starve yourself to death, you might as well know that it isn't going to work. Because the moment you lapse into unconsciousness, I'm going to cram you full of meat pies."

I delivered this statement with the lightness of a joke, and was pleased to see his smile widen by an inch at one corner. But then he held the smile too long, until his mouth began to quiver. He drew a hand through his hair, pushing hard as if to drive a thought away, his eyes growing damp. I saw him then as a man on the very edge of collapse, and I went to him, I laid a hand upon his arm.

He said, "There is such an emptiness inside of me now. So vast, so . . ." He shook his head. "And not only because of Sissie, not only that. But everything. All of it. The full frivolity of it, the folly of my life. Such a sorrowful little have I accomplished. So little good have I managed to do."

"Not true," I began, but he drew away, turned away from me and lurched back to his chair and fell into it. "My life, Augie, the whole of my life. It has been nothing but a mistake, beginning to end."

What was I to say to this? Should I have pointed out his accomplishments? Counted off the stories and poems and essays written, the books published? He would have opened his hands and spread them palm up to show me what all that work had won for him. A cheap room and a checkered reputation. No, I could point to nothing in his past that might bring him pleasure.

"I must go to Mexico," he said.

"Then fine, we'll go together. There is surely an office in Philadelphia where you can apply for your commission. And in the meantime—"

He held up a hand to cut me off. "I deserve no commission. No honors for me." And now he nodded, strangely pleased with himself. "I will go peddling my wares in the morning. I will sell every manuscript I have, if necessary, for a penny a page. In exchange for my passage south."

"I have a better idea. We can leave for Mexico from Pittsburgh." At this I lifted Brunrichter's letter from my pocket and tossed it onto Poe's lap.

His movements were lugubrious and painful to watch. I willed myself not to move nor say a word as he first gazed down at the paper without touching it, then cocked his head slightly so as to better read the lettering, then slipped a finger along the edge so as to lay the letter open.

"I went looking for you at *Godey's*," I explained. "A Mr. Longreve gave me that letter. We had hoped it might shed some light on your whereabouts. Otherwise we would not have opened it."

He did not nod, gave me no absolution for invading his privacy. What he did was to turn toward the window, better to catch the fading light. He then shook the folded paper open, and read.

I watched his eyes. They narrowed at first, but soon began to widen. It wasn't long before the corners of his tired mouth began to lift. The furrows eased out of his forehead.

There was life in him yet.

The change was immediate. That first evening together, while he nibbled at the sausage pie and pumpkin loaf, nibbled until both had disappeared—rediscovering with every nibble, it seemed, his appetite for the next—he spoke with greater and greater animation, holding to his original plan of ending this grievous journey of life in Mexico, but now with the added diversion of Pittsburgh and the money he would earn there, enough to secure our passage in comfort on a steamboat down the Ohio, then onward down the Mississippi all the way to the land of scorpions and saguaro. He spoke of leaving a last impression of himself as a writer and a thinker, of triumphing at the lectern, chilling his audience with the final awful cadences of the raven's beak against the window glass, of driving that beak into their hearts. He was well aware of the effect his poem could have on an audience, and knew well the macabre enhancement of the effect that had been provided by Sissie's death.

By the end of his first hour of speculation he had once again deemed himself worthy of a commission in the army, had all but appointed himself a lieutenant, with me as his adjutant. By the close of the second hour we had captured Santa Ana and were wondering aloud what to do with him.

He held Brunrichter's letter aloft and shook it in the air. "This!" he said. "This is *my* manifest destiny! Who would ever have thought salvation would call to me from a place such as Pittsburgh?"

In the celadon dimness of the room, with the sun now lost below the horizon, I answered with a smile. Had I possessed but an inkling of the actual destiny that awaited both of us in Pennsylvania, the agonies of flesh and heart that lay ahead, I would have torn that letter from his hand and reduced it to indecipherable pieces.

Chapter Three

He awoke me early, a light tug on my wrist. I opened my eyes to see him standing washed and dressed beside the bed, he in his black trousers and coat, the boiled shirt not radiantly clean but with collar attached, the room pink with morning light—the first sunrise I had missed in a good many years.

"A busy day ahead," he told me. "While you pull yourself together I'll be sending a wire to Dr. Brunrichter in Pittsburgh, informing him of our arrival within the week. If you will meet me downstairs in thirty minutes, there will be tea and buckwheat cakes waiting on the table."

I pushed myself onto an elbow. "You're looking spry this morning."

"Spry?" He laughed and slapped my hip. "I've returned from the maelstrom!" With that he went out the door and left me to make myself ready for the day.

And what a day it was. By the time I joined him in the tavern downstairs, its walls and ceiling smoke-stained, floor none too clean, the whole of it dimly illuminated by a few oil lamps and a dull-looking fire in the fieldstone fireplace, he was still grinning, apparently pleased to be alive again, even proud of himself for his feat of self-resuscitation.

As I pulled a chair to the table I asked, "You sent the wire?"

"And made a stop at the White Swan Hotel as well, where the Pioneer Transportation Line maintains an office. I have booked two seats for the Monday departure"—this day was a Friday. "We shall be in Pittsburgh by suppertime Thursday."

"I don't know much about Pittsburgh," I said.

"I expect to find it a primitive place. But stimulating nonetheless." He poured tea from a small cast-iron pitcher into a large clay mug, and slid the mug into my hand.

I nodded at the bulging satchel beside him on the floor. "Your laundry?" I asked.

"And I thought I could escape my critics by fleeing New York!"

He laughed at his own joke, to which I smiled, but uneasily, for there seemed something vaguely off balance about his humor that morning, something excessive and unhealthy. I was reminded of the bright blush of Virginia's cheeks when I first met her, a rosy glow placed there, I'd thought, by her soft femininity, only to discover that the source of her coloring was the same disease that would kill her.

"I intend to leave most of these manuscripts with an editor here in town," he told me. "If he pays me as little as a dollar a pound, it should be sufficient to defray the cost of our trip."

"You needn't worry about the money," I told him while slathering a half crock of butter over a mountain of buckwheat. "I've got more than enough for both of us."

He cocked his head, gave me a quizzical look. "My understanding was that you would be paid for your labor in room and board only, and that your patrons would see to your education."

I nearly choked on his use of the word "patrons," but

kept my bile to myself. Fortunately, too, I had a mouthful when he spoke, the chewing of which allowed me time to formulate an answer. "I was able to take on an extra job every now and then. There was always somebody wanting something done, and willing to pay four bits to get it done quickly. Building a country, you know."

This seemed to satisfy him. I found it endearing, though a bit embarrassing, that he was so ready to view me as an honest man.

He nibbled at some toasted bread spread with apple butter. "My only complaint is that you wrote too infrequently. Muddy nearly wore out your each and every letter from the reading of it."

"I guess there just wasn't much to write about. One day was pretty much like the others."

"Indians," he said. "Did you encounter any?"

"Shawnees mostly. Now and then a few Miamis. Deidendorf did some trading with them. In fact there was one family in particular I got to know fairly well."

He wanted to know all the details of our bartering, so I relayed the gist of it, substituting words here and there, not because I considered him a prude—I had seen too much of him for that—but because I was reluctant to have him view me as I did myself, a creature born to the underhanded and devious, a festering soul too ugly for the clean white light of day.

And he found my reiteration of our commerce fascinating, the simple exchange of goods for goods, no filthy lucre to soil one's hands or heart. I wondered how fascinating he might have found the truth, however, that the goods Pike and Wiley hauled out to the Indians' camp every fortnight or so—always on a Sunday evening when all good sinners were rattling the rafters with songs of praise and remorse—was a wooden keg filled with potato whiskey distilled in a small operation deep in the oak woods. Or that as far as I was concerned, the most lucrative reward of those trips was not the few dollars I made each time, money the Indians made from selling skins and hides, but that hour or so in the early evening when Pike and Wiley would sit around a roaring fire with our hosts, sharing the contents of the keg while I, accompanied by an Indian girl named Lula, sat on a log just far enough from the fire that its light did not illuminate the movement our hands made beneath the blanket thrown over our laps.

My relationship with Poe had not yet ripened to the point where I might share this experience with him. (And indeed, some experiences are never meant to be shared, but can only be diluted by the telling.) So we passed the rest of our breakfast time with plans for the day.

The first sight I must see while in Philadelphia, he announced, was Philosophical Hall in Independence Square. "The greatest minds of the country, from Ben Franklin on to this day, have been members of that society."

I tried to keep a jaundiced look to myself, but it did not escape Poe's eye. He said, "Perhaps the seven-pound wen on display at the Pennsylvania Hospital would be more to your liking."

"Seven pounds?" I asked, incredulous. "That's not an exaggeration?"

"That's what you wish to do after breakfast? Gaze upon a tumor?"

"But seven pounds! Where in the world did it come from?"

"From the neck and cheek of a very unfortunate individual."

"One more of these cakes and we can be on our way."

"If that is to be the tenor of our day," Poe said, "then I suppose I should scratch from the list certain architectural delights of the city."

"Such as?"

"The home of Betsy Ross."

"Scratched."

"The home of George Washington?"

"Scratched."

"The Second Bank of the United States? It's a lovely example of Greek Revival architecture, one of the finest around."

"Is that all you have to show me? A bunch of buildings?"

"There's always Peter the Mint Eagle," he said.

"An eagle sounds interesting."

"This one is stuffed. It used to frequent the Mint, as the story goes. Until one day its wing was seized in the flywheel of a coinage press."

"Now that sounds interesting," I told him, because we were both playing a game by then, he in the role of self-indulgent father, myself as mischievous son.

"Am I to show you nothing edifying?"

"You don't think a tumor and a dead eagle can be edifying?"

"I know what you might enjoy," he answered. "Down along the waterfront, on Carpenter Street, stands a high tower. Molten lead is poured through a mesh at the top of the tower. Can you guess why?"

"I haven't a clue."

"Because molten lead, when dropped from such a height, will form itself into perfectly round balls as it falls and cools. The size of the mesh determines the size of the balls."

"Lead shot! That's how lead shot is made?"

"Precisely. Some of which, made here in this city, is being used by our men in Mexico."

"Put it on the schedule," I told him. I mopped up a last small puddle of molasses with a last forkful of buckwheat cake. Poe by then had taken a small purse from his pocket and was counting the coins.

"I'm paying for breakfast," I told him, and patted my own pocket. "I have plenty of money." I leaned toward him and whispered, "Nearly eighty-five dollars."

"On your person?" he asked.

"Where else would I put it?"

"You must be very careful, Augie. That's a great deal of money to be carrying around in your pocket."

"I'll take care of it," I said, foolishly. "I worked too hard to get it."

Poe only looked at me askance, wanting to say more, no doubt, but holding himself back. It was not the first meal he had accepted from me, but the first I actually paid for, and in laying my coins in the thick hand of the barkeep I felt the stir of something gratifying, almost noble, a subtle whisper that the act of becoming an upright and honorable man might not be so onerous after all. If only I could discover a way to get my money by honest means.

Chapter Four

We were on our way toward Sparks Shot Tower on the waterfront, still five minutes from the Delaware River but in no hurry to get there, enjoying the clarity of a spring-like morning, pausing now and then to look into a shop window or, in Poe's case, to remark on the cherry blossoms straining to burst forth, the lilies poking pale green heads up through the dirt of someone's yard, and, in my case, to enjoy Poe's renewed appreciation of those sights, when I first became aware of how the street traffic seemed to be increasing its pace all around us, men alone or in pairs hurrying past at a brisk walk, laughing, carriages moving by at a speedier than normal pace, drivers applying the whip.

Within minutes we became aware that much of Philadelphia was rushing toward the river, men in business suits and women in long, whooshing frocks, customers and store owners alike. Even what must have been an entire classroom full of young children, squealing, pushing, pulling at each other as they trotted past us.

Trailing this group and moving with none of the children's grace but just as much eagerness was a stocky boy of fifteen or so, apparently a butcher's apprentice judging by the bloody white apron he wore, a red-faced and heavy-footed boy chugging like a steam engine.

I stepped into the middle of the sidewalk as he neared. "What's going on?" I shouted. "A fire?"

He was two full steps beyond me before he found the breath to speak, and then only the one word shouted over a shoulder, "Elephants!"

I looked at Poe, and Poe looked at me, his raised eyebrows a mirror of my own. Elephants? In Philadelphia? The moment was deliciously absurd. We turned and chased after the blood-splattered boy.

Parasols dotted the waterfront. Slouch hats, beaver hats, plus fours, and linen suits. But also raggedy children, dock workers, beggar men and burghers. Schoolmarms and ministers, hausfraus and prostitutes. A Seurat riverside added to by Lautrec, a scene sun-filled and gay. All soon to be drenched in the tar of catastrophe.

THE DAY THE PACHYDERMS CAME TO PHILADELPHIA

The entire menagerie came prancing down Ferry Street, some twenty animals in all, led by the Circus Ringmaster and a small brown monkey that rode on his shoulder. The Ringmaster was a tall man with a pointed goatee, as elegant as a seraph in his white trousers and long-tailed red frock coat. Behind him came a pair of high-stepping Arabian horses, feathered and festooned with bright ribbons, their backs straddled by a young man costumed like Ali Baba in billowing blue pantaloons and a flowing white shirt. Next came, pulled in a small wagon, a bird a bit like a peacock but smaller and more grandiose in its long trailing plumage, identified, not inappropriately, as a RARE BIRD OF PARADISE. Then a one-horned goat billed as THE LAST SUR-

VIVING UNICORN. A pair of lanky camels looking for all the world like long-faced imbibers wrapped in dusty rags. Midway in the parade, prowling back and forth in his rolling cage, came a Bengal tiger; atop his cage was a placard that read, to everyone's delight and terror, MAN-EATER.

On and on they came, an assortment of the earth's most exotic creatures. Each of the hundreds of spectators who lined the sidewalks to watch the passing menagerie then fell into line at its end, there to follow the most spectacular and improbable beasts of all, the two African elephants that brought up the rear of the parade.

The elephants were accompanied by their trainer, a small wiry man who shouted out interesting bits of information about his beasts, that they were a mother and daughter named Betsy and Baby. The mother was reputed to weigh nearly six thousand pounds—three tons!—and the daughter not yet four thousand. The mother sported short blunt tusks, the daughter no tusks at all. But in every other particular they were identical: in the stout legs, those thick limbs that for all their rigidity moved in a stately gait, slow and deliberate, the child holding by its trunk to the mother's tail, much as a mother and child of the human variety might stroll down the street hand-in-hand. Both wore loose gray skin with a greenish cast, so wrinkled and tessellated as to give it the quality of a cracked mud wall. Both had ears that flapped out periodically, almost rhythmically, like heavy sails of canvas. And in those ears, where the elephants' skin was least thick, veins stood out so clearly that the closest of spectators could discern the movement of the beasts' blood in the network of arteries.

Then, of course, there was the miraculous trunk, so odd yet so practical an appendage, as nimble as a jeweler's hand, able with equal ease to roll a log or to pick a pebble off the street. The trunk of the mother was always moving (the baby's being employed as a tether), either swinging in a lighthearted dangle just above the ground or rising into the air like a thick-bodied serpent, not to strike but to sniff the air or, on two occasions, to startle the crowd with a trumpeting blast, a brassy blare soon answered with a shriller blast from the child, as if the mother were asking, "Are you all right back there?" and the child responded brightly, "I'm just dandy!"

A female rider sat atop Betty on a brightly beaded blanket and small cushioned seat of red, holding on to a strap lashed around the pachyderm's girth. And from each beast there arose a steam of vapor into the early morning air, which gave these animals a look even more fantastical.

In time the entire parade made its way to the water's edge, there to be conveyed by ferry across the Delaware River and onto the New Jersey shore. While the first ferry was loaded and began its slow transport, the remaining animals lined up one after another, each accompanied by a trainer to keep curious boys from approaching too closely. A local urchin ran hither and thither passing out broadsides inviting all citizens of Philadelphia to attend the first night's show, a gala of "amazing feats and incredible spectacles" to be performed in a tent that would soon be erected not far from the opposite shore.

Upon return of the ferry for its second crossing, the ferryman expressed to the Ringmaster some concern that the pachyderms' weight would sink his flat-bottomed craft. The Ringmaster answered this with a loud proclamation that his wondrous beasts would swim to New Jersey.

The ferryman scratched his chin for a while, then wondered aloud if, owing to the speed of the current midriver, perhaps a better choice would be the sturdy new bridge a quarter mile north.

"Nonsense!" cried the Ringmaster. And in true Ringmaster fashion he then delivered an oratory on the miraculous nature of pachyderm anatomy, and described in such glowing terms the sponginess of elephant tissue, the natural buoyancy thereof, that the assembled crowd, reluctant to have the last of the morning's spectacles removed without a final flourish of drama, all began to cry out and cheer in favor of an elephant swim, a miracle of flotation!

With a nod then from the Ringmaster and the sweep of his arm toward the east, the rider atop Betty urged her forward, down the grassy bank and into the mud. First the mother and then the child at her tail waded into the river, each stepping as delicately as a bather into a chilly tub.

Forward they went. The rider periodically patted Betty's huge shoulder or pulled at an ear and shouted words of encouragement. And indeed it was a glorious sight to behold those great hulking beasts so gracefully plying the swift green water. Higher and higher the water rose on the gray flanks, until first the child's feet left the riverbed, and its great bulk was buoyed up. Soon the mother was afloat as well. And now Baby, in an effort to keep her trunk from submersion, released her mother's tail. The child issued a short blast, not of terror but, perhaps, of a rising concern. Betty answered with a trumpet's blare of reassurance, swiveling her huge head as far to the rear as possible.

That was when the current seized Baby and swung her off the course. She was spun to face downstream, and, without the comforting view of her mother's broad backside to guide her, the child panicked. Her movements, previously altogether graceful and smooth, became agitated. She jerked this way and that, legs lurching, trumpet shrieking, her huge dark eyes aglimmer with fear. She heaved herself toward the near shore and then the far, where, upon spotting her mother again, she appeared more terrorized by the distance between them than when she had not seen Betty at all.

The mother had turned now too and struggled to return to her child. The rider hammered a palm against the gray skin, hoping to turn the beast around. To no avail. Now both rider and Ringmaster shouted at the elephants and to each other. The Ringmaster, three-quarters across the river at the rear of the ferry, cupped his hands to his mouth and demanded, a bit absurdly, that the elephants follow him.

By now Baby was beginning to fail. Weakened by the powerful current, no doubt chilled by the water, her head dropped momentarily, submerging even the great knob of forehead until only the tip of her trunk was visible. From the evidence of the trunk, canted at a diagonal to the water's surface, Baby appeared to have capsized underwater. This observation was confirmed when the foot of one leg broke the surface. Betty lurched so vigorously toward her child that the rider was catapulted off and went down with a splash, down and completely under for a few moments, then to emerge several yards downstream, being carried swiftly away. She tried for a few strokes to fight her way back to the elephants but soon realized the futility of it and returned to the Philadelphia shore.

No amount of screaming from the Ringmaster could now turn Betty toward New Jersey. She plunged her trunk underwater, probing with it for her still-submerged child. Eventually she located Baby and the trunks emerged entwined, the mother holding the child's high. The crowd cheered and applauded.

But the celebration was premature, for the smaller elephant was no longer trying to swim, and the weight of its body moving in the current made it impossible for the mother to make for shore. She pulled and struggled a few moments longer, both beasts moving steadily downstream, all spectators running parallel to them down the bank and shore, the crowd now mute and helpless. In every mind was the knowledge of what had to be done, that Betty must release her doomed infant in order to save herself. Perhaps Betty knew this as well. But whether guided by instinct or intelligence, she would not concede, and held tightly to her daughter.

And then the mother's head dipped down as well, the eyes went under, leaving nothing but the powerful forehead above water, looking like a green-gray boulder being driven by the current. Within a minute's time, Betty, too, slowly tipped onto her side. And then came a deep and terrible silence, and the crowd stopped moving, and nobody spoke.

Both Betty and Baby were washed ashore just a hundred yards or so downstream from the bridge they might have strolled across to New Jersey. There was no brightness in their eyes as they lay there in the mud, no pulse of blood visible in their ears. Their hides were a duller gray now, even as the vapor steamed off their bodies, the trunks of mother and daughter yet entwined.

It strikes me as more than a little fitting that the final spectacle to assault our eyes before departing Philadelphia, that most civilized of cities, should have been the drowning of those two great beasts. Here was tragedy at its most absurd. And in what better incident to discern the hand of God? All tragedy is God's work, for only God, if He were inclined to do so, might prevent it.

On the other hand, is it fair to blame God for the damage done by that brief explication, composed in my own hand, of the elephants' demise? Some things, I suppose, must be ascribed to man himself—such things as jealousy, envy, and pride. If I plant a tree, for example, and on that tree a fungus grows, a blight, can it be argued that I, by planting the tree, created the disease that destroyed the orchard?

That is a debate best left to the philosophers. As for me, I must let the narrative suffice.

After the elephants' misfortune, neither Poe nor I had any appetite for entertainment. We passed the weekend in desultory conversation and lethargic activity, by cleaning up his room, packing his few essentials, sending a wire to Longreve in New York, and placing Poe's manuscripts with Mr. Godey, who grudgingly offered five dollars in the dim hope that he would find something publishable within the stack. Even more grudgingly, Poe accepted.

Finally, Monday morning arrived. Still in darkness we took our turns at the privy and the washbasin, then stumbled into the tavern for some tea and bread with blackstrap. Then to the railroad station to begin our journey. The train departed at eight, and since our car was not full, both Poe and I claimed window seats, his facing south, mine north, the locomotive west. On occasion he would point things out to me, or I to him, and we would hurry to the other's side to have a look. Poe's thoughts, far more than mine, were surely on the destination. Or perhaps his eyes shone only because of hope renewed, a purpose restored.

I, too, felt a low fire burning inside me, but not, like Poe's, an old fire, so frequently stoked. Instead it was something completely new to me, this ambition to preserve and understand an event by writing it, to take an image that was scalded into my brain, the last fervid glance from Betty's huge eyes before they sank beneath the water, to render that image in words that might somehow ameliorate the burn. We were not yet halfway to Cumberland, clanking along at a slow rattle, when I asked Poe if I might borrow some paper from his satchel, and maybe a stub of pencil if he could spare it.

He did not question my request until he had produced the items. "A letter to a girl in Ohio?" he asked.

"The only girl I know who might want a letter from me wouldn't be able to read it," I told him. "No, I just thought I might put down a few of my observations."

He smiled, but said nothing more, and soon turned back to his window.

An hour later, while I was still laboring over my words, he said, "All of the interesting scenery must be passing on your side of the train. What can you possibly see out that window worth writing about? There is little over here but trees."

I almost told him what I was up to, but held back, stopped myself, for I was not eager to share any of this just yet, by which I mean not merely the writing but the compulsion to engage in it, this growing ambition, this blossoming sense of myself that had not yet crystalized. A small part of me was trembling as I wrote, subtly quivering like a man on the verge of a momentous discovery, an explorer who knows that just around the next bend will lie the most momentous and startling discovery of his life.

I said only, "I would like for you to read this when I'm finished with it."

"Not poetry," he begged. "Not another Longfellow with his odes to woods and field."

"It's not poetry."

"Heaven help us!" he exclaimed in mock horror. "You've become a Transcendentalist! The flowers, the grass, the beauteous sky! All witnessed from behind the sooty glass of a noisy railcar. You will make the Frog-pondians proud indeed, Augie."

The dozen or so other passengers, all of whom had turned to catch his declamation (as was his intent), now awaited my response. I muttered, "I'm no more fond of Emerson than you are."

"Praise be to the Great Oneness!" he cried. "The boy is not yet lost!"

I doubt that any of the passengers fully grasped Poe's sarcasm, but they enjoyed his histrionics all the same, the flamboyance that I countered by speaking as calmly and softly as the rattling of our transport allowed. "If you will let me finish, I will show it to you soon."

He leaned across his seat so as to glance at the paper on my lap. "Are there any words left you have not yet crossed out?"

"I'm trying to get it right," I said.

He sat up straighter and leaned back in his seat, the side of his face fully lit by the sun. "When I composed 'The Raven,'" he said, his voice pitched louder and deeper now, as if to fill a lecture hall, "as well as my many many tales, every word flowed complete and perfect without a single revision, a gift direct from the Muse."

I might have contradicted him in this, might have remarked on the nights I had watched him toiling at his craft, trying out this phrase and that as a stonemason working to fill a hole with just the right stone will chip away at the edges, a flake here and a flake there, working patiently toward the precise fit. But then I took note of how the other passengers were reacting to him, those small derisive smiles, how to a man they had turned their backs to him in hopes of silencing him, an obvious crank.

What he hoped, I'm sure, was that one of them—all of them!—would cry out in a paroxysm of delight, "Edgar Allan Poe? Are you *he*, sir? Are you the famous author?"

That was the light he hoped to bask in, the light he always sought. He seemed to require it more desperately now than ever before, now that he was alone and bereft of the family that had shored him up. That light and the promise of it was the true reason he was traveling to Pittsburgh.

He would not find the light on this train. He watched as his listeners all turned away. He held his pose for just a moment longer, blinked twice (I could feel for myself the sting of humiliation in his eyes), and finally faced his window once again.

I bent over my paper and resumed my work. Two hours later, sensing some change in the air, I looked up to see that the train had stopped, we had arrived in Columbia, and that half our companions in the railcar had already disembarked. I felt vaguely disoriented, still half submerged in a fever dream.

Poe stood in the aisle, satchel in hand. "Shall I insist that the boat be held while you complete your masterpiece?"

I snatched up the paper in one hand, my bag in the other. "I'm coming."

The remainder of the journey would be completed by slow-moving packet boat, a small enclosed ark of a boat drifting down first the Juniata and Schuylkill Rivers, then through the Union Canal Tunnel over seven hundred feet long, and into the Susquehanna River. From there, as far west as Johnstown, a canal boat on wheels would be dragged along the Portage Railroad, hauled up mountain slopes by stationary steam engines, and pulled over level ground by a team of horses. In Johnstown we would again take to the water, canalling along the Conemaugh and Kiskiminitas Rivers until finally, gliding along an aqueduct, we would cross the Allegheny and enter into Pittsburgh.

All in all, four days of watching the trees go by. (Except for those fifteen minutes when, just west of Carlisle, our drift paralleled the Pennsylvania Turnpike and we glided past the dusty, fly-clouded, tail-swishing, low-mooing train of a cattle drive on its way to the slaughter yards of Harrisburg, it was not a trip remarkable for its exotica.) By the time we had been on the water for a half day, most passengers had tired of pointing out bald eagles and red-tailed hawks perched on high branches, of river otters and muskrats poking their heads up out of the water. We also witnessed more than our share of white-tailed deer, and could be roused to a window only when the word "Bear!" was shouted. Besides, not every passenger was blessed with a window. The interior of the canal boat was stuffy and hot, free of all decoration and adornment, the benches less hospitable than Episcopalian church pews.

"This canal boat is not unlike a communal coffin, is it?" Poe remarked. Several of us laughed, if sourly, at this observation. Only in hindsight do I see how prescient it was.

In Columbia, at the inn where we availed ourselves of refreshments before first taking to the water, I had slipped away from Poe long enough to purchase a pencil of my own at a stationer's kiosk, along with a half dozen sheets of good parchment. Later, on the boat, while Poe and the others dozed or read in the dim light or stared blankly at nothing in particular, I busied myself with making a clean copy of my composition.

This done, a good three hours after we had taken to the boat (the last hour was spent in nervous trepidation, the finished copy in hand), I returned to sit beside Poe. He had been drowsing, chin on his chest, but now opened his eyes, then turned his head toward me.

"Are we stopping for the night?" he asked.

"Not yet. We've got a bit of daylight left."

Now he noticed the paper trembling in my hand. "Is that for me?"

I could not quite bring myself to hand it over. "You told me once that I had the instincts of a writer. Do you remember?"

He nodded. "It was the day we first met."

"I assumed you were telling the truth."

"I have always told you the truth, Augie."

Finally, I held out the paper to him. "Tell me the truth about this."

He took it. Held it to the light. Read the first few lines. Lowered the paper and looked at me. "An account of the elephants?"

"It is."

He nodded. "It would help me to know, in assessing this chronicle, the purpose for which it is intended."

"I was hoping to get it published somewhere. In a newspaper maybe."

A smile twitched at his mouth, but he held it in check. "You intend to make your way through this world as a writer?"

"I guess that depends."

"On this."

"On that."

He looked at the paper again, now flat on his lap, but he was not reading. "It takes more than a writer's instincts to make a writer, I'm afraid."

"I know that."

"It requires years of hard work. Discipline and perseverance."

"I have to start somewhere, don't I? Well then, that's my start. Right there underneath your hand."

This time he lifted the paper to the light again. Fifteen seconds later he asked, "And will you be staring at me all the while as I read?"

I slid off the bench and stood. "I'm going to try to go up on top for a while. I need some fresh air. I'm suffocating down here."

A half hour later I returned to his seat, sneaking in like a thief. He kept his face averted, though I thought I could detect the insinuation of a smile on his lips. Whether it was a smile of pleasure or ridicule, I had no idea.

He asked, "Have you more paper?"

"I do."

He handed me the story. "Then start again."

I spent the remainder of that first day studying the marks he had made on my story, the circles he had drawn around certain phrases and redirected elsewhere on the page with long arrows, the lines drawn through other sentences, words changed, misspellings corrected. In the margins were comments to accompany the hieroglyphs. "A poorly chosen word." "Unclear."

"Maudlin." "You've remembered this incorrectly." "If you must steal, steal from a better writer."

I labored over every new word, every revised sentence. By the time the canal boat pulled to a dock at dusk that night and the weary passengers went tramping ashore, my second copy was ready. I handed it to Poe as we disembarked.

"Might this wait until after supper?" he asked.

"Of course, there's no hurry. Take as long as you like."

"Then let us fall into line. Surely somebody must be leading this parade."

Like sheep we followed the rest of the passengers along a footpath through the woods. A hundred yards or so back from shore set a roadhouse; there we were fed and given a room for the night, shared with four other men. All through supper I vacillated between exhaustion and euphoria, as drained by my intellectual toil as I was exhilarated by it.

In our room, a plain room furnished with one chair and three beds, I immediately went to the only bed not already occupied by two bodies and sat on the edge of it and pulled off my boots. Poe stood by the window, looking out at the darkness. I told him, "I don't mind sleeping on the floor tonight."

"Nonsense," he said. "Lie down there. You'll be up again soon enough."

"Aren't you coming to bed?"

"As soon as I've had another look at your masterpiece," he said. He searched the room for a candle but found none. "Well then. I suppose I shall do my reading downstairs."

In the past few moments I had become aware of an ache building in my chest, some low throb as I lay there watching him scour the room for a candle, my manuscript in his hand. Just as he pulled open the door to leave the room, I spoke. "Sir?" I said.

He turned back to me.

"I just wanted to thank you. For everything you've done for me. Everything you're doing. I've already learned a lot from you."

He nodded but said nothing, and soon disappeared out the door. I heard perhaps four receding footsteps, then silence, and then his tread returning. He looked around the threshold at me. "If we are to be professional colleagues as well as traveling companions, perhaps you had best stop calling me 'Sir.' "

I fell asleep that night with my eyes filled with warm tears.

It could not have been more than 4:00 A.M. when a thunderous knock on the door startled me and my roommates awake. "Breakfast in thirty!" bellowed the canal boat captain outside our door. "Departure in sixty!"

I sat up. The room was still dark but sufficiently moonlit for me to discern that the other half of the bed was empty. I put my hand to the mattress. Cold. And no indentation of Poe's head marked the pillow.

I arose quickly, having slept fully clothed but for my shoes and coat, made fully alert by a growing alarm that I would find Poe downstairs as I had found him in Philadelphia, reeking and helpless. Even at seventeen I understood the appeal of alcohol, the seduction of having to look no further than the bottom of a tall mug for one's strength, one's forgetfulness, one's surcease of misery. How many nights had I driven Wiley and Pike home from the Indian camp and dragged them to their bunks, with Wiley promising all the while to flatten Deidendorf at the next opportunity, just for the principle of it (a principle that invariably vanished with the mist of morning), and Pike weeping about a red-haired girl from Indiana who had gone to the creek for a bucket of water one afternoon and never returned? (More than once I had attempted, while hoisting Pike's stinking feet onto his bed, to ascertain his relationship to the girl, and how he was able to describe so vividly the way her hair, "as pretty as a sunset," fell forward over her shoulders as she dipped her bucket in the river. But there are some secrets that even a quart of potato whiskey will not wrench free.)

Less than a minute after the captain's call to awaken I was on my way out of the room, then down the dark and narrow stairway and into the tavern. The canal boat captain was seated at a table near the door, his platter of fried meat and bread lit by an oil lamp in the center of the table. He looked up at me and nodded, chewing vigorously, and spoke with his mouth half full. "Go on into the kitchen and fix yourself a plate."

I nodded in answer, though my gaze had already traveled to the other end of the room, to the table and chair closest the fireplace, where a stack of logs was just then beginning to take fire. There, slumped back in a straight-back chair, legs stretched out and crossed at the ankle, arms folded over his chest, was Poe. I approached tentatively, searching for evidence of his condition. On the table sat a pewter mug. I picked it up, sniffed for the scent of rum, smelled only tea. Nothing else lay on the table but for my sheaf of papers, the elephant story, weighted down by Poe's meerschaum pipe and his well-used pencil.

As noiselessly as possible I freed the papers and picked them up and slid closer to the fire. I knelt into the light. And squinted at the hieroglyphs with which he had once again adorned my composition, but this time not so prolifically. He had left at least half of my words intact.

"One more pass-through should do it," he told me, his voice hoarse with sleep, eyes still closed. And at that moment the heat of the fire washed through me and so warmed my chest and face that it was all I could do to keep from flinging myself upon him, seizing him in a hard embrace and kissing his unshaven cheek in gratitude. Little did either of us realize that had I done so, that kiss, in the not too distant future, would have come to be regarded as a Judas kiss.

That day's travel brought us to the mountains, our slow inching up one side, our cautious creep down the other. I cannot recall much of the actual experience, whether it was pleasant or monotonous, how the scenery was received by my fellow passengers, so immersed was I in my revision. But I do recall looking up from my work at midday, stretching my back, blinking, a bit surprised to find myself in a dim packet boat and not, as I had been all morning, standing on the banks of the Delaware in harsh sunlight. Poe was looking my way.

"You've done well," he said. "You've produced a serviceable little piece."

I do not know if it was his intention to lift me up with praise only to dash me down again, but that was the result of his remark. *A serviceable little piece*. Could a compliment have been any crueler?

Not only could, but was. Throughout the rest of that afternoon, he approached me from time to time and gave the thumbscrew another twist.

"It is really quite competent writing for one your age."

"It is hardly overdone at all."

"An engaging little sketch."

By early evening I felt as if a hundred barbed porcupine quills had been fired into my flesh. "Why do you call it a sketch?" I finally asked, able to tolerate his praise no longer. "A little sketch, a little piece, a little anecdote. Are you saying that it isn't finished or complete?"

At the time of this exchange he was seated by a window, sucking on his meerschaum, watching the smoke drift through the opening. "Oh, it's complete enough, certainly. For what it is, it is quite complete."

He was baiting me now, I felt sure of it. Still, the quills dangling from my skin had made me cranky. "For what it is? And what, exactly, is it?"

"What do you think it is?" he asked.

"I think it is a story. A true story."

"One might call it that, certainly."

"But you wouldn't?"

"What it lacks," he said, "is a foundation. An underlying purpose. One does not simply tell a story so as to hear oneself speak. There must be a reason for the story. A raison d'être."

"What about art for art's sake? Isn't that what you're always preaching?"

"This is your first effort at composition, Augie. We are not talking here about art. What you have composed is journalism. Reportage. Art is conspicuously absent."

"Well maybe that's what I was aiming for. An honest depiction of what I saw. Simple and true."

"If you were aiming for the simple," he said, "you have hit a bull's-eye."

We did not talk for the next three hours. Which is to say, I avoided all conversation. Again at dusk our packet pulled ashore and its passengers hiked stiff-legged and weary to the nearest roadhouse. Along the way Poe stepped to the side of the path so as to fall in beside me as I brought up the rear.

"You mustn't sulk," he said. "If you wish to be treated as a colleague, you must be prepared to accept the bitter with the sweet."

"Where was the sweet? I must have missed it."

"If I was overly hard on you, I apologize."

I was still too angry, too stung, to wave his cruelty aside.

"You have talent," he told me. "I have always known this about you. Your perceptions are as keen as any man's."

We walked in silence for a while, though I now began to feel a softening of my anger, a cooling of the heat that reddened my face.

As we walked he put a hand on my arm. "Let us not make too much of this," he said. "It was your first effort and it was a good effort. If my criticisms were too severe, it is only because of my deep affection for you. An affection so deep, Augie, that the least I ever want for you is perfection itself."

And now my chest ached with a different kind of heat.

"Have you ever found it yourself?" I asked, not as a challenge but an inquiry sincere. "Have you ever composed the perfect story or poem?"

He considered his answer. Then, after a sigh, "It is probably fair to say that what we crave most for those we love is precisely that which we ourselves have failed to attain."

And with that admission he healed the wound between us.

Unfortunately, the wound did not stay closed for long.

Chapter Five

Another roadhouse breakfast at 4:30 A.M. The tavern, despite its smoky lanterns hanging from the ceiling beams, seemed as dark and dank as a cave. And once again, Poe spent not a minute of the previous night horizontal, but this time, with no manuscript with which to pass his night, had sought out the usual solace.

At our table that morning he was more animated than anyone else in the room. Most of us were barely able to lift our heads, and so consumed our bowls of potatoes and eggs with eyes half-closed. In my presence, Poe took nothing but tea. But the vague scent that arose from him, and the restless nature of his gaze, at once furtive and fiery, were unmistakable. He could not keep his fingers from drumming nameless tunes on the tabletop.

Three other passengers shared our table that morning, all men. One was the canal boat captain himself, a Mr. Shook, a hard little bald-headed monkey of a man always in a hurry, his every movement brisk and sharp.

"Eat up, gentlemen, eat up. The sun's on its way and we must be as well."

"After Pittsburgh," said Poe, "is it then back to Philadelphia for you, Captain?"

"To Wheeling, sir. Down the Ohio to Wheeling."

"Some of us are traveling to Wheeling?" Poe asked the table in general.

One man raised his hand a few inches above his breakfast, but he showed no inclination to prolong the conversation. Captain Shook said, "In Pittsburgh I'll pick up several. Some for Wheeling, some for Cincinnati. Some for only God knows where."

After that the conversation lapsed. By this, our third morning, few had energy for idle talk.

Poe, however, had energy to burn. In lieu of other distractions, he turned to me. "Seeing as how you have your mind set on pursuing the life of a scribbler," he said, and here I looked up at him, not at all pleased to be singled out in this manner, not at all comfortable with having my ambition tossed onto the table like a slab of fatty ham, "I have devised a scheme for your advancement."

Here he paused to note how many ears had been piqued. Satisfied that all at the table were attentive, he continued. "Every great literary man needs a biographer," he said. "You shall be mine."

I feel certain that what Poe hoped for at that moment was not in any way to demean or ridicule me but to achieve for himself some measure of recognition from the other men at the table, at the least a question or two that might allow him to introduce himself, humbly of course, as a different kind of man than the rest of them, as a man not bound for the iron or glass works but engaged in loftier pursuits, a laborer in the vineyards of intellect and art.

A couple of our tablemates looked up at him briefly, but the only one to speak was Captain Shook. "Eat up, gentlemen. Let's finish up quick."

I admit that I felt sorry for Poe. His need for approval, for validation in the eyes of others, was sometimes pathetic. And so I asked, "What's a biographer do?"

Poe leapt on my question like a sparrow on a cricket. "You would write down the details of my life," he said.

"You would chronicle, past, present, and future, all the incidents of my life. In short, you would recreate my life for all to read."

It was the smugness of his tone that amazed me most, that imperious tilt of his chin that drove all trace of my sympathy away. Still, had I not been so exhausted by the trip, had I not even at that moment smelled the rum on his breath, were I, in short, not resentful of the changes displayed in him from the Poe I remembered and loved, his unpredictable fluctuations, I might have held my tongue.

"Sounds to me," I said, "like a lot of sitting and listening and writing down what I'm told."

He blinked. His head tilted back as if bumped.

And then I went too far. "I'm not about to be anybody's secretary."

His eyes narrowed. "All for the best. Since you are obviously not up to the task."

"What I'm not up to is wasting my life by writing about somebody else's. I've got my own life to live."

"You cannot count on elephants to drown every day," he said.

I turned to Captain Shook. "I'm on my way to Mexico to fight with General Scott. I suspect I'll find plenty to write about down there, don't you think?"

With that I shoved back my chair and stood, knocking against the table so hard that the plates and cutlery rattled. By the time I reached the door I had made up my mind to be done with Poe. I stormed outside and in the gray before dawn marched down the foggy path to the packet boat. The others arrived within a quarter hour. By then I had managed to unclench my fists, though my heart felt as hard as an iron ball.

* * *

One final incident before Pittsburgh. And, as it were, a harbinger of all to come.

In Freeport, north of Pittsburgh, where the Kiskiminitas River meets the Allegheny flowing south, our captain pulled ashore along a line of docks to tend to some matter of his own. We passengers took advantage of the stopover to disembark and stretch our legs, to wash our faces in sunlight and fresh air. All along the docks were small barges and other boats, packets and rafts and dinghies. By June any craft with a draft deeper than a canoe's would have a difficult time finding enough water to float the Allegheny, but March was not yet over and, because the spring melt had the Allegheny running high, river traffic was heavy.

Poe surveyed the fleet at hand, then looked into the sky—the sky was clear, with only a few high and wispy clouds, no threat of rain—then strode straightaway toward an odd-looking craft that to my eyes seemed the result of a collision between a barge and a steamboat. It had a wide deck and drew a shallow draft, with an awkwardly constructed cabin aft, its wheelhouse perched atop the engine house. At the stern was the paddlewheel, perhaps three-quarters the size of the wheel on a passenger steamboat. From rail to rail and bow to stern the boat was patched and tarred and splattered with contrasting hues of pitch and paint.

I watched Poe advance to the slip nearest this boat's wheelhouse and speak to the captain inside. I suspected that Poe was negotiating passage on the little steamer, and I experienced a sickening flutter of panic that I was the cause of his action. But midway in the brief conversation Poe pointed back toward me, and the captain leaned out of his wheelhouse to have a quick look. When he nodded, Poe reached for his wallet and emptied it out into the captain's hand.

Poe came briskly back toward the packet boat but did not even look at me as he passed. He went aboard, disappeared inside the cabin, and reemerged a few minutes later with both his bag and mine in hand. By now I had stood and come to the edge of the dock. He tossed my bag into my arms. "Let's go," he said. "We're transferring to the *Sweet Jeanine*."

"She doesn't look all that sweet to me," I said as I fell in behind him.

"Sweet enough. I can't abide another hour inside that oblong box."

"How much is my share?"

"It's been taken care of."

"I want to pay my share." I had seen the way Poe handled his wallet when dealing with the *Sweet Jeanine*'s captain, and I knew how little that wallet contained.

But Poe said, "A few hours from now we will arrive at Dr. Brunrichter's house, where I will have no need for money. And tomorrow night, after my reading, I will have been amply paid."

"Even so," I began, until he flashed me a look over his shoulder, and I decided to accept his generosity.

And so ended our first conversation since our joust at breakfast. Both of us, I think, regretted those impetuous words, yet an awkwardness remained between us. All morning long I had been searching my mind for some way to mend the rift without actually apologizing, which my pride would not allow, but again and again his condescending descriptions of my composition would return to me, and I would burn with resentment anew.

We placed our bags inside the wheelhouse and introduced ourselves to the captain, who did not reciprocate. He was a sallow man, wide in the gut, just like his boat, and equally attentive to his personal maintenance as to the *Sweet Jeanine*'s. I remember looking at the dirt that lined the creases of his neck and thinking that Jeanine must be very sweet indeed to tolerate the rank proximity of this gentleman in her life.

"Got my load coming anytime now," was all he said to us by way of introduction. "Don't wander too far off."

With that both Poe and I returned to shore. There he gave me a sidelong glance and said, "I believe I'll stretch my legs a bit."

He did not invite me to join him, so I merely nodded and stood my ground as he ambled down the shore. I watched him for a few moments, feeling somehow bereft, as sorrowful as an abandoned child. Then, suddenly recognizing this emotion, I grew resentful again, and resolved to rid myself of all unpleasant emotions, and turned and strode across the dirt lane that ran alongside the river, and hiked adamantly into the woods.

Some twenty or so minutes later, having spent most of that time chucking acorns at a fat red squirrel who sat on a branch ten feet above my head while shrilly scolding me for invading his territory, I headed back to the docks. There I found three wagons lined up along the road, their identical loads being carried one by one onto the *Sweet Jeanine*'s foredeck, and there being stacked in four tiers of descending number, four tiers of brand-new, empty coffins made of yellow pine, unpainted and unadorned but for the loop of heavy cord at the foot and head of each box.

Poe was leaning against the wheelhouse, watching this somber sculpture take shape. He stood with arms crossed, a half smile on his lips. It was then a strange presentiment began to overtake me. I cannot call it chilling because I felt no chill, nor can I call it heavy because it did not weigh me down with dread. What I felt as I watched those coffins going aboard, the clean, smooth boards as yellow as sunlight, their cleanliness in stark contrast to the rest of the *Sweet Jeanine*, what I felt was more of a nervousness, an itch of apprehension, exacerbated as much by Poe's cryptic smile as by the nature of the freight itself.

When the loading was done and the emptied wagons on their way down the road, I joined Poe aboard the steamer. Our captain, the only other individual aboard, uncleated the mooring lines, shoved his craft a few inches from the slip, then returned to the wheelhouse and set the paddlewheel in a slow, thumping churn. He backed us clear of the dock, gradually swung us around, and set us off down the Allegheny.

I waited silently beside Poe for a while, giving him an opportunity to be the first to speak. He did not avail himself of the opening. And so I asked, with a nod of my chin toward the coffins, "Where are all those going?"

"Same place we are," he said. He then turned away and went into the wheelhouse for a moment, only to return with his notebook and pencil. He leaned against the wheelhouse wall and immediately set to work on a rendering of the coffin sculpture.

I asked, "Any idea why Pittsburgh needs so many of them?"

He sketched for another thirty seconds without answering. Then said, "Climb up on top of those for me, will you, Augie? I am in need of a model."

His tone was as warm and familiar as ever, all trace of coldness gone. Still, I wondered if I had heard him correctly. "On top of *those things?*" I asked.

"Certainly a man on his way to war won't be afraid of empty boxes," he said.

It was all the challenge I required. I climbed, albeit gingerly, to the very top tier, and there stood, legs spread wide to steady myself against the steamboat's rock, hands jammed onto my hips.

The captain leaned out of his wheelhouse and shouted, "You topple them boxes and you're gonna haul them out of the river by hand!"

Poe told me, "Come down one tier."

I was more than happy to accommodate him.

"Now sit," he said.

I sat.

"Hmm, not right. Try lying down."

I did so.

"Not on your back, that pose does not work. Try lying on your side facing me. There, good, that's much better. Now then, elevate your left knee. Good. Now prop your head up on an elbow. Excellent. Remain just like that, if you will."

I spent the next ten minutes in that ridiculous pose, in constant danger of rolling forward off my narrow ledge. Finally Poe announced that I could come down if I wished, and I wished precisely that. I hurried to his side, legs peculiarly shaky, to see how he had rendered my likeness.

But the sketch displayed not me at all. He had, as he said, needed only a model. He had drawn himself in my place, himself in black suit and boiled shirt and stiff collar, the black tail of a frock coat draping over the edge of the coffin on which he lay so casually reposed.

Finished, he titled the sketch *The Conqueror Worm*. He then held it at arm's length for a moment, considering what he had done. Then he laughed derisively and ripped the sheet from the notebook and tossed it at my chest, where I trapped it between both hands.

"Something to remember me by," he said. And then he went to stand alone at the bow, his dark eyes glaring hard upriver, as if in defiance of all calamity ahead.

Chapter Six

The day grew hazy the nearer we came to Pittsburgh. The air sat heavier in my lungs, smoke-gray air from the blast furnaces in the distant forests where charcoal was made for the iron works built closer to the river. This cloud of smoke, renewed daily, lay like a perpetual gloom over the basin of the city, and the deeper into it we penetrated, the heavier grew the foreboding in my chest.

I would not say that I had begun to fear Pittsburgh, but rather that an apprehension of it, just short of premonition, had arisen in me. Disconcerting too was the new relationship that had developed between myself and Poe. It troubled me that my emotions toward him were now so frequently at crosscurrents with one another, a deep affection now and then subdued by resentment, pity, and even disgust. Through all my seven years as a farm slave, through all the abuses and routine miseries, what had kept me strong was the desire, the determination, not to let Poe down. Had I at ten, and thereafter in his absence, viewed him so differently than I now at seventeen saw him? Or had he in those seven years become more cynical, more arrogant, more bitter and distrustful? Had seven years of hardship and ridicule, the loss of his wife and the dissolution of his family, had all this fueled his desperation to the point that he had become less the Poe I remembered and more like one of his own tormented characters?

To each of these questions: Yes. Yes. And yes.

And now before us, Pittsburgh on the left, Allegheny City on the right, both muted in color beneath, or rather inside, the adumbrated sky that lay atop them. The first landmarks to catch my eye were the courthouse atop Grant's Hill, its dome and spire not tall enough to pierce the charcoal clouds, and, farther back on the opposite shore, the Western Penitentiary, as low and stolid and uninviting as the courthouse was noble and grand.

Then came the aqueduct, the very same one on which Charles Dickens had entered the city in 1842, crossing from Allegheny into Pittsburgh on the Pennsylvania Canal Line, there to behold before him an "ugly confusion of the backs of buildings and crazy galleries and stairs." The *Sweet Jeanine* made a slow swing out of midriver and aimed itself left, bringing me to face head-on all the confusion and baroque randomness described by Dickens but doubled, perhaps even tripled by now, a mere five years after his visit.

At river level Pittsburgh appeared a crazy quilt of

docks, some stable and complete, many not, a few of them still layered atop one another by the previous winter's ice jam and left there to rot. Moored to these docks was every kind of shallow-draft barge and raft and canoe and small boat imaginable, plus a few that remained unimaginable even as I gawked at them.

Old logs, broken barrels, flotsam of every type littered the shore and docks. It was an area so busy, so focused on upward growth, that all clean-up was left to the river itself. And the river was, to say the least, an indifferent housekeeper.

Rising up from the docks on both sides of the aqueduct was another crazy-quilt construction, but this one of wooden stairways and landings and loading ramps, each ascending to a congestion of wooden buildings, each building shouting for attention with a brightly lettered sign high on its wall: THE RAILROAD HOTEL, THE FOWLER EXCHANGE, DEVLIN'S TOBACCO AND CIGARS.

And the people, the citizens and visitors of Pittsburgh: At the dock level, burly bearded men in shirtsleeves, each one heaving this or that, carrying crates and kegs and barrels and bales either up the stairs or down, or easing them down the loading ramps with pulleys and ropes, or likewise dragging them up. From the deck of the *Sweet Jeanine* I could witness more of the same going on at street level at the top of the stairs, not only the rough and eager laborers of varied stock but also all manner of more dandified entrepreneurs, merchants and professional men of every ilk, gentlemen in frock coats and top hats, their faces clean-shaven or mutton-chopped or goateed, and often as not arm-in-arm with bonneted women, their long frilly dresses and four layers of undergarments swishing with every step, rustling like the water itself as these women strolled down Washington Street or promenaded across the canal's foot bridge.

Now that we were nudging close to a dock, I observed that Pittsburgh was not as uniformly enshrouded in smoke as it had seemed from upriver. Certainly it was not a sunny place, not even on the brightest of days, but here in the city proper the smoke did not hang so thickly nor so low upon our heads, and the local smoke arose from only a few high chimneys in the immediate area, from restaurant cookstoves and hotel fireplaces, with the blacker smoke of blacksmith shops or iron and glass works scattered farther up and down the river.

With all this clamorous activity, then, all this bustle and busy noise, how to account for the feeling Pittsburgh induced in me? A heaviness in my chest and limbs, a shortness of breath. A vague sense of oppression, as if the air itself were weighted and had begun to tighten around me. I knew nothing of premonitions at the time, of the way our bodies sometimes react at a cellular level to a looming darkness, the approach of disaster. But that is surely what it was.

The moment our bowline was seized by a boy stationed on the dock, a huge man standing next to him leaned forward to seize the rail not four feet from where I stood, and with the alacrity of a Macedonian lemur swung himself up and over the rail and landed with a smack of both soles firmly on our deck. He was the broadest-shouldered man I had ever encountered, thick enough across the chest to have been a prize attraction in one of Barnum's shows in New York City: *The Pittsburgh Strong Man! Stronger than a team of horses! Watch him snap a telegraph pole in half with his bare hands!*

An exaggeration, of course. But this was how he struck me. His arms at the bicep were as broad as my thigh, his fingers one-inch pipes. He wore dungarees and black boots and a chambray shirt with sleeves rolled nearly to the shoulder. And a battered brown hat, creased and double-peaked, looking something like a cross between a cowboy's Stetson and a crushed bowler. Slung from a loop in his waistband was a stout baling hook, the only tool of his trade other than animal strength.

"Good afternoon, gentlemen!" he boomed at Poe and me. He had a voice like a blunderbuss. "It's a fine day for casket work, isn't it now?"

With this he stepped atop the first tier of coffins and seized the braided cord from a box on the uppermost row, then turned both that coffin and the one next to it perpendicular to the row. He then faced us and, still grinning, backed up close to the two coffins he had positioned, reached backward with both hands, each hand seizing a braided handle, slid the boxes forward, and finally stepped down onto the deck with one long box balanced on the broad beam of each shoulder.

By now a gangplank had been set in place, and down it he went with his long thundering stride. Then up a wobbling staircase, two steps at a time, to a waiting wagon, where the empty coffins were deposited and moved into place. Then down the stairs he came again and onto the *Sweet Jeanine*.

Neither Poe nor I had yet moved. I wanted to see the same show again and would gladly have paid my two bits for the privilege.

The strong man gave me a wink as he seized two more boxes. It was all the invitation I needed. "Why so many?" I asked. "Is somebody building a house with them?"

His answer was delivered as lightly as my question had been. "Cholera!" he said. "That and murder—helps to keep the population down!" Then off he went with his two-shouldered load.

When he was out of earshot I turned to Poe. "Was he joking, do you think?"

"Not about the cholera, in any case."

I shuddered. "And the murders?"

Poe merely shrugged. By all appearances the heavy Pittsburgh air was not affecting him as it affected me.

It was then our captain offered his version of good-bye. Halfway down the gangplank himself, he shouted at us, "You can get off my boat anytime now."

We retrieved our bags. Poe said, "Our host will be expecting us to come by way of the canal. We will find him just off the aqueduct, no doubt."

We made our way up the same stairway the strong man had used, and in fact met him coming down. He offered me another wink in passing. I had the strangest urge to reach out and seize his hand. But I restrained myself. I nodded and continued on.

Then to the foot of Liberty Street, where a small crowd stood waiting for the next canal boat to arrive. We had beaten the canal boat by a full twenty minutes.

I spotted Brunrichter almost immediately. To claim that he was a mirror image of the man at my side would be claiming too much, but the resemblance was obvious. Though Brunrichter was starched and boiled where Poe was rumpled, and clean-shaven, but for his side whiskers, where Poe was bristled, both men shared the same slight physiognomy, the same broad forehead, thin mouth and tapered chin, the same fiery darkness in the eyes. I grasped Poe by the arm, then raised my finger to point his gaze toward Brunrichter. "That must be him," I muttered.

Poe, too, was taken aback, so much so that we came to a halt some ten yards from where the doctor waited, patiently watching across the aqueduct. "I am at a loss as to whether to be flattered or vexed," Poe said. "A man likes to think that he is unique in all the world. It is a bit unsettling to behold oneself in the face of another man."

The truth is that Brunrichter appeared a good bit more presentable than Poe. The doctor's clothes were finer, his carriage more aristocratic. He looked healthier and stronger, and certainly better groomed than Poe. But in Poe's mind's eye he no doubt saw himself (as we all tend to do) in a light more flattering than the one reality cast over him, and I said nothing to disabuse him of the notion. Instead I answered, "It's just like in your story, *William Wilson*."

"It is not at all similar," Poe said abruptly. "I need no conscience to haunt me."

Saying this, he seemed to recover all at once from the shock of Brunrichter's appearance and started forward again, his chin thrust high and a smile on his face. I remained a pace behind him, just so I could watch when he stepped up to the doctor and spoke.

Poe told him, by way of introduction, "You remind me of my brother Henry."

Brunrichter turned, saw Poe, and grinned broadly. "You remind me of myself," he said.

I joined them, standing just to the right of Poe, waiting to be introduced or at the least noticed. But Poe and Brunrichter continued to smile at one another, each looking like a man amused by his own reflection in a mirror. And then, for a moment, the strangest thing occurred. A dizziness swooped down on me, and I felt myself engulfed in a slow swirl of adumbrated air. This was no doubt due to the rigors of our trip, the sleeplessness and fatigue, the random and unhealthy diet. Or perhaps it was the smokiness of the Pittsburgh atmosphere, and the heavy palpitations it engendered in my chest. In any case, as I looked at Poe and the doctor smiling at one other, I was unable, just for a moment, to remember who was whom. For just a moment I experienced the peculiar vertigo of thinking that Brunrichter was the Poe I remembered from seven years past, vital and strong and optimistic, and Poe himself was the shadow image, aged and depleted, as half mad as a character created in one of his tales.

"And this?" Brunrichter said, noticing me at last. "Your valet?"

I bristled at the assumption.

"My protégé," said Poe, which prompted me to feel for him a resurgence of affection. "Mr. Augie Dubbins."

Brunrichter's eyebrows shot up. "Any relation to the venerable Auguste Dupin?"

"Dupin is Augie's namesake," said Poe.

Brunrichter reached for my hand. "I am very pleased to make your acquaintance, sir. Anyone who could inspire the genius of Dupin must be a fascinating individual in his own right."

He turned back to Poe. "Does he also share Dupin's powers of ratiocination?"

"He has a good mind," said Poe, "when he is not chasing after elephants."

"Elephants, sir?"

"It turns out that he has a great fondness for wildlife."

Poe's smile struck me as somehow sinister.

"Then you have come to the right place, young man. No city has a wilder life than Pittsburgh, if that is what you crave. As for your good mind, we can use that as well. Yours and Mr. Poe's especially."

He turned back to Poe, suddenly somber again. "Have you heard the news of our calamity?"

"I have heard of the cholera. We rode in with a boatload of coffins."

"And of our lost young ladies?"

"Lost how?" said Poe, and made an awkward attempt at a joke. "Misplaced?"

Brunrichter shook his head. "Vanished! Gone without a trace!"

Poe, at last, grew serious. "How many in all?"

"Six in as many weeks."

Poe closed his eyes for a moment, his thin mouth falling into a frown. I knew in that instant that he was thinking of his own Virginia, also gone without a trace. I felt something in my own heart sinking away with him, being drawn under.

When he opened his eyes again he said only, "Unhappy news."

To which Brunrichter replied, in a voice just as gloomy, "Unhappy news indeed."

I looked from one of them to the other, from Poe's gray eyes gazing downward, dull and weary, to the doctor's eyes of a similar hue but brighter, even lively as they stared at Poe, and again the dizziness swooped over me, but stronger and more violently this time, a smoky whirl of weakness in my brain, and I felt my legs collapsing but could do nothing to strengthen them, saw my field of vision blur, both men becoming ghost images half layered one atop the other, neither looking my way while the noise of the city swelled and came close, smothering me, and I gasped reflexively, sucking in the charcoal sky, and I felt myself falling, sinking down, sliding into a darkness miles and miles away.

Chapter Seven

I dreamed the dream of a seventeen-year-old boy, a warm and velvety dream of nearly stupefying pleasure in which Lula and I sat side by side wrapped in a rough Indian blanket, the campfire crackling, its heat paled by the heat of her hand beneath the blanket. . . .

And I awoke to find Poe leaning over me, his face close to mine, mouth smiling. Immediately I remembered my dream and slid a hand down to cover myself, felt a blanket there and pulled it up to my chest.

The moment my eyes had come open, Poe drew back and stood erect. Only then did he come into clear focus, and only then did I recognize that he was not Poe at all, but Dr. Brunrichter. He was quick to explain himself.

"No fever," he said. "And your heart is strong and regular. A day of rest will set you right as rain again."

I turned my head away from his smile. I would not call what I saw on his face an unctuous expression, but it was disconcerting still to see Poe's countenance on another man.

Pushing myself up on an elbow, I looked around. This was no hospital ward in which I lay, but the most luxurious quarters I'd ever found myself in, the bed a wide fourposter with a vaulted canopy of brocaded silk, the mattress thick with goose down, as were the pillows. The room was wide and spacious, brightly lit by a long row of windows. The walls were covered with a flocked material more like damask than mere wallpaper, a cream-colored background with a pattern of green climbing vines and tiny purple flowers. Over the length of the floor ran an intricately cut and colored Berber carpet.

I thought of my boots and how they must be dirtying the coverlet, and touched my feet together to ascertain if the boots had been removed. They had, much to my relief, though the relief promptly blossomed into embarrassment over the state of my soiled stockings.

"Am I in your home, sir?" I asked.

"You are indeed. And very welcome to be here."

"I fainted?"

"And in the bargain whacked your head on the cobblestones. Edgar and I loaded you into the carriage and brought you here. To the best doctor in town."

I put a hand to my head and felt a pad of gauze atop the knob above my left ear. "How much brain juice did I lose?"

Brunrichter laughed. "Not enough to worry about. There's plenty of juice left in you yet."

I started to sit up, but he held out a hand. "Lie there and rest for a while. I'll have tea and soup brought up to you soon."

"You needn't wait on me."

He leaned closer, as if to push me back down, but stopped short of touching me. "My advice is that you remain in bed. It will do you no good to be up and about so soon."

"Poe will be wondering."

"Edgar has already been apprised of your well-being. He is enjoying his bath just now, after which he will take his supper with me so as to discuss his presentation tomorrow evening. So, you see? There's nothing for you to do but to rest and heal yourself. In the morning I will introduce you and Edgar to my city."

I sensed, even in his gracious manner, that he wished to have Poe to himself for the evening. And that was fine. It was Poe who had been invited here, not me. I was a man of no distinction, no special genius for anything yet discovered. Besides, the bed was soft and inviting, and I had hopes of finding Lula hiding somewhere in all that goose down.

I eased my head onto the pillow. "As you wish," I told him.

He gave me a strange kind of bow then, almost Oriental, with his hands pressed together, thumbs against his chest. I fidgeted for a moment, feeling awkward, for it did not seem right or proper that this wealthy and accomplished gentleman should be bowing to me like a servant. In the end I attributed the gesture to his profound respect for Poe, and as a consequence I was made to feel even more remorseful over my earlier treatment of Poe, my churlishness and childish arrogance. If ever I could provoke a man like Brunrichter to be so admiring of me, only then would I have an inkling of the breadth and depth of Poe's gift. I resolved to make it up to him as soon as I was on my feet again. For if a man like Brunrichter could feel humility, then a man like me, spawned in a gutter and raised knee-deep in cow shit, should be its epitome.

It was a simple enough realization, and a simple

enough objective. And it would be the last uncomplicated thought I would entertain inside that house.

Tea and consommé arrived within minutes of Brunrichter's departure from my room, brought to me by a waddling, cherub-faced woman who introduced herself, with profuse apologies for disturbing me, as Mrs. Dalrymple. She had a wreath of white hair that seemed about to fly away like dandelion fuzz at any moment, and she sported a few white whiskers on her chin. But her mouth was kind and soft, and her eyes, though a bit too small for the roundness of her face, were still as hopeful as an infant's.

She set the tray across my lap and asked if she should feed me.

"It was just a knock on the head," I told her. "Not the first and probably not the last I'll receive."

"I thought you might be discombobulated from it. Can you manage a spoon?"

I took the soup spoon from her hand. "To be honest, I can't even remember fainting." I was suddenly so hungry that I barely got the last word out before shoving a spoonful into my mouth.

"Oh, this is heaven in a soup bowl," I said. "This is exquisite."

"It's not too hot?"

I shook my head only briefly, unwilling to interrupt the rhythm of my spoonwork.

"If that goes down all right," she told me, "I've got some chowder left from this afternoon. If you've a taste for something more filling, that is."

I pointed toward the window. "What in the world is that?" I asked.

She looked, squinted, stared at the glass for five seconds, then turned just in time to catch me lowering the bowl from my lips, the last of the broth drained away. Heretofore a bit shy, she now fixed me with a scowl that, because of the merriment of her eyes, could not conceal her pleasure.

"Is that the way your mother taught you to eat your soup, young man?"

"You wouldn't want to know the things my mother taught me."

"Oh I wouldn't, would I?"

"Not if you believe in an afterlife," I said, and held out the empty bowl to her. "Now then, as to that chowder . . . ?"

"And I suppose you wouldn't mind a few slices of roast beef to go with it?"

"I would indeed. Because a few is only half enough."

"And maybe you think you should have all of it?"

"I'll tell you what. Lift this tray off me and I'll follow you down to the kitchen. You won't even need to slice that beef for me. I'll chew it right off the cow."

She was trying hard not to laugh as she came for the tray. "I keep no cows in my kitchen, young man."

"You wouldn't mind a young bull poking around though, would you?"

She laughed so violently that she snorted. "Is that what you think you are, a young bull? My, my, we have a fine notion of ourselves, don't we?"

She reached for the tray then, but I held tight to its short stubby legs so that she could not lift it away. "Truly, Mrs. Dalrymple, I would prefer if you would allow me to join you in the kitchen. Truth is, I'm not comfortable being waited on."

"Used to it or not, if you want my chowder and meat

you will let go of this tray and behave yourself."

I held fast to the tray. "This bump on the head is nothing. I've taken worse knocks than this in my sleep."

"I'm sure I have no desire whatsoever to know what a young man does in his sleep."

I leaned close to her and whispered, "I'll bet sometimes you do."

She gasped at that and, releasing the tray, clamped shut her mouth, held her breath, and retreated from the room as quickly as she could waddle, her pale cheeks blooming suddenly like cherry blossoms in full sunlight.

•

"Your appetite for knowing things is near as big as your appetite for my beef," Mrs. Dalrymple said.

She had returned to my room not ten minutes after her abrupt departure, this time carrying a crock of corn chowder and a platter of sliced beef so mountainous that it had surely been constructed so as to shame me into submission. But I scraped every drop of chowder from the crock and forked one juicy slice of meat after another into my mouth. And all the while kept her there, perched primly on the window seat, with a steady stream of questions.

She enjoyed my informality, I think, and my playfulness. Her day was long—from six in the morning until seven at night, and even longer when she cooked for one of Brunrichter's frequent dinner parties. In any case she liked me and I liked her. (Did she remind me of Mrs. Clemm? Perhaps so. In fact now, when I look back on those days, I have to wonder if I am seeing Mrs. Dalrymple not as she was but as an imagined hybrid of Virginia and Mrs. Clemm, of Mrs. Clemm's compassion and generosity in the stout, soft body of a woman who had once looked like Virginia.)

What matters, however, is that Mrs. Dalrymple and I were comfortable with one another. As a result she answered my every question about that magnificent house in which I found myself, and about Dr. Brunrichter himself, his work as a surgeon at the Allegheny Hospital, his love of poetry and theater and music and science, his bottomless admiration for Poe. She told me that she was one of five employees all told, including Dr. Brunrichter's manservant Mr. Tevis, Mr. Keesling the stable master, and Marcus, the twelve-year-old stable boy. The fifth was Raymund, the Negro who maintained the grounds, but I was not likely to see much of him, nobody did, not even the rest of the staff.

"But his handiwork, now that's another thing entirely," she told me. "Come May he'll have this place ablaze with flowers and bushes. Mr. Keesling says that Raymund's an escaped slave, hopped off the Underground Railroad right here at this house. Course Mr. Keesling has seldom been known to be right about anything that doesn't apply to horses, so you can take that piece of information for what it's worth."

None but Mr. Tevis resided in the mansion, or Gingko Castle as it was called by Pittsburghers because of the pair of majestic Chinese gingko trees on the estate. Brunrichter was as rich as Croesus, she said, Teutonic by birth but related in some ambiguous way to the DeBeers diamond family. He easily could have afforded a staff of twenty if he wished, but he was an unassuming man, said Mrs. Dalrymple, who saw himself as a member of the working class, a man who drove his own carriage and despised such extravagances as footmen and valets.

"Which leaves all that extra work for me to do," she told me in a whisper. "Not that I'm complaining, mind you. As long as I can do it I'm happy to have the work. And he pays me well. Not that I have much need of money anymore. But I take it all the same."

She told me about her life as a widow who now shared her small home with two other widows in the neighborhood of Bayardsville, "twenty minutes away by foot. By these feet anyway. And all of it uphill no matter which direction you're going or coming from."

I wiped my mouth on a napkin made of finer cloth than the best of my two shirts. "And as to the young women . . . ," I began, only to be cut off by her laugh.

"Oh and that's what this has been about, is it? That's why you've been buttering me up with your nice words and all your questions. You've been working up to this, haven't you, Mr. Augie Dubbins? Well, if you're looking to me to help you bring a woman up here—"

"Mrs. Dalrymple! I'm shocked. I am shocked and offended. How could you ever suggest such a thing?"

"Why, I . . . I'm sorry. . . ."

"On the other hand, if you *want* me to bring a woman up here . . ."

She shook a stubby finger at me. "Keep it up, young man. I'll warm your bottom yet."

"And now who's flirting?" I asked.

"Oh my goodness! Now you just stop it!"

She was embarrassed but enjoying herself. And I enjoyed watching the rush of color to her cheeks and imagining how she would recount this conversation later that night to the other widow ladies with whom she lived.

•

"But honestly," I told her, "I was referring to the young women Dr. Brunrichter mentioned earlier. He said something about six young women who have disappeared."

She rolled her eyes and patted her chest; her expression was mournful. "Six in as many weeks."

"Just as he said."

"He's extremely troubled by it, him and all the other councilmen. They've been trying to organize a police force ever since this awful business began. Problem is, everybody wants protection but nobody wants to pay for it."

"There have been no bodies found?"

"Not a one."

"No ransom demands?"

"None that I have heard of."

"Is an investigation being conducted?"

"Of a sort," she said. "But seeing as how the watchmen in the various wards aren't often keen on cooperating with one another, the investigation is a fairly haphazard affair. There's been a handful of layabouts locked up over it—one fella had his head busted by the police for refusing to confess to the crimes. He died of it, God rest his soul. That was after number four, howsoever."

"And are the newspapers involved?"

"Oh, they don't shirk when it comes to calling for something to be done. Or for running stories and sketches of the poor missing girls. Mostly what they do is to keep the city in a state of fear."

"Are you afraid, Mrs. Dalrymple?"

"And why wouldn't I be? You think I'm too old to be murdered? Every woman in this city is half scared out of his wits."

"Has anyone suggested that perhaps these young women haven't been kidnapped but—how can I put this—have been introduced into a certain line of employment? In which case they are likely to be found in the kind of establishment no watchman would ever admit to frequenting."

"And I suppose that you, on the other hand, are just the man to be investigating these places?"

"If it will set your mind more at ease, Mrs. Dalrymple, I shall endeavor to do my utmost in that regard."

"Your utmost," she repeated, and tsk-tsked me. "I'm beginning to suspect that your utmost is like that Frenchman's balloon I read about last week. Full of hot air."

I clutched my heart as if fatally wounded by the remark.

She departed with the empty dishes and a low, sustained chuckle, leaving me with a very full belly, a soft mattress, and with thoughts of wanton women overflowing in my brain.

I dozed for a while, though not long, and when I awoke the gloaming was at my window. It was a gunmetal twilight, not delicately lit in pastels of sunset hue but of the color and chill of dull pewter. Upon awakening I required a few moments to retrieve my bearings and recall my whereabouts, and even afterward experienced that odd sense of displacement that comes from awakening in a strange place at the end of a long journey.

Yet enough light remained in the sky that I, now standing at the window, could see that my bedroom was located on the mansion's second floor, and that it looked out upon a rear yard. Some hundred yards or so out in that yard stood a line of hardwood trees, all thirty to forty feet high, all still quite skeletonal despite the buds of new leaves. A wind was blowing the high branches, shuddering the thinner limbs. And in the uppermost reaches of three of the trees, three adjoining trees near the western end of the copse, a gathering of grackles huddled, as shiny black as crows but only half their size.

The yards were spacious, with no other homes in sight. From my window I could see all or part of several outbuildings, most notably a greenhouse, a carriage house and stable, a small corral containing four sheep (these would be released daily, by Raymund, I presumed, and allowed to manicure the grounds). Also visible was a stone pad on which sat an anvil and other blacksmithing implements. Beside it, a redbrick bread oven.

By standing with my face close to the window and peering east along the glass I could see approximately one-fourth of an intricate hedge maze. It struck me as such a civilized accoutrement for a place like Pittsburgh, an enclosed and labyrinthine path leading, I surmised, to a comfortable bench at the secluded center, a place for meditation and reflection. Later I would discover that it was not a labyrinth but a true maze after all; that is, not with a single path meant to lead the walker to a symbolic center of his soul, but a series of convoluted switchbacks and dead-ends, such as might lead not to quietude but frustration, confusion, and even panic.

In any case, the outdoors beckoned. I had been in this room too long, despite its luxury. In fact the luxury itself made me ill at ease; I was hesitant to touch anything lest I somehow upset the elegance. Besides, my body was stiff with inactivity, stiff from four days on a boat.

I looked about for my boots, found them under a

chair, clean and brushed. Reshod, I eased open my bedroom door and stepped out into the hallway.

I will not bore you with my egress along that corridor and down the long, curved stairway except to say that it left its mark on me, a plain boy used to plain things, suckled on lust for the indulgences of others but weaned of that particular lust on the flatlands of Ottawa County, where I'd learned to covet freedom above all else, and came to recognize the impossibility of freedom when encumbered with the ballast of too much wealth.

In that frame of mind, and with that history etched into my psyche, how could a place like Gingko Castle not fill me with an odd mixture of emotions, of feelings that ran the gamut from envy to contempt? The high ceilings and parquet floors, the gasolier lights in their golden wall sconces, the marble statuettes placed here and there (being busts, I assumed, of Roman gods and goddesses, though for all I knew of mythology they might have been Greek instead), the elaborate oil paintings in ornate gilded frames . . . ?

The stairway descended in a graceful parabolic curve to the front foyer, and here I found the summation, the encapsulation of the mansion and all it represented. Here were but three items to catch the eye. First, hanging above the very center of the foyer, suspended on a golden rod from a ceiling at least fifteen feet high, was a chandelier so huge, so overdone, of such behemoth proportions that it made me wonder how the rest of the building withstood its pull of weight. All gold and crystal, it consisted of three tiers of hand-blown bulbs, each shaped like a wavering flame ten inches high, and inside which a gasolier flame fluttered brightly. At the center of the chandelier, hanging as if suspended by invisible wires, was a huge china globe, the sun in miniature, luminescent. The entire affair was both magnificent and grotesque.

The second item, the doorway. It was a double door, each half four feet wide by ten high, framed in red Barbadian mahogany, intricately scrolled. The door handles were solid tubes of glass four inches in diameter, curved into a loop and twisted like braided rope, and tinted the most delicate shade of rose. The door panels were of inch-thick etched glass, a fleur-de-lis pattern, exquisitely intricate but permitting no transparent view of the outside from the foyer, nor, conversely, from the outside in.

The final item on which my eyes fell, and which held my interest longest because it was not merely grandiose, not merely magnificent on a larger-than-human scale, but to my way of thinking, all too human, was a life-sized wood carving of the Delaware Indian chief Nemacolin (who, for the time being, I knew only as a nameless Indian).

I do not mean to imply that the sculpture was not magnificently done, that the folds of the Chief's robe did not appear to be made more of wood-grained velvet than of obstinate black oak, or that his head feathers, complete down to the last crenellation of each individual quill, did not appear newly plucked from a wild, if wood-grained, turkey. Or that Nemacolin's bare feet, even rooted as they were to a wooden base, did not look as if they might at any moment return to the soft matting of the forest.

It was the Chief's eyes that spoke to me, that looked up at me from the bottom of the stairs and drew me slowly down, that then held me there in the foyer, face-to-face with him. I know that trees have the oldest memories and the kindest hearts, but how could wood convey to me such remorse, such abject regret?

"Chief Nemacolin," said Dr. Brunrichter, who had walked up quietly behind me and startled me with his voice.

I turned. He was standing in the archway to the library, a snifter of cognac in hand. I leaned a bit to my left and now saw behind him, seated in a chair of maroon leather but leaning half out of it, his elbow resting awkwardly on the corner of a square Chickering piano, Poe. He sat there gazing sleepy-eyed, not looking in my direction but straight across the library, grinning (imbecilicly, I thought), one leg draped over the opposite knee. His face was flushed. He was wearing clothes I had never seen before, black trousers, a shirt almost too white for the room, a black silk cravat—clothes of a material far too fine for Poe's wallet.

"He blazed trails over the Allegheny Mountains for Christopher Gist, among others," the doctor continued, and raised his glass as if to toast the sloe-eyed Chief. "Helped to open up the West to Americans."

"His own people must despise him," I said.

Dr. Brunrichter was taken aback by my impertinence. "Hardly," he said.

"Of course, a man in your position could never subscribe to such a viewpoint."

I must have struck him as the most callow of youths, arrogant and ungrateful to boot. There I was with my belly stuffed with Brunrichter's food, my mind and body rested from his fine soft bed, my skull tended to and patched by his own skillful hands—yet I stood there impugning the man's open-mindedness, insulting him.

Even as I did so and heard my own voice, I had to wonder if perhaps one of Poe's imps had begun to work its perversity on me.

As for the doctor, he remained a good host, and indulged me. "Come into the library," he said. "Join us in a snifter and a cigar. You can enlighten me."

He seated me to the right of Poe, in an armchair of deep brown leather that faced the fireplace. Poe had looked up at me briefly when I came in, greeted me with the sleepy smile already on his lips, then returned to gazing deep into the fire of fragrant apple wood. Brunrichter, in the meantime, went to a small trolley table placed close to a window and poured another drink, brought it and a cigar to where I sat, and even struck a lucifer to light my cigar.

I could not help but notice that he was treating me, a yet unwashed boy, as his equal here, a gentleman, and though I scrutinized his face for some evidence that it was all a charade, I found none. I should then have been able to bask in the man's magnanimity, but I could not. Something rankled at me. Try as I might, I could not lay a finger on it.

I turned to Poe. "So what have you two been talking about this evening?"

Poe lazily raised his right hand, a cold cigar stuck between finger and thumb, and made a sedated attempt at a dramatic flourish. "Many things. Many things indeed."

Brunrichter added another stick of apple wood to the fire. Never before had I seen a fireplace so free of ash and soot stain, from the green-and-white tiles to the dark walnut mantelpiece to the heavy, ornate andirons. And yet the man himself, the master of this fanatical cleanliness, was himself a master of informality, the epitome of a casual demeanor.

He caught me gawking at the room and everything in it, saw how my eyes scanned one objet d'art after another to land, finally, on a collection of glass walking canes all leaning against one another in a corner like a display of wildly baroque icicles.

"We're very proud of our glassworks here," he told me as he resettled in his chair. "Some of the finest craftsmen in the country work here."

"But canes?" I asked. "Walking canes made of glass?"

He laughed. "Not very practical, I agree. And yet . . ." After a moment he stood again, went to the display and picked up one of the canes, brought it over to me and laid it across my lap. "The impractical is sometimes the most beautiful."

The tip of the cane was shaped as the pointed end of a serpent's tail and protected with a silver cap. The crystal clear body of the snake was entwined around an equally flawless crystal sassafras twig. The handle was, of course, the snake's broad head, its eyes tiny buttons of silver.

"There's no question that it's lovely," I said, and stuck the cigar in my mouth so as to have a hand free to feel the sinuations of the snake's glass skin.

"It's yours," he said.

I nearly dropped the cigar out of my mouth.

He waved a hand, dismissing any protest I might have uttered, and returned to his chair on the other side of Poe. All this time Poe had not taken his eyes off the fire. His lips had never lost their sad and crooked smile.

Brunrichter did not even allow me an opportunity to thank him for his gift. "Edgar and I have embarked upon a conspiracy," he said. "Will you join us in it?"

"A conspiracy?" I repeated. (Here you will need to picture me as I suddenly felt: an unshaven and unwashed youth, his clothes the same he had slept in for the past several days, a crystal snifter of cognac clutched in a hand whose fingernails were black with dirt, an expensive cigar in the other and similarly soiled hand, and a finely crafted and no doubt outrageously expensive glass cane balanced precariously across his lap. There I sat, unaccomplished in virtually every noble pursuit, a gutter rat with his tail still dripping from the sewer, and in the company of two distinguished and highly accomplished men, one of whom had just now invited me into a partnership. If I had felt vaguely rankled upon entering this room, I was by this time wholly disarmed of every sensation but that of awe.)

Brunrichter nodded. "The disappearances of which I spoke earlier. The six young women. Edgar and I, he with his intuition and me with my science, have determined to act as one mind so as to put an end to this crime."

"And me?" I asked. "How can I assist?"

"In any way you wish. Edgar assures me that you are a very perceptive young man."

"Mrs. Dalrymple tells me that the police investigation has accomplished little."

"And how could it do otherwise? Their lack of organization is appalling. Were it not for the constant admonishments from myself and other councilmen, nothing whatsoever would have been accomplished."

"And what has been accomplished so far?" I asked.

Again he smiled at my impertinence. "You are correct, young man. Nothing has been accomplished. That is why we are all so frustrated. Six young women have disappeared as if into thin air, and in most cases not even the exact locations of the disappearances are known.

"But you," he said, "being of an age, more or less, of these young ladies, perhaps you can keep an ear to the ground, as it were. As you travel about the city you might hear a bit of information the police have not been made privy to."

"If I do, I will let you know immediately."

"We would all be grateful for that," he said.

For a minute or so we sat in silence, Brunrichter and I drawing on our cigars, letting the smoke out slowly. Then the doctor leaned forward in his chair and spoke to Poe. "What kind of man, do you think, might be responsible for these crimes?"

A pause before Poe answered. "Brute," he said. "A savage brute."

Brunrichter nodded, then looked my way. "Would you agree?"

I was startled to be included like this, on an equal footing with these learned men. But I tried not to show my nervousness and to live up to the task. "Well, yes. An animal, to be sure. Who else could do such a thing?"

Again the doctor nodded, then leaned back in his chair. "Conceding that," he finally said, "by which I mean, conceding the brutish nature of the crimes, or at least the appearance of such, should we not also consider this brute a very clever fellow?"

I glanced at Poe, expecting his protest, but he merely sat there staring at the fire as before, his brow now furrowed.

Brunrichter continued, "To leave not a trace of evidence—I find that fact intriguing. No bodies, no buttons torn off and left behind, not so much as a single drop of blood to pinpoint exactly where one of the girls might have disappeared. The man must be a magician."

I could think of nothing to refute his logic.

"This is what troubles me most," he said. "A dumb beast is easy to track. But one so guileful . . ."

He swished the brandy in his glass, sipped from it, and then, a moment later, shook his head. "We must be even more clever than he," he said. "Our gravest mistake would be to assume too little."

The silence of the room felt ponderous. It was made so not only by the subject of conversation but by Poe's apparent mood, his lethargy. On previous occasions when I had witnessed him at his most morose or melancholy, there was, even then, an intensity to his emotion, a bright dark fire, if you will. But on this night no intensity of demeanor was visible, no flame. Only the cold, wet ashes of indifference.

Hoping to alter the climate of the room, I directed my next statement to Poe. "And what of our other plans in the meantime? To head south, soon after your reading tomorrow night?"

"Two readings," Poe said. "The second . . . a week tomorrow?"

"Next Saturday evening," Brunrichter confirmed. "At the Drury Theater. To be hosted by the Pittsburgh Institute for Arts and Sciences."

"Arts and Sciences," said Poe in a dreamy monotone.

"I hadn't planned to stay so long," I told them both.

Brunrichter said, "The choice is yours, of course. But you should know that you are welcome here, both you and Edgar, to remain as long as you wish."

Poe said nothing.

"Thank you but I . . . I really don't know what I would do with myself. I have plans to go to Mexico. To join the conflict there."

"If your intention is firm," the doctor said, "I won't attempt to dissuade you. In fact, if you wish, I might perhaps be of some assistance in that venture. There are two local militia outfits in Mexico already—the Duquesne Grays and the Pittsburgh Blues. If you will allow me to do so, I can arrange for you to be assigned to one of them. Would the rank of adjutant suit you?"

I could only blink in reply.

"In the meantime," said Brunrichter, "you absolutely must remain through Sunday. In the afternoon we shall have a picnic. And on Saturday evening—"

"A hanging!" said Poe, suddenly reanimated.

I almost leapt from my seat, so shrill was Poe's exclamation.

Brunrichter grinned at him, then reached across his armrest to pat Poe's knee.

And now Poe swiveled toward me. He waved his cigar at the doctor. "These Presbyterians, they take their pleasures sadly. Or was it seriously, Alfred—how did you put it?"

"Above all else, we take them humbly."

"Yes, yes, that was the word. I've never had much use of that word myself, you know."

"Nor should you, a man of your talents."

"Precisely!" said Poe.

And with that, a moment later, his body sagged again and he sank back into his chair, and his gaze returned to the fireplace.

Both Brunrichter and I watched him for a moment. Then the doctor leaned forward and spoke to me, softly, as if Poe, seated between us, could not hear.

"I can sense your concerns, Mr. Dubbins. And I share them. But I firmly believe—and I pray that you will come to appreciate this as well—I believe that Edgar is in a precarious state of health right now. He suffers grievously from the loss of his wife. For that reason, I think it best that he remain here in my care, and in the company of those who will delight in his gifts."

When I saw no flicker of awareness from Poe, no sign that any of the doctor's words had reached Poe's ears, I said, "He shouldn't be drinking. Sometimes all it takes is one drink and . . . there is no predicting the effect it may have on him."

Brunrichter nodded. "He is not a well man, I agree. I do believe, however, that, given time, I might alter the course of whatever it is that afflicts him."

"Well, I'm all for that," I said, and kept an eye on Poe's face, alert for any sign that our words had reached him, a twitch of his mouth, a curling of his lip. There was no such sign. "But to take him to a hanging? Is that wise?"

"He asked if he might accompany me. How could I refuse? He is, after all, an honored guest."

"And why do you have to go?"

"As a physician, it is one of my duties. To pronounce the condemned man dead. Hearing of it, Edgar thought it a wonderful opportunity for himself, because of the kind of tales he writes. You, of course, are more than welcome to accompany us. And to the picnic as well. It goes without saying that you will be a most welcome addition to each and every event. I might even say an essential addition. From what Edgar has told me, and he has told me much, you provide a stabilizing influence in his life. Perhaps the last remaining one."

I had no idea what to say to all this. I had made my plans and was eager to hold to them. But there sat Poe, the man I felt closer to than any other; the man who had witnessed far too much of the macabre already in his life, and had imagined all the rest of it; a man who could not be trusted to have a single drink. Yet there he sat, thoroughly besotted, as enthused about a hanging as about his own literary presentation. And, by all appearances, the very things he should be avoiding had in fact sedated him.

In all the hours we had been together, both earlier in New York and more recently on this trip, I had never before seem him so obviously at rest. His body was slack, even limp in the chair, his left arm hanging so low that the snifter with its ounce of brandy was resting on the floor. The cigar in his right hand, its ash long ago grown cold, had slipped from his fingers and lay on the carpet. His eyelids were open but heavy. His mouth, as if somehow it had slipped the bonds of its own natural gravity, turned up weightlessly at both corners. He had been in the home of Dr. Brunrichter for but a few hours, a half day, and, for the first time ever in all the time I had known him, the restless fire in him burned low. He looked content.

Who was I to refute a word the doctor had said?

"As you wish," I told him.

Brunrichter raised his glass to me. And then, like co-conspirators, we drank.

Chapter Eight

I slept late the next morning and awoke to a different house, a different climate. Whereas the previous evening had been distinguished by a dearth of human sounds, the morning, only an hour or so after sunrise, was clamorous by comparison. At the pitcher and basin in my room I splashed water over my face and slicked back my hair, then brushed my teeth, pulled on my clothes for the day, and ventured downstairs.

In the kitchen, from whence most of the clamor originated, I found Mrs. Dalrymple skittering like a waterbug between her cookstove and worktable, frying eggs and ham at one, kneading a huge bowl of dough at the other, all the while singing sweetly off-key.

" 'On Springfield mountain there did dwell a lovely youth, I knowed him well. Too-roo-dee-nay, Too-roo-dee-noo, Too-roo-dee-nay, Too-roo-dee-noo . . . ' "

I remained on the threshold for a minute or two, grinning to myself. When finally she spoke, she didn't even look in my direction. "If you think you're hiding around that corner, Mr. Dubbins, you'd be wrong. I smelled those clothes of yours coming from halfway down the stairs."

I stepped into the kitchen. "That fragrant, am I?"

She wrinkled up her nose. "Let me get these dough dodgers to frying, and then I'll find you something to put on that doesn't smell like it came from inside a dead dog."

"I doubt the doctor's clothes will suit my style."

"Are you suggesting that you have a style?" she asked.

There was nothing malicious in her tone nor in her character, so it was not possible to take offense. Nor could I rebut her observations. "First things first," I said. "Privy out that door there?"

"Back where you came from," she said.

"Pardon me?"

"The privy is indoors. Down the hall from your room."

I had never before heard of such a thing, and told her so.

"Go see for yourself. And when you're finished, pull the chain hanging from the ceiling."

With that she plucked a handful of dough off the ball, flattened it to the size of her palm and laid it in a skillet of sizzling lard. She did this twice more, every movement precise. With the third dough dodger frying, she turned to a shelf to seize a plate in her left hand, turned to the stove where, with her right hand, she picked up a flat ladle and flipped the fried eggs and a slab of ham onto the plate, flipped the dough dodgers over in their grease, slapped the plate down onto the table, seized the coffeepot and filled a mug half with coffee and half with cow's milk from a white ceramic pitcher, set the mug down beside the plate, turned back to the stove and, using a long fork this time, speared all three dough dodgers up out of the skillet and shook them onto the plate with the eggs and ham and then turned to me and said, "You going upstairs or aren't you?"

I had my eyes on the food—my eyes, my nose, my mouth and my stomach. "No hurry," I said.

She watched me a few moments longer, grinning, maybe waiting to see how long before the drool dropped out of my mouth. Finally I turned to her with plaintive eyes.

"Go on then," she said, and I, like a hound let loose from his chain at last, dove for the table.

She reminded me so much of Mrs. Clemm that I could not stop smiling even as I shoveled in the food. I was halfway through the feast before I paused for a breath. "Shouldn't I maybe wait for Poe and Dr. Brunrichter?" I asked.

"If you're angling for two breakfasts," she said, "you can think again."

I returned to my food.

"Besides which, the doctor is off to the hospital already. Left while you were still snoring like a baby. Mr. Poe will be taking breakfast in his room this morning."

"Is he ill?"

"Working on his speech is what I was told."

I nodded. "These appearances don't sit easy with him. He confided to me once that he now and then suffers from stage fright."

"Lord, and who wouldn't, what with all those faces staring up at you every second?"

We spoke no further until I was sopping up the last puddle of greasy yolk with the last piece of fried bread. "And you," she said. "What do you intend to do with this day?"

"Thought I'd maybe just sit right here until dinnertime."

"You'd better think again," she said.

"In that case, I have some plans for myself."

"If they don't require smelling like a wet dog six days dead, I suggest you let me do something about those clothes you got on. In fact, here's what you do. You go on upstairs and find that privy. There's a bathtub in there too. You put the stopper in the drain, then push on a big red button you'll see on the wall there. I'll start filling up your tub from down here."

"From here? How is that possible?"

She motioned for me to follow, then led me to the adjacent pantry. Here she showed me a large copper tank of water, a kind of boiler mounted over a small woodstove. She had me place my hand on the tank; it was hot to the touch. Connected to this tank was a hand pump.

"I fill the tub from here," she said.

"I never saw anything like this in Ohio."

"You won't find many of them in Pittsburgh either. But you can always count on the doctor to be trying something new."

In short, I spent the next hour or so reveling in the pleasures of indoor plumbing. No outhouse or washtub could ever thrill me again.

Later, newly outfitted in the dark blue trousers and plain white shirt Mrs. Dalrymple had laid outside the privy door, I set forth to discover what other wonders the city of Pittsburgh might have in store for me.

Dr. Brunrichter's estate, situated as it was on Ridge Avenue, in an unpopulated area that would later become the city's Eleventh Ward (at the time there were only five wards), enjoyed a commanding view to its west of the Allegheny River. From the front veranda I could see down to the Merchant Street Bridge, the Pennsylvania Canal Aqueduct and even the Hand Street Bridge. To the east, though perhaps twice as distant, lay the deeper Monongahela River. Where the two rivers converged at a place called, unpoetically but appropriately, The Point, here was where the tumult of the rivers' business climaxed.

Upon my arrival the day before, I had glimpsed enough of this business, the congestion and din and hurry, to want to see the rest of it. Pittsburgh's topography of hustle and confusion reminded me of the Manhattan I had known as a boy, and there was still enough of that boy in me that I longed to experience the familiar freneticism again. Besides, I did indeed have some plans for myself that day, and, in fact, for my every day in Pittsburgh. Plans that would, I naively hoped, ensure my future. What those plans did not include and were calculated to prohibit were my being, here or anywhere else, a mere appendage of E. A. Poe. I no longer delighted in the notion of being his valet—not his or anyone else's. What I intended to do, what I believed myself ready to become, was a man in my own right.

And so I set off toward the Point, the nexus, my beginning, my birth as a man, the place where that man would be born fully formed between the flow of two rivers.

But in every birth, a death, as Poe would have said. For every gift, its curse.

Of the remainder of that day there is little to remark. Not that I, with eyes so long narcotized by the dreary flat ness of Ohio, failed to find much of it remarkable. Heading straight for the Allegheny from Brunrichter's estate, I first crossed a wide grassy area, drained by the downslope but still slippery with dew. Then across an unpaved lane called Ferguson Road where, in advance of the first real street, called Liberty, lay an undeveloped expanse in the process of becoming the Pennsylvania Railroad Depot. Then down Lumeer Street, also dirt, on its dive toward Duquesne Way and the Allegheny River.

I was chased halfway to the water by a pig, a huge spotted sow who, once she had burst through a forsythia bush and set all that snorting lard and bacon into motion, had all she could do to keep her stubby legs in advance of the caboose as she pursued me down the hill. At one point she was so close to me, snorting spittle at my heels, that I swung into a side lane lest I be run over by her hurtling hams. She, unable to alter direction, kept going. She skidded and rumbled another thirty yards before managing to put the brakes on. When finally at a stop, she sucked air through her quivering snout for a while, and then, albeit reluctantly, she turned and, struggling like a hod carrier under a double load, plodded back uphill.

When we passed on opposite sides of the street she gave me a sideways glance and a snort, as if to insinuate that I was the cause of all her troubles. I laughed, unaware that, before the day was out, her sentiment would have spread.

To dispense, however, with the morning. Along the cobblestones of Duquesne Way I followed the river south, strolling first past the Merchant Street Bridge, and then, five blocks later, under the aqueduct, between the thoroughfares of Penn and Liberty. Here the major retail trade of the city was conducted, the glut of hotels and restaurants and taverns, the tailors and milliners, tobacconists, confectioners, stationery vendors, button shops, patent medicine shops, hackneys for hire, drays and handcarts, carriages and wagons—every conveyance conceivable, every imaginable product for sale.

Even here a few pigs wandered about at will, and perhaps twice as many chickens. I saw more dogs than either of these two, however, and more rats than dogs. No one but me appeared to give any of these animals so much as a glance.

I myself was more an object of curiosity to Pittsburghers than were their stray animals. Merchants sweeping the stones in front of their shops would pause to give me the once-over. They might grunt a hello in response to my own, but it was a grudging acknowledgment. Women, on at least three occasions, crossed the street so as not to walk too close to me. I was a stranger, a new face, and all new faces were regarded with suspicion, all appraised with the silent question, *Is he the one? Is he the murderer in our midst?* I wonder how they might have scrutinized me had I not bathed and put on fresh clothes that morning.

Three long blocks later I passed under the Hand Street Bridge. (I wonder now if, as I did so, I might have felt something tugging at my heart, might have felt some ineffable pull from a dark brick building up on Penn Street. I cannot now think of that building underneath the bridge, Miss Jones's School for Young Ladies, without having to swallow something hard and sharp that rises into my throat, something I can only assume to be a broken splinter of my heart.)

Then under the St. Clair Street Bridge and to the Point, where Duquesne Way rounded the blunt tip of land and became Water Street. From the Point as far up the Monongahela as Try Street, well past Roebling's wire suspension bridge, Water Street was piled high with freight, some of it coming, some of it going. On this side of Pittsburgh was conducted the bulk of the city's import and export trade. The Monongahela, thanks to a series of locks, was more routinely navigable than the

Allegheny, so the long wharf here was lined with one large steamboat after another, at least two dozen of them on that particular morning, as well as long trains of barges filled with sand for the glass works, coal or pig iron for the foundries.

I sampled it all, every scent and sight and sound of the raucous city. Knowing myself an innocent, I was scarcely bothered by the suspicion with which I was regarded. For how I loved the music of the dock workers' curses and shouts, the creak of overloaded wagons, the clop of horses' hooves. This was a roisterous symphony I could dance to.

I danced an even livelier step after an hour-long visit to an office on Fulton Street, my lone objective for the day. Livelier because I emerged from those dim rooms with my clothes stinking of the intoxicating perfume of tobacco smoke and ink, and with, more importantly, a new half eagle in my pocket, a five-dollar gold piece. I emerged, I imagined, as a whole new man, re-created and rechristened inside that office, and for the remainder of the day I did nothing but bask in the glow I thought I emanated—a glow, I thought, to banish the smoke and haze of odoriferous Pittsburgh, to freshen every breath I breathed. A glow, I thought, to render my seven years of servitude in Ottawa County inconsequential, my ugly boyhood in the sewers of Gotham as distant as a month-old dream. A glow, I thought, that might even cast a bit of healing light into a corner of Poe's midnight soul.

Despite my elevated spirits all the day, or perhaps because of them, I chose not to return to the mansion on Ridge Avenue until the supper hour had passed. I was determined not to be treated as an appendage of Poe, fed because Poe was fed, welcomed because Poe was welcomed. But he would be expecting me at his reading before the Quintillian Society, and in that I could not disappoint him.

Upon my return to Gingko Castle, I was met in the front lobby by Brunrichter's manservant, Mr. Tevis. He must have been stationed there to watch for me, for I was yet six paces off the veranda when the door came open, and he, with one broad arm holding the door against the wall, addressed me by name. He was not a tall man, an inch or so shorter than me, but broad of face and shoulders and chest, broad all the way down to the soles of his brogans. Nor was he corpulent. He moved with a lightness, even a delicacy of step. I might say that he was bearlike and possessed of an ursine grace. The heavy black suit he wore buttoned close to the neck, the heavy black hair and muttonchops, the thick stubble of whiskers that, though his face was cleanly shaven, adumbrated his countenance—all this, even the deep brown luster of his eyes, all this added to the bearish illusion. I liked him immediately.

"Have you had your dinner, Mr. Dubbins?"

"I have, thank you."

"Would you care for a bit extra before the evening? Mrs. Dalrymple tells me that you have a hearty appetite."

"It's been well appeased, thank you very much."

"In that case, sir, I have been instructed to convey you at your convenience to the Quintillian Club."

"You have, have you?" I remained standing on the porch, rather amused by his formality.

"At Mr. Poe's request. If you are so inclined, sir."

"Oh, I am inclined, all right. I have been inclined all day."

"Do you have appropriate dress?" he asked.

"I'm guessing that I do not. What would be appropriate?"

"A frock coat and cravat have been provided. You will find them in your chambers."

"Thanks to the good doctor, of course."

"Of course."

With that he waved me inside with a subtle turn of his hand. I slipped past him into the foyer, started for the staircase but then paused, staring up at the amazing chandelier overhead. Tevis closed the door, then waited half a minute before speaking.

"Shall I assist you, sir?"

I had been mesmerized by own reflection in the chandelier's crystal globe. The soft evening light, gone from lemony to amber, was coming through the glass window over the doors at just the right angle, coupled with the chandelier's own illumination and the lights from the rest of the house, to show myself back at me, small and contorted by the curvatures of glass, a dwarf inside a fishbowl.

He asked a second time, "Sir? Do you require some assistance?"

I blinked, looked away from my warped image, saw a less disturbing one in the hallway armoire, and answered, "Thanks for the offer, but I can change my own drawers," and bounded up the stairs two at a time.

Ten minutes later Tevis took me by carriage back down the hill. It was a brougham, driven from the outside, myself inside alone, which provided me no opportunity to talk with him further that night. I wanted to ask how Poe had seemed that day, whether nervous or calm, sickly or well, but since I could not I busied myself with fidgeting inside the clothes Brunrichter had provided, very nice clothes indeed but not what I was used to, so that even the silk cravat at my neck, soft and loose as it was, made me conscious of every nervous swallow of spittle. I was concerned not only about Poe's performance but about my own when I delivered my news to him, for I had devised a small bit of theatrics myself, call it a ten-second soliloquy, which I believed would mend all resentments and bring Poe and me shoulder to shoulder once again, as close as brothers.

I knew neither Poe nor myself as well as I believed.

Chapter Nine

The Quintillian Club held its bi-monthly meetings in what had once been a stone chapel adjacent to the Western University of Pennsylvania. I entered this building into an anteroom, a small lobby that opened onto the chapel, a room in the shape of a truncated triangle, wider where I stood, narrowing to the altar, lit principally with candles in wall sconces, plus here and there an attractive oil lamp with a glass shade the color of afternoon sky.

There must have been close to one hundred people crammed into that chapel, about half of them seated, the rest standing about in lively pockets of conversation. A long refectory table against one wall held several carafes of wine and platters of petits fours. From the air of festivity that came from the room, along with an occasional guffaw or shrill trill of laughter, I deduced that many of the guests had already helped themselves to the wine. I could only hope that Poe had not.

The chapel's pews had been replaced by several rows of straightback chairs, each comfortably padded with a red velvet seat and back cushion. All icons of religious connotation, save for the stained-glass windows, had been removed. Now, instead of representations of Christ or the Virgin Mother, there were busts of Plato, Shakespeare, and other long-dead masters of the rhetorical arts. The pipe organ, however, remained, as did a harpsichord. The smoke from the candles and oil lamps, and from the many pipes being puffed, clung to the rafters in a pinkish belly-lit cloud.

Where the altar had been was now only a lectern. Poe and Brunrichter and a half-dozen others stood together just to the side and a step below the lectern. Brunrichter was beaming at Poe, who stood there weaving a tale of some kind, or so it seemed by the way he waved his right hand about, up and down through the air as if to simulate the rolling motion of the sea.

The moment he spotted me he held up a finger to his small audience, whispered to Brunrichter, and then came striding toward me. Not until he had weaved his way past the many people between us did I notice that an empty wine glass dangled from his left hand.

He clapped a hand on my shoulder and grinned, I thought, unnaturally. "My boy!" he said, his voice too loud. "I am so glad to see you here. I was worried you might miss my triumph."

"Impossible," I said, and tried to return his smile, but failed, for my mood was no match for his mania.

He read the concern in my expression. "One glass,

Augie. Surely you would not begrudge me one glass in celebration. Even Muddy would have conceded one glass on a night such as this."

I should have kept my mouth shut. Who was I to set myself up as his caretaker? But the events of the day, and my inflated opinion of myself, fueled my impudence. "The wonderful thing about wine," I said, "is that a single glass of it can be very soothing to the nerves—"

He leaned close and interrupted in a confidential tone. "And despite all appearances, my nerves are in great need of a soothing influence."

"If it's only one glass then. So that your natural brilliance can flow more freely."

"But not so freely as to become a torrent of nonsense, am I right?" He squeezed my shoulder and laughed with his mouth wide open.

I should have known then from that single gesture, so anomalous on that thin, sad mouth, I should have known then that he was already intoxicated. But I, like Poe, like all of us, I suppose, saw life with my eyes focused primarily on myself.

"I have some good news to share with you," I told him. "But after the reading. When you have a few moments to yourself."

"Good news? Tell me now!"

"I think later would be better."

"Never keep good news until later," he said. "Good news can sour with time. So tell me now, and make this evening even brighter for both of us."

Nearly all of the audience in the chapel, those seated as well as those standing, were looking our way, smiling benignly, expectantly, as if my conversation with Poe was a part of the festivities. I stepped around Poe so that my back faced the chapel. I wanted this moment to be between only the two of us.

"Do you remember," I asked, "the first time I came to your house? The cottage you had out on Bloomingdale Road?"

"Of course," he said. But there was a vagueness in his eyes, and though I wondered for a moment if he did indeed remember that day, I quickly pushed my doubts aside. "It was the morning your story about Mary Rogers was published in the *Mirror*. You gave me a percentage of the money you had earned from that story."

"As you well deserved," he said.

I reached into my pocket then and pulled out the coin I had placed there. "I would like now," I told him, "to return the courtesy." I took his free hand in mine, turned it palm up, and laid a silver dollar in the middle of it.

He continued to grin at me. "The money I gave you was not a loan, Augie. There is no need to repay it. Besides, this is several times the amount—"

"This is not a loan either. It's a payment to my collaborator."

"On what did we collaborate?" he asked, still amused.

"On my story. I sold it to the *Pittsburgh Daily Chronicle*."

And now his smile twitched. "Your story?"

"About the elephants. The one you helped me to write."

A look of pain, quick as an arrow, flashed across his eyes. He glanced beyond me then, out over the heads of the audience, up into the smoke. Then fixed his gaze on me once more.

"Augie," he said evenly, all trace of humor gone, "you

did not inform them at the *Chronicle*, did you, that I had a hand in crafting that piece, that . . . ?"

"I told them I wrote it myself."

His face relaxed a bit. "As you did."

"Yes, but . . . but if you want your name attached to it—"

"No! No, it will be bad enough, a piece like that, just to have people assuming that I wrote it for you, a story about *elephants* of all things. . . ."

"Why would anybody assume that you wrote it?"

"How could they not? I've introduced you as my protégé, haven't I?"

"The byline won't carry my name."

He cocked his head.

"I chose to use a pen name. As a way of, I don't know, starting a new life for myself."

Again he looked up into the rafters. His voice was dark then, almost malevolent. "What name?"

I think he expected to hear a variation of his own name, or one that would similarly identify him with me. But I told him, "James Dobson."

His head jerked away as if slapped. His eyes came down out of the smoke, but filled with it. "James? You chose to call yourself *James*?"

"It's a lot better than Augie, isn't it?"

"Why not Jamie?" he demanded, his voice much shriller now, louder, his eyes injured and chin thrust high. "Why not christen yourself James Fenimore Dubbins and be done with it?"

"I wasn't even thinking of him," I said.

He seized the front of my coat so violently that two of the buttons popped off and clattered to the floor. He then rammed the silver dollar into my pocket, yanked his fist clear, and held it before him, between us, as if he wanted to strike me with it. Instead, after a few seconds frozen in this posture, his hand flew open, empty, fingers splayed, and he jerked away from me, took a long step past me and back toward the crowd. I turned to speak to him but could not, everyone was watching, every voice now silent and every eye on the two of us.

Poe was at that moment standing oddly postured, head low and shoulders awkwardly hunched, looking as if he had taken a stroke or two from a stiff cane against the back of his neck. His hand remained upraised before him, and though it was no longer aimed in my direction I could feel the threat of it even yet, holding me off, pushing me away.

And soon Poe, too, must have remembered the crowd so breathlessly waiting, for suddenly he pulled himself up straight, unnaturally straight, and marched stiffly toward the altar, where Brunrichter was waiting for him with a fresh goblet of wine.

I remained in the anteroom throughout Poe's reading. And every time he faltered during his recitation of "The Raven," my own eyes stung with shame. Twice then he forgot the proper phrases to his "Bridal Ballad," and as he stood there muttering, blinking, running a hand through his hair, I wanted to shout the words out to him, but bit down hard on my teeth and suffered the sour burn of my chest in silence.

He had floundered at readings before, this I knew from Muddy's letters. But tonight I was to blame for it. The consternation I had caused him. The sense of betrayal.

After "Bridal Ballad" he announced that he would next recite his "Sonnet—To Science," but instead meandered in his introduction and eventually launched into a rambling just short of incoherence. I could not fathom most of what he uttered, delivered either sotto voce or in a rapid tumble of words that obscured all meaning. But a few phrases emerged, provocative phrases that caused more than one head in the audience to cock sideways, elicited more than one startled gasp from a listener.

"A theory of everything," he said. "The Particle Proper we call God . . .

"A limitless succession of Universes . . .

"A plot of God . . .

"The annihilation and renascence of the Universe . . .

"With every throb of the Heart Divine . . ."

He went on like this for most of an hour. Initially I was embarrassed for him; to my eyes he appeared more of an insentient drunk than a literary genius. But perhaps the acoustics of my little room did not allow me to experience his presentation as the others experienced it. Or perhaps they had come to this chapel on that evening fully hoping and expecting a night of eccentricity. Certainly Poe's reputation for unpredictable behavior had preceded him here. So maybe his audience sat so intrigued for the very reason that he made no sense to them, and they, not willing to admit to themselves or others that the ramblings of genius were beyond their ken, nodded in approval, and even applauded enthusiastically from time to time.

What he delivered extemporaneously that night was the gist of a treatise called "Eureka," an attempt to unify all Art and Science. It was what he had been contemplating and composing in that dark room in Philadelphia all the days following Virginia's death, his explanation of God. The essay (of which I knew nothing at the time) was by then fully conceived but not yet published. Poe believed it to be his masterwork, the piece by which he would not only be remembered but by which he would rewrite the laws of Science and the perceived reality of all existence.

Nearly three-quarters through his presentation he happened to look up and notice the thrall in which he held his audience. If to my eyes he appeared bedraggled and nonsensical, to these Pittsburghers he was a prophet. It did not injure his case any that early on in his rant he denounced New Yorkers for their lack of receptivity to this same material, their "unparalleled obtuseness masquerading as arrogance." With the next breath he praised Pittsburgh for its "generosity of intellect" and its "raw and innate openness to Truth."

By the end of the evening they were on their feet for him. Ladies waved lace handkerchiefs in the air, while gentlemen pounded their palms together. Poe pushed the hair out of his eyes and smiled crookedly, as stunned by this reception, I think, as was I. Brunrichter mounted to the lectern to stand beside him while the applause continued, the doctor applauding as heartily as any.

A resentment began to swell in me then, and I did not like it. Such a roil of contradictory emotions. I resented Poe for not appreciating my own accomplishment of the day and for accusing me of a deliberate betrayal, the furthest thing ever from my mind. I resented Brunrichter for his sycophancy and for the contagion of that disease throughout the whole of the audience. I even resented Brunrichter's physical resemblance to Poe. Most of all I resented the fact that I was left to stand there alone in the back of the room, clothed in Brunrichter's clothing, isolated from the one man, the only man, whose approval mattered to me.

I did a stupid thing then. While much of the audience was still applauding and the rest of it inching forward to surround Poe, I strode into the chapel and pushed my way through to the refectory table. There I snatched up a bottle of wine and, eyes blurring with anger, I marched back into the anteroom and out the door. I looked back just once before exiting and saw Brunrichter's eyes following me, Poe oblivious to my egress. But as I rammed the door with my shoulder and shoved it open, I had a dizzying moment, as if I were drunk already, and said to myself *But wait! Maybe that was Poe watching you, and Brunrichter oblivious.* I did not pause to look back and corroborate this notion, however, but allowed my momentum to keep me racing forward into the night, bottle swinging up to my lips, as I set off toward the Monongahela, on the path of my undoing.

Chapter Ten

Several hours later. In golden light I climbed the streets back toward Ridge Avenue, all of Pittsburgh now quiet, a cool March morning, the light still soft enough for sleeping. I was quiet myself, a sweet inner quiet after a roisterous night.

I had fled Poe's reading to go trolling for the kind of company I knew best, and found it without much searching down on Front Street, one street back from the wharf. I made my first stop at a groggery called The Blind Dog, a place filled with burly, cheerful men and the women they loved or hoped for a chance to love, if only for an hour or so. I entered in a sour mood but soon found my temperament ill-suited to the place. Prosperity reigned in Pittsburgh, even for these wharf dogs, their whores and serving girls.

It was there I discovered the local brew, a weightless lager they called Iron City in homage to the foundries that were popping up all along the river. I discovered, too, that a mug of Iron City will blunt the bitterness of angry words, but two mugs will dissolve those words and wash them clean away. And by buying a few mugs for others in my vicinity I was quickly able to dispel the suspicion aroused by a newcomer and to make myself a welcome addition to the neighborhood.

I danced and sang, I ate and drank and danced some more. Other than my name, little was asked of me all night, and my name but infrequently. No longer an Augie, nor ready yet to be an August, and not spiteful enough, I suppose, to assume in corporeality the byline of James Dobson, I gave my name as Gus Dubbins. It was an easy enough name, plain and inoffensive. The first woman who asked it of me promptly converted it to Gussie, a diminutive I did not mind in the least, seeing as how she was twice my age and, perhaps more important, was seated warmly on my lap at the time.

This party continued on through the evening, from The Blind Dog to a second and a third tavern, all the way down to Try Street at the end of the wharf. There, at close to five in the morning, the countertop was cleared of beer mugs to make room for platters of fried eggs and thick slices of buttered bread, plus pots of coffee and tea and pitchers of buttermilk. By that hour I had already spent the last squawk of my gold half eagle, and I felt all the better for it.

A few minutes before sunrise I bid my few remaining celebrants good night and slipped away to meet the dawn alone on Roebling's Bridge. There I passed another quarter hour facing southwest, imagining myself on a steamer churning its way past the Point and into the Ohio, then down the Mississippi, where I would disembark just short of the Gulf of Mexico, James Dobson, wartime correspondent riding on horseback through sand and saguaro, high in the saddle on his way to his first bloody assignment.

Then back across the bridge and into Pittsburgh I hiked, not yet the James Dobson I wished to be but neither wholly Augie Dubbins, up Smithfield Street to Liberty, up Liberty to Ridge, sweetly exhausted, sweetly resolved (as only a youth can be) to the certainty of my future.

I entered Brunrichter's front lobby with all the stealth I could muster, meaning to steal quietly up the stairs, into my bed for an hour, then to rise and pack and be on my way again. My only regret was that I would not remain in Pittsburgh long enough to see my first story published.

Brunrichter, in his dressing gown and slippers, was sipping coffee in the library, his chair turned to face the threshold past which I was attempting to steal. He smiled when he saw me, and gestured toward the silver coffeepot beside him on its serving cart.

I wanted no conversation at that moment, no encumbrances of any kind. On Roebling's suspension bridge a revelation had occurred to me. I was not equipped for a routine of daily interaction, I understood that now. I was not equipped for any profession that might place me in routine proximity to others. I needed to be apart from mankind, an observer on the fringe.

The night before, in The Blind Dog and after, I first felt my apartness begin to assert itself, felt the observer in me take precedence over the participant. And in that detachment, I found a serenity.

I was now in no hurry to give up that serenity. But I was a guest in this man's house, in this man's clothes, if only for a short while longer.

"I've had some coffee already," I told him, and came as far as the threshold.

"One more?" he said.

When I did not answer immediately, he turned to the serving cart, poured another cup, then held it out to me. I came forward and took it, reminding myself that when he questioned me about my whereabouts all night, when he upbraided me for upsetting Poe before his reading, I must keep my anger in check, it would avail nothing, it would only delay my departure, hence my freedom.

"Help yourself to the cream and sugar," he said.

I did so.

"Edgar's reading was a great success, don't you think?"

"It seemed so to me." I stood beside an empty chair and sipped my coffee.

"But the activities afterward, the adulation, it went on too long."

"Oh?" I said.

"Not that he didn't revel in it. But it did exhaust him. The young women, in particular, were overly attentive."

"I'm sure he took no part in that at all."

Brunrichter smiled. "He does bask in the flirtation, does he not?"

"And is a master of it himself."

Brunrichter must have detected something in my voice, a tone I had not wished to convey. "You don't approve?"

I blame the weariness for loosening my tongue. "I only wish that he could be more . . ."

"Discreet?"

"No, no I was thinking . . . more complete unto himself."

"You have no need for other's approval?" he asked.

I raised the cup to my lips, and sipped, and wondered.

"In any case," the doctor said, "he will be sleeping for a while. Throughout the morning, I expect. I prepared a mild inducement to that end."

"But took none yourself?"

He shrugged. "I have a restless mind, always have. A few hours of sleep is all I require."

I nodded, and then, involuntarily, glanced into the empty foyer, the staircase, my gaze slowly mounting toward the top.

"Ah, you're tired too," Brunrichter said. "And I am keeping you from your bed."

"Yes, well," I began, thinking then that I should inform him of my plans, that I would be departing by noon. But I pondered it too long.

"I only wanted you to know," he said, "as you no doubt know already, that Edgar is not as strong just now as we might wish him to be. In my opinion, he is rather ill."

I responded with a quizzical look.

"The grief, you know. As well as the recent excesses in an attempt to assuage that grief."

"He needs to get some strength back, I agree. But otherwise—"

"Otherwise he is depleted. There is a lassitude to his movements, as I'm sure you have observed. However, despite the exhaustion he now feels, I am of the opinion that he requires more evenings like the last, by which I mean an atmosphere in which he is surrounded by admiration and respect—not ridiculed as he would be in New York, nor chided and coerced by penurious editors as he was in Philadelphia."

I wondered just how much of his life Poe had revealed to Brunrichter, just how naked were his confessions.

"An ambiance of heartfelt esteem," he said, "that is what Edgar needs most at this difficult time in his life."

He seemed to be asking for my permission, my approval of his thesis. And so I gave it. "I cannot disagree."

He smiled again. "And you, Augie. You are an important, no, an essential part of that ambiance."

To this I made no reply. Apparently he knew nothing of what had passed between Poe and myself the night before.

"You are his family now," Brunrichter said. "His sole connection to all he has lost."

If I was weary before this, the weariness now doubled. I felt a great heaviness press down on me, a pinching at the top of my spine.

"He enjoyed last evening so very much," the doctor said. "All that was missing in the festivities afterward was your company. He asked of you several times."

The weariness welled up in my chest then. It stuck in my throat and stung my eyes. "I thought he was angry with me. We had talked about something earlier and . . . I think I upset him greatly."

Brunrichter waved a hand through the air, as if my worry were a fly he could carelessly shoo away.

"I spent the night down on the wharf. Trying to forget, I suppose, how angry he had been."

"On Water Street?" he asked.

"Water, First, Second, all up and down the area."

"You weren't"—and he paused briefly, considered his words. "You weren't uncomfortable in such a milieu?"

"I grew up on the streets. Lower than the streets. Five Points in Manhattan. Pittsburgh's version is like a church picnic to me."

"Young women do not disappear from church picnics," he said.

"Sir?"

"You didn't hear the news while you were there?"

"News of what?"

"How strange that you, in the very midst of it, shouldn't hear. Edgar and I arrived home before midnight and already knew."

"Knew what, sir?"

"Another young lady. A child, actually. Barely fifteen years old. Last seen, we were told, just after nine. Returning home from a visit with a friend. On Diamond Alley, I believe."

"I walked down that street last night. This morning, I mean. Just a few hours ago."

He shook his head. "The women of this city have been cautioned, again and again and again, to refrain from walking about at night unescorted. They know the danger, and yet . . . What is it about youth that creates this sense of invulnerability?"

"Don't you remember?" I asked.

He smiled wanly. "I suppose I do."

Several seconds passed before he spoke again, and this time more vehemently. "Gaslights. We must have gaslights on every corner of every street in Pittsburgh. And I intend to see that we do. I will not let the council rest until it is accomplished."

I asked then how he had come to hear of the most recent disappearance.

"The operations of many of the watchmen are privately financed," he told me. "My fellow councilmen and I have arranged for these watchmen to keep us informed of the progress of their investigation. Or, in this case, the total lack of progress."

He turned away from me then, apparently lost in thought, his body twisted at the waist, chin resting on his hand, elbow on the armrest as he stared hard at the red embers in the fireplace. After a few seconds I set my cup on the tray and slipped out of the room. Before mounting the stairs I glanced back at him. He had now turned toward me but sat leaning forward, head lowered, gaze on the foyer floor, two fingers of a hand laid over his mouth. A tiny bead of moisture glimmered like glass in the corner of his eye.

Needless to say, I forgot my plans for an immediate relocation. No, not forgot. But I did forego them for a while, if a bit grudgingly, in the interest of Poe's health.

Chapter Eleven

He slept past midday, though not quite as long as I. After dressing for the day I ventured downstairs but found Mrs. Dalrymple's kitchen empty, no sight or sound of her about. I helped myself to a pair of fat rolls from the pie locker and slathered them with apple butter. With the grumblings of my stomach eased, I went looking for Poe and found him on the front veranda, seated in a posture that was not typical for him, by which I mean empty-handed, with no manuscript to fuss over, nothing but the scenery to occupy his eye. His acknowledgment of my presence there on the porch was slow, as was the turn of his head and his smile when I took a chair next to his.

I had determined that the best course of action was to clear the air between us, to talk about our argument of the previous evening and then to explain myself. I waited for him to broach the subject, any subject, but again, atypically, he seemed in no hurry to converse.

The day was clear and warm and the few wisps of cloud in the sky showed no signs of moving. The air, too, was still, though I felt a trembling in my gut.

"By all appearances you have a great many admirers in Pittsburgh," I told him. "And rightfully so."

His response did not come quickly, nor was his speech rushed. His Virginia drawl seemed accentuated by the drowsy afternoon. "In many ways this noisy little city strikes me as even more civilized than New York."

"It's not noisy up here though."

"It is very pleasant up here."

"So you plan to stay on awhile then? To present another reading?"

"The invitation has been extended, yes. And I am not averse to accepting it."

"No reason not to," I said. I listened for a while to a muted clanging of metal that rose to us from far below. The paleness of that distant sound seemed to accentuate how high above the clamor of commerce we sat, there on the porch of that lofty palace.

Then I asked, "What about this affair tonight? Have you any aversion to it?"

"Are you asking if I am eager for it?"

"I suppose that is what I'm asking."

"No, Augie. I am not eager to watch a man be asphyxiated and hanged." He pursed his lips for a moment and gazed into the naked treetops. "Howsoever," he said. "As a writer who has made the macabre his métier, whether by accident or not, I suppose that I do feel an obligation of sorts. Nor can I deny a fair measure of curiosity."

"Nor can I," I said.

This brought his first abrupt movement, a cocking of his head. "I have wondered of your interest."

"How could I not be intrigued—even though, in a morbid kind of way."

"Morbid indeed," he said. A brief pause, and then, "I vacillate between wanting you there and not. At times I think it might be good for you somehow. Edifying. At other times I feel certain that you must not attend."

I bristled at his use of the word "must." But rather than speak out, I spent the next several seconds entertaining every notion I could conceive of as to why he did not want me at the hanging. None of them satisfied. And so I asked, as evenly as possible, "Why must I not?"

"You are too young," he said. "It would not be appropriate for you, a lesson so harsh."

"Are you forgetting the many other harsh lessons I have witnessed? Harsher, I'm sure, than to watch a stranger hang."

I was referring to the time he and I had spent together in New York in the summer of 1840, the four murders perpetrated in a fortnight, one my own mother, one other by my own hand.

"Those you did not attend by choice," he said.

"Which makes tonight all the more acceptable. Because it is my choice. A choice I am fully old enough to make."

I had had no intention upon sitting down of antagonizing him further; I wanted only to placate, to reconcile. Yet there I sat balking at the first suggestion of a set of reins, though I knew in my heart that he had no desire to break or tame me, only to dissuade me, if he could, from the same descent into darkness that he too had begun as a very young man.

He smiled at me then, but I, unfortunately, already with my hackles up, viewed that smile as sardonic, a challenge. (Only now, so many years after the event, now with two sons of my own, one of them with his mother in whatever plane of existence, if any, this low and lonely one leads to, I now can see Poe's smile in a far different light. I see it as the same sad smile I offered up so frequently to my own children as they grew, the smile that says, *It is so hard for me to stand by and allow you to make your own mistakes, it is so painful. But I love you more than life and breath itself, so I must. You may do what you will.*

As young men we think we know all there is to know, that we can handle the worst life throws at us. Only with age does our store of certainties dwindle, our confidence diminish and our ignorance grow, until finally we realize how impotent and uninformed we truly are, and, accepting this, can count ourselves wise.)

At seventeen I was far from wise, and I viewed Poe's smile as a challenge to my courage, my ability to face without flinching another man's death. And so I stiffened at the gesture, shoved myself up and out of my chair, muttered something about needing to stretch my legs, and marched away toward the river, always toward the river, as if I expected mere water to wash my humanness away.

I returned to the mansion a few hours later, sufficiently mellowed by my ambulation that I was able to join Brunrichter and Poe for a simple but pleasant dinner of bread, cold meat, cheeses, and fruit (Saturday being Mrs. Dalrymple's day off), then afterward fine cigars and desultory conversation. And then we climbed into the doctor's carriage and, sharing whatever jovialities sprang to mind, including Brunrichter's comical rendition of a plantation minstrel song, we rode leisurely down the hill and across the river and onto the grounds of the Western State Penitentiary, and then we went though the massive gates, full of blithe and camaraderie, to watch a man we did not know be strung up by the neck to die.

The Hanging
by
James Dobson

The gallows of the Western State Penitentiary stand in the eastern corner of the prison's interior courtyard. These gallows are not new, though here and there a clean white board stands out among the older, grayer ones. Witnesses in attendance for the hanging are seated some twenty feet from the gallows, and during the early minutes of this event we stare at those white boards as if the wood's newness might suggest something hopeful. We are not sure what form this hope should take, but not in any case a reprieve, because we do not wish to go home disappointed. And in truth there is little hope or possibility of it evident inside these walls, and none of it at all in this courtyard on the evening when Leonidas Dixon is to die.

Convicted of the murder of a steamboat captain and three passengers aboard the paddlewheeler *Excelsior*, a crime committed in the autumn of 1846 and well-known to readers of this newspaper, Dixon is not the type of man to inspire sympathy. By all accounts having conducted himself in a low manner, being a brawler and liar and thief for as long as any Pittsburgher can remember, he is nevertheless considered by those who know him best little more than a third-class swindler, reliable in nothing but his devotion to John Barleycorn. His brother Maximus Dixon, employed as a blower in the Bakewell and Pears Glass Works, and also in attendance as a witness to the execution, informed this correspondent that Leonidas had never been known to hold a regular position before being taken on as a stoker for the *Excelsior*.

That employment, however, proved short-lived. It lasted a mere thirteen days before Leonidas Dixon, his face blackened with soot, strode into the pilothouse with pistola in hand, there to shoot down the captain in cold blood, one Percival Sidling, father of eight. Dixon then proceeded onto the deck where he divested the startled passengers of their personal belongings. Having done so, yet not satisfied with the amount of carnage thus wreaked, he then seized a fire ax and ran amuck about the deck for several minutes, swinging wildly at every person in his path even as the first mate ably guided the *Excelsior* toward shore.

Leonidas Dixon was successful in slaying three more men in their attempts to bring him down, and afflicted grievous wounds to twice as many others before he was finally knocked off his feet and subdued.

And now, at a few minutes before sunset on a warm spring evening, with the air so still that, beyond the prison walls, the song of a wren can be heard, and with a dozen witnesses waiting somberly for the appointed deed to be carried out, Leonidas Dixon, hands tied behind his back and ankles shackled, is led across the courtyard and up the gallows steps. Among those witnesses, in addition to the condemned man's brother and this correspondent, is local surgeon Dr. Alfred Brunrichter, and his guest, the illustrious author and literary critic Edgar Allan Poe.

Four members of the prison's personnel stand at attention to the side of the gallows, two men on each side. Another stands below the drop, though well to the side of it. A single guard accompanies Dixon up the stairs. The condemned man pauses only once as he mounts to the platform, gives his head and shoulders a shake, and continues on.

Dixon is now placed facing west, toward the setting sun and his small audience of witnesses. The charges against him are read aloud. Upon the recitation of each of his victim's names, Dixon is seen to grimace. When asked if he has any final words, he calls out loud and clearly through the stillness of the evening.

"You done it right, Maxie," he is heard to say. "I always thought you was the stupid one. But right now I'm thinking different."

Hearing this, his brother Maximus, who theretofore has sat stoically, now doubles forward in his seat and covers his face with a hand.

And then it is time. A black hood is pulled over the head of Leonidas Dixon. The noose is slipped around his neck and cinched snug. The guard steps away, leaving Dixon alone atop the platform.

When the nod is given, a lever is thrown and the trap door sprung. Dixon drops suddenly down. All of this is expected. What happens next is not.

Previous to the execution of Leonidas Dixon, the method of hanging in this state was known as "the short drop." By this method the victim falls only a matter of inches. Death is produced by a slow strangulation that can take several minutes to reach culmination. During this process it is not uncommon for the victim's face to become engorged with blood and to turn blue as a result of being deprived of oxygen. The eyes and tongue of the victim will protrude (hence the black hood) and the victim may be seen to struggle for quite some time before a total loss of consciousness ensues.

Because of the unpleasantness of this spectacle, and the longevity of anguish suffered not only by the condemned but by those who must witness his suffering, it was recently suggested to the penitentiary officials that the method of hanging known as "the long drop" be adopted here, as it has been throughout much of Europe. According to Dr. Brunrichter, this method requires a drop of between eight and ten feet, the exact distance to be calculated according to the condemned man's weight. The force produced by the fall is expected to cause immediate unconsciousness owing to a fracture of the neck and the spinal cord. The victim's heart may continue to beat for another quarter hour or longer before asphyxiation results in death, but it is presumed that the accused experiences no physical pain whatsoever.

Unfortunately, a miscalculation in the appropriate length of drop can result in an absence of instantaneous unconsciousness, as in the short drop method, or, as befell Leonidas Dixon, when the drop is too long, an even less desirable outcome.

The snap of the noose when Dixon fell was brutal and sharp. Dixon's body, from the neck down, broke free of the noose to crumple in a heap on the hard-beaten ground. His head, still mercifully enshrouded in its black hood, leapt upward with the coiled rope as it was suddenly released of all tension. A moment later gravity reclaimed its victory, and the black hooded head tumbled sideways out of the noose, and fell onto the body beneath it, and from there rolled onto the ground.

For a moment the courtyard remained preternaturally still. No man so much as breathed. Then there came a heaving sound from among the witnesses, and Maximus Dixon was seen to fall from his chair, having fainted at the sight of his brother's decapitation. This broke the spell of horror that had transfixed us all, and Maximus Dixon was quickly attended to, and in time revived and led away.

Dr. Brunrichter later invited those witnesses who cared to do so to examine the severed head. Mr. Poe and one other witness accepted this invitation, though out of scientific curiosity alone, in examination of the intricacy of musculature and nerves that renders human life so fragile and so precious.

Upon completion of Dr. Brunrichter's examination, the victim's head was reattached. The corpse was then placed inside an iron gibbet constructed to the exact specifications of Dixon's anatomy. The gibbet, with Dixon inside, has been placed at the head of Maynard's Island in the center of the Monongahela River, facing upstream, where it shall remain for the next several weeks as a deterrent to all individuals who might be contemplating a criminal life.

Chapter Twelve

I slept poorly that night, as might be expected, despite a cup of the special tea Brunrichter had prepared for Poe to help him relax, a mix of chamomile and what the doctor called "Indian herbs," plus a hearty measure of an Oolong and Darjeeling blend to give it body. In the library he'd poured out a cup for Poe, then, handing one to me as well, had said, "You've been upset by what you saw tonight. Your eyes are clouded."

"Not upset," I told him, but took the cup anyway, if only to wash from the back of my throat the sticky taste of blood. "But I can't stop thinking about it. I can see and hear every detail of that courtyard even yet."

"He is a writer now," Poe said from his chair, teacup close to his lips. "He has caught the writer's disease."

"Insomnia?" asked Brunrichter.

Poe nodded. "The imagination never sleeps."

"If I erred in inviting either of you to accompany me tonight, I apologize. I only thought . . ."

Both Poe and I waved the suggestion of error away. We were glad to have witnessed what we did, grateful for the sickening scene; that was the gruesome irony of it.

And as a result my dreams that night were harsh and convoluted. Each ended in sudden violence. Strange noises wafted out of the corners of my mind, chilling breezes from dark woods and filthy alleyways. Thoughts whispered like voices overheard through the wallboard, fragmented but threatening. At times I thought myself awakened by a shrill cry and lay there with an ear cocked to hear it again, and upon hearing it a second time arose to investigate, only to look back from the door and see myself still in bed. "Come back where it's warm," my supine self then said to the one naked and trembling by the door. "You're dreaming."

It was that kind of night. Laughable, terrorizing, exhausting. To this day I do not know if my most vivid dream of all was a fantasy or not.

I began this dream as a boy, a child of ten or so, asleep on my pile of rags in my room in the Old Brewery, deep in the anus of Gotham, a building damp and reeking and rank. My mother's snores rattled the chinking in the opposite corner. And then I was awakened by my mother's cry. But my consciousness, even as I sat bolt upright, told me no, that was not your mother, the voice too high and shrill. That was a girlish cry. *It's Sissie!* I thought. *Oh god, she's dying again!*

Dreams, as I'm sure you know, have no respect for the constraints of time or space.

In my dream, I then leapt up off the floor, meaning to save her, though from what or whom or how I did not know. I hurried in the darkness to the door. Reached for the latch. And grabbing it, looked down at my hand and saw that it was not little Augie's hand at all but a hand fully grown, a strong hand callused and browned from seven years of farm work. I looked back toward my pile of rags and saw instead a luxurious fourposter, now empty.

This was not the Old Brewery but a room in Brunrichter's house. Was I awake now? Was this the actual corporeal me standing barefoot and in a nightshirt, my hand on the cold glass knob?

And then the cry again, plaintive and shrill, though weaker this time. Was it real, or merely the echoing residue of a dream?

I convinced myself that it was real. I did this by reminding myself that Virginia was gone, Sissie could not be saved. But the urge to save her, the ache, this remained, logic be damned. I opened the door and crept out into the hallway.

If my room was dark, the hallway was even darker, a tunnel of pitch without dimension. I felt my way along, hand to the wall. Every time I touched a doorknob I gave the knob a silent twist, pulled open the door if it yielded, and peered inside. Every room was a black box, a tomb of absolute darkness. I continued on.

At times I seemed to be pushing my way uphill. At other times, in danger of sliding down. I walked for an impossibly long time, though it might have been only seconds elongated by my disorientation. I might, all this time, have been asleep in my bed.

But whether awake, half awake, or fitfully asleep, I soon found myself standing in an unfamiliar room, illuminated poorly by clouded moonlight through a tall narrow window. It seemed a sitting room of some kind, but small, perhaps eight by ten. I could make out a writing desk and chair, a mahogany secretary, a bookcase lined with leather-bound volumes.

During my stay in Brunrichter's mansion I had heretofore made no attempt to investigate the house, had slept in my chambers, taken supper in the dining room, breakfast in the kitchen, tea in the library. There must have been at least a dozen other rooms I had not yet viewed. So I was not surprised by the presence of this one, but surprised by what I can only describe as the density of its air, the great dark heaviness of every breath. I became aware of my own heart beating, slow and heavy. It felt in my chest like a large slow clock muffled in cotton.

I had come in as far as the center of the room when the windows went dark, and with them the room itself. A black cloud had obscured the meager moonlight. I waited for the cloud to pass, but the light did not return. My heart's pounding grew louder and more anxious. I began to feel claustrophobic and could not remember my way to the door. Suddenly my thoughts were as clouded as the moon.

Like a blind man I lurched to the side, hands feeling

for a wall with which to steady myself. Without visual reference I felt in danger of falling over. In time I found the wall, and crept along it slowly, like a bug scuttling fearfully over the boards, maneuvering past any furniture in my way. I remained at this activity for a time much longer than should have been required to return me to the doorway, feeling more dizzied all the while, more constrained by the darkness, more convinced that I was in fact dreaming, and therefore entrapped in some nightmarish maze without termination.

But then, beneath my hands, a door swung open with a dull clack. Eagerly I stepped into the opening, though it too was just as black as the room, and though my outstretched hands told me just how narrow this doorway was.

By putting out both hands only a foot or so beyond my shoulders I could touch the sidewalls of a narrow corridor, the boards rough, support beams bare. When the narrow door eased shut behind me, the darkness was absolute. On bare feet I advanced an inch at a time, fingertips picking my way along, toes sliding over smoothly worn wood.

The corridor seemed to turn, an angle here, another there, though in such darkness and with no clues other than those of touch, I could not be sure. Then came a set of stairs, but short. Strangely, I counted only four steps, scraping each with my heel. My hands and feet were my eyes, and with my hands I felt depressions in the walls, tiny alcoves whose purposes I could not discern, buttonlike protuberances that did not yield to pressure. In essence I was worse than blind, for I lacked the blind man's heightened acuity of hearing and touch and balance. My head was thick, all senses murky, and my fingertips half numb. Yet I could think of no option but to continue on.

Then more stairs. Or were they the same ones I had encountered earlier? Was I going up now instead of down?

Dead-end. The corridor stopped. My hands ran up and down the wall but felt nothing. A panic began to rise in me, a fear of being trapped here, buried, and I thought of the stack of coffins aboard the *Sweet Jeanine*—was that where I was? Had I fallen asleep in one of those boxes?

I rapped the wall with my knuckles, and indeed there was a hollow resonance to the sound, some emptiness on the opposite side of the wood. My hands ran all along the dead-end wall once more, tapping and tracing its surface, feeling for a latch of some kind. But nothing.

And then, unexpectedly, the wall came toward me, pushed against my hands. I stepped back so as not, I assumed, to be crushed by the wall's collapse. But immediately there was light streaming in at me, a brilliant light thrust so close to my face that I could smell the smoky oil, feel the heat radiating off the glass. I would have retreated but that a hand seized me by the wrist.

With the lamp now blinding me with light, I could not see the face of the man who held me, but I recognized his voice. "What are you doing in there?" Mr. Tevis demanded. He gave my wrist a twist as he spoke, and I contorted my body in compliance with the pressure.

"I'm not sure," I told him. "I thought I heard a sound . . . a woman's voice. I'm not sure if I did or not."

He blew out the lamp. And now I was blinded again,

differently but just as completely. He pulled me into a larger room. Said not another word as he dragged me quickly out of that room—a room I did not wish to leave, for it was pleasantly warm and smelled of fruit. I seem to remember a small table over which my hand trailed—I recognized the feel of oilcloth. And then out of that room and through another and soon we were mounting the servants' stairs to the second floor.

He led me straightaway to my bedroom, pulled me inside and up close to my bed. "Go back to sleep," were his only words. A moment later the bedroom door softly closed behind him.

But instead of lying down I went to the window to stand, that rectangle of gray light, the glass frosted on the outside, cold to the touch on the inside. I stood there looking out. In time I was able to see a few dim stars, diffuse pinpricks of white in the black-clouded sky. My heart still hammered like a cottoned clock. I shivered, my skin atingle with gooseflesh.

After a time I convinced myself that the stars were real. The glass I laid my hand upon was real. The cold was real. "You must surely be awake," I said.

Not without some trepidations, I looked back at my bed. It was empty.

I looked to the bedroom door. Closed.

All a dream? I wondered. All but the past few minutes, this slow dawning of awareness? Had I been out of this room at all that night, or walked no farther than from the bed to the window?

I climbed back into bed and pulled the covers to my neck, shivered and rubbed my feet together, in a hurry to get warm.

The stars were real, that was all I knew for certain. The bed was real and I was in it now.

It's all because of that hanging, I thought.

I wished for once that I knew a prayer, some repetitious rhythm to quiet a racing heart. In lieu of prayer I resorted to an old strategy, practiced often in my bunk in Ottawa County, and muttered the multiplication tables—colorless, odorless, unimaginative numbers—until I drifted off. Six times four is twenty-four, six times five is thirty, six times six is thirty-six . . .

Just before dawn I stood on Brunrichter's veranda, unable to sleep any longer. Truth is, though weary I was grateful to be awake, to be standing upright again in a well-lit and comprehensible world. My gratitude and relief were translated into an appreciation of the aesthetics of the new day. The river far below, for example, appeared never lovelier than at that moment, swollen and white, a river of fog overflowing its banks. Far to the east the horizon glowed orange and bright as a forge, and above the orange the palest of blues ascending seamlessly into sapphire. The beauty of that morning made me ache to be a watercolorist, a skill I could never acquire, and was rendered doubly poignant by my memories of the day before.

The hanging had been with me through every waking hour of the night. I could not count the times I had watched it happening again, that sudden and awful drop, the startling severance. In any case too many times for any man, even a writer, and even for a young one who might claim, with mug of ale in hand, that he cannot get his fill of human drama. Too many.

Chapter Thirteen

Of the next day, three incidents of importance.

Upon first waking, while the images were yet fresh in my head, and perhaps made more vivid from being replayed in incessant close-up in my mind's re-creations, I wrote down the story of the hanging as I remembered it. My objective as a writer was to place the reader of that scene beside me in the courtyard. Unlike Poe, who with his short stories and poems attempted to create an *effect*, a single emotion to engulf the reader as a chill fog might, my goal was simply to re-create the scene as accurately as my recollection would allow, and thereby permit the reader to generate his or her own atmosphere according to temperament. In short, I saw myself not as a tale maker, not as a creator of worlds imagined, but, more humbly, as a chronicler of facts. This was what I felt suited for. I was not long on imagination, and grateful for that shortage, considering how Poe had been and was tormented by his imagination.

If anything other than my own psychology could be blamed for causing me to forswear the imagination and for trying to live only in the world of the senses, it was Poe's enduring anguish. He lived as if tethered by the limbs to four wild horses named Grief, Loss, Fear, and Failure. In daylight hours these horses remained fairly quiet, sometimes even tractable. But only because they were nocturnal beasts, whipped by darkness into the most unpredictable gyrations of movement. Every night they tore Poe apart.

In the soil of imagination are planted, by whom or what or why we do not know, the seeds of all madness.

In any case, I awoke early and lit a lamp, and with a fine misting rain blurring the window I wrote the hanging and rewrote and reworked and re-created it until my spine ached as if stretched by the noose. The next day, a Monday, I would deliver it to the editor who had purchased my elephant story and, with luck, prove that initial success not a fluke.

This, I learned, is the alchemy of the writing act. To take an incident, in this case a man's execution, to take an incident that wounds the witness so deeply as to render him mute, stunned, frozen in horror, to take this incident that might damage him forever and then to transform it, through the magic of incantation, of words precisely chosen, into a prideful thing, a piece of work well done, a healing satisfaction. (Is writing an act of self-preservation? It is, it is. *Tomorrow I will kill myself. Today I must write.*)

But for now, at nearly 9:00 A.M., with the rest of the household excepting Poe off to morning services, the thing I now required, having written, was to refill the well that writing had depleted. Sustenance and stimuli. The world outside my own head.

I washed and dressed quickly. Then, feeling still a bit of a traitor toward Poe for having written again, and therefore not wishing to encounter him just yet, I tiptoed downstairs and, alert for evidence that he too was awake—of which I heard none—I eased out the front door.

In the market square four blocks off Water Street I

bought a meat pie and a sweet bun and enjoyed an ambulatory breakfast. I was discovering that nothing can whet the appetite more than a morning spent crawling on one's knees through the literary fields, planting row after row of words. It was then, as I ambled along the wharf just south of Roebling's Bridge, brushing crumbs from my lips, that the second auspicious incident of the day took place.

I recognized a man down on the docks as the one Poe and I had first encountered upon our arrival in Pittsburgh, the strong and cheerful stevedore of the blue shirt and brown felt hat. I watched him for a while as he went back and forth from the dock to a dray, each time carrying a small wooden barrel from the latter to the former.

"Last time I saw you," I finally said, having come to stand at the side of the wagon, "you were over on the Allegheny, and unloading caskets."

"And this time kegs of beer!" he said. "You'll avoid them both if you know what's good for you!"

His blue shirt was soaked through with perspiration, his broad face aglow with it. He appeared to take such joy in his work, humble as it was, that I could not help but feel a fondness for him.

"And how's a young man like yourself this fine Sunday morning?" he asked.

Throughout our entire conversation he did not break stride or alter his exquisite rhythm of labor, but continued to haul the barrels from the wagon to the dock and there to stack them in rows three deep and two high.

"I'm doing good," I answered, and noticed, not without some twinge of nostalgic pleasure, how easily I'd slipped back into my former manner of speech, unadorned and perhaps ungrammatical, that sweet understatement of the streets.

"Glad to hear it. On your way to church, are you?"

"Doing my best to avoid that too, along with the beer and coffins. Too much of any of them just ain't healthy."

He laughed. "Of the three, I'll take the beer."

"And this beer you're loading. Where's it headed?"

"Where does all beer go? Comes off the river one day, gets pissed back into it the next."

Now it was my turn to laugh. "You always work so hard on Sundays?"

"Only when there's money to be made from it."

On his next trip to the wagon he asked me, "Where's that accent of yours coming from?"

"I'm from Ohio lately. Ottawa County. But I was born in New York City. Lived there my first ten and a half years."

"And what's brought you to Pittsburgh?"

I must have pondered my answer too long, wondering which of my identities to reveal to him, for a half minute later he laughed so hard that a brace of pigeons burst into flight off the rooftop behind us.

"I never seen a man trying so hard to figure out what he was up to!"

I blushed hotly, but grinned all the same. "Truth is, I'm in the middle of trying to figure out that very thing. All I know for sure is, I'm on my way to Mexico before too long. I plan to get into that war down there before it's over."

There was a hitch in his stride then, perceptible only if you were watching him as closely as did I. "Last keg," he said, and heaved it onto a shoulder. "Time to sit and wait for the boat. Come down and join me if you've a mind to."

I followed him to the dock, sat beside him on a keg of beer. We faced north by northwest so that the morning sun did not blind us.

"What's your name?" he asked.

"Gus. Gus Dubbins. And you?"

"Buck Kemmer." He offered me his hand, large and rough and warm. "So tell me this, Gus Dubbins. Whose war is it you're so eager to fight in?"

"The war with the Mexicans."

"Not which war. I asked whose war."

"Zachary Taylor's, I guess."

"So if it's his fight, whyn't you let Zachary Taylor do his own fighting? What's he to you that you're willing to get yourself shot for him?"

"He's our President."

Buck spit into the water.

"You don't like him?" I asked.

"Don't know him. Never met the man. Never expect to. All I can tell you on that subject is, Anytime I offer myself up as cannon fodder, I'm gonna first have a damn clear idea of who I'm doing it for and why I'm doing it."

"Well, it's . . . it's for the adventure of it, I suppose."

"Being run through with a Mexican sword, or having your head taken off by a punkin ball—that sounds exciting to you, does it?"

"I don't intend to let that happen to me."

He nodded. Then he put a hand on my back and patted my shoulder. I considered whether he meant to comfort or congratulate me. Before I could reach a decision, he shoved me forward, and I went flying headfirst, legs kicking air, into the Monongahela River.

I came up spitting, spitting water but ready in a second or two to start spitting curses as well. He leaned forward and stuck out his baling hook for me to grasp, then hauled me out as easily as pulling a wide mouth bass up by its gills, and deposited me in a dripping heap on the dock.

"You intend to take that bath just now?" he asked.

I was still too angry to speak.

He knelt beside me. Looked me dead in the eye. Tenderly, then, with a delicacy I would not have thought his thick fingers capable of, he brushed a limp lock of hair from my eyes.

"Bad things happen," he said, his voice no longer loud, "whether we intend them to or not. Don't make much sense to go looking for them, now does it, son?"

Again I had no answer, though this time it was not anger that stopped my tongue.

A moment later a voice came to us from the riverbank, a voice that struck my ears with the same delicate tones as those of a church bell chiming over a springtime countryside. "And how am I supposed to panfry that?" she asked.

I looked first at Buck, who was grinning ear to ear: "I'm not all that convinced we should keep this one," he called to her. "Strangest-looking fish I ever pulled out. Seems to me we'd better hand it over to one of them professors you know. Let him cut it open, see what's in its stomach."

I turned to face her then.

And maybe because I faced fully into the sun at that moment, and took the sudden glare of it unshielded in watery eyes, maybe that was why I felt physically struck by her visage, literally thumped by it. Pole-axed, square between the eyes.

She was not beautiful. Yet she was beauty itself to me. She was not perfect. Yet she was perfection personified. If I had thought I'd been emptied by a morning's writing, made hungry by a good morning's work, my first glimpse of this young woman turned me inside out with hunger.

She was a girl of average height, somewhat more pretty than plain, with green eyes nearly emerald bright, a few pale freckles tossed across her cheeks. Her hair, beneath the wide-brimmed hat, was something like the umber of autumn, something like a sienna sunset. She was not a child—sixteen, I would later learn—but her smile was still young, too young for any trace of cruelty on those lips, those lips as full as summer itself.

(I have recently read, and tend to believe, now that I am old, too old for much of anything other than reading, and nearly too blind for that—I have recently read that what I felt on that afternoon, so sudden and startling, so impossible to predict, suppress, or re-create at will—I have recently read that what I experienced was nothing more than an animalian reflex, some imperative of self-duplication blasted from the medulla oblongata down the central nervous system and radiated into every cell. Something primitive and elemental, common to every living thing. This may well be true. Nevertheless, it is a magic.)

Of the conversation that followed between myself and Buck Kemmer's daughter, whose name was Susan, of our few minutes together as she delivered her father his noonday meal packed in a straw basket, nothing of the words that passed between us needs to be recounted here. What needs describing but never can be, can only be alluded to approached obliquely, too huge for words, is this approximation of what I felt: Upon my first glimpse of her, nothing else mattered.

What do we know of passion and love? What do we know that can be authenticated as fact, verified from individual to individual, tested and proven time after time by the most rigorous of scientific methods?

Not a whit.

Of passion and love we do not even know if one is a variety of the other. Or if the two are distinct, though they sometimes come into confluence. Is one to the other like a tumor on the brain, but a tumor whose tentacles have so enveloped and infiltrated the brain that they themselves become pathways for thought?

If, prior to my first exchange of glances with Miss Susan Kemmer, I had wanted to be a writer so as to fashion myself in some elliptical way more like Poe, I now wanted to be a writer for her alone, so as to impress upon her my gentlemanly facility with words. If previously I had craved the glory of battle among scorpions and sand, I now craved only the glory to be found as the object of her lingering gaze.

Was a baser desire tangled up with this as well? Even if my mouth denied it, the subequator of my body could not. But the fact remains: Suddenly, all life entered me through my longing for her. Every moment wore her smile superimposed upon it.

As adults, we are formed by our earliest passions. I, in the space of one week in my seventeenth year, discovered two unlike any others I had ever felt. Both would bless and curse me for the remainder of my life. One I would wear like a warm and rainproof cloak. The other like a thorn in my heart.

And now, the third important incident of the day, an incident colored, one might even say defined, by the previous two, for we perceive each moment not in its own light but in the light left over from its immediate past.

I do not mean to imply by this a belief in a cause-effect paradigm to our existence. Short-term, perhaps, a sequence of order can sometimes be identified. But in the longer scheme of things, accident and chance prevail. A life is shaped by the thing we call coincidence. An unexpected meeting. A coin found on the street. A sudden downpour that drives us into the nearest doorway.

Had I not been so pained by the sight of drowning elephants, for example, would I have felt compelled to find a means for expiating sorrow? Would I ever have dreamed of myself as a writer?

If a respected physician had not one morning happened to notice in his shaving mirror a resemblance there to the face of a writer he admired, would Poe and I not still be in Philadelphia, or perhaps New York?

The chain of all changes begins with chance.

It was chance, was it not, that had me return to Brunrichter's estate just at that moment, midday, when he and Poe were about to sally forth?

"In the nick of time," said Poe from the steps of the veranda, on his way down. Brunrichter, two steps below, held lightly to Poe's elbow, steadying Poe's descent—an unnecessary courtesy, it seemed to me, though there was a vague unsteadiness to Poe's gaze, a certain lassitude in his smile. Mr. Tevis waited just off the porch, a large and overfilled straw basket in each hand, a woolen blanket folded and laid over one shoulder.

The doctor smiled at me but said nothing.

"Come join us," Poe said. "We're off to have a picnic." He, like the doctor, was rosy-cheeked already. I did not think this bloom the result of Pittsburgh air.

"I've had a busy morning," I told them. "I was thinking of taking a short nap."

"Mrs. Dalrymple has prepared a substantial repast. Enough to feed one more, isn't that right, Doctor?"

Brunrichter did not answer for a moment, as if distracted. Then, "Of course," he said. "You will be most welcome."

Poe waggled a finger at my clothes, still limp and damp. "You mustn't put Augie close to a river. He cannot resist the urge to swim."

He then turned to Brunrichter and, as if I were no longer there, recounted his first meeting with "the boy," and told how the "grimy-faced urchin" had discovered, by way of a dunking in the Hudson River, the body of a young woman named Mary Rogers.

"Not the Mary Rogers depicted in *The Mystery of Marie Roget*?"

"The very same," said Poe. "More or less."

"How intriguing!" Brunrichter said, and turned to me. "Do all of your adventures involve the death of a young woman?"

Before I could answer, he spoke to Poe. "Has he told you, Edgar, of the happenstance of two nights past? How he happened to be in the exact location from which the latest of our own missing girls disappeared?"

"I would not call it the exact location," I said. "I was in the vicinity."

"But at the very hour she disappeared. More or less?"

I said nothing.

"An intriguing coincidence, would you not agree, Edgar?"

Poe smiled. I had the unsettling suspicion that he was seeing me again as a grimy-faced urchin. "Don't tease the boy, Alfred." But he could not leave it at that. "Unlike ourselves, he has shown no interest of any kind in attractive young women."

At this they laughed, Brunrichter heartiest of all. I was about to turn away from them when the doctor said, "Then by all means you must not join us, for we intend to surround ourselves with a bevy of young women through all this afternoon. Is that not what picnics are for, Edgar?"

"So you tell me," answered Poe.

"You would only be bored, Augie, in the presence of so much delicate flesh. Better to stay behind," he chuckled again, "and entertain yourself."

Was it this sophomoric challenge that caused me, in sophomoric response, to wave my hand with a flourish and answer, "Lead the way"? Or was it because both men were intoxicated, and I yet felt responsible for one of them? Was it because I sensed how much happier Brunrichter would be if I did indeed decline his invitation, and some truculent part of me wished to deny him that happiness, even at the expense of my own fatigue?

I did not know the answer then, and do not know it now. The human mind, for all its insights, can seldom see itself.

The picnic was held on a grassy ridge a bit more than a quarter mile to the rear of the mansion. From this promontory the Allegheny River was clearly visible in the valley below, a wide green serpent slowly coursing down greening valleys. On another elevation, slightly lower than our own and maybe seven hundred yards farther north, the grounds of St. Gregory's Benedictine monastery were visible—a stone chapel and four smaller wooden structures. The monks' herd of goats was to thank for keeping the grass of this rolling meadow cropped short, and also for supplying the monks' livelihood in milk and cheese and a sugary confection flavored with vanilla bean. The monks, Brunrichter told us, hoped to one day charter a college on their grounds.

Other than the monastery and the Brunrichter estate to the south, the land was clear of all buildings save one, the Brunrichter family mausoleum some fifty yards back toward the mansion. Brunrichter had walked us past it on our way to the picnic grounds, though it was not directly along our path.

"My final resting place," he had said of the huge octagonal tomb. Its Gothic dome would have made the building look mushroomlike and ridiculous standing alone there in the meadow, but for the sandstone porch that encircled the mausoleum, and the wide border of pink-white seashells that encircled the porch like a moat, the porch roof supported by a dozen marble colonettes, all surfaces filigreed and carved with intaglios, the entire edifice crowned with a bronze angel, kneeling, her wings spread and palms raised and eyes turned toward Heaven.

"Fit for an emperor," Poe remarked.

"My mother and father are inside," said Brunrichter, to

which we said nothing, though Poe put out a hand and touched the doctor's shoulder, and we all stood motionless, reverent, for the next thirty seconds or so.

Then Brunrichter said, cheerfully, "No visit from me today, however! Today we have a picnic!" With that he turned away from the tomb and marched off happily through the low-grown meadow. "Careful where you step, Edgar. There is deer and goat shit everywhere."

By the time we reached the picnic grounds, Tevis had already spread the blanket and was busily setting out the lunch. A half-dozen carriages sat side by side some twenty yards away, the horses staked and contentedly munching grass. The carriages' passengers, at least twenty in all, three-fourths of them female, were seated on their own blankets in a semicircle around the one Tevis had laid for Brunrichter and Poe, twenty eager faces all turned to watch Poe's approach. A pair of young spinsters—sisters, judging from the similarities of their broad Teutonic faces—actually applauded.

Despite the panoramic view and the serene atmosphere of the place, I regretted coming. I could tell by the crowd assembled that this picnic was to be another of Poe's public appearances, nothing more. No doubt he would recite a half-dozen poems. The young women would sigh, the matrons would smile and pat their bosoms, the men would nod sagely.

And I? I would linger long enough to eat—there was roasted pheasant in those baskets, and a leg of mutton—then slip quietly away. That there were indeed several young women in attendance, many of them quite comely, interested me not at all. There was but one young woman with whom I cared to share a word or glance or anything more, and this I intended to do, as soon as I could devise a way.

Chapter Fourteen

The picnic proceeded much as I expected, at least in the beginning, sedate and polite. Introductions were made by Brunrichter, but only for Poe's benefit, since everyone present already knew who he was, and Brunrichter deemed myself, like Tevis, unworthy of an introduction. The distaff side of the group was comprised of the daughters and wives of several prominent merchants, plus a few unescorted young ladies, all in frilly dresses and sunbonnets. Among the men were a Mr. Vernon, the vice president of the Bank of Pittsburgh, a Dr. Delaney, publisher of the literary paper called *The Mystery*, a Mr. Kane, publisher of the *Western Literary Magazine*, an elderly man named Gatesford, and a monk named Brother Jarvis from the nearby monastery. All were dressed for a casual day in the country, save for the monk, a rather slight and soft-spoken man, who wore a pair of gray trousers beneath a coarse brown cassock.

A red woolen blanket had been laid out for Poe and Brunrichter near the center of all the other blankets. Poe reclined there on an elbow, occasionally sipping from a glass of claret. In the beginning he spoke only when questioned directly, content to let the conversation wander through a series of local topics, its flow meandering like a stream over new ground, seeking its course. There was talk of the turmoil at the new cotton factory, of how local labor disputes had incited the women and boys employed there to demand the outrageous wage of three dollars per week—my own recently earned half eagle grew suddenly heavier in my pocket—and of how a few of those boys, their demands denied, had vented their frustration by smashing out a large window, only to be hauled off to the new jail adjunct to the courthouse on Grant's Hill.

Someone then called for the latest news concerning a young Mr. Foster, and an attractive young lady seated at Poe's feet, introduced as Miss Lydia Cavin and a close acquaintance of the Pittsburgh songwriter, was importuned to serenade us with one of Mr. Foster's compositions, a melodious ballad entitled "Open Thy Lattice, Love." She did so admirably enough, but it was, I think, the nervous quiver in her voice, coupled with a healthy figure and milk white complexion, that engaged Poe more. No doubt he heard an echo of Sissie's own dulcet tones in that serenade, for he was immediately taken by Miss Cavin, and his gaze, through all the ensuing talk of how sublime were Mr. Foster's melodies and lyrics, how tragic that he be forced to earn his daily bread in the outpost of Cincinnati, kept returning to her, his wistful smile a continuing compliment to her comeliness.

I recall, too, some talk about the city's newest literary paper, the *Pittsburgh Saturday Visitor*, published by the abolitionist and suffragette Jane Grey Swisshelm and filled, said old man Gatesford, with "antisocial bile aimed at the ruination of the American hearth and home."

This led to a discussion of contemporary letters in

general, and here Poe, enlivened by the warmth of Ms. Cavin's doelike gaze, was encouraged to give free expression of his antipathy toward those who presumed to be America's literary elite, the "titmice and tittlebats" of Gotham, the "Frogpondian euphuists" of New England.

I had the sense that there was nothing Poe could utter that would not be nodded at and smiled upon by those gathered around him. He sat like a sultan in the midst of an adoring harem. I stood like a eunuch on the fringe, a quiet disgust slowly accruing inside me.

In time, though none too soon, the food was unpacked, and this in itself prompted a sudden detour in the conversation. Most prominent among the savories that Tevis laid before us were slices of roast lamb, the edges crisp and rosemary-crusted, the meat pink and sweet, still warm from the spit.

"You will notice," Brunrichter said to Poe as Tevis prepared the plates, "that we have sacrificed a spring lamb on your behalf."

"How very appropriate," an older woman remarked, "so near to Easter!"

"And a holy lamb to boot," said the doctor, "supplied as it was by Brother Jarvis, and, we must therefore assume, as sinless as he is himself."

The monk gave a little bow of his head, totally unaffected by the doctor's ironic tone.

Vernon, the banker, was quick to seize on the opportunity for provocation. "What is it you people do with the blood?" he asked the monk. "You wash your hands in it, rub it on your doors, something similar to that?"

Brother Jarvis smiled calmly. "If by 'you people' you mean we Catholics, we do neither. Not literally, in any case. You are thinking, perhaps, of the Jewish people and the original Passover. When they smeared lamb's blood on their doors so that the Angel of Death would not visit their households."

"How disappointing it must be," said Vernon, "that Catholicism provides no similarly colorful alternative."

Brunrichter said, "Ah, but they have an even better one. All Christians do. It is called cannibalism."

Said Vernon, "I was raised an Episcopalian, and might be one still had we ever practiced such a treat."

"Did you never take communion?"

"I did."

"And what is communion if not a symbolic act of cannibalism? You eat the body of Christ, you drink his blood. Am I right, Brother Jarvis? Do you or do you not serve up your Lord on a platter every Sunday?"

The monk rolled his eyes. Apparently this was not the first time he had been baited with this argument. "And every Monday we enjoy the leftovers with a soup."

This brought a chorus of howls and shrill laughter, a few hearty slaps on the monk's narrow shoulders. The gaiety echoed over the meadow. I scarcely knew what to make of it all.

"Tell me, Edgar," Brunrichter said, "does the meat taste any sweeter for having been so vociferously blessed?"

"It is sweet indeed," said Poe, and with this raised his eyes to young Miss Cavin.

Brunrichter continued. "Brother Jarvis brought the animal to us last night, leading it by a rope. And all the way here he prayed over it." Now the doctor laughed, as if the memory were too delicious to stifle. "Even as Mr. Tevis sharpened his knife, Brother Jarvis kept muttering away—praying for *the animal's soul!*"

Brother Jarvis smiled. "Knowing what was soon to occur, perhaps I was praying for yours, Alfred."

"In either case, you were praying for something that does not exist."

The man named Delaney now held his plate out in front of him and cast a baleful eye at the small mound of meat. "Don't tell me that you experimented with this animal as well," he said.

"And why not?"

Delaney thought for a moment, then shrugged, then forked a slice into his mouth.

Mr. Vernon said, "Ms. Cavin is fairly new to our happy little group, and I can tell by the furrows in her lovely brow that she has no idea what we are talking about. Should we enlighten her?"

Said Brother Jarvis, "The good doctor conducts experiments on animals."

"Oh my," she said.

"Indeed."

Hesitantly she asked, "What kind of experiments?"

"Experiments in galvanism. He removes the head and attempts to keep it alive with electrical stimulation."

Her eyes grew wide. In short, she provided the horrified expression the men had hoped to induce in her.

Brunrichter said, "As always, Vernon, you oversimplify."

"You connect the head to a voltaic pile and try to make it talk. Or, in this case, *baaaaa*!"

Everybody laughed, except for Miss Cavin, who was looking a bit squeamish.

Brunrichter told her, "I excite arterial and muscular contractions."

"For what purpose?" she asked, her voice meek and strained.

"Because it reminds him of his first girlfriend. *Baaaaa!*"

The doctor allowed the laughter to subside. "Now that you mention it, the sound is remarkably reminiscent of a woman's cry. So much so that last night, when our lunch for today was first introduced to the knife, its bleating all but caused Brother Jarvis to drop to his knees with both hands clapped over his ears."

The bleat of a lamb outside my window—was this the cry I had heard in my dream?

I cast a look at Poe then, to see how he was taking all this banter. Was I the only person present who found this dialogue unsettling? Was this the way the civilized world behaved, this mutual exchange of insults and demeaning remarks? Poe, apparently, saw nothing amiss in it, for he continued to smile amiably at Miss Cavin and once reached out to delicately pat her hand.

"To answer your question," the doctor soon told her, and waited a moment for an appropriate silence to befall, and assumed a more somber expression. "The body," he then explained, "all bodies, are maintained by a number of organs, the greater two being, in ourselves and most other animals, the mind and the heart. Each works independently, ungoverned by the other. Sadly—and to my mind, this represents the major flaw in our anatomy—the most important of these two organs, the mind, cannot survive for long after the lesser one fails."

An older woman, the most outspoken of the group, now looked directly at Mr. Vernon. "Though I have known the lesser one to continue a full forty-seven years in the total absence of a mind."

Many of the women applauded. Mr. Vernon stood and took a bow.

When the banker was once again seated, Brunrichter continued. "It is my contention, Ms. Cavin, and I am not alone in this belief—in fact the work of Helmholtz and duBois-Renyard all but verify the same—my contention is that the activity of the heart supplies electrical impulses necessary to keep the mind functioning, in the way that a strong horse is needed to pull a carriage through the streets. But what if that carriage were made able to move of its own accord?"

"I don't understand," the young woman said. "What good is a mind without a body?"

"Hearts fail," said Brunrichter. "And when they do, the mind fails as well. But it needn't be so. What we will someday soon discover, I predict, is that the heart, in fact the body itself, is irrelevant."

"With the exception, of course, of your body," Vernon told her, and reached out to hold Miss Cavin's foot, which she immediately drew away.

"Well, sir," said Mr. Kane, as thin and stiff as a stork, "I won't believe it until I can walk along Liberty with Randolph Gatesford's head tucked under my arm while he and I enjoy one of our usual Wednesday night arguments."

Old Randolph Gatesford, his voice a croaking tremolo, said, "I am looking forward to that as well. I'll get around a lot faster then than I do on my own. Long as you don't get upset with me for being right all the time, and give me a good kick into the river."

Brunrichter said to Poe, "Mr. Gatesford has volunteered to be my first human subject. But not, we hope, for a good many years. When my research is further along."

"Better speed things up," said Gatesford. "I can't wait forever."

The conversation, I admit, had made me woozy. I had in the last few days begun to think of myself as a man of the world, yet here on a hillside in Pittsburgh people were speaking of things I had never imagined and wished that no one else had either.

I attempted to quiet the fluttering of my stomach by stuffing it with food. Yet the sour taste at the back of my throat would not be swallowed. Eventually I told myself, *One more pickled egg and off I go*. There was a heaviness in my chest and a lightness in my head, as if, atop that small hill, the air was insufficient to fill my lungs or sustain a coherent thought. I wanted to be elsewhere, on a simpler plane, at the level of water and mutual courtesy.

I was helping myself to that last egg, bent over near the corner of the blanket, hand reaching down, arse in the air, when the lady seated to Poe's left, middle-aged and stout, said (innocently, I assumed), "Wasn't that a wonderful piece about the elephants! In the *Chronicle*, wasn't it? Did you happen to read it, Mr. Poe?"

I froze, fingers pinching the egg. My gaze slid sideways and there met Poe's. His eyes glinted like gray glass. "I did," he told her. "I did indeed."

"And wasn't it wonderful?" she asked. "Didn't you find it so? I do not mean what happened to those poor beasts, of course, but the manner in which it was recounted. Didn't you very nearly feel that you were there to see it happen, Mr. Poe?"

He continued to smile at me. "The feeling was undeniable."

One of the gentlemen asked, "Who is this Dobson fellow? Does anybody know?"

"He's new, I can vouch for that. I read the papers cover to cover every day and this was the first I ever heard of him."

"I wasn't as charmed by his piece as you were, Anna. It struck me as somewhat flat in places."

"Flat? How could such a story be flat?"

"How did you find it, Mr. Poe?"

By now I had, with an excruciating self-consciousness, plucked the egg off its plate and retreated to stand several feet to Poe's rear. My face was burning, ears buzzing. Only gradually did it dawn on me that not a single eye deemed me curious. All eyes remained on Poe.

"I found it," Poe said, and paused, giving my heart time to beat a half-dozen times, had it been beating at all, "a promising start."

Brunrichter cut me a sidelong glance, a sardonic smile on his lips. "I would be interested to learn, Edgar, how you were able to discern that the piece represents a start. After all, we know nothing of this mysterious Mr. Dobson. Mightn't he be an old hand from a Philadelphia paper, for example?"

"The author is obviously quite youthful," Poe remarked, playing along. "This is not to say that, in his ability to craft a narrative, he is without talent. On the contrary. But the talent is raw. Unformed. Incipient."

"Amazing that you can deduce so much from the words alone!"

"Remember whom you are addressing," said the doctor. "Here before you sits the master deducer himself. The father of Auguste Dupin."

"An astounding creation," somebody said.

"Thoroughly original."

"The most fascinating character in all of modern literature."

The sycophancy was turning my stomach. Suddenly the vinegary smell from the half of pickled egg still in hand, its slimy texture, made me nauseated. (Maybe, in truth, I wanted the subject to return to my own writing and not to be so easily dismissed, flicked out of the conversation like a crumb flicked off the blanket.)

"Shall we perchance get to see the chevalier in a novel someday?" Ms. Cavin asked, the middle finger of her right hand stroking the hollow of her neck, her left hand toying with a lock of hair.

"Ah, a sustained work," said Poe. "A sustained work requires sustained concentration. Of which I find myself, regrettably, incapable."

"Hogwash!" blurted old Gatesford. "What about *Pym*?"

"The work of a younger and more energetic man." Poe swirled the wine in his glass. "These days, I'm afraid, there is a vague awareness in me, underlying all I do, that I am a fraud."

This was answered with a hail of vehement denials.

Brunrichter shushed the group, then held up a finger, providing Poe with the silence to continue.

"I am known for my hoax stories, am I not?" asked Poe. "That is how I began, in any case. My stories were intended to fool the feeblest of minds. The more feeble the stories, however, the more successful they were.

"I had always hoped that, along the way, I might engage in more honest writing. All I accomplished, unfortunately, was to dig my hole of fraud even deeper. Until now, when I am all but buried by my own trickery."

He was not posing now, was not milking the group for their sympathy or applause. How to account for this sudden detour into naked self-exposure I cannot say—unless it was the resemblance of the young woman, whose question had precipitated his turn toward misery, to his own lost Sissie—only that every person present felt how keen was his sense of failure.

Brunrichter was the first to speak. "It must be quite natural, from time to time, for a writer to grow weary of his own fabrications."

"You have given us so much pleasure, Mr. Poe. Surely you are aware of that."

"In my house, sir, we read your stories and poems aloud. We never tire of them."

"If you should ever stop imagining such tales . . . What a sad day it would be for us!"

Within minutes, the tone had turned funereal. I wanted to leave but I could not abandon him in this atmosphere, beset by sudden gloom.

I said, not loud, not anxious to direct attention to myself, "I remember what Mr. Poe once told me. He said that the finest writing emerges from the blackest turmoil. And that is why I anticipate that he will soon produce a masterpiece."

"Here, here!" came the cheers.

Poe turned at the waist and lifted his eyes to me. For just a moment then I saw in them the old affection we had shared. (Had I suspected at that moment how our relationship had and would be damaged, I wonder if I would have proceeded as I did.)

(And I wonder this too: What use is hindsight, when all it brings is regret?)

In any case, Brunrichter seized upon my statement to remark, "Indeed! His recent misfortunes notwithstanding, Edgar Poe is too much a genius not to turn calamity into art."

And now the coquettish Ms. Cavin spoke again. She gazed as adoringly as ever at her hero. "I have been meaning to ask you, Mr. Poe . . ."

"Edgar," he said.

She blushed. "I have been meaning to ask you. Is it your opinion that an . . . eventful life . . . is a requisite for a writer? Or is imagination alone sufficient?"

"An eventful life?" he repeated, amused. "Well, I suppose it is true that there is an allure, a romantic allure, to what you call an eventful life. But I can assure you, dear girl, and with all the confidence of an expert, that poverty and drunkenness and flights of madness are all more glamorous in theory than in the actual practice thereof."

Because his smile was so genuine, his audience laughed at this, though softly and respectfully. The girl, I can only assume, had been alluding to a whole different genre of romantic events than the ones with which Poe was most intimate, but she had the good taste not to correct his misinterpretation of her question, and indeed her gaze, still fixed on him, flamed ever brighter with hunger. He returned her look, and I thought to myself, now filled with magnanimity toward the man, *This is what he needs. This will do him good.*

How little I knew!

Brunrichter then said, "To return to the matter of Auguste Dupin. You might very soon see the great ratiocinator at work once again. Though not in a fictive capacity."

"And what do you mean by that?" somebody asked.

"Edgar and I have forged an alliance, if you will. We have agreed to join minds so as to discover and bring to justice the vile creature who has been terrorizing the young women of our lovely city."

"Bravo!" the old man said.

But Mr. Vernon chuckled. "I think what you will discover is that all six of these girls—"

"There are seven now."

"Seven?"

"The latest just Friday evening last."

"I hadn't heard. Howsoever, I still predict that all seven of these young women can best be discovered through a thorough search of the sporting houses of Manchester."

"A search for which you volunteer, no doubt!"

"Thank you for the invitation. I shall not take my duties lightly."

The men laughed heartily, the women hid their amusement behind mock gasps. I blushed, unnoticed, to hear this repetition of an earlier exchange between Mrs. Dalrymple and myself.

"Truthfully, though. Would you not agree, Mr. Poe, that in all likelihood these young women have disappeared only from the world, as it were, of virtue?"

"That is indeed a possibility."

"In which case, with my apologies to Brother Jarvis here, whose duty it is to exercise compassion and forgiveness, it strikes me that they are perhaps better left disappeared."

"I do not consider compassion and forgiveness a duty," Brother Jarvis told him.

"Of course not. Yet you are so much better at it than most of us."

"Perhaps because I try a bit harder."

"Touché," the man said. Then, "My point, Edgar, and I have small doubt that a man as worldly as yourself will agree, my point is that even whores have a place in our society."

The gasps that issued this time were not fraudulent.

"Mr. Vernon, if you please!"

"I apologize if my language offends you. I only wonder why it should. The word I employed is in fact a very serviceable word. And are we not all here lovers of words? The word I employed describes precisely who these women are, and just as precisely what they do. If we could learn to tolerate the word with a bit more compassion and forgiveness, perhaps we might learn to tolerate the service provided as well."

Brother Jarvis said, "Why do I suspect that your call for compassion and forgiveness is in this case not wholly altruistic?"

"I am an unmarried man, sir. So if I—"

"You have had your opportunities, Mr. Vernon."

More laughter. Vernon nodded and grinned. Then continued. "The human male is no different than the male of any other species. His physical needs are the same. And if those needs are not routinely satisfied, whether in the brothels of Manchester or elsewhere, he is likely to revert to even baser instincts. This is the nature of every male animal. And for which the animal himself cannot be blamed."

"By this logic," a pale young woman said, her first words of the day trembling with either timidity or anger, "even if the seven girls now missing are discovered to have been murdered, the man who did so is not to be blamed."

Vernon asked, "Would the murderer have resorted to such acts were other avenues of release readily available to him?"

"Are you implying that they are not? You who know the alleys of Pittsburgh and Allegheny City as well as anybody here?"

"I am saying that if a man were allowed to frequent such venues openly, without censure from society, he would never be driven to extremes."

"The young women in question were not prostitutes, sir."

"Were not. But can we now say, with the same authority, that they are not?"

After this, silence. Several women sat shaking their heads. A few of the men looked as if they wanted to nod in agreement with Vernon but did not care to be apprehended in the act by the women.

I, for one, became aware of an increasing animus toward Vernon. He was a distasteful man, brimming with the self-righteousness of the powerful and well-to-do. How ready he was to excuse his own excesses simply because they were his own. His every argument possessed an oily smooth quality, and it was easy for me to picture him skulking about the streets of Pittsburgh at night, waiting in a darkened doorway to lure a passing girl with his leisurely air of luxury.

But before I could further develop my appraisal of him, Brunrichter drove the conversation onward. "What is your opinion of all this, Edgar?"

Poe continued to stare at the shallow pool of claret at the bottom of his glass.

Brunrichter added, "Should we exercise our compassion, and allow the murderer to escape detection?"

Poe said, "As has been stated already, we do not know that a murderer exists."

"Very true. Perhaps he acted only as an abductor."

"Imagine," Vernon said, "seven young concubines all to oneself!"

"Mr. Vernon!"

"One for each day of the week."

"Dr. Brunrichter, please, you must make him stop."

"He loves to shock, my dear. He is doing his utmost to shock you."

"And succeeding very nicely."

Vernon said, "Come home with me and I will do even better. I too can excite muscular contractions, my dear—and I for one do not rely on galvanism to do so."

"Were you within reach, sir, I would slap your face for that."

"Come home with me and I will present both cheeks. In exchange for access to your own, of course."

The young lady's cheeks flamed red. "You should be careful of the way you talk, Mr. Vernon. Some of us might begin to suspect you as the abductor of the missing girls."

"I invite you to search my chambers," the banker told her. "And when you tire of the search, I will be very pleased to read something soothing to you while you rest. Are you familiar with the works of the Marquis de Sade?"

I felt my eyes narrowing as I studied the man. Would a true murderer or abductor be so foolish as to call such suspicion upon himself? Only, I reasoned, if he thought himself far craftier than his audience.

"All right, now," Brunrichter said. "We mustn't give Edgar the impression that we are all hedonistic fools. Not just yet, in any case."

Brother Jarvis said, "Might I suggest that we steer the conversation back toward the spiritual? The pursuit of art is a kind of spiritual quest, wouldn't you agree, Edgar?"

"Now Brother Jarvis," Brunrichter said, and waggled his finger at the monk, "as you know, I invite you along on these outings only as an object of ridicule. Not to introduce such tiresome subjects of conversation."

The doctor then turned to Poe. "Brother Jarvis and I have known each other since boyhood."

"Alfred was constantly catching small animals and taking them apart so as to see what was inside."

"I kept Brother Jarvis very busy with his prayers and burials!"

"It was probably you who turned me into a monk."

"Society should thank me for that. One less zealot roaming the streets."

This exchange was conducted without any trace of true malice. I could almost see the men winking at each other with every new insult. Until finally Brother Jarvis declared, "Life has not and never will be fully understood or explained through science."

"So you have argued ad nauseam. But perhaps we should bring Edgar into this discussion. Can you end our stalemate, sir?"

"Now you will lose at last!" said the monk. "For what is art if not a manifestation of the spiritual urge?"

Brunrichter leaned back on his elbows. "Edgar? Have you an opinion on this?"

Poe stroked his chin. He raised his eyes sufficiently to ascertain if the adoring young lady was still gazing on him adoringly. Of course she was.

"In point of fact," said Poe, "I have of late been coming

more and more to a formulation of the importance of science in our lives. The merely poetic, art for art's sake, does not move me as it once did. Perhaps because I have experienced too much that is antipoetic."

"Precisely!" said Brunrichter. "The more of actual, unsheltered life we are exposed to, the more we perceive that only science can save us."

"Yet science is nothing," Poe went on, "is as common as the rocks and the dirt, until it is elevated by the imagination."

"Hmmmm. Please continue," said Brunrichter, the perfect foil.

"Would you not agree," Poe asked Brother Jarvis, "that the universe is a plot of God? Just as a poem is a plot of the poet? And as a tale is a plot of the writer?"

"Life as a construction of the Divine imagination? Yes, I see what you are saying. And it's a reasonable analogy, to be sure."

"And yet," Poe said, "is it not a construction that, though highly imaginative and original, is founded on science?"

"Aha!" said Brunrichter. "The laws of nature! The laws of physical science!"

"Many of which we do yet comprehend in their full complexity," said Poe. "And so, if we are to understand this science, if we are to unravel this plot, as it were, we must indulge our own imaginations. We must look beyond the syllogism. We must make great leaps of speculation. Because what is provable and observable is, alas, an insufficient explanation."

"In time," said Brunrichter, "science will explain all things."

"Has it explained gravity?"

"We know what gravity does. We do not know why it does so. Or by what mechanism. But give us time and we will know it."

Brother Jarvis, however, was intrigued by Poe's premise. I, on the other hand, was more impressed with the increasing clarity of Poe's thoughts. Evenings and early mornings of late seemed to find him muddled and lethargic, but now, as the afternoon wore on, I detected more and more of the acumen with which I was most familiar. I noticed too that he spent more time staring into his wine glass than in lifting it to his lips.

"You are proposing," Brother Jarvis asked, "a merger of science and art?"

"I am not proposing it as much as I am suggesting that this is the nature of the universe. Let us look again at gravity, if you will. It is an invisible force that, so far as we know, is a kind of magnetism between all material bodies. The larger bodies exert their pull on the smaller ones—agreed?"

"Agreed," Brunrichter said.

"Is it true of our own bodies here on this hill? Of the relationship between the Earth and the moon? Of all the planets as they orbit the sun?"

"Of course it is."

"Then is it not reasonable to imagine that it must also be true of all suns, and of all the planets and moons that orbit them?"

"A perfectly logical assumption," said the doctor.

"And what of the larger suns to the smaller ones? Are their positions fixed? Are they immune to the forces of gravity?"

"Well, to our eyes—"

"To our eyes," Poe repeated. "Science says yes, the solar systems are more or less fixed in place."

"They move throughout space, perhaps, but otherwise . . ."

"This is what science tells us, yes, because this is what our perceptions have told science. But our imagination tells us something else. Our imagination tells us that if gravity exists within this solar system, it must also exist without. Which means that all heavenly bodies are being pulled one toward another, the smaller to the larger. And if we continue to apply our imagination to this formula, we see that at some point in time, far in the future perhaps but inevitably so, this process of attraction must, owing to the increased proximity of heavenly bodies, accelerate."

Brunrichter said, "You are talking about an end. An absolute collapse of the universe."

"Ah, but will it be an end? Must it be? Or might it be, instead, a unification? Might it, in fact, be a return to that original and singular entity from which all existence began?"

Brother Jarvis grinned. "Commonly referred to as God."

Brunrichter ran a hand through his hair and rolled his eyes. "Edgar, Edgar, Edgar. You have become, in one fell swoop, a poet, a scientist, a theologian, and a heretic."

Poe smiled at the adoring young woman. "And a thirsty one at that."

She blushed, but she did not drop her gaze from his, not even when he raised his glass to her and sipped. A part of me was happy that Poe might have some tender company for the evening, though another part of me was repulsed by his flirtatiousness and the girl's easy acquiescence. Truth be told, I was no doubt jealous of his success with the fairer sex. And especially with a girl not much older than I.

In any case, as the wine bottles went 'round again, I told myself that I had better things to do, and, though I could not articulate what those better things might be, I wandered away from the gathering. What I wanted, of course, was not debate or argumentation nor wine-enhanced frivolity, but the serenity I had glimpsed in Susan's smile. There was an aestheticism there as well, by which I do not mean a stinginess but its opposite, a fullness. A fullness of purity. Of simple and unadorned truth. Her smile to me was like the beauty referred to in Coleridge's poem; it was all I knew of life, and all I needed to know.

I am not making myself understood in this, and I apologize. It is a difficult concept to impart. Certain holy men, in far flung places, have a word for it, however. To them it is called satori.

To me it was, quite simply, contentment. It had struck me unexpectedly, a glancing blow. It goes without saying that, having experienced it once, I could never be happy until I found it again.

To that end, I slipped away from the picnic. Murderers, prostitutes, poets and scientists and monks all be damned—I needed only Susan.

Chapter Fifteen

"You back?" Buck Kemmer called to me from the dock. He was unloading bales of rags from a flatboat, standing with one foot in the boat and one on the dock, reaching out with his baling hook to grapple a bail and drag it close enough that he could swing it onto the dock.

"Don't you ever get tired?" I asked in reply.

"Ain't always that a weak mind and a strong back is an asset. Best to take advantage of it when I can."

I nodded and grinned, but said nothing.

"You know anything about work yourself?" he asked.

"Such as?"

"Such as how to do it."

"I've done my share."

"I see your mouth moving but you're still just standing there."

I went down to the dock and said, "What do you want done?"

"Slide these bales back on the dock some. Give me a little more room to work."

As I did so I asked, "What's the pay for this job?"

"You only just started and you're worried about the pay already?"

"A fair wage for a fair day's work, that's all I'm after."

"How about no pay for five minutes' work?"

"Wouldn't be the first time I worked for nothing." I busied myself then clearing the dock around Buck, dragging each bale well out of his way. That done, I hefted a bale—it was all I could do to lift it off the ground, seizing by both hands the thick cord wrapped around its middle—and toted it, awkwardly, up the steps to the street.

When I returned to the dock, Buck said, "Keep that up and we'll maybe renegotiate your wages."

"Now you're talking. How much will I get?"

"How about this: You get to ask me what you came here to ask."

"Who says I came to ask you something?"

"I'm a fascinating character, all right. You came back here 'cause you think I'm so pretty, is that it?"

"Well . . ."

"I'd advise you think twice before you answer that."

I toted a second bale to the street. Then, on the dock, I asked, "She have a beau?"

He said nothing, so I moved a third bale. When I returned he said, "She's got a lot of beaus. One of them's even a professor."

The floor dropped out of my stomach. Somehow it had never dawned on me that Susan and I had not been waiting all our lives for one another.

Buck, no doubt, saw me sag. "Prissy fella," he said. "Walks around with his chin up in the air. Like he's inviting everybody to have a look up his nose holes."

"Is she serious about him?" I asked.

"She's sixteen. It ain't her job to be serious about her suitors. It's mine."

"And are you?"

"About him? Yeah, I'm serious. I'm serious about wanting to give him a good arse-kicking every time I lay eyes on him."

I understood suddenly that he was taking the measure of me, watching how I handled myself with physical labor, the one thing he understood inside and out. Did I think myself too good for sweat? That's what he was asking himself. Because decent, honest men want for their daughters a man just like themselves, only better.

I picked up my pace, stepping more lively as I toted one bale after another to the top of the stairs. By the time Buck emptied the flatboat, I had moved a third of the bales. It was then the wagoner arrived. He sat at the reins, calming the horses, while Buck tossed the bales up to me and I stacked them securely in the bed of the wagon.

"You almost look like you know what you're doing," Buck told me.

"It's like I told you; I've done my share of work."

Within twenty minutes the wagon was loaded, Buck was paid his dollar, and the horses clopped off, straining at their traces. I remained standing there, sweaty and aching, while Buck returned to the dock, where he dipped a handkerchief in the river and washed his face with it. He returned to clap a heavy hand on my shoulder.

"Feels good to put in an hour's work, don't it, Gus?"

The name still sounded strange to me, but I nodded all the same, and rubbed my shoulder. "Felt better than that slap did."

He laughed. And then, an unimaginable thing—he started to walk away!

"Where are you going?" I asked.

"I'm going home, laddybuck. Home to my supper. You got a home to go to, don't you?"

Desperation made me bold. "I'd rather go to yours."

That one took him by surprise, I think. It surprised

even me. He blinked once, rubbed his cheek, then came marching toward me, long quick strides that made me think he was about to throttle me. Before I could so much as flinch he wrapped five fingers around my bicep and yanked me up close, his face only inches from mine.

"You say what's on your mind, don't you?" he asked.

"Only when there's something I want."

"Wanting ain't getting."

"I've got to try, don't I?"

He pulled me even closer. "You lay a finger on her, or even think of doing so, I'll tear this arm right off and beat you senseless with it—you understand?"

"Truth is," I told him, "I'm feeling pretty senseless already."

His laugh was so explosive that were I not anchored by his grip I might have been blown backward across the street. As it was he spun us both to the left, tossed a heavy arm around my shoulder, and sent us striding north.

"What is it makes a fool in love so lovable?" he asked, and I grinned dopily, too woozy to reply.

What can I tell you about the next two hours? Does it matter that their house was neat but small? Many are. The truth is that I cannot describe the features of those rooms with more than the sketchiest of details. I cannot tell you the color of the sofa I sat upon, or the texture of the fabric over which my nervous fingers ran a thousand times. Now, as then, when I see myself in their living room, or seated at their table, I see only the two of them in any light at all, as if they radiated their own illumination, Susan the brightest, smiling always, and her father in a softer light yet basking in hers as well.

We had a ham and cabbage soup that first night, I think, with carrots and onions, the broth thickened by potato starch. Surely there was bread as well. Cider and tea. I paid little attention to the food, for I had no attention to spare.

Susan was pleasant enough to me at first, friendly right from the start, though it was clear she viewed me as some harmless mongrel who had followed her father home because his hands smelled of fish. After all, here was a girl who counted a professor among her beaus. What would she want with a farm boy with callused hands?

For the most part I kept quiet and listened to their conversation. My training as a child—the backhanded slap, the snap of the leather strop—had taught me the virtues of holding my tongue. Occasionally, when I gleaned an interesting bit of information from the shorthand talk between father and daughter, I would hazard a question, politely, intending to display my inquisitive intelligence yet not too soon reveal my desperate desire to know every aspect of Susan's life.

She worked weekdays at Miss Jones's School for Young Ladies, located on Hand Street, under the bridge, no more than three blocks from where my feet had first touched Pittsburgh soil. She was an instructor for the younger girls, and in general an assistant to Miss Jones herself.

Buck wrinkled up his sunburned nose when the headmistress's name was mentioned. " 'We must have decorum,' " he said through his nose, his voice in falsetto, a nasally whine. " 'Decorum must be maintained.' "

"Papa, you promised," said Susan, but with head turned so as to conceal her stifled laugh.

It was all the encouragement Buck required. " 'Miss Kemmer, is this your idea of decorum? That child's hair is mussed, is it not? And that one—Child! Remove your finger from your nose at once! And the doorway, Miss Kemmer. There is a brutish-looking man on the threshold. Order him to leave, please. I will not have men gawking at me as if I am disrobed!' "

Susan giggled. "That man is my father, Miss Jones."

" 'Your father! Oh my. He is a handsome brute, isn't he?' "

"She did not say that, Papa."

"You can bet she was thinking it though. I seen the way she looked me over. Every time I come by the place, in fact."

Susan rolled her eyes at me. "My father suffers from the delusion that he is irresistible to women."

"It is not a delusion."

"Which explains why there are so many of them lined up at our door."

"There's none there, little miss, because I've worked so hard to chase them all away. I only need my one girl to make me happy."

She answered with a smile.

I asked, "Is it only the two of you then?"

She made no reply to this, nor did he. Some memories, no matter how old, always give us pause.

I told her, "I lost both my folks a good while back."

"Gus," she said, "I'm so sorry."

"Truth is, I never really knew my father. He went into jail for murder, never came back out. Was probably done away with in there himself. As for my mother . . . When I was ten I saw a man slit her throat."

She stared at me, horrified, her lovely mouth slightly open. Her father stared at me as well. I have to admit that I relished their horror.

"I ended up killing that man myself," I told them.

At this her gaze softened. "You're making this up."

"Oh, I killed him all right. Ran him through with a sword from a rich man's house. He was after me and Poe, wanted us both dead. So really, I had no choice in the matter."

I could tell by the flicker of lights in her eyes that she did not believe me. "Poe?" she asked.

"Edgar Allan Poe, the writer. He's here in Pittsburgh, you know. We came here together from Philadelphia."

I thrilled to the way she looked at me now. "Gus, if you are making this up . . ."

"I swear it's true. We're both staying with Dr. Brunrichter, up there in his castle on Ridge Avenue. The doctor set up a reading for Poe a couple of days ago. Today he threw him a picnic, which is where I was too before I came into town."

She put a hand to her bosom, that delicate but lovely bosom, and patted it as if to ease her breathing. I suppressed an urge to do the same, for I, too, just from looking at her so long, was very nearly out of breath.

"She wanted to go to that reading," her father told me. "Kept after Miss Jones to try to get them an invitation. Even asked her professor to try, didn't you, Susie?"

"He is not my professor, Papa. Though he might have been if he had been able to secure an invitation."

"I'll take you to the next one," I told her. "It's this Saturday. At the Old Drury."

I should probably have felt guilty for waving Poe in front of her like a fat worm before a hungry bird. But love is its own excuse and its own forgiveness.

Of course they insisted then that I recount the entire story of my relationship with Poe, including my mother's death, which I relegated to a kind of footnote to the investigation Poe and I had conducted seven years earlier in New York City. I told them how I had found the body of Mary Rogers under a Hudson River pier, had shown it to Poe, and how that discovery then led to at least three more murders, plus very nearly mine and Poe's.

By the time I finished the tale, I sensed that I had grown immeasurably in her eyes. All the better. For what good is history if we cannot elevate ourselves by it?

This story was followed, at their insistence, by a chronicle that I tried to limit to a mere summation, if for no other reason than to create an endearing illusion of humility, the story of my years between then and now.

"And since coming home from Ohio," Susan said, "you have been employed as Mr. Poe's assistant?"

"Not really his assistant, no. Though I do help him out when I can. Plus, he helps me with my own writing, you see, and together we—"

Again she interrupted, too startled for silence. "You intend to be a writer?"

This was precisely the opening I had been waiting for, had in fact been maneuvering toward since I'd found my way into the conversation. "In fact I published my first piece just recently. In the *Daily Chronicle*. It was about some elephants that drowned in Philadelphia."

"She read that to me!" Buck said.

"And as I recall," said Susan, "it was not authored by an individual named Gus."

Suddenly I did not like the name Gus any longer. From her mouth it emerged sounding homely and dull, a clunker on her tongue, and not the name of the solid, honest and erstwhile fellow I had aspired to be just yesterday.

"When I write I use the name James Dobson," I explained. "My real name is Dubbins. August Dubbins. Some people call me Augie."

"Augie is much preferable to Gus," she said.

"I like Gus," said her father.

"In any case," said Susan, and leaned back in her chair, and crossed her arms, and fixed me with a sidelong gaze, "you appear to be too many people for one individual. How can we be sure that it isn't all a fairy tale of sorts, intended to beguile a slice of pie from me?"

"We having pie?" Buck asked.

"Rhubarb, Papa."

"Well trot it out! What are we waiting for?"

"We shall have pie when the table is cleared."

He shoved back his chair and stood and whisked my soup bowl out from under my hand. In the meantime Susan and I continued to smile at one another, she waiting for my response, me savoring her attention.

"How about this?" I asked. "Two things. First off, my real name, August Dubbins. Being as how you claim to be an admirer of Poe's work, maybe you will recognize that name?"

She gave it some thought, then answered, "I do not."

"He named his famous investigator after me. The one from *The Murders in the Rue Morgue*. Auguste Dupin."

"Or," she said, "you named yourself after him."

"All right then. Consider this. I have written a second piece, also under the name of James Dobson. Tomorrow I will deliver it to the *Chronicle*. With luck, you will see it published there in a day or so."

"Is this your proof, Gus Augie August James? The promise that the writer named James Dobson will one day publish again?"

"I will bring it to you first," I told her. "You can read it. Before I take it to the *Chronicle*."

She eyed me suspiciously for a few moments, but her eyes were twinkling. "That should suffice," she said.

I felt huge with happiness.

"Where in God's name is that pie?" Buck asked.

Chapter Sixteen

Can a morning tremble? Can the air itself hang almost giddy with excitement? Something peculiar was afoot, to be sure, for there I sat on an empty crate on the Allegheny waterfront, close to the aqueduct, near where only recently hundreds of citizens had perished from cholera, and where seven young women yet remained missing, either kidnapped, shanghaied into prostitution, or dead—there I sat with both feet tapping the cobblestones, and thought this disorderly city, though clamorous and stinking, the finest place in all the universe. Let others enjoy their tobacco and applejack and rum and opium, I'll take love every time. Such sweet hallucinations of thought! Such tantalizations of the sublime!

Until 7:30 A.M. or so I indulged myself in every conceivable fantasy, every variation possible on the theme of marriage and perpetual bliss. Twenty minutes later found me pacing in the dooryard of Miss Jones's School for Young Ladies, a sheaf of rolled papers in my hand.

Twice I noticed Miss Jones observing me from a first-floor window of the large brownstone. She was tall and willow thin, dressed in a faded black frock and a collar that looked tight enough to choke a fishing worm. She had a head of wild gray hair, nearly all of it pushed or brushed or perhaps growing only at the very top of her head as if trying to escape from her scalp. She looked to me like nothing so much as an old cattail whose seed top has gone to fuzz. But I waved to her all the same, both times, and when, the second time, she did not draw away from the window afterward but stood there trying to evaporate me with the glare from her eyes, I broke into an impromptu jig on the hard-trampled lawn, just to show her there were no hard feelings on my part, that I was too happy to be slain.

The door burst open midway in my jig and out she marched onto the doorstep. "Stop it!" she shouted, her voice even more nasally than in Buck's impersonation, and as shrill as an ice pick. "Stop it this minute!"

I stopped dancing. Then flashed her my most fetching smile. Held out my hand and took a step in her direction. "Would you care to join me?" I asked.

She snatched a broom from behind the doorway. When she thrust it out in front of her, I had a hard time telling the two of them apart. "You get away from here this minute! I'll not allow drunken louts like you in my dooryard. Not now nor anytime!"

"I am not drunk, madam."

"Pixilated! I know it when I see it! Now get away from here and shame on you. You are a disgrace to your mother!"

That took some of the starch out of my smile. I considered informing her that my mother had been a whore and a drunkard whose greatest joy was in robbing me of my pennies and then beating me with a leather strap, but, for Susan's sake, which for the moment seemed inextricably entwined with mine, I did not.

As soberly as I could I answered, "I apologize for the dancing, Miss Jones. A tune came into my head all of a sudden. It won't happen again."

She brought her broom back to parade rest. "Be off with you now. My young ladies will be arriving soon. And you are not a fit sight for them to see."

"I have an appointment with Miss Susan Kemmer," I said.

"She has no time for that."

"Two minutes of conversation is all I require. And then I'll be gone. And with the humblest of apologies to you, Miss Jones, for disturbing your morning." I capped this last statement with a low bow.

She gave me a lingering glare, followed by a *Hmmmpf!* Then turned and entered the building and slammed the door.

She soon appeared again behind the window, arms clamped over her bosom, which, as far as I could tell, was not quite as prominent as the buttons on her dress. I kept my back to her after that and remained as still as I could muster, though the urge to throw a jig step or two was strong.

Fortunately Susan arrived within minutes. She was still some forty yards away when I spotted her, but even from that distance I recognized her immediately, aided by that peculiar telescopic sight that love often produces, a keenness of perception that goes beyond the merely physical. I hurried down Penn Avenue to meet her.

She smiled at my approach. "Have you brought it?"

I handed her the papers.

She paused there on the street, unrolled the papers, turned slightly so that the sunlight fell over her shoulder, which seemed to me the loveliest of all shoulders possible, so delicate and yet strong, so shaped to the curve of my palm, if ever my palm should be so lucky.

She read, " 'A Hanging. By James Dobson.' " Then she turned her eyes on me. "A common enough start for a forgery," she said.

"I am not lying, Susan. You know I'm not."

"I know no such thing."

"Yes, you do, I can see it in your eyes."

"You see your own foolishness."

"Is that what it's called? Then yes, I do see it. And I see yours too."

"Hush," she said, and blushed a little. "Let me read."

I watched her face as she read what I had written, watched her lovely eyes taking in my words, watched her lovely mouth soon lose its smile, turn gradually down, the lips forming into a slight pucker, her lovely smooth forehead furrow.

Finished, she said, not yet bringing her gaze to meet mine, "It's so horrible, Augie. Such a horrible thing."

I felt kicked in the stomach. I might even have moaned out loud.

"Oh no, I didn't mean—" She put a hand on my arm. "I mean the hanging itself. The awfulness of it. The way it happened. That poor man."

"He was a murderer," I said.

"I know, I know. But the way it happened. His head . . ."

"There's more to it that I didn't even write about."

"It could not get more horrible than this."

"The night it happened," I told her, "Dr. Brunrichter grabbed Poe by the arm and pulled him up out of his chair. Right up to the gallows. Brunrichter put his ear to the man's chest. Then he seized Poe and tried to make him do the same. When Poe resisted, the doctor took Poe's hand and pressed it over the man's heart."

"Why in the world . . . ?"

"Because the heart was still beating."

"No!" she said.

"The doctor seemed so excited by it. He turned to all of us and said, 'It does not yet know.' "

"And he was referring to the heart?"

I nodded. "The heart did not yet know that the man was dead."

She squeezed shut her eyes. A shiver ran through her, so that I ached to put my arms around her, hold her close, warm her with my strength. But of course I could not. Still, when she leaned toward me a little, I put out a hand and touched her lightly on the arm, and felt all of life coalescing where we touched, all contentment flooding in.

She opened her eyes again. "Is it true that he is out there now? In a gibbet on Maynard's Island?"

"Rotting away," I said.

She shivered again, and I felt it in my hand, all the way into my chest, and deeper still. "I shall have nightmares tonight. Thanks to your Mr. Dobson."

"I am James Dobson, Susan."

"I know you are," she said.

And so, it was a hanging, another man's grisly death, that first brought her close enough to touch. Would that it had been my own.

Chapter Seventeen

From Miss Jones's schoolyard, and with a heart as light as cloud wisp, I went directly to the *Pittsburgh Daily Chronicle*. My editor there, Mr. Lovesey, did not fall into my arms with rapturous gratitude after reading the piece, but he did sit quietly afterward, lips pursed, before telling me in his monotonic mumble, "We'll run it tomorrow." Whereupon he offered me a regular assignment of two pieces per week, to run each Wednesday and Saturday.

"I'm not sure I can find two stories every week," I told him. "These first two just sort of dropped into my lap."

"Are you a newspaperman or aren't you?"

"How about if they were to run on Monday and Friday? Gives me more time in between."

"Monday and Friday then. And while you're at it you can keep a sharp ear for any bit of news about those missing girls."

"I could talk with the families, I suppose."

"The families have been talked with to death already. Nobody knows a thing."

"Then . . . ?"

"Just keep your eyes and ears open, that's all you can

do. Sooner or later some fella's going to start bragging about what he's done to them. It's human nature."

I was reminded of Mr. Vernon's braggadocio at the picnic. Might it be less empty and frivolous than it had seemed?

"It's agreed then," Mr. Lovesey said. "Eight-fifty a week to start."

"But you paid me five for the first piece. Shouldn't it be ten dollars a week for two stories?"

"Drowned elephants pay extra. You won't be writing about drowned elephants every week. Nor even about men getting hanged."

"Does that mean that a hanging pays five dollars? Same as drowned elephants?"

"Three-fifty. Which brings you up to the sum we agreed on, eight and a half a week."

"The man's head came off," I said.

"A lucky coincidence on your part."

"I bet the *Gazette* would pay five." I made as if to reach for the papers on his desk.

He clamped a hand atop them. Holding them in place, he used his other hand to slide open a drawer, reached in, plucked out a half eagle and flipped it through the air to me.

I caught it, grinning. "Ten dollars a week then?"

"Eight-fifty!" he roared. I was shocked to hear him capable of such vehemence.

Then quickly he returned to his lifeless monotone. "Freak accidents, lucky coincidences, special kinds of mutilations, anything like that and you get a bonus. Track down those missing girls and you get a bonus. But your regular pay is eight-fifty. Take it or leave it."

I believed at the time that I would have no trouble

finding an abundance of bonus material. Not only because humanity itself overflows with it, but because I, it was beginning to appear, had been born to the macabre. Like Poe, I was a magnet for the grisly.

I believed, naively, that if I kept my eyes wide open I would be able to see carnage swirling all around me, while I, serenely observant in the eye of the storm, remained unscathed. Little did I realize then that these are the necessary illusions of youth—invulnerability, self-determination, control over one's own destiny—necessary lest we scurry like mice to the nearest cave, there to cower in impotent fear. Little did I realize that no one escapes the tornado of life unscathed. Even in its quietest moments the winds of that storm continue to rage, turning every object in existence into a projectile, a missile, so that even the most unlikely of them, even an airborne broom straw, can puncture an innocent's heart.

Chapter Eighteen

I saw little of Poe and Brunrichter over the next few days. The first assignment I gave myself was the very one Mr. Lovesey had disparaged—to interview the families of the missing girls. None was eager to speak with me, a mere writer with no authority, and on more than one occasion I was looked upon with contempt, my questions responded to with anger. At times it seemed I had presented myself to these families as a whipping boy, for upon me they vented their frustration with the police, demanding to know why nothing had yet been done, why those goddamn watchmen couldn't get themselves organized and do a better job of it. Nobody cared about their girls, they said. Nobody gave a damn. But just let some councilman's daughter go missing and then let's see how fast the watchmen scrambled.

Through it all I managed to piece together a bit of information. Two of the girls had been waylaid while returning from the homes of acquaintances, one coming home from a visit with a cousin, one after fetching a bucket of beer for her parents, one after delivering a bundle of knitting, another after cleaning a church. The first girl to go missing had simply gone for a walk after arguing with her mother about the color of a bolt of cloth they intended to buy for dresses.

All had disappeared from some street or alleyway below the aqueduct. This placed all of them within a twenty-minute stroll from Vernon's bank on Liberty. His residence, I could only assume, would be nearby. It also placed them within a twenty-minute stroll from most of Pittsburgh, but this was a fact I chose to ignore. I hoped somehow to link all the girls to Vernon because I disliked the man, had disliked him from the first moment I had heard him speak at Brunrichter's picnic. He had on that occasion displayed the arrogance and despotic nature of a well-to-do bachelor, used to satisfying his own selfish needs and no others, and I would have been thrilled to discover that the families of all seven girls did their banking with Vernon, thereby providing him the opportunity to know the girls at least by sight and name, enough to excite his nefarious urges. Unfortunately, only two of the families used any bank at all, and only one of those used Vernon's.

In the end, after exhausting the patience of every family member who would speak to me, I learned little of consequence. By all appearances, each young woman seemed the victim of a random kidnapping, of some madman who prowled the streets in search of an occasion to strike. My questions accomplished little more than to drive the grieving families even deeper into their grief.

And so, after my first day as an honest newspaperman, I was left with no option but the one employed by the police themselves, which was to sit back and wait for a bit of usable evidence to appear, to eventually float to the surface like a drowned horse. As a slightly dishonest newspaperman, however, another option remained.

Next day, a few minutes before the noon hour, I stationed myself within view of the front doorway of Vernon's bank. I hoped that he would return home for his midday meal, thereby leading me to his place of residence. I would then scrutinize the building, assess the number of servants employed therein, and determine how best to use those privateering skills of stealth and sneakery acquired as a gutter rat in Manhattan. I was a much bigger rat now, not so light on my feet as I had been at ten years old, but I did not doubt my ability to gain entrance to any edifice in Pittsburgh. In fact the prospect of a bit of brigandage—all in the service of journalism and truth, of course—thrilled me more than just a little.

As luck would have it, Vernon did not return home at noon but dined instead at a small tavern a block north of the bank. I was forced to return to the bank later that evening, at the business's closing hour, in hopes of finally following Vernon home. But instead he returned to the tavern. And there spent the next two hours swilling lager. I admit to having a mug or two myself while hidden behind a beam across the room from him.

He was a man of huge appetites, both in beer and in victuals. And, even more telling, in the way he gathered others around him, calling fellow businessmen to his table so as to fill their glasses from his own pitcher, regaling them with loud stories that grew even louder as the evening progressed, laying a hand on the arm or hip of every waiter girl to pass within reach, and, on two occasions, pulling one of them onto his lap.

The light outside was in its gloaming by the time he departed. Into the lavender dusk we went then, back past the bank with Vernon a dozen strides ahead of me. He kept a slow but fairly straight line and did not meander side to side, not drunk but thoroughly relaxed and sated.

And finally to his house, just a block and a half beyond the bank. It was a solid two-story structure of yellow brick, with a small covered porch out front and a tiny yard boxed in by a low white fence. The house was completely dark, and no servant met him at the door.

He unlocked the front door and stepped inside, turning to the right but remaining framed there in the open doorway. There must have been a small table there beside the door, for I watched him bend down and a moment later a glow erupted, a lucifer had been struck. He used it to light an oil lamp, adjusted the flame, filling the room with light. Then he closed the door.

I moved closer, watching the movement of his lamp past the windows. Another lamp was lit, but it remained stationary while the first lamp disappeared toward the rear of the house.

I checked quickly to see who might be watching me,

saw no one looking in my direction, and sprinted forward, leapt his low fence, and made my way to the rear corner of the house. Soon the back door swung open and Vernon emerged. He came out into the yard and, singing to himself, crossed toward the privy.

He went into the outhouse and shut the door. Yellow light shone through the vent holes shaped like a half moon and four stars. Vernon continued to sing in a low baritone.

I looked at the house's back door, standing open, a soft light coming from deep inside. I could stroll inside unnoticed if I wished, it would be as easy as that. But to what avail? At best I would have a few minutes to search the house, and surely the light from the oil lamp, as I carried it racing from room to room, would arouse somebody's suspicion. Better to wait until daylight, I reasoned, when Vernon was at his bank. I could then search the place at my leisure. All in the service of journalism and truth, of course.

Next morning, I did just that. At half past nine, by manipulating both ends of a piece of stiff wire, I persuaded the lock on Vernon's rear door to snap open. I stepped into a kitchen warm with morning light and still redolent of his breakfast coffee. The empty cup, along with a small pan, a bowl and spoon, all having been washed clean, sat drying on the enamel counter beside the sink basin. I guessed that he had breakfasted on coffee and oatmeal, and found it amusing that a man so gluttonous by night would be so miserly by morning.

I also wondered why he employed no servants but kept his own house—not lavish by any standards, not even my own; in fact it was downright ascetic—when he could easily have afforded several. Was he merely a spendthrift? Or were there more execrable motives at play here?

Into the front rooms then, a dining room and adjoining parlor, each furnished quite plainly with the barest minimum of pieces, nothing new, nothing bright or welcoming. And nothing, I observed with disappointment, conspicuously damning.

Up the stairs I went, moving quietly, though I knew I was alone. Three of the bedrooms were empty, completely empty, the walls bare and the scarred wooden floors uncovered. Only the final bedroom gave evidence of habitation. And here, too, was evidence of Vernon's other half, the self-indulgent side of a puzzling personality. A thick braided rug covered most of the floor. Two cherrywood dressers, one with a large mirror, and the bed with its wide feather mattress, covered the rest of the floor.

But I merely glanced at these furnishings, scarcely took them in at all. I had not even crossed over the threshold and into the room before my breathing quickened and my heart began to race. For there on one side of the bed, laid out and smoothed like the skin of a radiant ghost, was a woman's underdress, what I thought of then as a petticoat because at seventeen I had no names and little familiarity with women's undergarments, especially with any so impractical as this, a pearly, brilliant and silky white, with lace across the bodice and over the slender shoulder straps, the fabric as delicate as any I had ever seen, the entire garment from the hem of the skirt to the turn at the top of the shoulder straps laid out and smoothed by Vernon's hand so that not a single wrinkle creased it.

I was trembling as I tiptoed forward. Perhaps I even giggled, I felt that giddy, that triumphant. Beside the bed I lowered myself to a knee and eased my face close to the bodice and sniffed. The faint scents of powder and lilac, dizzying, intoxicating. Yes, yes, a woman had worn this petticoat—a young woman, one of the missing women, *yes!*

Unthinking, heedless of the consequences, overcome with what I thought of as my victory, I stood and snatched up the garment, my trophy. It felt almost slippery to the touch and weightless as a whisper as I crumbled it into a ball and crammed it inside my shirt, so cool against my skin. Only when I was several blocks away from the house, making my way toward Ridge Avenue and the safety of my own room at Brunrichter's place, did I feel the idiotic grin slipping from my mouth, feel the corners of my lips turning down as if something heavy in the city below was yet attached to me there, pulling like fishhooks.

Regret ballooned in me. What had I been thinking? Truth was, I hadn't been thinking at all, else I would not have touched that underdress. What good would it do in my hands? I could not show it to anyone, could not turn it over to the police, could not trot it out before each of the grieving families to ask, *Was this your daughter's?* Any of those actions would prompt the question, *And how did you come to possess it, Mr. Dobson?*

My career in Pittsburgh would be over before it got started. Not a soul would trust me were the news to get out that James Dobson, budding journalist, was also a sneak thief, a burglar, a looter of women's unmentionables. And if none of the families could identify the underdress—and on second glance the silky garment struck me as something more befitting a banker's paramour than a merchant's or day laborer's daughter—what then? Word might spread that I was trotting around town with a woman's undergarment in hand. Word might spread to Vernon himself, and he would speak discreetly to the watchmen employed in his bank, he would have me beaten, arrested, perhaps even worse. He might do as little as to spread a rumor, in fact not a rumor at all but the truth so subtly nuanced toward the salacious, that I had gone to the trouble of breaking into his house only to steal no money, no silver candlesticks, nothing but an airy underdress left behind by one of his intimate acquaintances.

I would be made a laughingstock. Ruined not only in Pittsburgh but as far and wide as the story might carry. And worst of all, far worse than all that, Susan's eyes would be opened to the blackguard at the heart of me, and she would turn her back on me forever.

A half-dozen explanations came to me then as to why a silky underdress might be laid out across a bachelor's bed. Among the more credible ones: It lay there awaiting his mistress, whether another man's wife or simply a progressive young woman such as Lydia Cavin, who visited Vernon on occasion and could not risk carrying her lingerie to and fro; or it lay there as a memento of an earlier tryst, or as last vestige of a lost love who had spurned him; or it lay there as an incentive to a lonely man's self-pleasure; or, finally, the one I preferred, if only because I was feeling so mean-spirited and low suddenly, it lay there because it was Vernon's own nightwear, the wardrobe of a secret midnight life.

Had I searched Vernon's bedroom more carefully I

might have found evidence to validate any one of those possibilities. But no, I had been too impetuous for that. Stupid, stupid man.

The garment was worthless to me. It proved nothing—nothing but my own foolishness. Come evening Vernon would return home to discover the underdress missing; for a few moments he would go dizzy with confusion and fear—had he mislaid it? Where could it be? He would search everywhere, in every unlighted crook and corner of the house, in a panic that his secret, whatever it was, had been discovered. And in the end he would arrive at the only conclusion possible: the garment had been stolen. His house, his privacy, his secret life had been violated.

Would he suspect me? There was no reason to do so. Yet my guilt made me itchy with nervousness. I crammed the underdress into the bottom of my battered valise and vowed that, when next I found myself alone in the house, I must turn it to ashes in Mrs. Dalrymple's stove.

Chapter Nineteen

For the rest of that day and the ones to follow, my daylight hours were engaged in strolling the city in pursuit of other stories, an activity that helped to distract me from the voice that kept reiterating what a fool I had been. From the docks to beyond the city limits and back again I walked, trudged, hopped rides on wagons, a peripatetic scavenger of mischief and mayhem, of stories to tell. My face soon became a familiar one atop Grant's Hill, where I routinely visited Chislett's magnificent courthouse and the adjacent jail, nicknamed Mount Airy. After the hanging piece came out, the personnel of those two buildings took to greeting me by name. Or, rather, by pseudonym.

"Mornin', Mr. Dobson."

"Here about that stabbin', Mr. Dobson?"

"Wagon rolled over down on Findley, Mr. Dobson. Broke a woman's back, it did. Leastways that's the story her husband's tellin'. And wasn't he lucky to come out of it with nary a scratch!"

In short, because the young Mr. Dobson had kept a cool head when another man lost his (in decapitation by hanging), the world of journalism opened wide its arms to him. People everywhere were eager to share their tales with me (especially if the telling of them painted the speaker in a pure light and tainted others by contrast). And I, like all ambitious men, was eager—no, make that desperate—desperate to have a name that commanded respect, even if the name had to be invented. Especially desperate now that the scoundrel Augie Dubbins had momentarily taken over while in the banker's bedchamber, and in the action of a few seconds had shown the damage he could do to both Dobson and himself.

I did my best to put the episode out of my mind. Though I would keep my eyes and ears open for any talk about the missing girls, I would do far better, for a while at least, to tend to other business.

When on occasion I did return to Brunrichter's estate, typically in the evening hours after a supper with Susan and Buck, I usually found Poe and Brunrichter in the library, ensconced in smoking robes and slippers, enjoying their brandy and pipes. (Previous to this Brunrichter had favored the cigar, but he switched to pipe smoking because Poe preferred the meerschaum.)

Neither man ever broached the subject of my hanging story. Nor did either of them question my comings and goings, save for the one time when, early in the week, as I crept past the library doorway and toward the stairs, hoping to avoid further human interaction for the day so as to savor alone a recollection of my time in Susan's gaze, the doctor called to invite me in for a cognac. Only when I stepped to the threshold did I see that Brother Jarvis was also seated inside.

"Thank you," I said, "but I believe I will retire, if you gentlemen don't mind."

Poe looked especially mellow that night. His eyes were calm, gaze peaceful, mouth relaxed. His face over the past few days had gradually lost its gaunt expression, the features and lines softening. I was gladdened to note that, though he drank with Brunrichter most every night, not once had he displayed a tendency toward any of the unpredictable or aggressive behavior that alcohol previously had provoked in him.

He asked, his voice slow and thick, "Are you finding sufficient interests to keep you occupied, Augie?"

"I'm doing newspaper work now," I told him, in part to see how he might react to the notion.

My news made no impression on him. He nodded and smiled, already staring at the fire. A moment later he looked up at me again and asked, "Hmmm?," but I said nothing more, and his gaze soon lost its focus, and he turned away, his head lolling drowsily, and smiled at his host.

I found this brief exchange unsettling. Had his affection for me, his concern, his interest in my welfare been abandoned altogether? Where was his curiosity, his penetrating questions? Had we grown so distant that he no longer cared?

"We have again been discussing the local mystery," Brunrichter told me. "Are you sure you won't join us?"

"Thank you, no. It's been a rather long day."

"What we cannot agree upon," the doctor said, "is the motivation for the crime. Have you an opinion on that?"

"Not, I'm sure, an original one. Seven young girls disappear. The motivation seems obvious."

Brunrichter smiled at Brother Jarvis. "Another vote for carnality." He then turned to me and asked, "What of simple loneliness? A desperate and excessive loneliness, to be sure, but might that not, too, motivate a man to force a woman's company?"

"Seven times?" I answered. "I cannot fathom such a need."

"Perhaps," Brunricher said. "Perhaps not. My point being simply this: There must be numerous other reasons, in addition to that of a sexual compulsion, why a man might commit such acts."

"I cast my vote for monetary gain," said Brother Jarvis. "It is my contention that the young women have been sold into a kind of slavery—"

"Ah, carnality again," Brunrichter interrupted.

"Yes, Alfred, a slavery of carnality. Whether they remain on this continent or another, it's impossible to predict."

The doctor lay his head back against the chair but kept it turned so that he could look my way. "The greatest flaw among religious men is that they view every act in either black or white. If it isn't good, it must be evil." He smiled, awaiting my response. He wanted me to join him, I think, in attacking the monk. But I had no enthusiasm for an attack. I merely shrugged.

"What about anger as a motivation?" Brunrichter asked. "What about hatred? Inquisitiveness? Dementia? Perhaps, even, in a twisted way, love itself?"

Brother Jarvis said, "Perhaps even demonic possession."

"Oh, please," Brunrichter groaned.

He continued to gaze at me a few moments longer, softly smiling, then turned his head slightly and stared at the ceiling. "As Edgar himself agreed not ten minutes ago, the human mind is a very complex mechanism."

"As is the human heart," Poe mumbled.

He had been listening after all! I was startled to hear his voice, muted though it was.

"'Thus spake the poet,'" said Brunrichter. There was no mistaking the derisive tone of his words. Then, "The human heart, my friend, as I have attempted to show you, is a small piece of machinery. Nothing more."

"The heart," said Brother Jarvis, "is the seat of the soul."

At this Brunrichter laughed, a loud, scoffing, chuckling sound. He sat forward in his chair again and aimed a finger at the monk. "This is the point at which all your beliefs inevitably collapse," he said, and went on to chastise Brother Jarvis for his reliance on faith as a source of knowledge, for attributing all good to God and all evil to Satan, both unprovable entities, mere conjectures, superstitions of a lazy mind.

I soon became invisible to the three men, even as I lingered in the doorway. Their conversation shifted now to a debate about the nature of the human soul, where in the body, if not the heart, it might be situated, and of what material it might consist, how much it weighs and whether or not it purveys an odor. These questions were all offered up by the doctor, of course, who repeatedly challenged the monk to answer in specifics and to avoid any "abstract declarations of faith." Poe joined in the conversation only when questioned directly, and seemed, to my ears, to cast his allegiance to whichever side posed the question.

Later that evening, in my room, I was overtaken by a profound melancholy as I wondered about the paradox at work within my own soul, the way I so enthusiastically courted stories of human tragedy by day and sought the purest of loves by night. And I wondered too what effect this dichotomous behavior might have on me, what I might have lost in becoming a new man, this James Dobson. I wondered whether what I hoped to gain by it would be irremediably tarnished or diminished by what I had given up.

Chapter Twenty

Came the night of Poe's second reading in Pittsburgh. I had spent the morning scouring the city for tales of misfortune—I was already filing one story every other day, writing with the raw ferocity of a man possessed—and had passed the first part of the afternoon at Mount Airy, questioning a new prisoner there, a particularly perfidious individual in whom so many of Pittsburgh's hopes were invested.

Earlier that day, while I ambled through the courthouse, poking my head into this or that room to inquire of recent crimes, accidents, litigations and freakish events, a clerk in the High Constable's office informed me that a man named English had been apprehended during the early hours of morning after a ruckus at a waterfront pub. Within minutes of being manacled he had confessed to the murder of the seven young women.

"What's the evidence against him?" I asked.

To which the clerk replied, "The man confessed. Even told how he did it."

I had been wrong about Vernon, that was the first thought that came to me. And with it, a disappointment, because I had wanted so badly for the banker to be the villain. On the heels of this thought came an opportunistic one: Be the first to get the story. Of course I raced next door to Mount Airy and arranged for an interview with the prisoner (and, even as I did so, wondered with a kind of awe about this detachment in me; wondered why my first or even second thought had been of anything other than compassion for the families of the missing girls. Maybe this James Dobson was no different than the gutter rat after all).

Accompanied by a guard I was led down the short hallway off the main lobby and into a small anteroom, empty but for the plain wooden table where two more guards sat playing dominoes. A heavy door was unlocked at the end of this room and I was escorted into the cell block and down another corridor, this one lit by gaslight. It was flanked on each side by a half-dozen thick doors of solid oak.

Mounted on each door at approximately five feet off the stone floor was a rectangular panel that could be slid open or, as all were at present, bolted shut. The guard led me to the last cell on the right side, unbolted the panel and slid it open with a bang. Cautiously he peeked inside. It took him awhile to locate the prisoner.

"Look for him under his bunk," he told me, then stood to the side so that I could peer into the cell.

The small room was neither bright nor exceptionally dim. A shaft of dusty light slanted down from somewhere high above the center of the cell, but I, with my field of vision circumvented by the size of the panel, could not locate the source of illumination. The prisoner, on the other hand, was distinguishable as a long shadow beneath the plank bed secured to the wall on my right.

"Mr. English?" I called into the cell. "My name is James Dobson, I write for the newspaper. I'd like to ask you a few questions if I could."

"My name is James Dobson, I write for the newspaper!"

The man's voice when he said this was higher than I expected it to be, almost feminine, and there was a lilt to it, an undulating music not indicative of the local tongue. I guessed him to be a native of the British Isles.

To the guard, who was grinning broadly, I said, "Is his name English? Or is that his citizenship?"

"Whyn't you ask him?" he suggested.

I put my face to the opening again. "Could you tell me your name, sir?"

"Pudden'n tane! Ask me again and I'll tell you the same!"

"Is your surname English?"

"Is your surname Dobson?"

"Yes, it is. And my first name is James. What's yours?"

"Marco Polo Ponce de Leon!"

Again I cast a jaundiced eye at the jail guard, whose head was bobbing up and down now as he chuckled at my reaction.

"The man is insane," I whispered.

The guard replied, "All the same, he's the one. Just ask him. Ask him if he done it or not."

"Mr. English?" I said. "You are being held here for kidnapping the seven missing girls. Did you do it?"

His response sent a shiver as sharp as a dagger down my spine. "Elma, Harriet, Kizzie, Linda, Mercy, Penelope, and Wilda."

Not only had he correctly identified the first names of each of the missing girls, but he had put those names in alphabetical order.

"Didn't I tell you?" the guard said.

I asked him, "The names have all been printed in the papers, have they not?"

"What is that supposed to prove?"

I addressed the prisoner again. "And what did you do to the girls, Mr. English?"

"Same as you would. Same as any man."

"Which is what, exactly?"

"I kissed their titties and made them cry!" His laugh was as shrill as a nail scratching slate.

I spent another twenty minutes with the man, posing one question after another, but no candor could be coaxed from him. I went away from Mount Airy uncertain if Mr. English was thoroughly mad or brilliantly disingenuous.

Afterward I found a quiet spot to the rear of Grant's Hill to make some notes for myself. Unfortunately, I had been apprised at Mount Airy that I had not been the first to learn of Mr. English's incarceration and therefore would not be the first to report of it. This absolved me of any obligation I might have felt to write of it, and for that I was grateful, for I was not convinced that English was the culprit he claimed to be. Not especially eager to be made a fool of again by saying in print that he was or wasn't the girls' kidnapper, only to be proven wrong, I concentrated instead on outlining another story I had been told, that of a woman who reputedly was living four to five leagues north of Pittsburgh as the common-law wife of three brothers, to whom she had borne five children thus far. But there was something about that story, too, that made me uneasy, and I finally realized that the source of my unease was the phrase with which this family had been described, "as happy as ducks in water." I was finding it difficult to equate their happiness with either criminality or sin. And since my editor had not charged me with reporting on situations of happiness, no matter how unconventionally obtained, I eventually scratched that story idea from my list and decided to allow the family their peace.

The one good thing that had come out of my few minutes in Vernon's bedroom was that I now questioned how far I might go in pursuit of a story, to what lengths I was willing to descend. It had occurred to me that, to be an effective writer of the type I hoped to be, I must also become at times a criminal of sorts, a pickpocket of secrets, a thief of dignity and privacy.

The dilemma handcuffed me as I sat there atop Grant's Hill. I scribbled a few worthless notes for myself but could decide on no story to write, could find no firm moral ground on which to stand. In mid afternoon I decided to return to the mansion on Ridge Avenue. Brunrichter, I knew, would still be at the hospital, and Poe, I knew even better, would be on pins and needles as he anticipated the evening's presentation. He was to speak that night at the Old Drury Theater, a venerable old stage house, and to an audience much larger than that of the Quintillian Society. Brunrichter had told him to expect a gathering of at least three hundred eager admirers.

I found Poe in his room, in just the condition I had expected, as nervous as a bug in a hot skillet. The door to his room stood open, and I came upon him as he stood before the mirror, already dressed for the evening in a finely made black frock coat, a stiff white shirt and black silk cravat, a look of quiet terror in his eyes.

I tapped lightly on the doorframe. He reacted with a start.

"Only me," I said.

He released a feathery breath. "Come in, my boy, come in. I am so glad to see you. I am rather at loose ends here, with nothing to do but to worry."

I went to the small padded bench at the foot of his bed, sat there and said nothing, watched him fuss with his cravat for a while, then unbutton and rebutton his coat. No matter which way he pulled at his clothing, the fit did not satisfy him.

"You look fine," I said.

"Too tight and I cannot breathe. The air gets stuck in my throat and my voice goes as high as a woman's. Too loose and I appear a sloven."

"You should try to relax. There are four hours left before the reading."

He groaned. "Two hours before dinner. Another two before the reading. I will never survive without a glass or two of wine." He turned away from the mirror. "Come and join me downstairs."

"Could we stay here for a minute or two? And speak privately?"

He looked down into my face, saw something there that touched him, something that took him out of himself for a while, beyond his own fears. He then went to the rocking chair by the window, turned it to face the bed, pulled it to within a few feet of me, and sat.

"We haven't had much time together lately, have we?" he asked.

"You've been busy," I answered.

"In truth, not at all. Except for the reading last week and the activities of the weekend, what have I done?"

"I assumed that you have been getting to know the city. Seeing its sights."

"Only those that can be seen from my window," he said.

"Have you been writing?"

"If so, I have been doing it in my sleep."

"Well, sleep is good for you. It's been a long, rough spell for you."

"I worry that I sleep too much. It is sometimes noon before I awaken, and another full hour or more before I feel anything but dullness in my brain. By the supper hour I feel reasonably fit again, but then, afterward, the lethargy returns, the dullness, and the next thing I know I am awakening, dully, to yet another day. Somehow I have lost a full two-thirds of the time we have spent in this house; I cannot account for it at all."

"You've been ill since the last of January," I told him. "You're recovering still."

I had reminded him, without thinking, of the date of Sissie's death. Not that he required any help in recollecting it. "Sometimes," he said, "I sit here in this room, hour after hour, and I think of her. It is all the energy I can muster, just to hold her in my thoughts."

"How could you help but to think of her? I do as well."

"But is it healthy to dwell on her as I do? That is what I wonder."

"Does it bring you comfort?"

"Truly? I would have to answer no. It brings me . . . it brings me something other than comfort, that I should be enjoying a room like this, a house such as this, when, all those years, I was able to give her so little."

"You gave her everything you had."

He sat with one elbow on a knee, and rubbed a hand across his eyes.

We sat in silence for a while. A minute or so later he lifted his face away from his hand and sat a bit more upright. "But you," he said. "Was there something you wanted to discuss with me?"

"Everything," I told him.

At this he smiled. It was good to see that, for a while at least, the old Poe could be resurrected.

"In general, though, I came to keep you company through the afternoon."

He wagged a finger at me. "You know my proclivities well."

"We all have our proclivities," I said.

For just a moment his countenance darkened. "Some more nefarious than others."

He could be moved so easily from one emotion to its opposite, swung by just a nuance of word from optimism to despair, from selflessness to self-pity.

"In truth," I said, "I have a request of you."

Again he brightened. He liked nothing better than to be of use.

"I have a friend who would very much like to attend your reading tonight. With your permission, of course."

"My permission is hardly necessary."

"I would like it all the same."

"And of course you have it. My permission, my blessings, my whatever you need. Did you imagine you would offend me somehow by bringing a guest unannounced?"

"It seems that everything I do of late has that potential."

Even as I said this a warmth ballooned in my chest, while another one stung my eyes. The look on his face suggested that he was experiencing a similar heat.

"It isn't true, Augie. Though if it seems that way, then the fault is mine. And I apologize."

"Maybe it's just that I'm feeling, I don't know, in the way here."

Poe leaned closer to me and spoke just above a whisper. "Dr. Brunrichter tends to exert a rather proprietary influence, does he not?"

I nodded.

He slapped my knee. "But not on my heart, young man. Never on my heart."

And now the warmth was in my throat. I swallowed hard.

"Speaking of the heart," said Poe, and he leaned back in his chair now and gave me a devilish smile, "tell me of your friend."

"Her name is Susan," I said.

"And is that all you know of her?"

But no, I knew more. I knew so much and yet so little. I knew every lift and turn of her mouth by now, but I did not know the taste of that mouth, the way her lips might part when pressed to mine. I knew the rise and fall of her breasts when she smiled at me from across the supper table, but I did not know the sculptured beauty of those breasts beneath their layers of cotton and muslin, did not yet know the way their flesh would fill my hands and their warmth would fill my soul. I knew the way her fingers, so lovely, long and thin, would hold a cup, a fork, a patent pen, but I did not know the way that hand might fit my own, knew only that the fit, when at last our fingers dovetailed, must surely be seamless and divinely precise.

What I related to Poe, of course, were all the superficial facts I knew about her. He understood the rest without being told.

"She is a great admirer of your work," I said. "If you could speak to her tonight, just a word or two . . ."

At this he stood, so quickly that it startled me, and went to his satchel beside the bed, rummaged through it, then pulled out a volume, his *Tales of the Grotesque and Arabesque*, published the same year I first met him in New York. He carried this to his writing desk, where he wrote an inscription on the flyleaf. He fanned the ink with his hand, then brought the book back to me, held open so that I might read:

For Susan,

Who though she has stolen the heart of one I dearly love must be forgiven nonetheless. For in truth a father's love cannot be diminished, but is by his son's loves multiplied.

Edgar Allan Poe

The inscription was more for me, I think, than for her. I bowed my head and hid my eyes. I could not speak.

He placed the book in my hands, then turned away and went to the mirror. When I ventured to look up again he was removing the pin from his cravat, then fussing with it needlessly. "And now we know," he said with a smile, "where you have been spending all your time."

I nodded. A few moments passed. Deliberately, if awkwardly, I changed the subject. "Did you hear that a man has been arrested for the murder of the seven girls?"

His brow wrinkled.

"Do you remember about the girls?"

"Vaguely," he said. "As in a half-remembered dream."

"A man was arrested this morning. Apparently he's confessed to it."

"I would like to read that story," Poe said. "Have you the newspaper?"

"It's probably not in the papers yet. Tomorrow at the latest. But I spoke to the man myself."

A pause before he replied. "Why in the world . . . ?"

"I'm working for the newspaper now, remember?"

"When did this come about?"

"I told you a few nights ago. Don't you recall?"

"You are *writing* for a newspaper?"

"The *Daily Chronicle*. I told you this."

"I think not."

"But I did, I know—," and then I stopped myself. I would not argue with him, not tonight. "Well, perhaps I didn't. Perhaps I only think I did because I've wanted so badly to tell you. Because I want you to be proud of me, but I'm also a bit afraid that you won't be."

He spoke in a voice absent of all censure. "Why would

I not be proud of your accomplishments? Can you tell me that?"

"The name," I said. "The name I write under, James Dobson. It was my understanding that you objected to the name."

"James was your father's name, was it not?"

"So I was told."

"And Dobson? As close to Dubbins as you might get, without actually getting there, of course."

"Precisely my intention."

"I fail, then, to understand your concern," he said. "It is a common practice for a writer to employ a pseudonym. How many have I employed myself? And you. In truth you had little choice but to assume another name. Had I not already appropriated yours for Monsieur Dupin? I left you little option but to re-create yourself. So why should you be concerned? I am proud of everything you do. Sissie would be proud as well. And Muddy! We must save a copy of everything you write and send it to her."

"How I would love that," I said.

"How she will love it!"

He turned back to the mirror then and fussed with the cravat awhile longer. Finally he tossed it aside. "Damn this thing! I have never known silk to so chafe like a noose!"

He looked my way. "A glass of claret before supper, what do you say to that? We will sit on the front veranda and sip our claret and you can tell me all about this writing you do."

"There's not much to tell of it. You've read my work, the elephant piece at least. I don't think my writing much appeals to the poet in you."

"You have a plainspoken style," he told me. "It is forthright and true."

"I can't claim your gift for words, that's for sure."

"Plainspokenness will serve you well. Better, I hasten to add, than my gift for words has ever served me."

"Until now," I said.

"Now is an illusion, my friend. But what a bountiful illusion. So come; downstairs we go. To indulge ourselves awhile longer. Before the illusion of this feast vanishes altogether."

We spent a wonderful hour together that afternoon, two men unrelated by blood yet as close as father and son. And it was no illusion, that feeling we shared. We basked in the waning light of a golden afternoon and sipped our sweet claret and spoke nothing more of mad Englishmen or murdered girls but only of our riotous times together in Manhattan, the risks we had taken, the people we loved. And in that lemony light of spring I imagined our soft sweet hour as a new beginning, and never suspected, young fool that I was, how such contentment could serve as portent of an end.

Chapter Twenty-one

By evening the news that the murderer of seven young women was locked safely away had reached every corner of the city, and as if with a mountain breeze the climate of Pittsburgh was refreshed and lightened. The pall of fear, if not the gray smoke that seemed to embody it, was lifted. Noticeably more women strolled the street, some singly, others arm in arm. Had I been asked for a word to describe this recharged atmosphere, I would have said that it fell just short of exuberance.

Owing only in part to this revivified ambiance, Poe's reading was a great success. He was, as always, severely nervous at the start and recited too quickly, hurrying the words. But the audience was receptive, as such audiences will be. If in every such audience there are a few ungenerous souls who come hoping for fodder to validate their cynicism—come hoping to spot the poet's frailties and fumblings so as to claim "You see? He is no Junius Booth, is he now? His words are flat, his sentiments shallow. His is a minor art after all."—if there are those few who will not be happy unless they can walk away grumbling, and there are always those few, the rest had come out of respect for the work and were rewarded for their patience when Poe's voice gradually strengthened, when the confidence that infused the poems themselves, the confidence of solitude, infused the man as well, that benign symbiosis of art, and the voice of the poems presided over the voice of the poet.

He recited "A Dream" and "Dream-Land" and "Eulalie," and with those rhythms gently rocking, like a man at midnight walking through the graveyard of his thoughts. . . .

Well, it was contagious, as all fine writing must be. It was hypnotic. The large room, every seat occupied, sat hushed. And when Poe read *The Tell-Tale Heart*, his timbre rising with the narrator's fear, his own eyes dilating, the terror upon him, there was not a rustle of petticoat in the house, not a scratch of restless foot across the floor. Until that point in the story, of course, when Poe put a hand to his own throat, pulled at the choking cravat and shouted, ". . . tear up the planks!—here, here!—it is the beating of his hideous heart!" And then came gasping, swooning, a quivering of the air. Women reached for their escorts' hands. Men gripped their armrests.

If Poe committed any misstep that evening it was with the material that would soon be known as "Eureka," the treatise in which he proposed a unification of science and art, joined at the nexus that is God. Wisely, though, he read only briefly from his notes for that massive compilation and limited himself, in keeping with the theme of the night, to the passage in which he intuited the fate of the universe, that moment when the principal force of gravity will suck together all heavenly bodies into one "climactic magnificence" of destruction.

The audience was puzzled by this, I could read it in their faces. Was he spinning another story? Another tale of madness?

And then he puzzled them further by adding a strangely optimistic endnote: "Are we not, indeed, more than justified in entertaining a belief—let us say, rather, in indulging a hope—that the processes we have here ventured to contemplate will be renewed forever and forever and forever; a novel Universe swelling into existence, and then subsiding into nothingness, with every throb of the Heart Divine?"

I wonder if he even meant to recite "The Raven" that night. He had looked out upon the audience at the close of his "Eureka" material and saw so many sitting there with heads cocked, as if trying to fathom what he had meant by that last strange bit. There was no applause, no shouts of "Bravo!" Maybe they were stunned by his peculiar assertions, though more likely only confused. (He would try out the material again the following February, this time in New York City, where even his supporters would label the material "a mountainous piece of absurdity.")

In any case he was astute and sober enough to realize, judging from the Pittsburghers' reaction, that this was not what they wanted that night, this intellectual exercise in hope, in the mind's long reach for meaning. They wanted to be spooked, to be pricked by fear. (I think he despised this shallowness but felt mired in it, for it was, as a rule, his only source of acclaim.)

In the audience's silence he stepped away from the podium, moved, as if feeling his way through darkness, to the very edge of the stage. Stood there for a moment gazing down at his feet, looking for all the world like a man about to topple forward (I shifted in my seat, ready to spring to his aid), when he then lifted his gaze to just above the heads of the audience, looked beyond them and beyond the theater's walls, raised a hand to his forehead, remembering something, some dread encounter, and he spoke: " 'Once, upon a midnight dreary. . . .' "

With those words the audience returned to him, all in a rush. Faces relaxed, smiles were renewed, heads nodded. Here was a throb they could understand and even feel, this throb of loss and misery, this haunted thing of life.

Susan's lips mouthed the final word in unison with him. As did my own and everybody else's. A hundred mouths spoke, " 'Nevermore.' "

Then silence. A chill ran through us all.

Poe stood with head bowed, a slender man, used up, depleted.

Brunrichter was first on his feet, but by no more than half a second. The hall exploded with applause, a thunder of ovation that did not wane until our hands were sore. He had chilled us to the bone, made every one of us, when we stepped away from that chill and shook it off, so grateful to discover that it had all been just a trick of words, a collusion of imaginations. Poe's own climactic magnificence.

Susan was bewitched by him. Is there any other way to say it? And all the members of the Quintillian Society, they clung to him as if he were their personal own, as if they were somehow responsible for his genius.

When he came down off the stage he was immediately swarmed by admirers, yet still managed to signal to me. I brought Susan forward, leading her by the arm as if she were drugged. She could scarcely bring herself to look at him when introduced.

We stood with our noses nearly touching, the three of us, pressed on all sides by Poe's devotees. "You must come to the house with Augie," he told her. "There is to be a reception at the house. Only a handful are invited. Come to the house in an hour or so. I can better greet you there."

He was turned away from us then, Brunrichter's insistent hand upon his arm.

I led Susan to the side of the room, where the path to the door was unobstructed. Outside, with the door shut behind us, the smoky night air seemed charged with energy.

"Did you hear?" I asked. "You've been invited to the reception at the doctor's mansion."

Still she trembled. She pulled the shawl about her shoulders. "I couldn't go, I can't. I'm just—"

"He has a gift for you."

"Mr. Poe?"

I nodded.

"He doesn't even know me."

"He has a gift for you all the same."

"Because of you," she said.

"Because of you."

She put a hand to my cheek. Now it was my turn to be bewitched. "I will have to ask Father," she said.

"I won't allow him to say no."

Would there be no end to my mistakes?

Chapter Twenty-two

Her father was not at home, the small house dark.

"Good for him," she said.

"Good that he's not here?"

"He's gone out with friends. I suggested he do so, though he said he would probably not. But he works so hard and takes too little relaxation."

"Is he nearby? We could go looking for him."

"He will be at the Dog and Rooster down the street. But no matter; I will leave him a note."

She lit a coal oil lamp, and in its sooty glow sat at the table with paper and pen.

A minute or so later she said, "I think this will do," and held the paper out for me to read.

"Dear Father," she had written, her script small but not cramped, elegant without a single baroque loop of flourish, "The reading was wonderful. And now I have been invited to attend the reception for Mr. Poe! It seems that Mr. Dubbins is not the exaggerator we had both assumed! I expect to be home before the Cinderella hour, but if I am not, do not be concerned. The newly redeemed Mr. Dubbins is my escort. Your loving daughter, Susan."

I handed the letter back to her, and thanked darkness for concealing my intractable grin. "So I have been redeemed in your eyes?"

She laid the letter on the table and weighted it in place with an earthenware salt mill. "I hope you do not intend to give me reason to think otherwise," she said.

"I believe you know by now what I intend."

She smiled to herself but said nothing more. She stood, leaned close to the lamp's chimney and blew out the flame. In the sudden darkness a hollow feeling swooped over me abruptly; a kind of grief, I know no other way to describe it. The lightness of her scent and how it always weakened me; the small, neat snugness of her home, with nothing visible for those moments save the glow of embers in the fireplace; the chill of the unlit street upon my back—which of these forces so emptied me, so turned me inside out with sudden despair and longing, I cannot say. But as she came toward me at the door I reached out for her suddenly, I seized her hand and brought it to my lips, I held her hand to my mouth and wanted to weep for the emptiness I felt, that deep, black, inexplicable ache of wanting her.

She did not pull her hand away. She put a hand to the back of my head, touched me lightly there.

I came out of the emptiness only gradually, as if rising from murky water. She did not hurry my ascent. And when finally I lifted my eyes to hers I was fully filled again; by her smile remade.

"We had better get started," she said. "We have a long walk ahead."

"You will do no walking tonight. Where might I hire a carriage?"

"In daylight hours there are many places. But now . . ."

"It's not yet half-past nine."

"There's a livery two blocks from here," she said.

"Would you like to wait until I return with the carriage?"

"It isn't necessary, Augie, really. I'm a strong girl. I can walk to the reception. A carriage ride will be so expensive."

"Consider it a gift from a friend of mine."

"Not Mr. Poe again!"

I took her by the arm. "A man named Dobson. A journalist. Have you heard of him?"

She stepped into the street with me. "They say he will be famous one day."

"Is that what they say?" and I pulled shut the door.

"As famous as Mr. Poe."

"Surely not."

"It's what they say."

We talked like that most of the way, her hand on my arm. I felt such a dandy, such a prince. There was nothing I could not do.

"Perhaps he will be famous," I said. "If he can find a few more men willing to give up their heads in the service of literature."

"Or even one who, having given up his head, might then engage in an act even more spectacular."

"I once saw a headless chicken fly thirty feet up into a tree," I told her.

"You did not."

"But I did. And was told that it happens quite frequently. The chicken's body, you see, doesn't know that the head was chopped off. But, sensing danger, it tries to escape. And a reptile's heart, for example—I've seen this too. You can cut out a turtle's heart and hold it in your hand and it will continue to beat."

"Is that true of all animals?" she asked, and shivered, a quick tremor passing from her hand and into my arm. "Is it true of us as well?"

"Only in Poe's stories," I said.

"And in the story of the Headless Horseman."

"I once met Washington Irving, you know."

"Oh, Augie."

"I did! And James Cooper too. In fact, now that I recall it, I very nearly punched him in the nose for insulting Poe."

"You are a terrible prevaricator," she said.

"I am a very good prevaricator. Except that in this case I am telling the truth."

"Augie, no—did you really? You met them both?"

"Why would I lie? I am newly redeemed—you said so yourself."

"I did, yes. But what can a girl from Pittsburgh know?"

The walk to the livery stables took us not quite five minutes. For another twenty we waited for the proprietor to pull on his trousers and boots and join us at his carriage house, an old barn whose heat-charred exterior walls showed how narrowly it had missed the Great Fire of two years earlier. He was a suspicious man, slow to speak (and perhaps to think), whose every response was introduced by a repetition of what I had said a moment earlier.

"I would like to engage a carriage for the evening," I told him.

"Engage a carriage," he said, and worked his jaw around as if trying to locate the next mouthful of words. "The way the two of you is dressed, you'll be wanting a Victoria."

"That will be fine," I answered.

"That will be fine, yes." After chewing on the phrase for a few seconds, then, "I could let you have a phaeton."

"What about the Victoria?"

"What about the Victoria?" A pause. "Don't have one. Nor a coachman neither."

"In that case the phaeton will have to do."

"The phaeton will do." Up and down went the jaw, side to side. "Little late to be hiring out."

"We'd only need it for a couple of hours."

"A couple of hours, yes." To watch the man think was an agonizing process, akin to watching a bucket of water being drawn from a dry well a hundred feet deep. "Which puts me in my bed when you return with it."

In this manner the negotiations continued. After a long while Susan stepped forward to intervene. I have no doubts that with a single smile and a few soft words she could have melted away all resistance and obtuseness in the man, but I was seventeen and had many things to prove, not only to her and the world but to myself. I pulled out my wallet and nonchalantly displayed a sizable stack of paper money—my entire life savings, hard-earned over seven years of field work, moonshining and petty thievery.

"I will pay twice your normal rate, sir, if you can have a carriage ready within the next five minutes. Plus a dollar extra for your trust that, two hours from now, I will return the carriage to the barn and put your horse back in her stall, all without having to wake you from your sleep."

"Without waking me from my sleep," he said. He nodded, tongue sweeping off the walls of his cheeks, until finally the gist of my offer struck home, and his eyes lit up, and he turned toward the barn door and hastened to lift the latch.

Before long Susan and I were moving briskly up Liberty Street. Our horse's clops on the cobblestones were the only sounds in the night, other than those of the howling dogs alerted by our passage.

"You handled that very well," Susan told me.

"I was hoping you would notice."

"You were hoping I would notice," she repeated solemnly, and then we rocked against one another laughing.

A few moments later she laid a hand on my arm. "You seem older than you are," she said. "Father thinks so too."

The words thrilled me nearly as much as her touch. "Older than your professor?"

"He isn't my professor, Augie. And he is nearly thirty years old."

"Have you kissed him?"

"August Dubbins! Don't be impertinent."

"I'm just curious is all."

"Curious? Only curious?"

"Only curious," I said, and watched out of the corner of my eyes for her reaction, which was precisely the one I longed for, a slight pouting of her lips.

I added then, "Curious as to whether I will have to shoot the man or not."

She laughed again. What music! "You shall not have to shoot anyone on my account," she said.

"No one?"

"None worth shooting, in any case."

We rode in silence for a few moments. The night was aglow, so warm on my cheeks, such a fire in my heart.

"And me?" I finally asked.

"And you what?"

"When will another man have cause to shoot me?"

"Why, never, I hope."

"What I mean is . . . your professor, for example. If he felt the same way I do, that is. About having to shoot someone . . ."

"Your wit and candor suddenly desert you," she said with a smile. "Why is that?"

"I'm glad to be able to amuse you."

"What is it you really wish to say to me, Augie?"

I pulled in a deep breath. "I want to kiss you, Susan Kemmer."

She said nothing. Smiled a slow, delicious smile.

I waited as long as I could. "Well?"

"Well what?" she asked.

"Well, how do you feel about what I just now told you?"

"It pleases me," she said.

"And?"

"And what?"

"Damn it, Susan—"

She turned suddenly, eyes glaring.

"I'm sorry, I didn't mean to curse."

"I think you did."

"You're right, I did. In fact I feel like doing it again."

Instead of making her angry, my response appeared to defuse all anger. Her smile returned but was directed at the road ahead. I decided to let the matter drop for a while, to savor the smile as the most I was likely to get.

But not two minutes passed before she asked, "Do you still want to kiss me?"

I turned to her, unflinching. "I will never stop wanting to kiss you."

If any of my words that night had the potential to sway her, those, I thought smugly, would surely do it.

She did not sway.

My frustration was explosive. "Well?" I demanded.

Her smile was cherubic. "Just curious," she said.

Chapter Twenty-three

That carriage ride, as I now look back on it, marked the end of our innocence. We rode through the hard dismal gray of Pittsburgh and into the bucolic hills, up out of the haze of smoke, moving at a clop ever closer, we thought, to the stars overhead. We did not realize that the stars will appear even brighter when gazed upon from Hell.

Music came to us through the windows of the doctor's house, music as bright as the gaslights twinkling through the glass. The closer we approached, the louder was the laughter, too, and the chatter of all the celebrants inside, some two dozen or more. There was no room at the long hitching post for another carriage, so I tied our horse to the wheel of a Dearborn.

"Isn't this exciting?" Susan asked as I led her onto the veranda. "The night seems so magical—I can't stop trembling."

I sensed something in the night as well, a certain disquietude that struck me, vaguely, as not so magical as she imagined, and, had Susan been any less enthusiastic, I might have paused before flinging open the door, might have taken an extra moment to ascertain if the trembling, mine as well as her own, should be interpreted as an inducement or a caution. But I wanted to give her happiness. I wanted her to think me a man who lived in the very heart of it.

I escorted her into the foyer, where she gawked wordlessly at the massive chandelier blazing with the brightness of a dozen tiny suns. For a moment I was content to gaze upon her face, my own source of wonderment, until some of the laughter from the adjacent library took on the quality of a shriek, and I turned toward the threshold, and she with me.

I do not know how to describe the scene we beheld there without lapsing into caricature. What the room contained was itself a caricature of gaiety and licentious behavior. It goes without saying that I was not then a prude and never would be, and were it not for Susan's presence at my side I would surely have looked differently upon the scene, would probably have thrown myself eagerly into the fray. But there was a delicacy to Susan that I cherished and wished to protect. She was unsullied by the world, and I, who had been drenched in its sullying influences from the moment of my first breath, I wanted her to remain that way. She seemed to me like light itself in a pitch-black world. How could I allow that light to be dirtied?

A quartet played in the corner of the library, the musicians deliberately oblivious to everything but their music—I think it was one of Mozart's chamber pieces they played—a countermelody to the behavior of Brunrichter's guests. Extra divans and chairs had been squeezed into the room, extra individuals squeezed onto each one of them. Suffice it to say that wine and rum were in no short supply, that men had thrown off their coats and ties to stride or sit or sprawl in shirtsleeves and suspenders, many with women at their sides or in their laps, every body lax and unstable, men and women alike puffing on fat cigars. A few individuals sat stretched out nearly supine, a pad of gauze still over their noses and mouths, having recently been visited by or anticipating a visit from Mr. Vernon, the banker, that pillar of society, who with a small bottle and dropper in hand moved about the room administering dose after stupefying dose.

Poe's reception had degenerated into an ether folly. Those guests not stupefied by ether were wild with alcohol or intoxicated by those components of the smoky haze that smelled nothing like tobacco. The host, Dr. Brunrichter, was nowhere to be seen. As for the guest of honor . . .

Susan spotted him a moment before I did. Her fingers tightened around my arm so that I turned from the scene of a young woman who, having undone her bodice, was fanning the two halves back and forth. She was the same young woman who, less than a week earlier, had struck me as so demure and reverential at the picnic for Poe. Miss Lydia Cavin. Now she was cooling herself by opening and closing her dress in the face of a corpulent man bent over close to her breasts, a glass of wine in each hand, held out as if for balance.

In any case, Susan's small gasp turned my attention to her. When I looked her way she said, "Behind the violinist. On the floor."

(I am failing at this description, I know. It no doubt strikes you as a comic scene, a roomful of inebriated fools. You would have to know Poe as I did, you would have to know his weaknesses and failings, the darkness he carried, to understand the malevolence of this tableau. All of this was as poison to him, but a poison he could seldom resist.)

Poe had collapsed in the corner between the violinist and the wall. He was on one knee, forehead pressed into the corner, one hand braced against the wall, the other arm limp at his side, his fingers occasionally fluttering up and falling helplessly down. I could see him in profile, saw how his eyelids fluttered, how the side of his coat and one pant leg was soiled because either he or somebody else had been sickened by the ether or alcohol or another of the drugs.

"Wait for me outside," I said to Susan, and without turning to watch her exit I strode into the room, shoving men and women aside. I was angry but it was a cold, unswervable anger. I seized the startled violinist by an arm and firmly but calmly made him rise and move aside. He looked once into my eyes and then complied without protest. Then I leaned over Poe and slipped my hands beneath his arms.

"Stand up with me," I told him.

He turned his head slowly, lifted his baleful eyes at me. He muttered something but it made no sense and did not matter. All that mattered was that his eyes were so clouded with sadness. He was lost in despair.

He offered neither resistance nor cooperation. I pulled him to his feet. At that moment he seemed so slender and frail in my arms. I could feel the sharpness of his ribs beneath my hands.

Moving backward then, neither of us fully upright, I half dragged, half carried him toward the foyer. If an individual blocked my path I let him know by a thrust of my shoulder that I would not be constrained. Near the threshold Mr. Vernon interposed himself in front of me. He stood there grinning, and raised up his bottle of ether in one hand, a white handkerchief in the other. I went rigid with anger.

"Move out of my way," I told him, "or you will soon wish you had."

He gave this a moment's consideration, just long enough for the fool in me to form a thought about the petticoat, to think about uttering some reference to it. Fortunately, Vernon's hesitation lasted no longer. He turned aside to let us pass, and I managed to keep my mouth shut.

I managed to pull Poe out into the foyer and beneath the blazing chandelier. I backed us to the stairway, climbed to the first and then the second step. As I dragged Poe toward me, lifting his heels clear of the first step, I happened to lift my gaze to the entrance, the open doorway. There, watching, fingers to her lips, was Susan.

I did not hear Brunrichter descending behind me. Until he spoke. "Mr. Dubbins. You have decided to join us."

I turned sharply, pivoting as much as I was able so as to look him in the eye. He stood two steps above me. "What have you given him?" I demanded.

"Nothing he didn't request, you can be sure."

"You know his condition!"

"Better than you," he said.

I jerked my chin toward the library. "This is a disgrace."

"Do not lecture me, young man."

"This is contemptible. And so are you. Get out of my way."

He smiled at me but he did not move. He then raised his right hand above his shoulder and flicked his fingers, summoning, I now saw, Mr. Tevis, who had been waiting at the turn of the stairs above. Tevis came down quickly, and, for just a moment, I glimpsed behind him, before he ducked away behind the corner, the face of Brother Jarvis, the monk.

I had no opportunity to puzzle out this situation, however, before Tevis was upon me. He seized the back of my coat and jerked me away from Poe, who sat down heavily on the stairs. Brunrichter slid past me before I could recover, and in a moment had taken Poe by the hand to lead him back into the library.

As for me, I had no fondness of being handled roughly, and so returned the favor as quickly as I could regain my balance. I grasped Tevis by the lapels and, squatting suddenly, hauled him toward me, ducking my head between his legs so that he tumbled over me headfirst, thumping to the foot of the stairs.

He righted himself in an instant and came at me again, but now Brunrichter emerged from the library. "Stop!" he said.

Tevis froze but kept his grim eyes locked on mine.

Brunrichter smiled. He nodded toward the doorway, where Susan yet remained. "You are frightening your lovely young friend," he told me.

"And you are killing Poe."

"Don't be silly. I am his doctor and his friend."

"His doctor? He has no need for a doctor."

"He does indeed. His melancholia, his lethargy, the pains in his abdomen, his oversensitivity to sound and touch—you look surprised. Could it be that I see him more clearly than you do?"

"You see what you choose to see."

"I know him as well as I know myself. For that reason I, and only I, have been able to identify his disease. And I am treating him accordingly."

"I'm taking him out of here tonight."

"You will not."

"Do you think you can stop me?"

"You have been stopped already. And if you persist, Mr. Tevis shall be obliged to stop you permanently."

Tevis stepped toward me then, putting his back to Susan, blocking her view as he unbuttoned his jacket and pulled it aside to reveal the ivory handle of a small pistol protruding from his vest pocket.

"Shall we continue this discussion in private?" Brunrichter asked.

"I have nothing to discuss with you."

"Then I bid you good night."

"I'm taking my things. I won't stay here any longer."

"As you wish," he said.

"I'll be coming back tomorrow for Mr. Poe."

"He will be here. But he will not wish to leave."

A dangerous thought then occurred to me, and I lacked the maturity to hold it back. "Perhaps I'll bring James Dobson along as well. Will that make a difference?"

He flinched. Then, imperiously, "Why would the presence of a newspaper hack matter in the least?"

But my intimation had struck home; I saw it in his momentary lapse of aplomb.

And with that, plus an ill-considered smirk, I turned away from him, strode up the stairs to my room. There, in the darkness, I gathered up my few possessions and stuffed them into my bag. Last to go was Poe's slender volume of stories, which he had inscribed to Susan. I paused by the window to open the book, to read by moonlight what he had written there, his first overt expression of love for me.

On that same page, as a kind of bookmark but so much more, I had placed a small black feather. A year earlier that feather had been mailed to me in a letter from Muddy, sent, she said, as a memento from Poe, his way of acknowledging his debt to me, as he conceived it, for my part in the inspiration for "The Raven," a poem composed one rain-dark, windy night in Poe's cottage off Bloomingdale Road. Mine was a minimal inspiration yet one I cherished, the good fortune that had put me there in the room with him as he, slumped over the kitchen table, came halfway out of a troubled sleep, convinced that Death himself was rapping on the window, come early to whisk Virginia away, and then the relief in Poe's eyes when I told him, "It was just a crow, don't worry, I chased it away."

For a moment I considered removing that feather

from the book, keeping it my own. But to give it to Susan would not be giving it away, merely passing it forward to another part of myself. And so I closed the book, feather inside, then placed the book in my bag, and I left that room forever.

Poe was no longer in sight downstairs, not, as I expected, in the library, where the celebration continued unabated. The front door had now been closed, but through the etched glass I could see shadows on the veranda, and upon exiting I found Susan there in conversation with Brunrichter, he with one hand on her elbow, the other holding her hand lightly by the fingers, holding it with all the nonchalance I had never been able to muster. That he, who had known her only minutes, knew her in fact not at all, felt privileged to take that hand into his own when I, longing impotently to do so all these days . . .

In an instant I was enraged, and saw the world through a tincture of blood. I barreled into him, shoulder first, and sent him flying against the porch rail.

"Augie!" Susan cried. She might have said more, I heard nothing but the roar inside my head.

I was deaf and blind to everything but my rage and the object of my rage. Without a moment's hesitation I dropped my bag and was upon him, seizing his coat so as to haul him up off his knees. Strangely, even as I drew back a fist, he was grinning at me.

And then, an explosion against the side of my head. Tevis's swing had come over my right shoulder, a blast of thunder on the corner of my mouth, rattling my jaw and spinning me away. I staggered hard against the wall, head full of sudden lightning that blinked as suddenly out. Pitched in blindness, I felt my legs caving in beneath me, my field of vision flooded with a blackness broken only by the red swirls of pain.

How I made it to the carriage, I do not remember. Two recognitions eventually returned to me: the sense of movement, of jouncing along at a brisk gait, my bottom bouncing on the seat board; and, secondly, of a slick heat in my hand, its trickling tickle on my wrist.

We were on our way down Bedford, not yet as far as the Basin, whose stink I would have noticed had my nose not been full of blood. My hand, held to my nose, was full of blood as well, my sleeve soaked with it. I could feel the front of my shirt sticking to the skin.

"Put your hand back over your nose!" Susan scolded me. "Tilt your head back!"

She was driving the carriage, reins in one hand, other hand atop the brake lest our horse, trotting vigorously downhill, should be spooked by the carriage pushing hard from behind.

"Where are we going?" I asked, still in a daze.

"Where do you think?"

Only by the tone of her voice could I know that she was angry with me. As to why she might be—I sat quietly for a few moments and picked splinters of memory out of the confusion.

"Who was it hit me?" I finally asked.

She flashed a scathing look.

"It wasn't Brunrichter, was it? I would've seen it coming."

"*Why* did you behave like that?"

"He had his hands on you."

"We were talking! He was introducing himself. Apologizing for the misunderstanding that had occurred between you two."

"There was no misunderstanding," I said.

Once again she whipped her head my way, only long enough to administer another stinging lash with her eyes. Then she faced the street again. "Why did you attack him?"

I found it incredible that she could be so obtuse. "You have never held my hand like that."

"You have never reached for it," she said.

So I reached for it.

She jerked away. "Pinch your nostrils," she said. "And just please be quiet."

We rode in silence to her front door. There she laid the reins in my lap, climbed down and went inside. I did not move, unsure of what was expected of me. Did she mean to leave me in this manner, without so much as a word of good night?

She had left the door standing open, which I took as a good omen. Through it I watched as she lit a lamp, then carried it into her tiny kitchen. A moment later she returned to the carriage with the lamp in one hand, a dampened cloth in the other.

She climbed up beside me and held the lamp to my face, looked me over critically, then laid the cloth—I might even say she shoved it—against my nose.

"Clean yourself up," she said.

The cloth was cold and dripping. With it I scrubbed at the blood caked under my nose and over my chin. "Why are you so angry?" I asked.

"Why am I so angry? Why are you so stupid?"

It did not seem a question begging to be answered. I said nothing.

"Your shirt is ruined," she said. "You have blood all over you."

"I think it's stopped now though."

"Your nose might well be broken."

"He didn't hit me all that hard."

"Oh, just stop it," she said.

"Who was it hit me anyway?"

"The man in the foyer earlier. The one you knocked down the stairs."

"Tevis," I said.

"I do not know his name, we were not introduced. Introductions were not conducted—or don't you remember that either?"

Now that our movement had ceased, the pain caught up with me, a ballooning throb of pain all along the side of my face. Even my teeth hurt. And in my stomach a sour nausea was building. All of this I attempted to hide behind a stony expression, for I did not want her to see me grimace, did not want her to see me weak.

"You know what was going on in that room," I told her. "You didn't really want to go in there, did you?"

"We could have just left. We could have just had another nice carriage ride together."

I pressed a hand to my stomach. The sickness was coming. I wanted to stay with her forever, but I had to leave, and soon. "May I call on you tomorrow? To apologize?"

"I never would have taken you for a ruffian," she said.

"Susan, it's very complicated. You need to understand."

"Please don't start making excuses."

"If your father were here—"

"You are not my father's escort, you are mine! So tell me. Why should I forgive your deplorable behavior, whether tomorrow or ever?"

Did she need to hear it said? Apparently so. "Because my heart is not my own."

"And what is it you mean by that?"

"How many ways must I say it? I am in love with you!"

Why, I wonder, does that phrase, no matter the intonation, have such a halting effect on us?

Why do we not employ it more often?

She leaned back and looked at me. The night was dark, but she was luminous.

"Come back tomorrow," she finally responded, and softly. "After you have washed your face and changed your shirt. I will consider your apology then." With that, she started to climb down.

"Wait, I have a gift for you. The one from Poe." I patted the front of my jacket, felt nothing in the pocket, and then remembered. "But it was in my bag. I must have left it—"

"Your bag is here," she said, and produced it from under the seat.

I reached for it but she said "Wait," and nodded toward my bloody hands. "May I?"

"Of course. It's on the very top."

She opened the bag and took out the book, held it, I thought, a bit too reverently. I found it more than a little irksome that she should appear so overwhelmed by a mere object, and for the first time I was truly jealous of Poe's talent, I wanted it and more for myself. And, of course, I felt immediately guilty for those thoughts, betrayer of a friend.

"There's an inscription," I told her. "But don't read it here."

She held the book to her chest. "Will I ever have an opportunity to thank him?"

Him, I thought. Why not *you?* But said, "I will make certain of it." And then I continued, because it was necessary for all of us, "The way he was tonight. The way you saw him . . ."

"I understand," she said.

"That was not his doing. I'm convinced of it. He would never degrade himself like that."

"Augie, I understand. He is a very great man. I think no less of him."

I let a moment pass. Then asked, "And of me?"

She considered her response. "I think you are more unpredictable than I first assumed."

"Is that good or bad?"

She said nothing for a moment and kept her eyes lowered. Then she picked up the lamp, held it low so that I could not see the full expression of her face, and stepped away from the carriage.

"Come back tomorrow," was all she said.

She went inside then and closed the door. I watched the light move across the window, watched it steady as she set the lamp on the table, knew that she was pulling out a chair now, laying open the book, leaning over it.

My chest felt swollen, my heart too big for its cage. I picked up the reins and gave them a snap.

Chapter Twenty-four

"The hours of folly are measured by the clock," said William Blake. "But of wisdom, no clock can measure."

After leaving Susan's house I relived the minutes of my own folly that night, relived and tried without success to reconfigure them as I drove slowly about the town, aimed for no destination other than wisdom itself, which, if it existed at all on that particular night in that particular city, eluded me without fear of capture.

I had acted impetuously, yes. Without deliberation. I had acted out of passion, not logic. And for my bellicosity, two consequences: First, I was further separated from Poe, and so driven away from him now that the rift might never be mended. Second, I had proclaimed my feelings for Susan, and saw, or imagined I did, heard in the softening of her tone and in the sudden dimming of her anger, the possibility of reciprocated feelings.

Did the second end balance out the first? Did it justify the means?

I was torn between misery and bliss.

In the end, after an hour or two of purposeless driving, the only wisdom I glimpsed was this: The distance between misery and bliss is no wider than a heartbeat.

I returned the carriage to its barn, as per my agreement with the livery master. The gelding was unhitched and led to an empty stall, where, as it nibbled from a trough of oats, I wiped it down with a rag I found hanging from a nail. I was in no hurry to leave the earthy warmth of the stable, to retire from the friendly nickerings and the hay and horsy smells, because I had nowhere else to go. In the morning I would find a boardinghouse, some place close to Susan, some simple room overlooking the river, no ostentatious mansion on the hill. But for the remainder of the night I found comfort among the beasts—among which I counted myself as one.

I lay in a corner made soft with hay. My satchel, my life's belongings, became, that night, a pillow. My only other possession was the dampened cloth given to me by Susan to clean my face. I accomplished that task as best I could, scrubbed the blood off my face and hands, then folded the cloth over, the stain of my blood inside, and slept with its coolness against my mouth, the scents of water and blood like a subtle camphor to my swollen nose, as well the fragrance too of Susan's hand—a scent, I hoped, that by morning might mend all that was broken in me.

I awoke with the horses, who started their nickering before first light. Minutes later I was out on the street, searching for more permanent lodgings. And what a comfort there was to that notion of permanence, of settling down in this roisterous city with a wife, a family, of becoming a newspaperman with a regular beat. Maybe, with time, I might become even something more. Me, a fat and satisfied burgher, bouncing grandchildren on my knees!

A few days earlier I had been anxious for slaughter, for bullet and bayonet. Now all that had been erased by a young girl's smile.

Three streets off the Monongahela Wharf, smack between Smithfield and Wood, I came upon the Second Street Temperance House. Its handlettered sign in the yard advertised comfortable beds for travelers, private rooms for families. A thin white smoke came wafting out the kitchen chimney, which told me that the proprietress was up and about, probably frying great slabs of ham and setting the coffee to boil.

I was not in the least put off by the establishment's title. Though I had never been of a temperant nature in the past, the notion of abstinence was one that would surely please Susan (and amuse her father). Besides, the boardinghouse could not have been more ideally situated, ten minutes each from the Kemmer home and the offices of the *Chronicle*, and a mere twenty-minute stroll from Miss Jones's School for Young Ladies. (When you are in love, every coincidence seems ideal.)

I crossed the yard, moving jauntily despite my bruised and swollen face, strode to the back door and, with the new sun bleeding orange all across the horizon at my back, I rapped on the door frame.

The woman who answered the door was tall and shapeless, not old but haggardly, gray of hair and eyes and complexion, her liveliest color the raw redness of knuckles on both otherwise sallow hands.

I smiled and told her, "I'm looking for a room for a few days. Maybe more."

She did not answer immediately, perhaps had not even heard me. Her gaze was locked on my shirt front, her mouth grim.

I plucked at the blood-stiffened cloth, flicked my fingers at the blackened stains. "I had a . . . bit of trouble last night. Nothing serious."

She considered my smiling countenance, nose as red as a beet, lip swollen and cracked, the blue of a bruise beginning to color my jaw. "We've got no room here for sporting men."

"I wasn't drinking," I told her.

"You've been brawling."

"Not a brawl, no. A misunderstanding."

She studied me a moment longer, then began to back away, to close the door.

I wrapped a hand around the door frame so that she would be forced to crush my fingers in order to shut me out. "Missus, please. I am not a brawler or a drinker, I assure you. Present appearances to the contrary, you will get no trouble from me. And to prove that I am a man of honor, may I pay you now for two—no, let's make it three nights' lodging?"

Even as I reached for my wallet, she backed away from the door. By now she was standing near the center of the kitchen, a warm and smoky room. I could hear meat sizzling in a skillet, could smell not only meat but coffee on the boil, biscuits in the stove. I stepped over the threshold and set down my satchel. With my other hand pulled out my wallet and flipped it open. Smiled my most fetching smile (though swollen-lipped and sore).

"All I've got is a bed on the second floor," she told me in a tone meant to suggest that the bed might be flea-infected, or worse. "You'd have to share it with Hirsch. Works for Bakewell. He's a fair-sized man. Would make nearly two of you."

But I was not to be put off. The perfumes of breakfast had already seduced me. "That will do just fine."

"Two other beds in the same room. Two men a bed."

"An equitable distribution," I said.

She gave me now a curious look. My vocabulary struck her as at odds with my appearance. Which was precisely the effect I had hoped for. If she could find no words to welcome me, neither could she find the ones to send me away.

I saw her looking at my hair then, and I put a hand up in the direction of her gaze, felt something as stiff as a broom straw in my hair, and pulled away a slender stalk of hay. When I looked at it I saw, as surely she did too, the dried blood caked under my fingernails.

"A man made unwanted advances toward my fiancée," I told her. "I intervened, of course, only to have one of his confederates punch me in the nose. That was the extent of the brawl. All this blood you see is my own. It's not as bad as it looks."

All the while I continued to smile and to hold my wallet open before me.

Eventually, her gaze came down to my wallet and the paper stuffed inside. A few moments later she nodded. "You can't go up to the room yet. Not till the others are up and around."

"I have all morning to wait." I nodded toward the stove. "And breakfast?"

Again, that pause. And then, "Three nights, you said?"

The rates were posted on the sign out front, one dollar a day, breakfast and supper included. I withdrew the script from my wallet and held it out to her. She balled it up in a fist. "Pump out back where you can wash up," she said.

I thanked her with another smile, left my satchel on the floor and made my way to the rear yard. First to the outhouse surrounded on three sides by lilac bushes, still brittle and bare. Then to the pump with its frost-limned handle, as cold as a toothache in my hands as I worked the lever up and down until a heavy gush of water gurgled out and into the wooden tub set there to catch it. The tub leaked at such a rate that it was necessary to fill the tub to the brim so that I had time to hunker over it and splash my face a few times before the tub had drained. The water was as close to ice as water can be without freezing. Three quick splashes were sufficient to rob me of all breath and set a black dizziness aswirl in my head.

I was anxious to shed my blood-stiff shirt and wash all trace of blood from my body, but that would have to wait until my belly was full and I could better tolerate the prick of icy water. For now a general dampening would have to do.

Teeth chattering, I returned to the back door, slapping my cheeks so as to spark a little warmth and feeling into my face and fingertips. Strangely, the kitchen now stood empty. And the coffeepot was boiling over on the stove.

I went in and found a rag and lifted the pot off the stove. And now I smelled the biscuits burning. I opened the oven door, pulled out a tray of blackened lumps. She had moved the skillet, however, so the slab of ham as large as the frying pan had survived. It lay there in its pool of grease. I stared at it and wondered what to do.

Only one solution occurred to me. I found a plate, a fork and a knife, and I carried the ham to the table, and there sat, and administered to the ham the fate it deserved.

Several minutes later, with nothing but a shallow gleam of grease remaining on the plate, I turned my thoughts to the ruined biscuits, and was wondering if some part of them might be salvaged so as to sop up that grease, when a noise at the door interrupted my musings. There in the doorway stood a man in a square blue jacket and black trousers. Sewn onto his jacket was the blue-and-white patch of a ward constable. He was not a tall man, not as tall as the mistress of the house, who was standing there behind him, but he was twice as broad as her, his stomach as wide as his shoulders, his buttocks even wider. He was a comic-looking pear-shaped man and I would have smiled a bit more broadly had his eyes reminded me more of a man's and less a snapping turtle's.

"You always eat other people's food, do you?" he asked.

"I'm a boarder here. Isn't that right, missus?"

The constable plunged ahead two steps, one thick trunk of leg stabbing forward, the other dragged and swung to follow. He stopped but one pace from my chair. "What's your name?" he demanded.

I started to turn in my chair so as to better face him, but with a lunge he closed the final distance and stood behind me, put a thick hand to the back of my head and shoved it around so that I faced the table again, my body bent slightly forward under the weight of his grasp.

"Eyes forward! Now what's your name?"

"August Dubbins," I told him.

At this, some noise from the woman, a kind of grunt and exhalation.

I tried to crank my head around so as to look at her—Why would my name provoke such a response?—But the constable's thumb and pinkie held my neck in their claw, his three middle fingers splayed across the back of my skull. And then, unbidden, an anger welled in me to be handled in such a way, held like a boy by the scruff of the neck. I stiffened, felt every muscle balk at the man's touch, felt the muscles of my legs pushing up, felt the violence ballooning inside me, and even as my body thrust itself up against the man's hand, driving it back, my brain commanded it to Sit still!, and might have been heeded had I simply been allowed to rise to my feet, to stand and respond to this insult like a man. But before my knees could unbend, before the seat of my pants had barely cleared the chair, the constable's hand came off my skull, and an instant later something exploded against the side of my head, a fulmination of blackness that devoured every thought in its thunderous crack, and all further inquiry into the matter was silenced.

Chapter Twenty-five

I awoke to the blank and unblinking eye of God.

The eye is sometimes blue, as it was that morning, but a cold and distant blue, a bit curious, perhaps, about the creature lying so low beneath it. But hardly concerned.

Imagine yourself as you peer through a microscope's lens at a dung mite stuck to a glass slide. Now imagine yourself as the dung mite. If you can imagine that, you can imagine the sensation to which I awoke in my cell at Mount Airy, the jail atop Grant's Hill, flat on my back on a narrow plank bed in an otherwise bare six-by-eight-foot room, awakening at first to no recognition but pain, an aching in every joint and a thunderous throbbing of my head, then opening my eyes to behold bare gray walls rising up close on all sides, rising high to a vaulted ceiling that culminated in a narrow, oblong window that gave the room its only light, a window filled now with the pale blue eye of God as it peered down in divine dispassion at the vermin blinking and moaning below.

Some time passed before my senses returned. I smelled the mustiness of damp stone, the staleness of enclosed space. The air, though hardly fresh, was cool, warmed only by the shaft of dusty light slanting in from high above.

I did not sit up or otherwise move until the realization formed that I was in a jail of some kind. For a moment I almost laughed, remembering how, during the earliest portion of my life, before I met Poe, I had always expected to end up in just such a place. But there was no humor to the soreness of my body, the pulsating burn in my head, the tenderness of ribs that ached with every shallow breath. I could not account for the latter except with a dull and dreamlike remembrance of being kicked at and dragged, but the incident of the former was my most recent conscious thought.

I had been seated at the kitchen table of the Second Street Temperance House, having used the front of my hand to wipe ham grease off my lips so as to better speak, my head turning in resistance to the constable's grip, that grip then falling away, jerked suddenly away, giving me but a half moment of relief before I sensed the man's other hand whipping up into the air, the sibilant sound of some object suddenly unsheathed, a quick hissing as he pulled his truncheon through a belt loop and swung it at the side of my head.

So, I had been arrested. For eating the woman's ham? But I had paid for my breakfast—why hadn't she told the constable this? Did she mean to deny it now that she had my three dollars in her fist?

More time passed before I was able to sit up and brace my feet against the floor. How much time, I have no idea. Every tiny movement constituted an hour's worth of pain. Every thought preceding movement was contemplated a dozen times before thought became act.

A thick ridge of welt ran along the right side of my skull from ear to forehead. My hair was matted with blood, a sticky clot that had run down my back and pasted my shirt to my spine.

From where I lay I managed to turn sufficiently to find the door, a heavy affair of dark, blank wood, with a sliding panel, closed, for communication with whatever waited outside that door.

I stood, meaning to go to the door and hammer upon it until a satisfactory resolution was obtained. But upon standing, I quickly sat down again. Then did the same thing a second time. The floor slipped and undulated beneath me. I do not recall eventually completing the journey to the door but I must have done so, for at one point I opened my eyes to find myself leaning hard against the wood, forehead to the panel.

The sliding panel was locked, of course, and would not succumb to my weak pummeling. Nor would the door itself.

My next conscious thought was of lying again on the plank bed, staring at the exit and trying to remember if I had yet indeed made my way to the door, or whether I had only considered doing so. In either case, no further movement was in the offing. I ached deep inside, low in the back, and when I tried to probe the place with my fingers, a bubbling of nausea rose in my stomach, so that I lay motionless in that awkward position, hand trapped beneath my spine.

The most I could accomplish was to turn my head so that my eyes roamed upward, every inch of movement a grating in my neck, a scrape of skullbone over wood. To that oblong gaze of blue high above, I asked, "What for?"

As is usually the case, there was no answer.

When I slept, I dreamed of pain. Never had my entire being so ached and throbbed. Few external noises reached me through the thick walls of my cell, but the few thumps and shouts that did also found their way into my dreams. One dream in particular has stayed with me all these years, perhaps because what happened upon my awakening was as much a nightmare as what had preceded it.

I dreamed I was in the barn in Ohio, Deidendorf's barn. My job was to fork hay down the square hole in the floor, down into the stall from which the cattle would be fed. But in my dream the stall below was not a feed bin but a bedroom, Virginia Poe's bedroom, and on her bed she lay dying of consumption. Even as I forked the hay down atop her she lay there looking up at me, eyes full of forgiveness. I did my best to pitch the hay away from her, but the hole in the floor was not large and allowed little freedom of movement. Some of the hay always landed on her face and body. She was too weak to push it away. Bit by bit I was burying her. Deidendorf stood at my side, rifle in hand, and barked at me to work faster. I did so, crying, still just a boy in my dream, eleven or twelve years old. Every time I slowed or hesitated he jabbed the tip of the rifle barrel into my ribs.

The barn itself was a peculiar affair. (Years after this dream I would first encounter the paintings of Hieronymus Bosch and think to myself, *Here's a man who's seen my dreams.*) The rafters were lined with pigeons softly squabbling, their perches white with excrement. The hayloft was stacked with unpainted coffins like the ones Poe and I had seen on the steamboat. And all throughout the barn, on various improbable levels from floor to high ceiling, like a cross section of the Old Brewery in Five Points where I had lived as a boy, were individuals I remembered from those days, the diseased and dying on their beds of rags, the drunken and drugged, the imbeciles and crippled. A young whore yellow-eyed and feverish but working hard to earn her ten cents for the day. An old man squatting over a chamber pot, his face shiny with sweat, hands trembling.

In my dream I was aware of what lay outside of the barn, the Mexican desert, a flat, sere landscape sun-bleached and clean. But here inside the barn all was filth and stink, a rank greasiness of shadow. Everywhere I looked my eyes fell on something squalid and ugly. I had no choice but to gaze down into the hole, to watch the hay mounding up around Virginia, as high as her shoulders now, her ears, nearly covering her innocent face.

My shoulders ached as I pitched down the hay, my ribs ached, my head throbbed with the squabble of a hundred pigeons. "Faster!" Deidendorf barked. "Get your work done!"

I stabbed the pitchfork into the mound of hay but too hard, the tines sank into the plank floor, stuck there. The pitchfork quivered in my hands, stinging. I could not pull it free. And now Deidendorf pulled a harness off its nail on the wall and began to beat me with it, leather and buckles biting into my flesh, over my shoulders, lashing across my back. I recognized the smell of that leather, recognized the way it cracked against my skin, just as my mother's strop had done.

And now I wanted to wrench the pitchfork free only to turn and plunge it into Deidendorf's belly. But my hands were slick and the pitchfork remained stuck fast.

With every lash of the harness the barn rumbled all around me. The entire structure creaked and wobbled. Faster and faster Deidendorf beat me, screaming in my ear, turning my name into a profanity. Dust and feathers and pigeon shit rained down over me. Walls and floors creaked and split, tumbling Old Brewery residents out of their chairs and beds, sending them crashing to the barn floor, broken and moaning while they too cursed my name. The caskets in the hayloft rumbled against one another, slid this way and that, lids popping open, boards splitting open, spilling out skeletons and dust. I struggled to free the pitchfork, wept like a child because I could not. The harness flayed my back and shoulders. The barn, board by board, tumbled down all around me.

I let go of the pitchfork finally and covered my head with my arms. Felt every blow as the entire structure collapsed. But somehow I remained standing. The dust swirled in a storm around me, blasting my skin, filling my wounds. Every breath burned like fire. Finally, when I thought I could stand the torment no longer, I uncovered my head, looked up, and there beheld the pale blue eye of God, the oblong window of my cell. I was sitting up on the side of my bed.

Was the dream over? Not quite yet. For there in the corner of my cell, seated at a small table, the one from his kitchen in the cottage on Bloomingdale Road, was Mr. Poe bent over a piece of parchment, vigorously scribbling.

"Are you writing me?" I asked. "Are you writing this dream?"

He said nothing. Did not even look my way.

But the rattling of my dream continued, the banging and shouting. It was now at the door of my cell, wanting in. The panel slid open with a bang and I heard my name, a curse that filled the room. Poe at his table was smiling.

But there at the door, his face filling the panel opening, was a flesh and blood man, no dream at all, his face scarlet with rage, eyes hideous with hate.

Buck Kemmer.

Whether something in his indecipherable shouting conveyed to me what had happened to cause his anguish and outrage, or whether I merely deduced as much, somehow knew it in the heart's deep wisdom, felt it in the shudder of my bones, I cannot say. My thoughts were not yet wholly rational, nor would they be until the following day. Suffice it to say that somehow, by word or murmur or by the ineffable intuition that accompanies love, I understood.

I covered my face with my hands, and I wept, I wailed, I collapsed into a bottomless pit of grief.

With every breath, I prayed that the pain of that grief would erase me.

We hold love so dear, I suppose, because the anguish of losing it is so terrible. There is no other hole so deep or black, no maw of hell so engulfing.

My tears evoked no sympathy from Buck Kemmer. If his voice softened, it was only because of a shortness of breath. His sentiments underwent no change. He cursed me with every epithet he knew, while I, having fallen forward onto my knees on the rough cold floor, pounded forehead and fist against the stone.

When finally I settled into motionlessness, and Buck too had exhausted himself into silence, I asked, though it hardly mattered, "How, Buck? How did it happen?"

This unleashed another flood of venom from his tongue. He ended by promising, "If you ever get out of there, I will kill you myself."

I must have been a terrible sight by then, forehead skinned and bloodied, cheek bruised, nose and lip swollen, shirt stained black with blood front and back. But he felt not an ounce of pity for me, nothing but a murderous contempt. Still, I raised my eyes to him. If anything mattered to me at that moment—and, in truth, nothing much did—it was that he be made to understand. I needed someone to share my misery with, or else I could not bear it. And I knew that no soul in the world could feel as incinerated as mine, with the single exception of Buck Kemmer's.

"I didn't do it," I told him.

He grunted at me, too furious for words.

"Whatever happened, Buck, it wasn't me."

He slammed one fist and then the other into the door. The thunder shook the stones beneath me.

I put out a hand to the side of the bed, seized the scarred plank, dragged myself up onto my feet. I doubted I could walk as far as the door. My center was gone, the core of me blown away as if by cannonball.

Yet I staggered forward.

When he thought me close enough, he stuck an arm through the opening, lunged at me, hand straining for my throat. Nothing more than instinct made me jerk away.

A guard outside the door shouted at Buck to pull back. He did not. Then came the sharp crack of a truncheon slammed across his shoulders. Buck winced but he did not reclaim his arm.

"Let him be!" I shouted. "Let him kill me if he wants to!"

The guard laughed. "You volunteering for it, are you?"

"If that's what he wants," I said, "let him do it."

"It's nothing to me," the guard said, invisible to me behind the door. Then, to Buck, "If he's stupid enough to get that close, have at it."

"You think I won't?" Buck asked.

The guard said, "I would if I was you."

I let a moment pass, did not yet move within Buck's reach. Felt the guard stepping away from the door, absolving himself of all responsibility. Buck's arm withdrew until only a hand was visible, and then, above it, his face appeared in the opening now.

I told him, "I'm coming forward, Buck. But first you should know this. I didn't do it. Whatever happened to Susan, I had no part in it. I would sooner be cut to pieces, an inch at a time, than to ever do anything to hurt her."

His face became a mask, I could not read it. No matter: He would either strangle me or embrace me. I think I longed more for the first than the second. In any case, I moved closer to the door.

His fingers, gripping the panel's frame, now flexed, went stiff and splayed. He was thinking about reaching for me, about crushing my throat in his powerful grip. He lifted his hand away from the frame, knotted it into a fist. Then suddenly he drew back and again slammed that fist into the wood.

"Here now!" the guard shrieked. "Take it easy on that door!"

Buck looked in on me a final time. His mask of torment nearly finished me off. Then he turned and stalked away.

"Buck!" I cried, because I could not help myself, and thrust my head into the opening so as to call after him. "Tell me what happened to her!"

The guard raked his stick across my face, driving me back. And slammed the panel shut.

* * *

Sometime later, maybe midafternoon, the panel came open again, easing quietly this time, even cautiously. On my bed I continued to stare at the blank window high above, and waited for the visitor to speak. When he did not, I raised myself up enough to look his way, a hard expression on my face, a look of annoyance at being interrupted in my abject grief.

Poe stood at the door. His eyes were wounded, dark, his mouth a crooked frown. He was gazing at me, I thought, as one might gaze upon a small animal, a rabbit or squirrel that has been crushed beneath the wheels of a wagon, barely but yet alive. A look of regret and revulsion.

"I didn't do it," was all I said.

He closed his eyes to this. Shook his head slightly. Then moved away.

A guard looked in at me and grinned.

Next day, the first gray light of morning. A clank and scrape in the corridor outside my door, coming gradually closer. Breakfast on its way. But I was more ravenous for information than for food, and stood waiting at the door.

"What's going to happen now?" I asked the moment the panel came open and the guard took his preliminary peek inside.

He was a different guard than the one from last night, but of a similar temperament. He thrust in the bowl. "Court meets first Monday of the month."

"What is it I'm supposed to have done?"

"You forget already?"

I stared down at the bowl of food in my hands, nauseated. Oatmeal, a slice of bread spread with lard. Even the odors were sickening. "Is she dead?" I asked.

"Dead?" He laughed. "You drove that gaff clean through her!"

Again I staggered, put a hand to the door. The bowl tilted sideways. The bread slid to the floor.

"What everybody's wondering," said the guard, "is did you do the other business before or after you put the hook in her."

I moaned, I think; went numb. The bowl fell from my hand and everything on it spilled to the floor, metal bowl and spoon clattering away even as I dropped to my knees gagging, the echoing ring a distant chiming in my head as I heaved and vomited against the door.

Chapter Twenty-six

Because I cannot be specific about the passage of time during this hazy episode of my life, I apologize. Any individual who has ever been pitched in grief will understand. Time becomes fragmented by delirious thoughts. Or perhaps, time loses relevance. Nothing matters, not hunger, not the stink and soreness of one's own body. The misery is its own soporific, a narcotic that causes the sufferer to lapse in and out of sleep. At the moment of awakening there is a brief lightness, almost a giddiness as you think, "I was dreaming." But then it all comes back at you, rushing like a bull with horns lowered, and one of the horns catches you straight through the heart and lifts you up, holds you there, suspended, impaled and impotent, as the bull shakes his head furiously and with this movement widens the hole, until again the pain is too much to bear and you lapse again into the temporary blessing of sleep.

Is this what God is? The bliss of unconsciousness?

From one of the guards I managed to wrench a bit of information. He found my ignorance humorous, and played along, I think, to see how far I would carry it.

"The gaff that was used," I asked. "What kind of gaff was it?"

"I suppose you don't remember taking it down from beside the door."

"Buck's baling hook? Is that what was used?"

"You could've at least pulled it out of her when you was done."

I nearly swooned, but could not let myself give in. "And where was she at the time?"

"Where would she be? Considering what else you done."

"She was in her bed?"

"Stuck there, I'd say. Until her father come in and found her like that."

At some point on the second or third day—the sky had turned overcast (though not as dark as my thoughts) and I was unable to guess the hour—Buck Kemmer returned. He looked in at me as I lay on my bed.

The first thing he said to me was, "Haven't they even let you wash yourself yet?"

By this I knew that he had come to an understanding. He had sat alone in his small dark house, remembering his daughter's scent, the way she moved and the delicacy of her smile, and he remembered the way she had looked on me, the things, perhaps, she had spoken to him in secret, and he recalled the look in my eyes each time she was near, and he came to realize somehow that I, in my own dark room, was doing the same, and that in all the world there was only one man who might understand his grief, because, though perhaps we loved her differently, we loved her the same.

I rolled over and sat up, then crossed as quietly as I could to stand close to him, and whispered, "Where's the guard?"

He drew back for a look. "Setting down the hall. Ten, twelve feet."

I continued to speak softly. "Have you searched the house?"

"For what?" he asked.

"For anything. Anything that doesn't belong. Anything that might tell us who was there after I left that night."

He put both hands on the panel's ledge. His face was haggard, eyes red. He had not shaved since last I saw him. "What happened that night?" he asked. "She said not to expect her home before midnight, but I come back around half-past ten and . . . she was . . ." He choked down the rest, swallowed it, bitter as bile.

"I brought her home around nine."

"You didn't go to the party?"

"We went. But only for a few minutes. It wasn't the kind of party you would have wanted her to attend."

"And then you took her home?"

"And said good night at the door."

"If only I had come home sooner," he said. Then, "I shouldn't have gone out at all."

But I would not allow him any of the blame. I wanted it all for myself. "I'm the one who left her alone, Buck. I should have sat with her until you returned."

His face, which I had never before seen without a smile, seemed less broad and full somehow, pulled in upon itself, shrunken, his brow creased, eyebrows knitted, lips puckered. It made me think of Poe's theory of the universe, the way all matter would be drawn back to its center, where it would swallow itself. Poe had called that center the Particle Divine. I called it Grief.

"You had better not stay here long," I told Buck.

"The guards won't stop me from coming. One of them told me that if it was up to him, he'd give me fifteen minutes alone with you to do whatever I liked."

"Don't let them think you've changed your mind about me."

He nodded, but I could tell that his mind was clouded, thick with the fog of sorrow.

"I'm not even sure where I am, Buck. It's not the penitentiary, is it?"

"The jail," he said, "alongside the courthouse. They won't take you to the penitentiary till after the trial."

"And how secure is this jail? If I could somehow get out of this cell, I mean."

He looked up and down the corridor. "There's one guard at the entrance to the cellblock, two more in a room outside his door."

"Just as I remembered it. So then—there's no way out?"

"None I can see."

"You will have to do the work then."

He looked at me with plaintive eyes. "I don't got the brain you do," he said. "I wouldn't know where to start."

"I need to know what makes them so sure I'm the one they want. What's the evidence against me?"

"You were the last one with her." And now his expression turned doleful, full of shame. "I'm the one told them that."

"It can hardly be enough to hang me on."

"They'll do what they want. Evidence or not."

"Find out for me, can you? Talk to the guards. Act like you want to be sure I'll get the noose for this."

"I'm not an actor neither."

"You can do it, believe me. You have to. If we're ever to find out who's really responsible for this."

He set his mouth in a grim frown and nodded stiffly. Then, "There was something else you asked me to do. I forgot it already."

"Search the house," I said.

He nodded.

"Thrust a lamp into every corner. A man cannot come into your home and do what he did there and leave without a trace."

"All right," he said. But I had to wonder if he would remember any of this by the time he reached the street. Instead he would probably wander aimlessly for the next several hours, maybe go to the docks and beg for work, for anything to keep him from having to return home, back to those cold rooms where the fire had now gone out, back to where Susan's presence and her final chilling moments were so keenly felt.

"The funeral is today," he said.

It struck me like a blow to the stomach, filled me with new sickness.

"I need to go buy a shirt," he said.

I pressed my hands atop his as he clutched the panel's ledge.

"The church on High Street," he said, "that's where she'll be. Beside her mother there."

I could think of nothing to say, no words, no words.

"I need to see about getting her a little marker of some kind. See if they'll let me pay for it on time."

I reached for my wallet then, was about to tell him to buy the finest block of marble he could find, to hire the finest artist to engrave her name—but my pockets were empty. Somebody had taken my wallet and everything in it. Probably the constable who arrested me. He certainly would have picked up my valise as well, carried it away from the boardinghouse so as to rifle its contents in search of anything valuable. So my life's savings were gone. Everything gone.

And then I remembered the underdress. That silky, weightless thing, a moment's impetuosity. And now I would be hanged by it.

Exhaustion washed over me, exhaustion and nausea. "Come back tomorrow if you can," I said to Buck.

He nodded. "I'm going to tell them to let you wash yourself. Let you clean off that blood."

"No, you mustn't. Not a kind word about me—remember?"

He blinked, too depleted to even nod. "Looks like they beat you pretty good," he said.

I touched my scabbing forehead. "Some of it I did myself."

He did not respond to this, but something changed in his eyes then, a shifting of light, a subtle darkening, which gave me to know that he understood too well the desire to harm one's self. He had been thinking about it for a good while now, no doubt, had been thinking about how to end this agony, how to silence all cursed thought.

I pried his fingertips up off the wood, gripped them in

my own. "We have a lot of work to do now, Buck. Remember that. We have a lot of work to do for Susan. We're the only ones who can." Even as I said these words I heard the hollowness of my voice, the lack of belief.

But the light hardened in Buck Kemmer's eyes, flared and strengthened.

"Come back tomorrow," I said.

He slipped one hand free, patted mine. Then gripped it fiercely for a few seconds. Then released me and stepped away from the door.

"Goddamn you to Hell!" he shouted, and the corner of his mouth twitched in a mournful smile suppressed, and he turned toward the exit and with a halting gait, mechanical, he marched away.

Of what use is the sun if it does not illuminate her smile? What purpose the moon if it cannot light my path to her?

Of my own tongue I have no need if it will never speak to her again, never touch a kiss upon her lips, her neck, her breast.

I want only what I cannot have, can never have because there is no God so great or wise or merciful enough to grant it to me: To trade my death for hers.

How can she be gone?

How can life, all life, not be gone with her?

A day in every waking minute. My jailers came and went, brought morning and evening a tray of tasteless food. A man dressed like a constable but with no insignia on his stiff blue coat came to speak with me briefly, asked me to tell him what had happened that night, then stood outside my door stone-eyed and stoical while I recounted the incident at Brunrichter's mansion. I left out the reason for our sudden departure from the mansion, said only that the doctor, in my opinion, had had too much to drink and behaved in a forward manner toward my companion, and that I, admittedly, had overreacted by intervening physically, only to be slugged from behind by Mr. Tevis. Next thing I knew I was saying good night to Susan at her door and promising to call on her the next day.

"Is that all?" the man asked.

"That's all there was to it."

He slid shut the panel and did not return. I was an animal being held for slaughter.

I lay on my bed and stared at the high window, gazed into a sky that changed unpredictably. Pale blue, gray, cloud white, midnight black. Its color did not matter. The sky was empty.

As my head gradually cleared, a few thoughts arose. Only one man might have raised an uproar for my release, but he believed me guilty too. So I could not count on Poe. He had been so unlike himself these past several days, so subdued. He seemed, almost, as if at all times a part of his mind and most of his energies slumbered. Nor did his lethargy seem the stillness of melancholia, which is a dark and heavy stillness, suffocating. His seemed more a colorless calm of insentience.

What was it Brunrichter had said, that he was treating Poe's illness? Treating him how? With some analgesic that, even as it dulled Poe's pain, loosened his every connection with the world?

I had no doubts that on the occasion of Poe's one brief visit to me in my cell, when he looked in on me with his hopeless gaze, even then Brunrichter had probably been at his elbow, subtly pulling him away. The doctor saw Poe as a kind of twin, the completion of his own incomplete self, and he meant to keep Poe in Pittsburgh indefinitely. This attention had done Poe a lot of good, yes, had surrounded him with admirers he sorely needed, eased his troubles in myriad ways. I could find no fault with that.

What rankled, I suppose, was that Poe had found a better friend than me. All the way from Philadelphia the distance between us had widened, and into this gulf Brunrichter had stepped, filling it up entirely, shoving me aside. I resented Brunrichter for wanting to be so like Poe, or wanting Poe like him, and the irony of this resentment was the fact that I, in striving to become a writer, had been aching to be more like Poe myself. This effort, the writing, had become the final wedge that had driven us apart.

But what did any of this matter now? The writing did not matter, nor did Brunrichter's friendship with Poe. What mattered was that the city that had so eagerly embraced my mentor and lifted him up and away from me had just as eagerly thrust me down into a gray-walled isolation, labeled me as murderer, beast, while the true beast of Pittsburgh still blithely strolled its streets.

Another day. My whiskers had me clawing at my face, causing flecks of dried blood and scabrous flesh to be raked off by my fingernails. A macabre kind of entertainment it was to sit on the edge of my bunk and watch the black flakes fall between my knees, to see how much of myself I could scrape onto the floor.

My forehead, beaten raw two days previous when I had repeatedly banged it against the floor, was slow to heal. Each time a layer of blood coagulated over the abrasions I picked it off and bled anew. There was no small amount of masochism to this practice. The physical discomfort was like a nearer music that, though superficial, muted the darker and deeper music within.

That afternoon Buck Kemmer came again. I stood close to the open panel so that we could whisper without being overheard. He was wearing a new white shirt, its collar buttoned tight around the neck, the fabric still stiff but soiled and wrinkled now. I suspected that he had been wearing that shirt since donning it for Susan's funeral, had slept in it, or maybe only lain awake in it all night.

I knew nothing about funerals at the time, had never attended one, and could only imagine how Buck had passed the night afterward, doing what I would have done if not confined: an aimless walk all up and down the riverbank, for no reason but to separate myself from anyone who wished to comfort me, an exhausting walk until my legs gave out, then staggering back to the churchyard in the stillness of deep night, back to that mound of fresh earth, to remain there through the darkness so as to watch, with first light, as the earth gave up its warmth to the morning air, a fine white vapor rising into the eggshell dawn.

Before speaking into the panel, Buck jerked his head down the hallway, jabbing his chin in the direction of a guard. "That one asked me why I keep coming back," he whispered.

"And what did you tell him?"

"I said I just like to look at you. So that I can picture you dangling from a rope."

An icy tremor ran through me as I envisioned a somewhat different picture, my body dropping too fast and too far, hooded head suddenly separating to snap upward with the unencumbered rope. . . . But to Buck I said, "That's good. You said the right thing."

"He told me I won't have to picture it for long. Said they've got you dead to rights."

"They don't have a damn thing," I said, though I knew otherwise. "How could they?"

"I only know what I've been told."

"Which is?"

"First off, that lady at the boardinghouse. Said you showed up there all bloody and strange-looking. Scared the life out of her, she said."

"There wasn't much life in her to be scared out, if you ask me."

"Then the livery master, Ben Findley, who I happen to know."

"You talked to him?"

Buck nodded. "Said you didn't bring the horse and carriage back till close to midnight. Though you claim to have left Susan off at the house at half past nine."

"What is that supposed to prove? I rode around town for a while, thinking about things. I paid him damn well for the use of that carriage!"

"Says he thinks you spent the night in his barn. Uninvited."

"Where else was I supposed to go?"

"Says he found blood all over the hay. Not to mention on the carriage itself."

"That's my blood! Brunrichter's man coldcocked me. I bled like a stuck pig."

"I reckon that's not the worst of it."

"What is?"

"What the doctor told the police."

Finally, something that made sense. I had expected Brunrichter to lie. He could not report that he had stopped me from removing Poe from the party because he might then be asked why I would attempt to do so. Well, because we were having a right old debauch, my good man. Rum, opium, ether—randy old goats and frisky young ewes—many of the most respected citizens of our fair city, all in utter abandon of normal restraints. I fail to see why Mr. Dubbins took such umbrage.

Hardly. No, Brunrichter would certainly lie. But what would he say?

"Said you came there feeling your oats," Buck told me. "Left Susan waiting in the carriage while you went waltzing in and started carrying on, loudmouthing Mr. Poe about something or other. Said you tried to pick a fight with him. When the doctor asked you to quiet down, you took a swing at him, he says. That's when his man stepped in and put an end to it."

Buck watched my face closely as he related all this, studied me for my reaction.

"You believe any of that?" I asked.

"Doesn't sound like the Gus Dubbins I know."

I thanked him with a mirthless smile.

He added, "Course, I don't know you all that well."

At that small joke, my heart leapt. I was not, after all, alone.

"According to the doctor," he continued, "you was also in the neighborhood of where the last of them missing girls disappeared. Says you told him that yourself, that you were right near there at the time they figure it happened. He says you seemed to be bragging about it."

"I was there . . ." Suddenly my head grew thick again, so clouded that I could not recall much of the conversation in question. "I was in a tavern nearby, I think. On Diamond Alley, wasn't it?"

"People see you there?" he asked.

"Dozens of people."

"You can name them?"

Name them? They had all been strangers to me then and were strangers still. Could I count on a single one of them to vouch for me, to state unequivocally that I, who meant not a whit to any of them, had been present in the tavern at the very moments, known to no one, when the girl had been assailed?

"Thank goodness for English," I said. "He's already confessed to having done it."

"There's talk of letting him go."

"You can't be serious."

"They say he's not in his right mind."

"He's a raving lunatic! Which is what a man would have to be to murder seven girls."

Buck answered with a twitch of his mouth, a grimace.

"So now they suspect me of all of them, don't they?"

"Your friend Mr. Poe has sworn you were with him."

"For the first five at least."

It was the way he looked at me then, the way he held his head, a question in his eyes, that told me there was more to come, the coup de grâce. I waited for the fatal stroke.

"Then there's that thing they found in your bag."

My pulse beat hotly against the scabs on my scalp. I smelled the rankness of my skin. "They show it to you?"

He nodded. "To ask was it Susan's."

"Which it wasn't. So they probably showed it to the other families as well."

"They did."

"And?"

"Nobody recognized it."

"Then they can't use it against me."

"What they figure is, somebody just don't remember it. Or one of the girls had it without telling anybody."

I could make no reply but to shake my head, incredulous even yet that I could have been so profoundly stupid as to take the underdress in the first place.

Buck said, "Me, I figured you had it because you planned on giving it to Susan one night."

There was a tremulousness in his voice when he said this, a quiver that gripped my heart. Though it was an effort to do so, I lifted my head and looked him square in the eyes.

"The only night I would have given her a gift like that," I answered, "would have been on our wedding night."

He blinked once, and the fear in his eyes faded out. Then he asked, "Why'd you have it then?"

"There's a friend of Brunrichter's by the name of Vernon. A banker. There was just something about him, I don't know, some quality . . . He was talking about those missing girls once and, the things he said about them, it made me suspect him is all. Made me think he might be responsible. So I broke into his house one day, looking for evidence. I saw that underdress on his bed and . . . I took it. Without even thinking what I might do with it. Turns out I couldn't do a thing."

"Are you saying maybe he's the one kidnapped those girls?"

"I don't know what to think anymore. I can barely keep a thought straight in my head."

Buck responded to my statement with his own look of helplessness, eyebrows raised above a plaintive gaze, mouth crooked as if to ask, *What can I do about this mess?*

"All right," I told him, and strained to focus my thoughts, to locate one small point of clarity in the miasma. And the only point of clarity I could see was Susan. Susan was all that mattered. "Your home. Did you do the search?"

"I did," he said.

"What did you find?"

He shook his head.

"Nothing?"

"Nothing of any good."

"But something? Surely you found something?"

"It's in my hat," he said.

"Turn sideways just a bit, with your back to the guard."

He did so.

"Now take your hat off—be natural, Buck, not too fast. Hold it down in front of you. Good, good. Now give me what you found."

"Should I just hand it up to you?" he asked.

"Can the guard see what you're doing?"

"Not unless he can see through me he can't."

"Go ahead then. But slowly. Don't let your shoulders move."

He brought the fingertips of his right hand to the bottom of the panel opening. Between finger and thumb he held a small black feather. Something snagged in my chest when I saw it. Something jagged pierced my heart.

"I gave that to her," I told him. "It was inside the book I gave her that night."

"It's nothing then?"

"No. It's nothing."

He read the anguish in my eyes. "Maybe you'd like to keep it," he said.

I closed my hand around it, withdrew it from his fingers and clasped it tight.

"The only other thing was this," he said. He held it on the tip of his index finger, a broken piece of shell no bigger than a fingernail, its edges smoothed and upward curving, suggesting a concave structure, the outer surface a subtle pink, the interior as white as pearl.

"I thought it must've come off one of my boots," he said, "from down on the docks. Except that it isn't a mussel or clamshell, is it? It don't look like either of them to me."

I placed it on my own fingertip, concave side down, and held it to the light. It looked familiar somehow, but I could make no connection, could not remember where I might have seen such a shell.

"It's from out of the river, ain't it?" Buck asked.

"I don't know. It seems awfully clean, doesn't it? There's not a trace of mud on it anywhere I can see."

I studied it awhile longer, but in the end it told me nothing. A broken piece of shell. Probably given to Susan by one of her students.

My hopes, meager as they were, sank further. Again I turned to Buck, meaning to hand him the shell piece along with the bad news that nothing could be gleaned from it. But he was staring hard at my hand, brow knitted.

"What are you thinking?" I asked.

"What book?" he said.

"I don't understand."

"You said you gave her a book that night. The one with the feather in it. Except that there's not a new book anywhere in the house. I know every book there."

"*Tales of the Grotesque and Arabesque*, by Poe. He inscribed it for her. I gave it to her just before we said good night."

"It's not in the house," he said.

"You're sure about this?"

"The feather was on the floor underneath her bed. That shell was in the kitchen, stuck between two boards. There wasn't no book."

He watched me for a moment, waiting for an explanation. I could not piece together a coherent thought.

"Somebody killed her for a book?" he asked, too loud. "For a goddamn book?"

"Shhh, no, no. No, it wouldn't have been like that."

"Then why?"

I held the raven's feather in my left hand, the broken shell still stuck to a finger of my right hand. I closed both hands into loose fists then, closed my eyes so as to better let the images come to me. And that is all they were, mere images, fleeting pictures in my mind, not sufficient for conclusion or even theory. But they raised a question or two.

"Now what's got you thinking?" Buck asked.

I looked at him again. "Are you ready to do more?"

"I'll do whatever it takes."

"Two things. First, are you familiar with the hills behind Dr. Brunrichter's estate?"

"Only from a distance. I know where they are."

"I want you to go there, Buck. Find some roundabout way. Make certain no one spots you. But go there and take this shell—put out your finger. There, take that shell and go to the hills about a quarter mile behind the mansion. You'll see a mausoleum there, and that's where you need to go. Don't let yourself be seen."

"He's not behind this, is he? Is that what you're saying?"

The fire flared in his eyes then, and because I knew the kind of rage that might come upon him, knew what he might do with it, I told him, "No. No, I'm certain he's not."

"Then what am I to do with this?" he asked, meaning the shell.

"All around the mausoleum there is a border of seashells."

"Sonofabitch!" he cried.

"Buck, hush! You have to be quiet now. We have to take this one step at a time."

"You do think it was him, don't you?"

"It wasn't him! Now listen to me. Do you want to do this for Susan or not?"

He glared at me then, furious that I should doubt his devotion to her. I did not. I only doubted that he could channel his emotions appropriately to our needs.

Then, finally, holding himself in check, he asked, "What is it I'm to do?"

"Just see if it fits is all. See if that piece of shell might have come from the mausoleum or not. You'll be able to tell."

"And if it did?"

"Then we'll know something we didn't know yesterday. But first, before you do that. First I need you to do something else."

He waited.

"We need another person to help."

"Who?" he asked.

"I don't know who. But it has to be somebody you can trust. Somebody we can both trust. And it has to be somebody who can. . . ." I struggled with how to say it.

"Somebody who can move in higher circles than you and I. Somebody of a higher station in life."

His brow was wrinkling again.

"There are people who need to be questioned," I said. "Successful, prosperous people. The kind who would never speak to you or me. And even if they did, who would never tell us the truth."

"Who would I even ask? That kind of person would never deal with me in the first place."

"I don't know, Buck. But you have to think of somebody. And when you do, send him here. Have him come to see me at the soonest possible moment."

"What would he tell the guards about why he's coming here?"

"Buck, I don't know! The two of you will just have to figure it out!"

"I wouldn't know who to ask," he said.

I was exhausted. Depleted of argument. I took a step back, let my gaze wander away to the blankness of wall. Blankness and surrender.

"All right," he said then.

I felt a smile come. "You also need to eat something," I told him. "Change your shirt. Take care of yourself."

"Look who's giving advice," he said.

And all through the long afternoon afterward I clutched that small black feather atop my chest. Raven's feather. From a bird both reviled and worshipped. Devourer of carrion. Soothsayer. Truth teller. Midnight messenger of the untimely dead.

There is a place in one's self that can be reached only when you lose everything that has mattered to you. It is as if you had been sitting in a spacious and sunlit room, with a feast of bright tomorrows laid out before you on the table, and you are standing there with a cigar in one hand and a snifter of cognac in the other, ready to take your seat and fill your plate, when suddenly the floor collapses beneath you and you go tumbling down through darkness to land in a small dank hole, alone in the deepest of places, while shattered crystal and ash rain down upon your head.

In that place, after the shock of initial impact wears off, after the reality sinks in and you accept that the situation cannot be easily undone or time turned back, you no longer care what becomes of you. It is not courage because courage requires that you act in the face of your fears. But you are not in the least afraid. You lie stripped of all hope and all of your previous ambitions.

For my part only one thing remained to be accomplished in my life. I needed to murder the individual who had murdered Susan. If I perished in the effort, all the better. I also accepted the fact that if I succeeded in the effort, success would not matter much either, but only until the satisfaction gleaned from it was devoured by the loss that did not end.

Yes, the pleasure of success would be temporary but it was the only pleasure I could anticipate ever again. All other pleasures had been rendered null and void. What did writing or riches or anything else avail in the absence of love? What did guilt or innocence matter? I was not driven to clear my name. My name and my future were no longer relevant. The only name that had meant anything to me was one I had fabricated, and it was gone now too, blown away like a dandelion's wisp.

And if somehow I succeeded in my final ambition, what then? Then . . . movement. Nothing more. Whether by foot or boat or rail I would set myself in motion, always away from but never toward anything in particular, until I was acted upon in such a way that required a reaction. I would make no precipitating maneuvers of my own. I would turn myself into a cipher, a zero, a slowly rolling nothing.

Maudlin? Yes. But such was the only comfort I could muster there at the lowest latitude of my soul. The world is dark, indelibly dark, when you are only seventeen and believe with all your heart that you will never be happy again.

Chapter Twenty-seven

It could not have been more than two hours after Buck's visit to me than the panel door slid open with a bang. I was lying faceup on my bunk, staring into God's cyclopean eye, which at the moment was clouded over, milky with indifference. A few minutes before this I had been inspired by the raven's feather clutched in my hand and had come up with a scheme of action and was waiting for God to blink as a sign of his approval. That is, I promised myself that if a bird flew past my window, any kind of bird at all, I would do what I had devised.

The plan was simple enough: At evening mealtime, when one of my jailers came to push a bowl of bean or cabbage soup through the opening, I would respond by hurling out the contents of my chamber pot. With any luck at all this would so enrage the guard that he would rush headlong into my cell. If my luck continued to hold, and it probably would not, I might subdue him before he could bash my brains to a pulp. After that, how I would make it through the next door and the two outer guards, I had no idea. In truth I had no real hope of escape, no hopes at all. My mood after Buck's departure had quickly plummeted, so that I now considered a death by beating preferable to one more night of this damnable impotence.

And so I lay there watching for my omen. Instead, the panel door slid open with a bang. And in the opening, adorned with its usual sneer, the pockmarked face of my midday guard.

"Wake up!" he told me.

"Bring me something to eat."

"Hungry now, are you? I knew you couldn't hold out."

"Bring me some food!"

"You'll eat when it's time to eat. Till then you can scrape up what's on the floor."

"Fuck you," I told him.

"Sit up!" he barked. "Got somebody here wants to pray for you."

"Pray for this," I answered, and made an obscene gesture.

He laughed. What could I do or say that he hadn't experienced before? A moment later he stepped to the side and said to the person there, "I ain't responsible for the way he's going to talk to you. Just remember that."

The face of Miss Jones then appeared in the opening, a hard and angular face, her thin neck black-collared, gray hair black-bonneted. Just the sight of her astringent countenance was a shock to me, and not a pleasant one.

"Have you a favorite passage from the Bible?" she asked. Her voice coming into the small enclosed room seemed a jagged kind of shriek, a caw thrown down from a brittle branch.

I felt inclined to shock her in return. "*The Song of Solomon*," I answered.

She showed no surprise, not the slightest discomfort. And answered, "I think not."

She brought a heavy Bible up to the opening and rested it on the panel's ledge. "*Revelations*," she said. Now she turned to the right and spoke to the guard, whom I could no longer see. "You should stay as well," she told him. "It will do you good to hear this."

He laughed again, this time just one explosive "Hah!" Then his footsteps echoed down the hall. Miss Jones continued to watch after him. A few moments later the guard's chair, at the end of the hall, scraped shrilly over the floor as he dropped himself into it. She called, "You should come back down here and listen to this!"

In my mind I could picture his wave of dismissal.

"I insist that you come down here!" she said. "You must provide an example for this young man!"

"You do what you came to do," he called to her, his voice an impatient boom, "and leave me out of it!" The chair legs scraped again, this time the longer squeak of a chair being jerked and twisted so as to face away from her.

Miss Jones sniffed once as if insulted. Then she turned to face me once again. With her head framed as it was in the aperture, her features appeared more exaggerated than ever, heronlike, a long beaked face on a serpentine neck.

She lay open the Bible. "*The Revelation of St. John the Divine*," she said. "We shall begin with chapter two."

"I'm not interested in this," I told her.

She began anyway. " 'I know thy works, and thy labor, and thy patience, and how thou canst not bear them which are evil.' "

"Come take her out of here!" I screamed.

The guard down the hall laughed mightily.

Miss Jones continued to read. " 'And thou hast tried them which say they are apostles, and are not, and hast found them liars.' "

I told myself, *I should not have to suffer this as well.* I lay there awhile longer, jaw clenched, and began a low rumbling moan in an effort to drown her out. She read even louder.

" 'Nevertheless I have somewhat against thee, because thou has left thy first love.' "

"Damn you," I muttered, then swung my feet onto the floor, and stood and crossed to her, meaning, if necessary, to shove that Bible out into the hallway, Miss Jones preceding it. I was but one long stride from doing so when, with a flick of her bony finger, she dislodged a slip of folded paper from between the Bible's pages and sent it trembling to the floor.

She continued to read, did not slow by a beat or lift her eyes to me. The paper lay there on the stones, no accident.

I sank to my haunches, picked up the paper, unfolded it. Only two words were written on the paper, words penned in an elegant script, a very womanly hand, both words underlined. At the top of the paper she had written *Names?* And midway down the center of the page, *Questions?*

My brain fogged momentarily, but just as quickly the fog evaporated. She was the person Buck Kemmer had sent! Miss Jones! I felt suddenly giddy with the absurdity of it.

Strange how a manner and countenance so annoying can become in an instant so endearing. What an actress she was! I wanted to kiss that parched hard cheek of hers.

I rose and moved closer. I signaled, by scrawling my finger through the air, that I required a writing instrument of some kind.

She slid a bit more of the Bible inside my cell. With her left hand she fingered a thick stack of pages and lifted them slightly, revealing the stub of pencil secreted beneath them. I slipped a finger between the pages and slid the pencil out.

She read on. "'I know thy works and where thou dwellest. . . . Repent; or else I will come unto thee quickly. . . . And I will give him the morning star . . . .'"

And as she read I wrote what names I could remember. Vernon, of course, was first on the list. Then Kane Gatesford. The girl, Lydia Cavin. Soon afterward I gave up on trying to remember individual names and scrawled *Any and all of the Quintillian Society*. Under her second notation I wrote: *How long did Poe's reception continue? Was Brunrichter ever absent from it? At what time and for how long? Did any of the other guests leave soon after my departure?*

I prayed for a clearer mind but I could think of nothing more to write. So I refolded the paper along its crease and slipped it into the Bible, along with the pencil stub.

She read a few moments longer, then finally stopped. She closed her eyes as if to bless me with a silent benediction. I whispered, "Be careful how you ask those questions. Don't make anybody suspicious about—"

Her eyes flew open. "Do not presume to tell me how to conduct my business, young man."

The guard's chair legs squeaked. I could sense the man looking her way. And so I put my hands on the Bible and slammed it shut and shoved it up against her scrawny bosom. I gave her a wink and shouted, "Get her out of here now! I don't have to put up with this!"

"Oh you don't, do you?" came the guard's reply. His footsteps thundered down the hallway.

Miss Jones pulled back from the door, held the Bible flat against her chest. "Never mind," she told the guard. "This vile young man is beyond redemption."

"Didn't I tell you so?" he said.

Miss Jones strode away without giving me another look.

I stuck my head out the opening. "Bring me something to eat!"

In answer the guard, who was closer than I had thought, yanked out his truncheon and took a swing at me. I ducked inside. He laughed again, then slammed and bolted the panel door.

I took my supper without complaint that evening. The barley soup was barely warm, with little islands of congealed fat floating atop it, the barley overcooked to a mush, the broth all but soaked up by the chunk of bread laid atop the soup. Even so I gulped down every drop of it.

I did not heave the contents of my chamber pot in the guard's face because I no longer felt entirely alone in my plight, no longer felt abandoned to an unjust fate. Though outside those stone walls I could not have felt more secure than in the company of Buck Kemmer, his physical bulk did me little good where I was, and his capacity for the type of careful, deliberate maneuvers that might eventually free me had engendered little in the way of confidence. But he believed me, and that was confidence enough. Miss Jones, on the other hand, though as brittle as a charred stick, possessed an iron will and a keen intelligence. So now there were three of us.

With every spoonful of soup I sat anxious for further news from Buck, an indication of how his search of the mausoleum had gone. I expected him shortly before supper, then during, and then after. Something had gone wrong. Had he been apprehended while skulking about Brunrichter's estate? Or had he in fact not even made it that far, but was instead conveyed by a father's irreconcilable grief to one of the waterfront groggeries, where even now he flooded his misery with rum?

Worse yet, had he reached the realization that fluttered and whispered through my own consciousness that neither justice nor revenge could ever undo the loss, and that his anguish might be undone by one act alone? Had he therefore taken a knife to his own throat, just as I might yet decide to do, but only after exhausting every possibility of first taking that knife to another's?

I had lived most of my seventeen years steeped in hatred. Hatred was a part of my veinwork, and the desire for revenge was the blood that flowed through it. Those few days of something like dignity that I had long ago enjoyed in the company of Poe and Virginia and Mrs. Clemm, and the few sweet hours of something like joy in the company of Susan, they were as foreign to me now as the ancient wonders of Egypt. I expected to see a pyramid about as much as I expected to feel clean and free and content with the world. Which is to say, Never.

I did not mind the solitude of my cell. Those stone walls seemed nothing more than a physical extension of the interior walls that isolate us from one another. About this, John Donne was wrong. Every man *is* an island. There can be, for the fortunate ones, moments of contiguity, moments of union, but they are only that, transient, and when they pass or are stolen from us we are pitched into a silence even more profound, even more impenetrable from the outside.

And here is the ultimate cruelty: Not only can we never truly know one another, never truly see into the bared essence of another human being nor communicate to them our own, neither can we communicate our own to ourself! A human being is a bifurcated creature—and perhaps, if there is a spirit (my hope in this regard remains small), even trifurcated—one whose principal parts, the body and the mind, can know each other only superficially, as mere acquaintances, sometimes affectionately, though often not.

My hair grows. My beard. But am I the one who does it? Do I make or inspire them to grow?

The length of my arms. The shape of my feet. How much say in that is mine?

My stomach, for a reason known only to itself, might suddenly double up, knot up in pain like an angry fist. Does it tell my mind why? Does the mind bother to inquire?

I eat a chunk of bread, drink pallid soup, I chew, swallow, forget about it. Next morning, there it is again, reconstituted. Am I responsible for this process?

This body, this stranger to myself. This thing that tastes and touches and sees and smells and aches and calls itself me, but isn't.

Yet the other part confounds me more.

I use my mind to think, to think about itself. But the thing has no eyes of its own, no ears. It casts no reflection. The thing cannot know itself. Nor can it explain to me, neither to the me it is nor to the other, the visible and unthinking me, what or how I am.

I can think, yes. Why can't I *know*?

And the greatest mystery of all, the heart. Is it mind or body or separate from both? Do not tell me that the heart is an unthinking organ, a mere mass of pulsing muscle. It is that, yes, but why, with happiness, does it lift up inside my chest, why does it beat wildly with excitement and passion, why does it thrum so ominously with fear? Why does it *feel* and give form to the very emotions the mind cannot explain?

What causes love? We do not know.

How can a heart so pierced as mine or Buck's not bleed to death?

How can so much love and so much murderous hatred exist side by side and not devour one another completely?

How can a heart die, again and again and again over the course of a single day, yet continue to beat?

We do not know.

We do not know.

We do not know.

* * *

The night bled in through the eye of God and stilled myself and all around me. I counted three stars framed in the distant window, three dim pricks of light softened and blurred by cloud. There was nothing else to look at, nothing else moving in my universe, and so I watched until one of those stars had crawled beyond the window's frame, and only two remained. These two I watched a good while longer, holding my eyes open and not allowing them to blink, until my eyes stung and teared and the muscles in my face began to ache. And finally I accomplished my one objective for the night, to exhaust myself sufficiently to sleep, and I closed my eyes at last.

It is a dream, I told myself. A shrill scratching in my dream, cat's claw on glass. Repetitive. I listened to it in my sleep for a good long while, trying to turn my sluggish mind toward it, to seek it out, all to no avail. It culminated in a muted cracking sound, a snap. And with that snap I realized that I had come awake, was lying there curled on my side, eyes open to the darkness.

I listened awhile longer. Nothing. I drew a hand to my face, felt its warmth, then reached out in the blackness and touched the cold wall not four inches away. Yes, I told myself, you are awake.

But there seemed some difference to my cell, and to me. I rolled onto my back then, looked up, saw nothing, could not now distinguish even the shape of the window high above me, so uniformly black my surroundings. But the air—was it cooler now? Freshened?

I felt a draft wash over me. Sat up. Placed stockinged feet upon the floor. Heard nothing.

But the draft was there, no dream. I felt it on my face, smelled it in the faint smoky odor of Pittsburgh air.

I stood, crossed cautiously toward the door, hands outstretched to feel my way. Found the door, touched it, ran fingertips up and down the wood. No, the panel was closed. Locked tight.

I turned. Walked back into the center of the room, hands raised, fingers spread to catch the mysterious draft. There, I felt it again! But where was it coming from? I moved a step to my right. Nothing. Two steps to my left.

And suddenly something in the night attempted to seize me by the wrist, brushed roughly against my wrist so that I jerked away, jumped back, then stood there waving my fists in front of me, swinging at air lest the thing attempt to grab me again.

It did not. I could hear my own snorting breath, shallow inhalations quick and terrified. Could hear the drum of blood in my temples, heart thunking in my chest.

The thing did not approach.

I stood there so frightened that I wanted to shriek, my tongue too paralyzed to make a sound. And I admit to thinking to myself, *All those stories of Poe's—could they have been true?*

I don't know how long I stood there frozen. Maybe half a minute. Maybe more. Eventually I calmed myself enough to become embarrassed by my fear, and then angered by it. I stepped forward again and swung hard at the air.

And felt it again—there! The thing was still there!

But it moved away when my fist made contact, it

yielded to my touch. It moved away . . . but then returned. Cautiously now I opened my fist and moved my fingers toward it, felt a rough and not unfamiliar texture. More important, the thing made no attempt to seize me. I turned my hand toward it now, gingerly wrapped the tips of my fingers around it, then took it into the palm of my hand, put both hands on it, held it tight. And very nearly laughed out loud.

A rope. A thick braided rope, hanging down from the ceiling.

A rope had been lowered to me through the high black eye of God.

Because I wanted to shriek with joy but could not, I sent that shriek into my muscles and pulled myself up hand over hand, shinnying up one pull after another, holding tight with my ankles and knees as well. Almost giggling, I thought, *The Indian rope trick—I've read about this!* and neither knew nor cared what strange plane of existence I might tumble into on the uppermost side.

I poked my head up through the hole, through the window I had been thinking of contemptuously as the eye of God, and into open night. There, sitting awkwardly astraddle the roof slates, one hand wrapped tight around the rope he had looped about the chimney, the other hand clutching the thick plate of glass he had pried loose, was a shadow so large it could only belong to Buck Kemmer.

"Watch out for the edges," he whispered hoarsely. "The metal's sharp."

"The opening's too small. I'll scrape my hide off."

"Your hide or your neck. Choose quick."

I chose to keep my neck intact, and, considering the way men are hanged at the penitentiary, my head too. I wriggled, squirmed and twisted to get my shoulders clear, and in the bargain flayed a long strip of flesh off my left shoulder and arm. But then I was out, and oozing like a worm up beside Buck.

"Watch those slates," he said. "They're slippy."

"I forgot my shoes."

"Better take off your socks."

I pulled them off and stuffed them into a pocket. The slates were as cold as ice on my skin, but how I reveled in the chill. "Which way now?"

Buck handed me the pane of glass then, perhaps two feet long by a foot and a half wide, while he hauled up the rope, coiling it around an elbow as he reclaimed it. This done, he balanced the coil atop the roof's peak and pressed it flat with both hands so that it would not slip away.

Then he took the glass from me. "Grab hold of my waistband," he said, "so that I don't go falling in." I did so, and he leaned toward the opening, inclining forward an inch at a time as he lowered the pane of glass back onto its metal frame—an impressive feat of balance and strength.

When he sat back, finished, he released a low huff of relief.

"How'd you get the glass out?" I whispered.

"Got a friend works at Bakewells. Borrowed a few of his tools." He tapped the front of his shirt; the tools inside made a clinking sound.

Now, half crouching, he used the rope to pull himself up to the roof's peak, then sat there, knees hugging the slates, and motioned for me to do the same. After I had joined him he pointed to the rear of the building. "We'll go down over there."

"What's on that end?"

"Kitchen and pantry."

"What time of night is it?"

"Time to get the hell out of here," he said.

We walked duck legged, hunkered low, straddling the peak, hands riding the cold slate tiles. Midway Buck loosed the rope from around the chimney, tied the loose end around the coil and then draped the coil over his head, wearing it like a horse's collar.

Several anxious moments later we reached the back edge of the roof. I leaned forward over my stomach but could see only darkness below. Both sides of the roof sloped off too steeply for us to contemplate working our way down with any degree of deliberate movement.

"You'll have to turn around and go over the edge butt first," Buck instructed. "Slide off over your belly. About four feet down you'll feel a ladder underneath you. It's set up on the roof of the pantry."

"You carried a ladder too?"

"I brought what was needed."

Only then did the magnitude of Buck's labors dawn on me. "You could have gotten yourself killed."

"I might yet. Now shut up and go. Give me your hands, I'll steady you."

More skin came off as my belly scraped over the roof's cornice, but that was the least of my concerns. I eased down as quietly as I could, feeling the wall with my toes, imagining that at any moment my weight would pull Buck off his tenuous perch to send both of us plunging into a noisy heap. But never was an anchorage so secure as the one provided by Buck Kemmer that night. I am confident that even had his arms popped from their sockets he would not have let me slip.

My toes finally found the first rung of the ladder. Then the second. A minute later I was standing firmly, if with watery knees and trembling hands, atop the much flatter pantry roof. I leaned then against the ladder, doing what I could to steady it as Buck climbed down.

It was sheer brute strength that allowed him to push his body over the roof's edge and into empty space, to hold it there secured by nothing more than ten fingers pinched like pinions into the tiles. Then at last he was beside me, and without a moment's hesitation he whisked the ladder away from the wall, crossed to the edge of the pantry roof, and noiselessly let the ladder down through his hands until it touched hard ground.

"Go to the Hand Street Bridge," he told me. "Wait for me underneath it where it crosses Duquesne."

"I'll wait for you on the ground. Help you carry things."

"You'll not. Now go before I throw you off this roof."

He grabbed me by an arm and thrust me toward the ladder. I scurried down. The first shock of ground beneath my feet, even cool, hard-trampled earth such as it was, strengthened and steadied me.

I looked up at Buck's great black silhouette as he stood above me. "Go!" he said.

I turned and ran.

At Seventh Street, having upbraided myself the entire way, I turned and went back, meaning to help Buck with his load. But he was gone. The ladder was gone, the rope, all trace of him gone. I crept to within three feet of the pantry's small porch, saw its interior still pitch dark, before I was convinced that he had made it safely away.

And then, the strangest urge came over me. Or perhaps it was not strange at all, but merely human. An urge to demean those who had demeaned me.

What I did next was immature and foolish, I admit. I blush even now to remember it. The act was made even more foolhardy by the fact that all evidence of my disdain would have been thoroughly dried by morning, and surely went unnoticed by all but the local tomcats who, sniffing an intruder in their territory, would have covered my mark with their own. I knew all this even as I walked softly over the porch boards, soaking them with my scent.

I saved the last of it for the pantry door itself. And then, because of a scuffling sound from somewhere out in the yard, a stray pig perhaps or a wandering goat, I hopped off the porch and once again broke into a run, buttoning up on the go, half pig myself but determined that never, not ever, would I be anybody's goat.

By the time I reached the Allegheny waterfront my feet were stone-bruised and half frozen. And the exuberance of my escape had by now been replaced by a chill, so that as I cowered against a piling beneath the Hand Street Bridge I hugged myself and shivered. The night smelled of river fog, that dank, cloying scent of dead fish and mud.

There were no streetlights here, the only illumination a meager sprinkling of candles and oil lamps burning in small houses and shops. I guessed the time at maybe three in the morning, but it was only a guess, based on nothing, for the moon and stars were obscured by heavy clouds, my own innate clock obscured by an escalating anxiety.

Realistically I did not expect that my absence from the jail would be discovered until morning. The guards maintained a fairly lax routine, trusting to the security of the heavy cell doors and most inmates' inability to fly or leap eighteen feet into the air. At sunrise, however, the order would go out to watchmen in every ward that a murderer was on the loose. Apprehend at any cost. Shoot on sight.

A quarter hour passed with no sounds other than the liquid hammerings of blood in my temples, the river pulsing against the docks. Then, startling me, though I had been listening intently for just that sound, footsteps. I strained even harder to hear. They were quick footsteps, heavy, coming from the west, long strides over cobblestone. I moved to the opposite side of the bridge piling, flattened myself against it, tried to quiet my breath.

The footsteps came upon me quickly, then stopped. By my guess the individual stood not six feet away. His feet scraped as he turned. Ten seconds of silence. His feet scraped again. He was looking for somebody.

"You here?" he whispered.

I slipped around the piling and went to him. "You have a voice like a meadowlark, Buck. I never noticed that before."

Buck Kemmer did not pause to chuckle. He seized me by the wrist. "This way."

We hurried inland, keeping underneath the bridge. I asked, "We going to the school?"

"Quiet," he said.

We were indeed headed for Miss Jones's School for Young Ladies. As we skirted the front schoolyard I could not help but glance at the spot where, a lifetime ago, I had stood to wait for Susan, my heart thrashing with hope, my body warm with desire. Now, in passing that spot, I was cold inside and out.

Buck led me to a low basement door at the side of the building, affixed to the building on a slant so that the door's near end touched the ground while the top of the door stood less than three feet higher against the side of the building. He reached down and pulled the door up and then pushed me forward down those five steps to another door, this one vertical. I seized the knob but the door was locked.

"Wait," Buck said. He lowered the first door behind us, enclosing us in absolute darkness. The space we shared was barely large enough to allow for a yawn, so he had to squeeze past me to stand before the second door. He rapped on it with his knuckles, once, then twice more, then three times more.

A key turned in the lock on the opposite side. Then the door came open and there stood Miss Jones looking tall and brittle and terrified. The room behind her, the furnace room, was lit by a single oil lamp on a small table. She had hung black cloth over the basement's two small windows.

"Here he is," Buck told her, and pulled me inside.

As Buck closed and locked the door behind us, Miss Jones gestured toward the table and chair in the center of the room. "Sit here," she told me.

I crossed to the table, the basement's earthen floor no warmer to my feet than the ground outside. But atop the table was a small iron kettle, and from it came a warming scent of stew, of potatoes and gravy and onions and meat. Even before dropping my buttocks onto the chair

I reached for the pot's lid, lifting it up only to have Miss Jones jerk the lid from my hand.

Without explanation she laid before me a blank sheet of paper and a patent pen. Then took from the pocket of her shapeless frock another piece of paper, unfolded it, and smoothed it out beside the blank sheet. There was writing on the second sheet. She jabbed her finger at it. "Copy this over in your own hand. Quickly now."

I read what she had written. *As recompense for the loss of your skiff A.D.*

"What do I need a skiff for?" I asked.

"Write," she said, and jabbed at the paper again.

I turned to Buck. "I'm not leaving this city, if that's what you're thinking."

"For Christ's sake, Gus—sorry, Miss Jones—write the damn note!"

I did not like to see such fear on his face. And so I wrote, because Miss Jones's words did not sound like my own, *In exchange for your skiff A.D.* I waved the note through the air a couple of times, drying the ink, then handed it to Miss Jones. "I wouldn't have used the word recompense," I told her.

She sniffed, only mildly affronted. She then folded the paper in half, folded it a second time, and handed it to Buck, who stuffed it in a pocket and then went quickly out the basement door.

She relocked the door behind him. Then stood there for several moments leaning against it, fingers pressed to the wood.

I told her, "I'm not leaving this city. Besides, I don't have any shoes."

She turned and looked at me. Blinked twice. Then said, "You can eat now."

I required no second invitation. I lifted the lid off the kettle and beheld a feast of brown gravy and chunks of brown meat, a symphony of carrots, potatoes, onions and yams.

"There's no spoon," I told her.

She clicked her tongue, whether at me or herself I did not know nor much care, then hurried across the room and up the stairs. I could hear her above me then, yanking open a drawer, the clatter of cutlery. With my fingers I fished a chunk of meat from the pot and popped it into my mouth and almost swooned from the rich peppery taste of it.

Her footsteps came tapping down the stairs again, so I chewed and swallowed quickly and wiped a sleeve across my mouth. She came to the table and held out the spoon. "You had the decency to wait, I hope."

"Miss Jones, please. I am not a barbarian."

At this she sniffed again, then drew back a step and looked me up and down. Obviously, judging by my scent and appearance, I was nothing but barbarian. "I will bring you water and a razor in the morning," she said. "And a pair of shoes."

"And what will the janitor do when he finds me here?"

"There is no janitor. Susan and I tended to all the duties here."

She looked for a moment as if her face might lose its composure, as if it might suddenly break apart at all those seams and wrinkles. But she blinked, she inhaled sharply, she held herself together. "Eat," she told me.

I did so. The pot contained twice as much stew as I could comfortably eat, but I continued to spoon it in long after my waistband had expanded, devouring every chunk of meat and scrap of vegetable if for no other reason than to show Miss Jones how grateful I was for her hospitality, for her trust in me, the love for Susan she could express in no other way.

I scraped the last spoonful of gravy from the pot, placed the spoon in my mouth and sucked it clean, then dropped the spoon clanging into the kettle. Miss Jones had spent the past ten minutes seated on the steps rising to the kitchen, staring at her hands clasped atop her knees, eyes closed as if in prayer. But she looked up at the sound of the spoon's chiming.

"Best I ever had," I told her, and said to myself, *Except for Mrs. Clemm's.*

She said, "Half of that was intended for Mr. Kemmer."

My stomach bubbled. "Well why in the world didn't you say so?"

"You should have inferred as much."

"I was too hungry to make any inferences. You should have told me."

"It isn't natural for a man to eat that much."

I would have argued further but for the gurgling of my stomach. She was right; it wasn't natural. "Is there I place I can lie down?" I asked.

"There's a pallet laid out behind the furnace."

I pushed back my chair and stood, then crossed to the rear of a cast-iron wood boiler. There, against a stack of neatly cut and split logs, she had prepared my bed. I went down on my knees atop it, then collapsed sideways onto the heavy quilts, my head on a goose feather pillow. The wood-beamed ceiling was not half as high here as the one in my jail cell, and for a view I had only a stack of wood to my left, the black bulk of the furnace to my right, but the blankets were soft and clean, the furnace warm with a low fire, and for the first time in a long while I actually felt a smile coming to my mouth. I remember looking at the firewood and thinking, *I'll bet Buck did that,* because the wood was so uniformly split and so perfectly stacked. *That's the way Buck would do it.*

Unfortunately my moments of relative ease were short-lived. Soon other thoughts prevailed. *Here you are in hiding again.*

I did not at seventeen feel significantly different about hiding out than I had when I was a boy, which is to say that I was angered by the need to do it, made to feel ignominious by my desire for self-preservation. It came to me then that nearly everything of importance in my life had been accomplished in darkness and had required a period of concealment until the danger had passed. Was this, I wondered, the way my life was going to play itself out, the pattern I was destined to repeat?

Such did not seem appropriate for a man who, a week past, had been trying to do some good with his life. I would rather have been the kind of man who worked his small wonders by daylight, who could then at nightfall take to his bed and sleep in something like contentment until another day began. And it had seemed for a few days that I might indeed be just that type of man, a writer of stories true and unusual, to be read by people at their morning and midday meals. But apparently that had been a temporary illusion. Apparently I possessed an affinity for the darkness that was just as strong as Poe's, just as binding.

It was an exhausting thought. Even more so when the emptiness and impossibility of Susan broke over me like a sickening wave, colder and darker than my basement hideaway could ever be, and I had to turn my face into the pillow to muffle the choking sounds I made, as if I were being slowly suffocated by my darkness.

Chapter Twenty-eight

I awoke with a start. The room was pitch-black now, the single lamp extinguished. I do not know what had awakened me so suddenly, whether a dream noise or a real one, but I came awake by sitting up abruptly, gasping for air as if I had been underwater too long, so deep I might never have broken the surface.

Almost immediately I sensed that I was not alone. Near the foot of my pallet, somebody sitting. He moved his chair slightly, made the wood creak, to let me know he was there.

"You owe me for a flat boat," he said. His voice was soft in the darkness. Warm. There was a sadness in it too, a weariness, but it held no anger.

"I told you before. I don't want anything to do with a boat right now."

"It's already done."

"What is, Buck?"

There was a pause before he spoke. "I punched a couple of holes in the floor of it. Hated to do that to a perfectly good boat," he said. "Another man's property."

I thought I understood him then, but said nothing.

He continued. "Set it adrift out into the river."

"How long before it went down?"

"Couple of minutes. Current should take it quite a ways yet."

"So now I'm a boat thief as well as an escaped murderer."

"You're likely to be a lot of things before this is done with," he said. "But that boat weren't stole. You paid a silver eagle for it."

"Who put up the money?"

"I did. But it was Miss Jones's idea. She's the one come up with it. Pretty clever, if you ask me."

"If it works it is."

"No reason it shouldn't. A man wakes up in the morning, finds a note and a silver eagle shoved under his door. Note says here's some money for your boat I took. So he goes to where his boat was tied up and it's not there."

"It won't stop them from looking for me."

"At least they'll be looking down the Ohio somewhere and not here."

I began to wonder what Poe would think of me when he heard the news, how my disappearance would erase all doubts he might have harbored concerning my guilt.

Buck must have intuited my thoughts. "They'll be asking Mr. Poe to study that note you wrote. Identify your handwriting and all."

"That was a good idea Miss Jones had."

"Clever lady, like I said."

"Where is she now?"

"She's got a sleeping room upstairs. This is her home as well as her school."

"She must have thought the world of Susan to do this for me."

Buck said nothing. He swallowed thickly.

I told him, "Maybe Poe will tell them I'm on my way to Mexico. That's what we talked about doing."

"That would be good," Buck said. "Couldn't hurt."

We sat in silence for a while. Then I asked, "Did you go to the doctor's mausoleum today?"

"Yesterday," he said. "Right after we talked about it at the jail."

"And?"

"It's what made me decide to break you out of there. Except that now it don't seem to make any sense to me."

"What doesn't? Breaking me out, or what you learned at the mausoleum?"

"I'll show you in a bit," he said. "When there's light."

"Tell me what you found."

"In the morning," he said.

His resolve was tangible, as solid as his presence. "Then at least tell me this much, Buck. Has Miss Jones talked yet with anybody from the party? The party at Brunrichter's place?"

"Wait till morning," he said. "She'll come down then with something for us to eat, and she can tell you herself."

"Why can't you tell me now? I won't be able to sleep anymore anyway."

"It'll be better if we can see each other's face when we talk."

"If you tell me now, I can think about things in the dark."

"The things you think about in the dark won't be of no use to you in the daylight. Trust me."

He let a moment pass, then continued. "This is no way to have a conversation," he said, "whispering like hooligans."

In a sense Buck had already become a hooligan, a

criminal on my behalf. The difference was that Buck felt no ease in the darkness, found no solace in invisibility. As a creature of the sunlight he preferred all things open and exposed. Me, I was born to be nocturnal.

But I took no pleasure from the knowledge that I was constructed that way.

I told him, "There's no reason you have to spend the night here. You could go home to your own bed, you know."

"I know," he said.

And we let it go at that.

After a while I asked, "What time do you think it's getting to be?"

"Couple hours yet before the sun's up. Better get yourself some sleep."

"That goes for you too."

"Not me," he said. "I don't like what I see when I close my eyes."

"You can't stay awake forever, Buck."

He made no reply to this. Nor could I come up with a convincing argument to counter his silence.

I eased back down atop my blankets finally, hands crossed atop my chest, and stared at where the ceiling would have been had I been able to discern it. I discovered that by staring into the darkness without effort and letting my eyes relax I could deepen the blackness and push it higher, turn it into a kind of midnight sky not a few feet but hundreds of feet above my head, a sky without ceiling that went on soft and black forever into the unimaginable reaches of empty space.

And as I lay there with no companion but for the sound of Buck's breathing I wished for some small break in the monotonous blackness above. It did not have to be an eye of God gazing down on me; any pinpoint of light would do, any small indication or suggestion of the Particle Divine.

But I was just a boy then, and I have long since forgiven myself such desires.

Miss Jones started moving about before first light. Not that I could have seen the sunrise anyway, what with the black cloth draped over the windows. But if you are quiet and attentive you can feel the morning changing at dawn, you can sense the subtle difference just as old salts can sense a change in barometric pressure. If there are animals to watch, they will tell you too. Birds are especially useful.

Outside Miss Jones's school there were several trees in the yard, two stately oaks that I could remember, and another three or four tulip maples. The birds had returned to those trees early that year, chickadees and phoebes and sparrows. Softly they began to twitter that morning, one or two singing at a time, just before Miss Jones's feet first scraped across the floor overhead. In a half hour the birds would be in full chorus. Their exuberance always made me wonder if they had been taken by surprise by the sunlight, if their brains were so small that they had forgotten that the miracle of sunrise had ever happened before.

Was that such a bad way to be? I wondered. Maybe it was a blessing to have a brain so small it could retain no memories more than a few hours old. How many people did I know who could awaken each morning with a songbird's exuberance? Was memory, and therefore regret, a natural consequence of intelligence?

This thought gave me yet another reason to feel no

great pride in being human. In truth, any pride that managed to survive my first seventeen years had been wiped out in the events of the past few days. If my history, both recent and older, had taught me anything, it was that mankind's intelligence contributes little to this world but misery.

In one of Poe's tales he wrote of a visitor from a distant planet, a wise and witty fellow who, if a bit sarcastic, was nonetheless compassionate and well-meaning toward us humans. But in this depiction of a superior mind, I think Poe erred. For if we study our own planet we can conclude that no evidence exists to prove that intelligence makes a species more tolerant or compassionate.

It then seemed to me (and seems to me still) that somewhere between the automatic aggression of the very small-brained—the viper, the crocodile, the snapping turtle—and the selfish and deliberate cruelty of the large-brained—man—there is an optimal middle ground of wit. The cow, for example. As a farmhand in Ohio I had spent numerous hours in study of the cow, who must surely be the most contentedly stupid creature on earth. Beat her flank with a stick and she will maybe roll her head your way, appeal to you with those huge trusting eyes, and issue a low "Mooo!" on her way to the slaughterhouse. But provoke the powerful crocodile, or provoke a powerful man, and the response will not likely be as innocuous as a moo.

No, intelligence does not render us docile or sweet. Intelligence makes us irritable, short-tempered, impatient, and arrogant. If a superior race from some distant planet ever does make a call on Earth, no amount of mooing will ever save us from the slaughterhouse.

In any case, such was my mood by the time Miss Jones rose from her bed to begin the day's ablutions. I listened as she shuffled toward the rear door, paused to pull on her boots and, I imagined, a heavy flannel robe, then shuffled outside to the privy.

When a few minutes later the rear door opened and fell shut again, Buck told me, "You'd better go now if you have to. While it's still fairly dark."

I wasted no time in taking care of necessities, though I had to run to the privy barefooted over frosty ground. When I returned, Buck hurried to do the same. Miss Jones was waiting halfway down the staircase by then. "I've got a washbasin up here," she told me.

"Do you think it's safe to come up?"

"Stay away from the windows," she said.

She led me to her tiny kitchen, where, as I filled myself with the scent of a thick slab of frying ham, I washed my face and hands in heated water and scrubbed at my teeth with a finger. The abrasion on my forehead was scabbing over, and the yellowing bruise on my cheek was no longer tender. None of this made me feel new but at least I felt put together again, haphazardly perhaps and with a few mismatched parts, but nonetheless complete.

Complete and stomach empty. "Is that ham for me?" I asked. "I mean for me and Buck?"

She was standing at the woodstove, alternately tending the ham and, in another skillet, frying slices of buttered bread. On the cooler edge of the stove top sat a pot of mush, and on the sideboard a quart of milk with two inches of golden cream on top.

"Buck and me," she corrected.

I misunderstood. "Isn't there anything for me?"

She gave me a censorious look. "I had been told that you are a writer."

"That's true, I am."

"Then if you expect to eat in this house, you had better remember the proper grammar. The correct phrase is not me and Buck, but Buck and me."

"Ah, of course, I knew that. I mean I know I should have said Buck and me. It's just that it's so easy to slip up, to . . ."

"To revert to your primitive ways?" she asked.

I smiled sheepishly.

"At least you didn't say Buck and I."

"Or I and Buck, which is even worse. I'll bet it sets your teeth on edge, doesn't it? Whenever somebody speaks improperly."

"I arrived in this city twenty-seven months ago," she told me. "My teeth have not been off edge since."

I grinned and nodded, thinking it a joke. But she did not smile. "You may return to the basement now," she told me. "I will serve your breakfast there."

"It would save you some trouble if we were to eat here in the kitchen, wouldn't it?"

"It would not," she said.

Back down the stairway then and into the dungeon-like cellar. Despite the wood-burning boiler down there, the place seemed very much like a cell, and a dread seeped into me with every step descended.

Until I saw what Buck had spread across the small table for me to view. He was standing there beside the table now, the oil lamp burning with a high flame. Along the nearest half of the table, between the lamp and me, were a dozen tiny pieces of broken nautilus shells, ribbed and curved, all of a similar size and the same delicate pink hue.

I stood close to the table. "From around Brunrichter's mausoleum?" I asked.

"They are," Buck said.

"They look just like the one you found in your house."

"Which is there among them now. See if you can pick it out."

I studied them a moment, but soon gave up. "It's impossible to tell."

"I guess that's the point here, isn't it?" he said.

I pulled out a chair and sat. "Question is, what does it tell us?"

"It tells us that whoever was in my house was also at that mausoleum one time or another."

"It could well have been me," I said.

But he did not wish to consider this possibility. "Let's just say it wasn't. For the sake of argument. Who else could it've been?"

"Are you sure those shells can't be found anywhere else around here?"

"I've lived along these rivers all my life. I'd know."

"Could Susan have brought the shell into the house herself?" I asked. "Stuck in the tread of her own boot, for example?"

"When was she ever up to the mausoleum?"

"But maybe she picked it up in another place. From outside the mansion, for example. Where it had been carried and dropped by somebody else."

"She was only there that one night, wasn't she?"

"That's all, yes."

"According to what the doctor told the police, she never even lighted from the carriage."

"But she did. I walked her onto the porch myself, and then into the foyer."

"Why would he lie about that?"

I explained the doctor's motivations in obscuring the events of that evening, the harm it might do his reputation were the true nature of the literary reception to become widely known.

"So maybe he killed her just to keep her quiet about it," Buck said. "So she wouldn't tell nobody what she saw."

I shook my head. "I'm the bigger threat to him. Anyway I doubt that those parties are much of a secret. Not among the rich anyway. So it's not gossip he would fear but a more public kind of criticism. As I might provoke in a newspaper piece."

Buck stood there rubbing a bristled cheek. The hollows of his eyes looked black, even in the yellow light of the lamp. "Couldn't of been him anyway," he muttered.

"Why do you say that?"

He nodded toward the staircase, down which Miss Jones was descending one slow, deliberate step at a time, a wicker tray held before her, heavily laden with two plates of food and two steaming mugs of tea. She said, "Dr. Brunrichter was not absent from the reception."

"You spoke with the guests?" I asked.

"I spoke with four guests, to be precise." She same to the table, stood there holding the tray bosom high, unmoving, until Buck lifted the lamp out of the way and then swept the broken seashells into his hand. Miss Jones set the tray in the center of the table.

"All four guests confirmed that, following your hasty departure, Dr. Brunrichter and Mr. Poe alike returned to the library. Mr. Poe was made comfortable on the divan, where he remained for the evening, sometimes sleeping and sometimes not. Dr. Brunrichter entertained his guests with several selections played upon the Chickering. One of the young ladies sometimes accompanied him vocally."

"What about Tevis?" I asked. "He's the one who slugged me. Did you ask about him?"

"I did not, but he was mentioned. By Mrs. Verhoven, to be specific. She informed me that the doctor asked his Mr. Tevis to station himself at the library door in the event that you might return to cause further disruption. Mrs. Verhoven expressed her regrets that you had conducted yourself like a ruffian. She remembered you from a picnic several days earlier, at which time, she said, you conducted yourself as a fine young gentleman should."

Buck gave me a fierce look. "Could they all be lying?" he asked.

Miss Jones continued. "Scarcely an hour passed between Mr. Dubbins's departure from the estate and your return to your own home, Mr. Kemmer. Within another thirty minutes, the police, alerted by you, had arrived at the estate in search of Mr. Dubbins. At which time they found Dr. Brunrichter still at the piano, and all guests still in attendance."

Now nobody spoke. The smell of the food there in front of me, so appetizing only minutes earlier, was turning my stomach. As did the notion that Susan's death could be ascribed no rationale. The fact that life is meaningless is one I had already come to suspect, but that even the best of us might die needlessly, with nothing gained from our demise, nothing learned—this was too bitter a truth to be made to swallow.

Eventually I looked across the table and raised my eyes to Buck, whose gaze had gone vacant, utterly blank of hope. "We should have some of this fine breakfast," I told him. "We won't have another chance to eat until after the students leave."

"There will be no students," Miss Jones informed me. "I have canceled all classes for the week ahead."

I nodded. Neither Buck nor I reached for our plates. I have no doubt that he was as hungry as I, but it was a two-sided hunger, and the deeper one would not permit the lesser to be satisfied.

"I need to talk with Poe," I said then.

"Impossible," said Miss Jones. "You could never go to him now."

"But he could come here."

"Could," said Buck. "But why would he?"

"He is still my friend. I know he is."

"And Brunrichter's friend as well."

"The two things aren't necessarily incompatible. Look, I don't care for the doctor's manner, I never have. But apparently he had nothing to do with Susan's death. I don't like him because of the way he's trying to take control of Poe. Plus, Mr. Poe is sick. And I don't trust the medicines he's being given. He's been no more than a shadow of himself ever since we came to Pittsburgh. That's another reason why you need to bring him here."

But Buck was shaking his head. "The police catch you a second time, they're going to chain you to a wall."

"Prudence," said Miss Jones. "We must be prudent in everything we do."

"We need his mind," I said.

"Have you not already stated that his mind is clouded?"

"But if we can get him away from his medicines for a day or two . . . get him away from the wine and brandy . . ."

"You jeopardize your freedom," said Miss Jones. "Ours as well."

I turned in my chair, looked up at her, lifted a hand and laid it lightly atop her wrist. She stiffened at the contact, as if to pull away. But I drew her brittle arm away from her body, enclosed her hand in both of mine. Her fingers were as cold and hard as sticks, her knuckles like stones. But from the palm of her hand came a warmth, a low-banked heat, ageless and aching. I pressed the heat of my own hand into it.

"Miss Jones," I told her. "Because of what you have done for me, your love for Susan, there is nothing you could ask of me that I would not do my utmost to provide. I am in your debt forever. But I must make this one last request of you. Please. We need Mr. Poe."

"We have the three of us. That should be sufficient."

"We have your wisdom, it's true. Your cleverness. Your educated mind. And we have Buck's strength. His loyalty. A father's determination."

"We have your fearlessness," he told me.

"Maybe fearlessness, maybe foolishness," I said with a smile. "In any case, what we have together is a great deal. But we need more. We need an eye that can see into the very heart of darkness. We need an ear attuned to evil in all its seductive voices. We need a man who knows how to straddle the worlds of light and darkness, and a mind that can peer into both worlds at once."

"Can we trust him?" Buck asked. "That's the only thing I need to know."

I looked again at Miss Jones, my hands still wrapped around hers as I waited her answer.

Half a minute passed. Finally, as if struggling against the pull of gravity, she raised her free hand and brought it to rest atop my own. Her thin lips smiled. Of Buck she asked, "Our Susan trusted Mr. Dubbins, did she not?"

"She did," Buck said.

She patted my hand. "Then we shall as well."

Vanity, thy name is Poe.

On a sheet of her finest stationery, Miss Jones wrote this:

My dear Edgar,

Imagine my surprise to learn that you, too, are stranded in Pittsburgh! My steamboat departs, however, at noon. Can you meet with me here? Please, you must, for I have great news for you—a position to secure your place in history!

Yours most affectionately,
Rufus
by the hand of M. Lignelli,
Secretary to Rufus Griswold

If anything could cut through Poe's narcotic fog, it was an appeal to his ambition, made by the one man most frequently his champion (and just as frequently his nemesis or rival). Though I had never met Griswold I had heard of him through Muddy's letters, of the many times he had come to Poe's aid with an assignment, a loan, a letter of introduction. He was therefore the only individual I could think of who might be called into action as the proverbial carrot on a stick.

It being a weekday, I surmised that Brunrichter would be busy at the hospital. But just in case he was not, and felt inclined, as he surely would in that case, to accompany Poe on his visit to another literary figure, I asked Miss Jones to append this postscript: *Whatever you do, Edgar, come alone, lest this windfall be jeopardized. But come—and quickly!*

Would Poe, if he had his senses about him, be suspicious of this note, seeing it as vague and possibly spurious? Probably so. But I was counting on Poe's hunger for security and advancement to allay any doubts he might entertain.

Buck then carried this note, thrice-folded, sealed with wax, and wrapped once with a strand of red ribbon, down to Penn Avenue, where the aqueduct ended, and where a line of hacks were queued for the morning's first passengers soon to disembark the Main Line. Then, handing over yet more of his hard-earned savings, he hired a driver and sent him off in his cab to the mansion on Ridge Avenue, with instructions that if Mr. Poe were still asleep he was to be awakened immediately and delivered personally of the note from his old friend and colleague Rufus Griswold.

Upon completion of this mission, Buck returned first to his own house, and then to Miss Jones's basement to wait with me. He tossed a pair of boots at my feet.

"They won't be a perfect fit," he said.

"You can stuff them with newspaper," said Miss Jones.

I told her, "Better bring me a week's worth."

She returned soon enough and gave us also a deck of cards with which to distract ourselves. Unfortunately we could concentrate on no mere game and spent most of the next hour seated across from one another at the small oak table, each of us building his own shaky house of cards, story upon story, only to watch them tremble and fall.

Horses' hooves in the schoolyard. Miss Jones's footsteps hurrying above us like muffled gunfire as she crossed to the front door. There she paused, waiting for the knock.

Tap tap tap. Buck and I sat motionless, breathless, as we stared at one another. Would that be Poe at the door, or the hack driver come back empty-handed?

Miss Jones's voice through the floorboards. I could not hear the words but there was something in her tone, something subdued, almost reverential. I remembered how her hand had quivered when she'd penned the note to Poe—she, a humble (figuratively speaking) school teacher, in correspondence (though fraudulently) with the renowned author himself!

I gave Buck a hopeful look, the hint of a smile. We each leaned back in our chairs, ready to rise, heads cocked toward the stairway.

And then I heard it. The front door closed and two pairs of footsteps crossed the bare wood floor. Two! The hack driver would have been sent away, which meant that the second set of footsteps could only be Poe's.

I rose slowly from my chair, careful that the legs did not squeak. Tiptoed to the stairway. Mounted the first step. Felt my knees weaken, heart begin to race. How was he going to react to the sight of me? How would he react to this duplicity?

I nodded to Buck. Now he rose too, made his way silently to the cellar exit and sneaked outside.

The voices upstairs became louder and clearer with every step I ascended. Poe—yes, Poe!—was asking why

Mr. Griswold had chosen to meet him here rather than in his cabin aboard the steamboat. Miss Jones feigned ignorance. She bid Poe sit, make himself comfortable. She would fetch the tea, she said. Mr. Griswold would be arriving any moment.

At the top of the stairs I paused. Strange how I felt at that moment. There were tears in my eyes, butterflies in my stomach. The man still meant a great deal to me, no matter how indifferent to his approval and trust I strove to appear.

I opened the door, peeked out into the kitchen. Miss Jones, setting cups and sugar bowl atop her wicker tray, glanced my way, then jerked her chin toward an adjoining room.

A couple of slow breaths, just to steady myself. How I detested my body when it weakened like that, going stiff and clumsy and hot with trepidation. In defiance of those reactions, I strode forward.

Poe was seated in Miss Jones's library, a small room lined on three sides with crowded bookshelves. Arranged in a circle in the center of the room were two padded armchairs, their seats and back cushions covered with hemlock green cloth, and eight straight-backed chairs. Poe was seated rigidly in an armchair, a hand on each knee as if to brace himself up, eyes turned away from me toward the bookcase on his right.

I stepped over the threshold. Softly I said, "Good morning."

His head turned slowly, mouth already crooked in a lopsided smile. He studied me for a moment. The only alteration of expression was in his eyes, which narrowed just slightly as he squinted to see me better. Ten seconds passed before he spoke. "Augie?" he said.

How dulled his senses were. How like a dream I must have seemed to him.

I came into the room, crossed to him, stood before him for a moment, then lowered myself into the armchair next to his (thinking even as I did so, *I wonder which of these was Susan's chair?*). He still regarded me with a quizzical look, but his eyes were void of the sparks of surprise.

"I apologize for not being Rufus Griswold," I told him. "I am very sorry for this deception."

He looked at me a moment longer. Blinked. And said, "Rufus should be arriving shortly."

It made me wonder how much of the past few days he was actually aware of. Did he remember visiting me in jail? Or understand that I was being hunted as a murderer?

The front door eased open then, a long slow squeak of hinges. Buck, I knew, was coming inside. He had been charged with the responsibility of preventing Mr. Poe's egress were he to make such an attempt. But there was small chance of that at the moment. Poe was subdued to the point of mesmerization. I marveled that he had been able to get this far.

"Do you know where you are?" I asked.

Again, a delay preceded his response. "I was told that Rufus is here."

"Yes. Does anyone else know that you have come here to meet Mr. Griswold?"

He thought about this for a moment, then answered, "The housekeeper."

"Mrs. Dalrymple?"

"Mrs. Dalrymple," he repeated.

"Does Dr. Brunrichter know?"

"Mrs. Dalrymple will inform him."

"Of course. And will she tell him where?"

He thought about this, closed his eyes, swayed softly in his chair, hands still clamped to his kneecaps. By now Miss Jones was standing in the doorway, holding her tea tray. Buck peered over her shoulder.

A few moments later Poe's body jerked and his eyes flew open, his right hand going to the armrest, gripping it tight. "Are we departing?" he asked.

I laid a hand on his arm. "Not just yet."

And now, close up, I could see the glazing of his eyes, could smell the peculiar odor of his breath, almost almondine. There was a laxness to the muscles of his face. His hand began to slip from the armrest.

"Are you feeling all right?" I asked.

And he told me, "Very tired, Augie. I am always so tired."

"Would you like to lie down for a while?"

"May I?" he asked.

I helped him to stand.

"This way," said Miss Jones. "Upstairs. He shall have my bed."

Along the way, as we climbed slowly to the second floor, he draped an arm around my shoulders. He leaned his head against me. "Augie," he said.

I said nothing. To be cast in this position again—the memory choked me with emotion. I remembered the other time I had led him, in just this manner, out of a Five Points groggery, where he had been drugged with opium. Afterward, the next day, he had labeled me his fidus Achates. I was ten at the time and assumed that "fidus" meant the same as Fido, that he was calling me his dog, his little puppy, and so desperate was I for affection that I secretly thrilled to the appellation. I rejoiced in it still. Yet wondered by what name, this time, he would call me in the morning.

"We should write to Muddy soon," he told me.

"Yes. We will."

"To tell her of our good fortune."

Again I did not speak. Halfway up the stairs he laid a hand on the wall, considered the ancient cherry paneling. "Whose house is this?" he asked.

"It belongs to Miss Jones."

"We are acquainted?"

"She is a great admirer of your work."

And he answered, "Aha!"

Side by side up the stairs to the second floor, Miss Jones leading the way, Buck following behind us, hands outstretched to prevent Poe from tumbling backward. At Miss Jones's bedroom Buck chose to remain outside the door, too embarrassed to even look inside a lady's boudoir.

Miss Jones and I sat Poe on the edge of her bed, removed his shoes, helped him to lie supine. Before I drew away, he clutched at my hand.

"What is it?" I asked.

"Sissie," he said.

"Yes?"

"Sissie is gone."

"I know," I told him.

"It took," he said, "such a very long time."

I nodded. What could I say? "She's out of it now."

At this, he smiled. He closed his eyes and let go my hand. "*Requiescat in pace*," he said.

And we left him to his peace.

Chapter Twenty-nine

Poe slept off and on throughout the day, just as I imagined he did in the doctor's home. He seemed a bit more alert each time he awoke, and from this I determined that whatever medicines he was given each morning were calculated to keep him placid during those hours when Dr. Brunrichter was not available as his companion.

"I think we'll see a change in him come evening," I told Buck and Miss Jones.

"And what do we do until then?" Buck asked.

I shrugged. "We play cards."

Buck rubbed a cheek with the flat of his hand. "No offense to you, Augie, but I wasn't built for all this sitting still we've been doing. I think I'd better go down to the docks and find some work to do."

"Keep an ear out for news of my escape."

"You can bet on that," he said.

And so I was left on my own in the basement. Miss Jones supplied me with a writing tablet and pencil, should an epistolary urge overtake me. From time to time throughout the long hours until evening, she brought me food and drink and a bit of news concerning Poe.

"He awoke asking for rum," she told me in the morning.

"And did you give it to him?"

"You will find no rum in this house, young man."

"I'm glad to hear it."

"I gave him a cup of chamomile tea. He seemed content enough with that instead."

At midday he called out for Mrs. Dalrymple, and when Miss Jones appeared at his bedside he took no notice that she was the physical antithesis of Brunrichter's housekeeper but only asked her, "Is it time for my medicine yet?"

She answered that it was and fed him a cup of chicken broth. His forehead, she told me, was beaded with perspiration. The movement of his eyes never rested, but his gaze seemed unable to focus well.

"He didn't protest?" I asked. "When you gave him the soup instead of his medicine?"

"I believe he contemplated doing so. Until I informed him in no uncertain terms that I was his nurse from now on and he would do as he was told."

And of course he would. Just as he had always acquiesced to Muddy and never raised his voice to her. In the presence of any woman he would behave with great civility, even docility. He treated them all as the gentlest and most precious of creatures, even when there was little gentleness apparent.

"Take that broom from the corner and sweep," she told me after clearing away my own soup bowl and mug.

"Sweep what? The floor itself is dirt."

"Sweep down the ceiling beams. There's likely a spider or two up there."

"I've got nothing against spiders," I told her.

"I will not tolerate sloth, young man. You can sweep or you can find another place to pass your time."

"Speaking of time, what day is this?"

"It is the first of April."

"April Fool's Day?"

She gave me a look that, had I not turned sideways to her, might have burned a hole clean through me. "There will be no pagans in this house, Mr. Dubbins. You may practice your sacrilege elsewhere."

"I'm not a pagan, Miss Jones. Please resume breathing."

"Are you an atheist?" she demanded.

That one gave me pause. But finally, when it seemed her eyes could glare no longer without bursting into flames, her nostrils flare no wider without splitting her nose apart, I responded with what she needed (though a part of me must surely have been hoping to rile her even more). "Anglican," I answered.

She blinked once. "I do not hold with the papists," she said.

"Protestant Anglican."

She cocked her head at this, swiveling her pointed chin upward by thirty degrees or so and glaring at me cockeyed. Her resemblance to a heron, poised to stab its beak into the water, was remarkable. "I am unfamiliar with the Protestant Anglicans," she said.

"It's a Midwest movement. Reform. Highly progressive."

"And what are the tenets of this faith?"

"Only one. Salvation through denial."

"Denial of what, might I ask?"

"Of all things," I said.

"All? How can one deny all things and yet retain a faith?"

"It is very difficult," I said.

"I fail to see the logic in it."

"It is an extension of your own belief, Miss Jones, that all things are possible through God. For if one accepts the possibility of all things, one must necessarily accept the possibility of nothing, because nothingness is a part of the All. In fact it is the primal part. So, by denial of all things, we are paying reverence to the original Nothing, which was, in its initial and unified form, the Everything."

She laid a hand to the side of her face, as if to keep herself from swooning. "The day after tomorrow is Good Friday," she said. "How will you observe it?"

"With the ultimate discipline, of course. By denying that it exists."

Fifteen seconds later she nodded slightly. "I would like very much to discuss this with you further."

"Unfortunately, the act of discussing the subject negates the denial of that subject. I've already lapsed in my discipline by telling you as much as I have."

"It is a very strange faith you practice, Mr. Dubbins."

"Impossibly rigorous," I said.

"Are its roots in the religions of the East, perhaps?"

"There are no roots."

This puzzled her for only a moment. "Of course. I see. You are compelled to deny even the origins of your religion."

"What religion?"

"Enough!" she said, and turned on her heels and, still shaking her head, went stiffly up the stairs, leaving me to my basement, my broom, and my spiders in the ceiling beams, their webs too small to see.

When I was with Susan and lived every moment with the possibility of Susan I had been aware of something building inside me, something new that at its peak might well have changed me again just as Poe's unexpected friendship had once changed me. That possibility was gone now, irrevocably gone, but as I whisked invisible cobwebs from dark corners, feeling myself enshrouded in a less observable darkness—though perhaps I should not say enshrouded but filled, for this particular darkness lay well beneath the skin—I was forced to acknowledge that there is something about love that turns it into a focal point, turns it into the brightest of lights in the center of a large room, illuminating all those objects you had never before noticed and giving each of them an individual relevance.

With Susan I might easily have accepted the notion of a divine beneficence because with her light filling all my dark corners I would have seen beauty and relevance wherever I looked. Some people, who through their lack of luck or their own hard nature cannot find an earthly love, find a divine one nonetheless, perhaps as a substitute, or because it is the only one available to them. But that was Miss Jones's kind of love and although I liked her very much despite her sternness and old maid's brittle ways I was not constructed to love as she loved.

These, in any case, were my thoughts as I swept clean a room in no need of sweeping. Afterward I stoked the fire in the furnace, and then, with a head full of thoughts, sat at the small table for a while. I, like Buck, was not used to inactivity either, and I did not know what to do with my hands. I could build a house of cards and watch it fall down time after time, or I could employ the paper Miss Jones had provided.

Here is what I wrote, my manifesto of aloneness:

Premise:

It is an observable and well-documented fact that the human condition is now and always has been marked by an abundance of physical and emotional pain, with sorrow, misery, and cruelty. Therefore, as to the role of Divine influence on the human condition, one of the following must apply:

1. There is a God who is powerful enough to alleviate all pain, sorrow, misery, and cruelty from the human condition, but
    a. He is unaware of the human condition. Or,
    b. He is aware of but indifferent to the human condition. Or,
    c. He is concerned with the human condition but is too busy elsewhere to lend assistance. Or,
    d. He is aware of but entertained by the human condition. Or,
    e. He is aware of but has decided not to interfere in the human condition, because
        1. humans are irrelevant to the Divine Plan. Or,
        2. human pain, sorrow, misery and cruelty are a requisite of the Divine Plan. Or,
    f. His efforts to improve the human condition are routinely subverted by a power of equal or greater but opposite intent. Or,
2. There is a God, but, even in the absence of a power of opposite intent, he lacks sufficient power himself to counteract the forces of human nature. Or,
3. There is no God.

Conclusion:

The human condition is not likely to be improved through Divine intervention.

Early evening brought another kettle of soup from Miss Jones, this time a thick concoction of leeks and potatoes, ham and carrots. The first spoonful made me want to believe there is a God after all. How else to explain how a woman so parsimonious of laughter could produce such happiness for the tongue?

"You're an excellent cook," I told her.

She said, "If I decide to take on a task, I make certain to do it well."

I attempted then to engage her in conversation about her past; I thought she might be as hungry for companionship as I. "What did you do before you came to Pittsburgh, Miss Jones? Have you always been a teacher?"

"One is never always one thing or another," she answered. With that she stepped back against the staircase and stood there with arms crossed over her bosom until I had scraped my bowl clean. She then came forward to retrieve the bowl and spoon.

"I need to go outside again," I told her.

"You may use the chamber pot upstairs."

"I won't do that," I said.

"There are as many as ten children a day inside this building, Mr. Dubbins. Yours would not be the first pot I've emptied."

"All the same, I would prefer to take my chances on a dash to the privy."

"You cannot wait till nightfall?"

"I cannot wait another five minutes."

So she fetched down her longest overcoat and widest bonnet. Then I, properly costumed, did a lively spinster's stroll out to the privy. Afterward I was so reluctant to return to the dank enclosed spaces of the basement that I lingered awhile at the hand pump. I washed my face and hands and filled my belly nearly to bursting with cold water.

Then came a moment when, looking up into the lavender light, an unexpected stillness came over me, and I thought how beautiful the sky appeared at this time of evening, how lovely the budding trees, and I sensed something of the promise of another spring. But it was a short-lived contentment, ten seconds at the most, for just as suddenly I thought of Susan, and all the images I wanted to suppress sprang full and vivid inside my head.

And then, perhaps because the light was fading, perhaps because I had given up on God, perhaps because I saw myself as a ridiculous scarecrow of a figure in old maid's clothing, or perhaps none of that but just because Susan was gone, a terrible nausea overtook me there at the pump, a sudden and violent nausea that kept me doubled over and heaving for another three minutes.

Stomach emptied, soul turned inside out, I felt no less sickened. I pumped water splashing onto the ground until long after Miss Jones's fine soup had been washed away. Then doused my face and hands and mouth again. Then, weakly now, clinging to the cold metal, aching in every joint, I heard the nausea speak.

You never even kissed her, it whispered. *And now you never will.*

I thought of walking away from there, of flicking off the bonnet and shucking the coat and strolling off to whatever fate awaited me. If no one laid a hand on me before I reached the river, I would walk into the water. And why not? What did the continued beating of my heart avail?

Only one thought gave me strength enough to return to that basement. It was a black thought, yes, and blood-soaked. But it steeled me for another day of living.

Poe was sitting on the basement stairs when I returned from the yard, sitting four steps from the bottom, elbows on his knees, his face in his hands. I knew him by the posture only, for the oil lamp had not yet been lit and he was little more than silhouette, a shadow hunched over with one of Miss Jones's afghan shawls draped around his thin shoulders.

He lifted his head when I latched the door behind me, but he did not speak. So I crossed to him and stood waiting at the foot of the stairs. He was shoeless and wore no collar.

He looked at me for a while, chin in his hands now, one finger poised between his lips. Then he said, "I had forgotten how tall you've grown."

His voice was weak and his eyes were weak and he lacked the strength to sit erect. The finger trembled against his mouth. "Can you tell me what I am doing here?" he asked, and smiled his crooked smile at me, the sheepish smile that said he blamed himself for his current situation, whatever it was.

"How much do you remember?" I asked.

"A great deal. Unfortunately, no one memory is connected to another. My mind is a jumble of broken pieces."

"It will pass," I told him. "With rest and good food, you'll soon be straightened out again."

He nodded. "That woman upstairs . . ."

"Miss Jones. It is her hospitality you now enjoy."

"I had the impression, awhile back, that she was Muddy."

"It's been awhile since you've seen Mrs. Clemm. A month at least."

"And how long, precisely, have I been in this place?"

"You came this morning."

"It seems much longer."

"Do you remember why you came?" I asked.

He told me he had a recollection of sorts but that he placed no faith in it, and asked instead that I explain not only the why but the where and what-for of our current situation.

"Do you remember coming to see me in the jail?" I asked.

"I had thought that a dream."

And so I reminded him of my incarceration. I recounted the events that followed his reading at the Old Drury, my confrontation with Brunrichter, Buck's discovery of his daughter's body, my arrest the next morning, and my subsequent escape. He eyed me steadily throughout, sometimes turning his head slightly this way or that. He was drawing energy, I think, from my candor, my obvious need for his assistance. He appeared to sit a bit straighter as I spoke, and placed both hands atop his knees so as to straighten his spine.

"Forgive my trickery," I said, "but it was necessary to bring you here."

"Apparently I was eager to be duped. Besides, your circumstances warranted a bit of subterfuge."

"And yours," I said.

He raised his eyebrows.

"Consider the way you feel at this moment," I explained.

"Do you know how I feel?"

"I can only speculate."

"Please do so."

"As if you are just now awakening from a week-long fever dream."

Again he smiled. "A fair enough appraisal."

"You have been drinking a great deal," I told him. "Principally in the evenings. With Dr. Brunrichter. By all accounts you sleep through most of the day. Because, I assume, of the medications the doctor has prescribed to alleviate your condition."

"My condition?" said Poe.

"He told me, on the night of your reception, when I objected to the state I found you in, that he has been treating you for melancholia and brain fatigue. Were you not aware of being given medication?"

He thought for a moment. "Awhile back—and forgive me, the days are a blur—a while back, it was at breakfast, as I recall . . . Yes, I rose early, as I usually do, and at Alfred's invitation I joined him at the table. Mrs. Dalrymple served me a cup of tea that was particularly aromatic. But, seeing that Alfred was having coffee, I asked for that instead. Alfred commented that I was in all likelihood allergic to coffee, hence my nervousness. 'The tea will soothe you,' he said. 'It's a special herbal blend.' "

"I believe I sampled it once myself. It was made with Indian herbs, he said."

Poe nodded. "I have had a cup every morning. Even this morning . . . yes, it was this morning, wasn't it? I was at my breakfast, sipping my tea, when the hackney driver arrived with the message from Rufus. Or rather," he said, "from you."

I kept silent, not wishing to force any thoughts upon him.

"Alfred could not have known," he said, "how strongly the concoction affected me."

I said nothing.

He raised his eyebrows. "You surely don't mean to suggest," he said, "that he intended to debilitate me?"

"I mean to suggest nothing."

"He is concerned only about my health and vitality."

"His concerns strike me as overly keen."

"In what way?"

"I am drawing no conclusions from this," I told him, "but allow me to state a few facts. Dr. Brunrichter has, from the very beginning, been envious of our companionship."

"That is not a fact," said Poe.

"Consider it. And you will see that it carries the weight of fact."

He answered with a half shrug, a palm raised weakly, but too weakly to wave the notion away.

"Second, he has allowed and perhaps even encouraged you to drink with him every night. I have seldom seen you two together when you were not sharing a carafe of wine or enjoying a cognac."

"In moderation, it is good for the blood."

"It is not good for your blood," I said. "And he is well aware of your sensitivity to alcohol. You spoke of it your first night there. And I have made it clear to him as well."

"And when you did," asked Poe, curious now, "what was the doctor's reply?"

"That he was your doctor and knew what was best for you."

"He referred to himself as my doctor?"

"Which brings me to my third point. When did it become your habit to sleep through every morning?"

"I rise before seven, as I have always done."

"Yet while in the doctor's house you return to bed soon after breakfast. How do you account for that?"

"You are getting excited," he said.

"I am getting angry, as I believe you will too. Consider this. Brunrichter has begun to dress like you, has he not? To wear his hair as you wear yours?"

"We share a certain . . . physiognomy."

"Which he accentuates at every turn. Consider his initial letter to you—what was the phrase he used? That you and he are closer than brothers? The same man in two bodies? He has orchestrated your every move since you came here, even to your virtual immobilization when he is engaged elsewhere!"

Again Poe's posture sagged. He rubbed a hand over his eyes, then against his cheek. Several minutes passed before he spoke.

"I find that I can neither agree nor disagree with your observations," he said. "Perhaps when my head is clearer . . ."

I went to the table and pulled out a chair. Lowered myself onto it. Drew the oil lamp closer. Then picked up a lucifer. But I did not strike the match. I could feel Poe's eyes on me still, and for that reason I chose not to interrupt the darkness.

"If in the end you are proven correct," Poe finally said, "even so . . . how does this relate to your dilemma?"

"In as much as it points to the doctor's eagerness to be rid of me," I said. "He is so eager, in fact, that he was willing to lie when questioned by the police. And by lying, to see me convicted of murder."

The final word caused him to jerk his head up an inch or so. "Your Susan," he said. "I had forgotten, I . . . I am so sorry, Augie. So sorry."

"You know I had nothing to do with it."

"I know you well enough to be certain of that. And if the girl's father himself can put his faith in you . . . But how do we remedy this injustice?"

"When the hack arrived for you this morning, was Dr. Brunrichter about?"

"No. None in the house but for Mrs. Dalrymple."

"Not Tevis?"

"I saw no sign of him."

"And so you told only Mrs. Dalrymple the reason for your departure?"

"It was she who delivered the note to me. So yes, she knows."

"And has no doubt shared the information with Dr. Brunrichter by now. He will be expecting your return at any time. But if you do not return—"

"Why would I not return?"

Something flopped in my stomach, a heavy twist of sourness.

Poe said, "I will inform him that the medications are no longer necessary. And I will convince him of your innocence. I will insist that he retract his earlier assertions."

I sat there shaking my head. An anger was welling up in me again; not toward Poe, nor even Brunrichter, but toward the situation itself, the convoluted mess of it, the malevolence that would allow a young man's love to be subverted by a pustulation of jealousies, deceit, bitterness, and fear.

Poe was the first to speak. "What would you have me do, Augie?"

"Help me," I said.

"That is precisely what I mean to do."

"Then you cannot go back. You must not."

"He will wonder—"

"Miss Jones can send another note. As Rufus. No, you can send a note. In your own hand. Explaining that you have joined Mr. Griswold for a few days, but that you will return thereafter."

"And what do we gain by this subterfuge?"

"We gain . . . an opportunity to work together, as we did in New York. Buck and Miss Jones and I will gather the pertinent facts, and to these you will apply the ratiocination. If only for Susan," I pleaded. "I understand that it might be difficult for you, because you met her only briefly—"

"I know her through you," he said.

I nodded, but said nothing more. My throat was choked, my eyes too warm.

Finally he said, "Miss Jones mentioned something awhile back about the availability of soup."

"Potatoes and leeks. It's very good."

"You've eaten?"

"I have."

"Perhaps she would allow me to take a bowl to my room."

"I am certain she would."

He sat there a few moments longer, then put a hand to the wall and pulled himself to his feet. "Is there more we should discuss this evening?" he asked.

"It can wait," I told him.

"My head will be clearer in the morning."

He turned and slowly mounted the steps. Near the top he paused. I could see only the lower half of his body. He came back down a step, but not enough to bring his face into view.

"I wish to apologize," he said, and spoke haltingly, choosing his words, "if in some way my negligence has brought all this upon you."

I wanted to tell him that not for a moment did I hold him responsible. I wanted to tell him that his presence and his trust in me were as much amelioration as I ever hoped to receive. I wanted to tell him this but my chest ached and my eyes stung and I could not speak.

He went softly up the stairs and gently closed the door.

I had also wanted to tell him that I blamed myself, not him nor anyone else, for bringing catastrophe upon us. I had done so not through negligence but ardor. It was I who had brought Poe to Pittsburgh and into this imbroglio. It was I who, by loving Susan, had delivered her into the hands of a murderer.

I wanted to tell Poe my own worst fears, that if an order exists in this world it is of a kind that turns good intentions to disaster and steers all things toward annihilation; and, last, that I, in the blackest and bleakest heart of myself, so longed for annihilation that I would probably drag him in with me.

Chapter Thirty

The evening grew long and Buck did not return. I sat and then stood, I paced and then lay down. I played with the deck of cards. I ruined several sheets of Miss Jones's stationery by trying to sketch a likeness of Susan's face, only to end by scratching out my feeble lines.

Where in the world was Buck Kemmer?

At perhaps three hours after sunset I crept to the top of the stairs and eased open the door. The kitchen was empty. Into the hallway then, where I followed the lure of light to a nearby room. Miss Jones was seated, prim and rigid even in her solitude, reading by the light of an oil lamp, a pair of spectacles perched near the tip of her nose.

I tapped lightly on the door frame, and she looked up from her book. "Excuse my interruption," I said.

She waited for more.

"Have you heard from Mr. Kemmer lately?"

"Not a word," she said, and closed the book, marking the page with her finger. "Are you concerned?"

"I am."

"As am I."

"I was thinking I should maybe go looking for him."

Again she was silent. I imagined she was forming an argument in opposition to my proposal, so I sought to change the subject. "What is it you're reading?"

"*Twice-Told Tales*, by Hawthorne. Mr. Poe recommended it to me. I was lucky enough to find a copy this afternoon at the stationer's."

"You will enjoy it," I said.

She pursed her lips before speaking. "So much darkness and brooding."

"A good book all the same."

"I was referring to your temperament, Mr. Dubbins. Yours and Mr. Poe's. How do you manage to live in the midst of so much darkness?"

"It wasn't of my making," I told her.

"Are you sure of that?"

I had not gone there to argue, and so said nothing. The truth was clear to me, and that was sufficient. "I won't be out long," I told her, and turned away.

"Where do you propose to look?"

"At his home, I suppose. Then, the waterfront. There's also a public place he goes to on occasion. I'll look there as well."

"You must not show yourself in public."

"I know," I said.

We did not speak then, yet she held me in place with her gaze. I cannot describe it as stern or critical but it was a hard gaze all the same, penetrating, or at least attempting to penetrate, to peer into me in a way I could not myself.

Finally I asked, "Is there anything else?"

"The church on High Street," she said.

"I beg your pardon?"

"I would look there first, were I you."

And that was where I found him, a long shadow in gauzy moonlight, motionless on his belly in a corner of the small enclosed space to the side of the church. Susan's grave had no headstone, only a small cross of white marble, donated by parishioners. Buck lay on the grass between her grave and the next, her mother's, one arm extended in each direction. At the head of each grave he had placed a few Easter lilies. Their small, drooping flowers looked gray in the moonlight.

I backed away before he could notice me. If he was sleeping, let him sleep. If awake, even more reason not to disturb him.

I walked a long time that evening, glad to be free of the basement for a change, but feeling confined nonetheless. I walked well up the Monongahela waterfront, keeping to unlighted Bluff Street, walked angrily and briskly until I finally had to admit to myself that the walking did no good, it took me nowhere I needed to go. So I went to the river's edge and stared at the water for a while, a wide black moving thing, undulating like a serpent.

It is believed by some that the serpent is an agent of wisdom, of secret knowledge from underground. When the serpent tempted Eve, for example, he tempted her with wisdom, the knowledge of good and evil. But I already knew all I wished to know of evil. I knew too much.

And so I lifted my eyes to the heavens instead. But nothing moved in the night sky, no sign of life whatsoever, no hiss of promise, not even the slithering sibilance of the river. In the end there were no answers at all, no explanations, no apologies no matter which direction I looked.

I sank to my haunches only inches from the water's edge. Picked up a water-smoothed stone. Hurled it into the water, close to my feet, accompanied by a muttered curse. Again I did this, and again, heaving each stone so close to where I sat that its impact splashed muddy water back into my face. I wished I could embrace the earth as Buck was doing, and find some peace in that gesture. But I could not. And because I could not reach the sky with either stones or obscenities I pummeled the river instead, and soaked myself with muddy tears.

A hand on my shoulder, nudging me awake.

Typically in those days I awoke quickly, fully and suddenly alert, but that morning I was a long time coming up and out of the darkness. I was asleep but could feel some external force pushing against my shoulder. Then, still asleep, I recognized it as a hand jostling me. Then, as I worked my consciousness toward that hand, wading toward it as if through deep mud, I recognized that the hand was outside of my sleep and I literally had to will myself toward wakefulness, climbing up through dark layers of an unremembered dream.

I opened my eyes to find Poe on his knees beside my pallet, watching my face. There was some light in the room, enough that I could read his expression, a crooked smile of anticipation. I blinked several times, feeling still disembodied, a part of me struggling to catch up with the rest. All I could think to ask was, "Is it morning?"

"It will be soon," said Poe.

I rubbed a hand across my face, and finally sat upright. Poe said, "There's tea upstairs. Come join us."

He stood and moved away from me then, and a few moments later I heard the stairs creaking with his ascent. I sat there trying to clear the fog from my head. Reached for my boots and put them on. Stood, looked about, remembered where I was and why. Then, by the light of the lamp on the table, its flame turned low, I made my way outside for a quick trip to the privy. The chill air helped to revive me, as did the acrid tang of smoke in the air. The morning was still gray, no blush of sun along the horizon.

By the time I returned inside and up the stairs to the kitchen, my disorientation lingered only as a kind of dullness clumped in the back of my head.

Poe, Buck, and Miss Jones were all seated at the kitchen table, all looking very somber in the lamplight. Spread out across the table were the tiny pieces of seashell Buck had gathered at Brunrichter's mausoleum. As I pulled out a chair, Poe reached for the teapot and poured a cup and slid it toward me.

I asked, "How long has everyone been awake?"

Poe was the only one to answer. "I have been reminded of the hazard of a clear head. It will not rest."

I loaded my tea with sugar, then nodded toward the scattering of shell pieces. "What do you make of these?"

"Quite a lot," Poe said. He then turned to Miss Jones. "Have you a writing instrument I might borrow? And a sheet of your stationery?"

She rose from her chair. "I have some lovely new Thoreau pencils. I'll put a point on one for you."

Poe muttered to himself as she left the room. If Buck heard the grumbled curse—"the damn Frogpondian euphuist"—it surely meant nothing to him, yet he made no inquiry. Only I knew how strenuously Poe despised the Transcendentalist and how much it would irk him to employ a pencil manufactured in the Thoreau factory.

Soon Miss Jones returned and laid a sheet of paper beside Poe's teacup, and atop the paper the long, square-sided pencil of unpainted red cedar. "The hardest and blackest graphite in America," she said.

Poe, to his credit, only grunted. He rubbed thumb and forefinger together, then, probably recoiling inwardly at the touch, picked up the pencil and began to write.

"Here is what we know," he told me, haltingly, as he wrote. "A tiny piece of shell, found in the home of Mr. Kemmer. The shell, judging by the pearly septa you can see here, is the type inhabited by the cephalopod of the genus *Argonauta*, found only in ocean water."

I sat back in my chair. Poe, expecting such a reaction, explained, "I once contributed to a book on the subject of shells and their inhabitants. For use in the schools."

"That's one I didn't know about."

"You and many others," he said. "Howsoever. When we consider the shell's nonindigenous relationship with the area, plus that it matches perfectly these numerous other shells taken from Dr. Brunrichter's estate, we can assume, logically, that the shell found by Mr. Kemmer and the shells from the mausoleum share a common origin."

"Which doesn't in itself prove anything," I said.

"Correct. But consider this as well. Also discovered in Mr. Kemmer's home was a small black feather—given to you by me, as I recall—which you had placed inside the book I inscribed to Miss Kemmer. The book itself has not been found.

"Again, a fact that alone tells us little. But, when considered in the light of other observations, including yours, Augie, related to me last night, perhaps they speak more clearly."

"You mean the things I said about Brunrichter?"

He nodded. "The past few days are the haziest in my memory, but the events of our initial days in Pittsburgh remain fairly clear. I recall, for example, our picnic. I recall Dr. Brunrichter's discussion concerning his experiments, the obvious delight he took in explaining that his research was conducted on wild rabbits, which, when snared, will cry out, he said, sounding much like a human baby."

He paused for a sip of tea. As if by signal, we all drank. And by that I knew that Poe was once again in charge.

"He and I continued the discussion that same night, and other nights as well," Poe said. "We talked of his theory regarding the reanimation of the brain through electrical stimulation. He seemed to consider Shelley's morbid tale less a fiction than a primer.

"And do you recall meeting a Mr. Gatesford at the picnic?" Poe asked.

"The elderly gentleman," I said.

"More important, the one who has consented to be the doctor's first human subject, upon the man's mortal demise, of course."

"Just like in *The Facts in the Case of M. Valdemar*."

"I regret to say that the doctor claims my story as the source of his inspiration."

"He's obsessed with you."

Poe nodded, but mournfully. "He confided in me that he considers me a scientist in the guise of a writer, my stories the theories upon which much of his research is applied. In which case, if your suspicions prove correct, Augie, then I must bear the ultimate responsibility for his actions."

After a moment's silence, Buck put out a hand, laid

his huge callused palm atop Poe's, and patted it tenderly. Absolution.

Poe continued, his throat a bit hoarser. "Next we come to the hanging at Mount Airy. You remember it, of course."

"Vividly," I said.

"Did you know," he asked, "that Dr. Brunrichter was the individual responsible for plotting the table to determine the height of the man's fall?"

"I believe he told us that."

"Does it surprise you that a man so meticulous in his observance of details would make such a gross miscalculation?"

"You think he did it on purpose."

"I recall how avidly he dragged me to the body afterward. How excited he was when he bade me press my ear to the man's chest to hear a heart still beating."

"It seemed to me a cold thing to do."

"Cold indeed," said Poe.

He busied himself then with his writing. Afterward he looked up at me. "How many household servants does Dr. Brunrichter employ?"

"Mrs. Dalrymple and Mr. Tevis."

"And they live at the estate?"

"Mr. Tevis does."

Poe nodded. "On what day of the week is Mrs. Dalrymple given a rest from her duties?"

"Let me think a minute."

"On Saturday," he said. "She leaves the house after supper on Friday and resumes her duties first thing Sunday morning, preparing breakfast before she and Tevis and the doctor attend their worship services."

"I didn't know that."

"And do you know on what day of the week each of the seven missing women have disappeared?"

I did not know, but said nothing, and sat and waited.

"On Friday evening!" cried Miss Jones. "Every one of them disappeared on a Friday night!"

From the look she now exchanged with Poe, the nod he gave her, it was clear that this information had been pieced together earlier, at Poe's request, by Miss Jones herself.

"But not Susan," I told them. "It was a Saturday night for Susan."

"Nor has Susan disappeared," said Poe. "Her body was not removed."

"So are the two things related or not?"

"Logically, the two cases are so dissimilar as to bear no relationship to one another. Howsoever . . . Let us consider a previous fact. The disappearances all took place on a Friday evening. Mrs. Dalrymple is absent from the mansion from earlier the same evening until nearly a day and a half later. Does this suggest anything to you?"

"He wanted the house empty when he brought the women there."

"Now consider this: The doctor's animosity toward you, which I am now prepared to accept as real. His infatuation, shall we call it, with my works and my physical appearance. His lies to the police concerning your behavior on the night of Susan's death. What, if anything, does all this suggest?"

"He killed her because he wanted rid of me."

"I vaguely remember his reaction when we learned of your escape. Even in my near-somnambulistic state, I was secretly gladdened by the news. But he. He ordered every door and window in the house bolted shut. He went so far as to arm himself with a pistol."

I seethed, but said nothing.

"His mood was much improved when, not long after, we heard that you had stolen a boat and made good your escape from Pittsburgh."

Buck said, "That boat wasn't stolen. I paid good money for it."

"I misspoke," said Poe. "My apologies."

Buck gave his head a crisp nod.

"As to Dr. Brunrichter, however. He was beside himself with relief. 'The coward!' he cried. 'The coward runs from me!' When I asked him, 'From you, Alfred?' he answered, 'From the truth, of course. From the fate he so rightfully deserves.' "

"He wanted me jailed. And hanged for murder."

Nobody moved or so much as nodded. I could not bring myself to look at Buck except out the corner of my eye. He was sitting there now with head bowed, the tears falling unrestrained onto the tabletop, between two fists clenched harder than marble. His daughter had died only because her death provided a convenient opportunity for Brunrichter to remove me from his life.

Poe said, "Two different crimes with two different motives. But related, perhaps, by the proclivities of one individual."

Miss Jones said, "A problem arises. Each of the people with whom I spoke assured me that Dr. Brunrichter never left the house on the evening of Susan's death."

Poe said, "We know that Mrs. Dalrymple was never about the house on a Saturday. The same does not hold true, however, for Mr. Tevis."

"You're sure of this?" I asked.

"I am indeed. On the Saturday before the picnic, for example, my morning tea was brought to my room by Mr. Tevis. When I inquired after Mrs. Dalrymple's health, Tevis answered that she'd spent Saturdays at her own home. 'She,' he said. Not 'we.'

"And this is also of interest. On the Saturday following the most recent disappearance, the doctor spoke with me briefly that morning, but only to apologize that he would not be able to keep me company throughout the day, for Saturday was his reading day, as he called it, devoted to those journals that would keep him abreast of the latest medical and scientific advances."

"Reading, my foot," said Miss Jones. It was as close to a profanity as she was likely to mutter.

"So it was that fella Tevis then," Buck said. "Doing what Brunrichter told him to do."

"But wait," said Miss Jones. "I was told that Mr. Tevis was stationed outside the library all through the night in question."

Poe said, "No doubt the doctor loudly issued that order. But can any of the evening's celebrants say with certainty that Tevis did not then sneak away from his post, as he had secretly been instructed to do?"

And the rage ballooned inside me again, just as, I'm sure, it was swelling in Susan's father. "What now?" I asked. "What do we do about it?"

Poe said, "I return to the mansion."

My jaw dropped.

"Only briefly," he explained. "To gather up my things. And to look, if the opportunity presents itself, for the book I inscribed to Susan. To find that book would be evidence conclusive."

"You know he has it," I said. "He knew I took it from

your room. And Tevis would know how obsessed Brunrichter is with you, and would have grabbed it for him."

"The logic of this particular is weak," said Poe. "I could have inscribed a hundred copies to the doctor personally. Why would he risk discovery of the book by having it stolen? Or by accepting and retaining it even if he did not instruct that it be stolen?"

But I was working on a logic of my own. "The mind of a madman," I said.

"Sadly," said Poe, "that is what makes it impossible to fathom."

Miss Jones told him, "You have been doing a fine job so far."

And Poe answered, "It is hardly a virtue, Miss Jones, to know too much of the way a madman thinks."

Soon after, Poe was on his way to Ridge Avenue. As he told us later, he hid himself in the bushes beyond Brunrichter's front gate and there waited until the doctor came down the lane in his phaeton and set off for the hospital. Poe then crossed briskly to the house and entered through the front hall without knocking. He found Mrs. Dalrymple in the kitchen, cleaning up after the doctor's breakfast. She was startled by his unannounced arrival.

"Mr. Poe! Well my goodness gracious—where have you been all night?"

"My apologies," he said. "The meeting with my friend lasted much longer than either of us expected. It did not seem fitting to return at so late an hour."

"Have you had your breakfast?" she asked.

"Not one so good as yours, but yes, thank you, I have eaten."

"I should send word to Dr. Brunrichter that you've returned. He went off to his duties just a few minutes ago. I'm surprised you didn't pass him on the street."

"Yes, how unfortunate," said Poe.

"He told me that he paced half the night waiting for you to come home."

"My regret is inexpressible."

"In any case you're back again, none the worse for wear as far as I can see."

"Unfortunately I cannot stay. My friend Mr. Griswold and I have not yet concluded our business."

"I thought he was leaving at noon yesterday."

"That was his intention, yes. But, as I said, our business is not yet concluded and he has decided to stay over. But he must leave today, and very soon. I have agreed to accompany him part of the way, and then, in Cincinnati perhaps, I will disembark and return."

"We can expect you back tomorrow?"

"Let us say, instead, on Saturday. Though I would not be surprised to be gone until the day after."

"On Saturday or Easter Sunday then. I'll be sure to let the doctor know."

"Easter already! How quickly the days have gone by."

"I must say that you're looking fitter than ever I've seen you," said Mrs. Dalrymple. "You've got some color in your cheeks."

"I am feeling much better, thank you."

"It did you good to see your friend."

"It did indeed. And now, if you don't mind, I will fetch my bag and be off again."

"You go right ahead. Are you sure you wouldn't like some breakfast first?"

"I regret that I cannot spare the time."

"A cup of tea? The doctor left your powders should you return."

"Today," said Poe, "I am going to do without my medicine."

He went to his room and quickly stuffed all his belongings into his bag. Then, after making sure that the way was clear, he stole into the doctor's room and raked his eyes over the hundred or so books shelved against the wall. There was no sign of the one he had inscribed to Susan.

He had only begun to ransack the dresser drawers when Mrs. Dalrymple came thudding up the stairs, crying out, "Mr. Poe! Oh Mr. Poe!"

He froze at the sound of her voice, his hand poised beneath a pile of boiled shirts.

She paused near the top of the stairs to catch her breath. Then called to him, gasping every third word or so, "I've sent the boy from the stable to the hospital with your message. I'm sure the doctor will return at once if he can do so. He was so distressed by your absence when he went off this morning."

Poe withdrew his hand and eased the drawer shut. He crossed to the threshold and smiled at Mrs. Dalrymple. "I had planned to leave a note for Alfred on his nightstand. But you have saved me the trouble. Thank you."

She beamed. "You might as well have a bite of breakfast now. The doctor won't be long."

Poe responded with a deferential smile, he said, which sent Mrs. Dalrymple back down the stairs and waddling happily to her kitchen.

Poe did not dare linger. He returned for his bag, then to the kitchen where he made a quick apology, and all but raced out the door with Mrs. Dalrymple following behind, waving her hands and imploring him to reconsider.

Out the gate and finally out of Mrs. Dalrymple's view, Poe hurried back to Miss Jones's School for Young Ladies, staying well away from the most direct path between the hospital and the mansion. He came straightaway to Miss Jones's basement but found the room dark and empty. We heard him fumbling his way through the basement and up the stairs. A few moments later he emerged into the kitchen, thence to a small room off the main parlor, where Miss Jones and I were playing a game of cribbage.

"She's allowing you to stay upstairs now?" he asked.

I grinned. "Unable to resist my manly charms."

"Any more talk like that," said Miss Jones, "and you and your charms will march right back down into the cellar."

Chapter Thirty-one

A chill gray morning. I had begun to detest the weather of Pittsburgh, the adumbrating smoke that never allowed an unfiltered blue to shine through. To wake to the scent of smoke every morning, to inhale it in your sleep—such a fragrance does not fill the mind with thoughts of goodness and purity.

Because we had no specific plans for the day, Buck had gone off to find some work. I envied him the routine of labor, of bucking crates and kegs and barrels, channeling all of his restlessness out of the mind and into the muscles.

Poe assumed that Dr. Brunrichter might try to catch up with him on the docks, might go so far as to check the manifest of all steamboats scheduled to depart that morning. Poe, of course, had been deliberately vague in the information doled out to Mrs. Dalrymple, and was confident he had given the doctor no cause for alarm or suspicion. Still we thought it best to lay low for an hour or so, until Dr. Brunrichter, if he did go looking, had exhausted his hopes of deterring Poe and had returned to the hospital.

Shortly after Poe's return to Miss Jones's place, she excused herself to leave Poe and me alone. I fiddled with the cribbage board while he fiddled with his thoughts.

After a quarter hour of cerebration, he finally spoke. "A realization of some importance has occurred to me," he said. "Do you recall having ever witnessed Mr. Tevis at the mansion when the doctor himself was not present?"

I thought about it for a moment. "Brunrichter was always somewhere in the house," I said.

"But Tevis lives there, does he not?"

"So I was told."

"Surely he doesn't spend his day at the hospital with the doctor."

"I wouldn't think so."

"Yet Alfred drives himself each morning." He stroked his cheek. "I myself never once left the house unless accompanied by the doctor. If Mr. Tevis had been about during the day, I certainly would have noticed him."

"Remember, though, that you've been half asleep most of that time. Seems that whatever was put in your tea every morning it was meant to last till midafternoon or so."

"It dulled my senses, yes, and slowed all movements.

But it did not render me unconscious. At midday Mrs. Dalrymple would ring a bell to announce mealtime, and I would rise and dress and make my way downstairs."

"And afterward? Until the doctor came home?"

"The effects of the drug would gradually diminish."

"How did you spend your time while you waited for the doctor?"

He smiled sheepishly and shook his head in self-abnegation. "Sitting on the front veranda, staring into the distance like an opium fiend."

"Just the way he wanted you," I said.

"One thing I am certain of, however. Throughout the day, the house was empty but for Mrs. Dalrymple and myself. I would sometimes hear a man working in the yard, at the forge or stable—"

"That would be Mr. Keesling," I told him. "He and his boy manage the outbuildings."

"A boy, yes. I once watched the two of them rounding up the goats from the side yard." He paused then, having lost the train of his thought.

"You were saying something about the house being empty?"

"Yes! Yes, all day long there was no one in the house but for Mrs. Dalrymple and myself. Tevis would appear perhaps a quarter hour before the doctor's return each evening, always with a glass of claret in hand for me. An aperitif, he said. Which I, alas, never refused."

Again Poe shook his head. But I would not allow him to lapse into the despair of self-criticism. "Brunrichter enjoyed telling you about his research, did he?" I asked.

"It entered our conversations regularly."

"Where does he practice his research?"

"Where?" Poe repeated.

"Did you never ask?"

"My curiosity, if you recall, had been blunted. But I assumed, I suppose, that there were appropriate facilities at the hospital."

"Yet I remember his statement that, while at the hospital, his day was—what did he call it?—an uninspiring routine of setting broken bones, lancing boils, treating burns and cuts, and so forth. If the day was particularly exciting, he said, he might get to amputate a finger or two."

Poe was nodding slowly. "He spoke of his work and his research as if they were separate endeavors. Unrelated."

"But you know of no facilities for research in the mansion?"

"I never felt compelled to investigate."

We contemplated this information in silence. But I, unlike Poe, think more clearly when my thoughts are allowed to unravel through audible speech. "So what does this mean?" I finally asked.

"It is a clear case of something or other," said Poe with his lopsided smile.

"If Brunrichter doesn't conduct his research at the hospital or at the mansion, he must do it somewhere else. Maybe that's where Tevis is all day."

"Alfred leaves the house at seven each morning," Poe said. "He returns shortly after five each evening. Which leads me to wonder not only where but when he conducts his research?"

"His reading day," I said. "When Mrs. Dalrymple is not around."

Poe's head began to nod. "And on that day he remains in the mansion. Somewhere in the mansion. On the one day when Mrs. Dalrymple and all other servants are given the day off. All save Tevis."

"Do you think Mr. Keesling might be able to tell us anything? Or the Negro, Raymund?"

"Even if they could, neither of us can chance going there to ask."

I banged a fist on the table. "What damn good is it to be out of jail if I can't even move?"

"Patience," Poe said.

"For what?"

He continued to speak calmly. "We know that whenever Alfred is at the mansion, Tevis is as well. We know, too, that every morning after Alfred departs for the hospital, Tevis also disappears. Not to the hospital, or so we must assume. And tomorrow is Friday. Alfred will attend to his patients as usual. We can surmise that Tevis will be absent from the house for roughly the same hours. I propose that, come tomorrow morning, we attempt to follow Mr. Tevis to wherever it is he passes his days."

Finally, I thought, a plan of action. But it would not come soon enough for me. "And until then? What am I to do until then? Sit here and play cribbage with myself?"

"You and I, in a while, will avail ourselves of a deliciously long walk. Do you remember all the miles we enjoyed together in New York?"

"Every one of them," I said.

"We shall soon do so again."

"When?"

"The moment our friend arrives."

"Buck?" I asked.

"No, our other friend. The one we both have loved even before we knew one another."

He smiled when he saw my forehead furrowing. "Darkness," he said. "Our most reliant and dependable friend."

By midafternoon Buck had returned, unable to keep his mind off Susan any longer. Of all of us there at Miss Jones's house, Buck was having the worst time of it.

"The work don't seem to help no more," he told us. "There just ain't no reason to do it." The strain was evident in his once-robust face, the now baleful gaze. His hands sometimes trembled.

"After Susan's mama died, it was all I had for a while, the work. But I was working for Susan then, you see. The work had a reason to it."

"And now you must work for yourself," said Miss Jones.

Buck shook his head. "I was never the one that mattered. Never going to amount to more'n what I am. It was only because of Susan that the work meant anything at all."

Poe, who knew as much of grief and loss as any of us, stood behind Buck's chair and laid both hands upon the big man's shoulders.

"Used to be," Buck said, "a fella would bark at me down on the docks and I'd just laugh it off. Now a man can't even look my way without me wanting to smash a fist in his face. I came close to doing just that three times today. It's why I finally had to walk away. I show up tomorrow, don't know if I'll be allowed to work or not."

"Tomorrow there is other work to do," Poe said.

Buck answered, "There's only one kind of work I care about now."

"Precisely what I had in mind," said Poe.

I then told Buck and Miss Jones of our plan to follow Mr. Tevis next morning. We would need three men to keep watch over each of the mansion's exits.

"He better hope he don't come my way," Buck said.

"You mustn't interfere with him," said Poe.

"I can't promise I won't."

"You must promise. Or else you do Susan no good."

He bristled at first, his neck stiffening, but Poe's hands rubbed back and forth across Buck's shoulders, and in time Buck began to relax. He was eager for violence, that much was clear, especially to me, who understood the desire well. What both of us needed was to contain our violence until it could do the most good.

Miss Jones cleared her throat. "If you gentlemen will be going out later, you'll need your supper earlier tonight."

"Who's going out?" Buck asked.

Poe answered, "Augie and I are in need of some movement. We'll be taking a stroll after nightfall."

"Do you have room for another? It's not easy for me to sit still nowadays."

"Your company is always welcome," Poe told him.

I had thought that what Poe had in mind was an aimless perambulation, that we would walk until we wearied of walking, then turn back for a few hours of sleep in our beds. But it soon became obvious, not long after we set out that night, that he had a clear destination in mind. In fact, he had plotted our course with the help of Miss Jones, who, he admitted, had advised him on the least conspicuous route.

The moon was little more than a gauzy wafer in the black sky as Poe led the way up Pike Street and past the

Merchant Street Bridge. The city of Allegheny glittered across the river in a sprinkling of lamp and yellow candlelight. Glowing embers sometimes swirled up out of chimney stacks, only to blink out a few moments later.

"Miss Jones was inclined to think we would encounter no watchmen in this part of town," said Poe.

Buck said, "If there's any here, they'll be few and far between."

We walked on for several minutes. I was thinking how lovely it would have been to be taking this stroll with Susan, her hand in mine.

"We should've brought some dinner pails to carry," Buck said. "We'd of looked like three tired gobs coming home from the iron works."

"The best invisibility," said Poe, "is conspicuity."

Buck gave me an elbow then, and, when I turned, a quizzical look. I told him, "If we act like we're not trying to be sneaky, nobody will suspect that we are."

On Martin Street, at the rear end of the railroad depot; Poe had us turn away from the river and toward the center of the peninsula. It then became clearer where we were headed. I asked, "We have some business with the doctor tonight?"

Poe chuckled. "Not precisely, no. We shall be visiting his ancestors instead."

Another elbow jab from Buck. "The mausoleum," I explained.

Poe wanted only to look at the small building again, hoping to nudge his mind toward some more solid recognition. As if by agreement we stood to the side of the crypt, with the building between us and Brunrichter's mansion a quarter mile away.

"I was paying small attention when we walked here on the day of the picnic," Poe said.

And I told Buck, "That was the day I first met Susan."

Poe moved closer to the building then, onto the seashell border and then onto the narrow porch. He tried the door. It was locked.

"What is it you're hoping to find here?" I asked.

"In truth," he said, "I do not know."

He stood looking toward the house for a while. Two windows on the first floor were aglow with lamplight, and one window on the second floor.

"Maybe we should have a peek over that way," I suggested.

Poe shook his head. "Tomorrow will be soon enough."

"Not soon enough for me," Buck said.

In the end, no insights were forthcoming. We stood there shivering in the dark. Finally Poe said, "I should have liked to have met the young songwriter, Mr. Foster, were he in town. Sissie used to sing one of his melodies for me. Would you know which one it might have been, Augie? I can't recall the title."

I did not want to tell him that he was remembering incorrectly, that it was a Pittsburgh girl who had sung the song to him, and only days ago. Better to let the sweeter memory, though false, remain. I told him, "I believe it is called 'Open Thy Lattice, Love.' "

He nodded. And I was struck then by the fatalistic air of his earlier statement, and now heard in it Poe's certainty that he would never have the chance to call on Stephen Foster. In other words, he believed that tomorrow would bring an end to every trace of hospitality the city had heretofore accorded him.

Chapter Thirty-two

A morning as gray as three-month-old grief, as damp and chilled as fear. Poe wanted us in position outside Brunrichter's mansion before the sun rose, and so we had hiked briskly up through the fog, three silent men with hands shoved deep in their pockets, necks tucked and heads lowered. We passed a dozen or so working-men on their way downhill to the docks and small factories along the shore, sullen men off to another day of backbreaking labor. Buck made sure to stay at the rear of Poe and me as we walked abreast, his head close to our backs, his hat pulled low over his forehead lest he be recognized.

On the edge of somebody's yard a pig glowered at us. I thought it the same sow that had chased me once before, but there were three of us now, and she merely snorted. Somewhere down the hill a rooster crowed.

We thought it likely that Mr. Tevis would exit the estate through the front gate, so Poe positioned me there because I was the quickest. I hid twelve feet off the ground, stretched out in the branches of a sprawling black pin oak. Before sending me up into the tree Poe had said, "Alfred will come out in his phaeton a few minutes before seven. We should expect Mr. Tevis not long afterward. What we do not know is whether he will be afoot or astride a horse or in a carriage. So you must be prepared to move very quickly to ascertain his direction. But not at the expense of allowing yourself to be seen."

The night before, we had agreed upon a signal to each other, a whistle in imitation of the common wood pewee, two short whistles followed by a longer one upward lilting. We had practiced the signal in Miss Jones's basement until able to distinguish the individual calls. Buck's was deeper and more forceful than either mine or Poe's. Poe's was nothing if not melancholy.

And now, with me safely concealed in the tree, Poe crept away to take up his position in view of the side entrance. Buck went to the rear of the mansion where he could watch the stable and carriage house.

Perhaps twenty minutes passed, though it felt like twice as many. The sun shone pale and diaphanous through the rising fog. And then, the clap of a horse's hooves. Coming around the side of the building, a small, light carriage pulled by a single horse, the horse led by the stable boy.

The boy stopped the carriage in front of the porch and stood there waiting another two minutes until Brunrichter emerged and climbed onto the driver's seat. I noticed as the carriage passed beneath me that the doctor was not wearing his hair in the same style as Poe, that is, parted on the side and combed forward so that it lay across his forehead, but brushed severely back, as on the day we had first met him. And I wondered if he adopted Poe's hairstyle only in the evenings, if he became Poe's doppelganger only when at his leisure.

I suppressed an urge to drop a gob of spit on the man, and willed myself to remain motionless.

He passed out the gate and down the street. I waited. And ten minutes later, coming out the front door, striding briskly, still pulling on a pair of calfskin gloves, came Tevis. He was whistling as he passed beneath the tree, whistling in such a sprightly fashion and moving so jauntily, so utterly at ease with himself and the world, that although he wore the same face and the same physiognomy as before, I scarcely recognized him. That is, I knew it was Tevis but how startled I was to see him strolling by with such insouciance, all trace of a manservant's rigidity and formality gone.

Because he was afoot I could not risk shinnying down from the tree until he was a good twenty yards away. And even with my feet on solid ground I did not dare whistle yet, not until I had stolen inside the gate where Tevis could not see me were he to turn and look. Nor did I wish to be spotted from inside the house by Mrs. Dalrymple. So I crouched behind a slender arborvitae, and only then let sail my whistle.

I signaled twice, *me-oh-whee! me-oh-whee!*, waited for fifteen seconds or so, then whistled twice again. Soon I saw first Poe and then Buck scurrying toward the front gate, both bent low as they ran. I hurried ahead of them to the street outside the gate and had another peek in Tevis's direction.

Poe came up and seized me by the sleeve. "Go on ahead," he told me, "and don't lose sight of him. Neither allow us to lose sight of you!" With that he shoved me forward.

I admit to the exercise of no great skill in my pursuit of Tevis. Nor if so, was any necessary. Not once did he glance over his shoulder. Nor did he seem in any great hurry to get where he was going, and in fact stopped twice along the way, first at a bakery, where he made a purchase that was wrapped in white paper, and then at a general store, from which he emerged with a larger sack in hand.

By the time Tevis came out of the second store, Poe and Buck had caught up with me as I waited on a corner. We had come to a spot nearly midway between the two rivers, with a commanding view of the courthouse on Grant's Hill. From there we followed Mr. Tevis no more than three full blocks to a dwelling on Crawford Street. Here, directly in front of a small stone house, Tevis opened the gate and crossed into the yard, went onto the covered porch, unlocked the front door, and stepped inside. The door fell shut behind him.

Poe, Buck, and I turned to look at one another. Buck asked, "What can he be up to in there? Meeting somebody?"

Poe said, "He carries a key to the door. Perhaps he lives there."

"I thought he lives at the doctor's place."

Poe scratched his chin. "Let us go off in different directions again. There is nothing more to be seen from the front. Augie, go to the right, and Buck, the left. I will come at the house from the rear. In ten minutes, more or less, we will meet back here to discuss what we have observed." He did not wait for acquiescence but set off smartly for the street corner.

There was nothing for me to see on the right side of the house. Even standing at the neighbor's gate, in full view of the populace, I could detect no movement within the stone house. I did not dare remain so conspicuous long, however, and soon returned to my former spot behind a tree, where I nervously waited for the minutes to pass.

Buck was the first to return. "Anything?" I asked.

He shook his head. "I couldn't get close enough to see into the windows."

Anxiously we waited for Poe. Ten minutes elapsed not once but twice. Finally Buck said, "Down there," and directed my attention some fifty yards down the street, which Poe was now crossing at a leisurely pace, making certain by his slowness that Buck and I had seen him. Then, instead of returning to us, he set off toward the Allegheny, but not without a glance or two back so as to assure himself that we were following.

Buck said, "He's headed back to Miss Jones's, I think."

We convened in the small parlor at the rear of the schoolhouse. When Buck and I arrived, Poe and Miss Jones were already seated. I strode into the center of the room and said to Poe, "Well?"

Before answering, he looked past me to Buck, who had remained just off the threshold, hat in hand. Miss Jones told him, "Come in, Mr. Kemmer, please. You needn't always wait to be invited."

He came two steps forward.

"Please be seated," she told him, smiling. Then she looked at me, and her smile shrank. "Gentlemen should always take a seat before engaging in a conversation."

I reminded myself that this was Miss Jones's house, and I held my tongue. I took a seat.

Poe then spoke. "I observed the rear of the house for several minutes. After which, Mr. Tevis emerged."

"Where did he go?" I blurted.

"Not far. In the rear yard there is a small wrought-iron table with two chairs. Atop this table Mr. Tevis placed a plate holding two small cakes."

"From the bakery where he stopped."

"No doubt. He also set down the larger sack he had

been carrying, and from it he pulled three smaller bags." Poe paused now, unable, even in a situation like this, to avoid taking advantage of the dramatic effect.

"Seeds," he finally said.

"Seeds?" I repeated.

"He had laid out a garden plot in the rear yard. And a very nicely worked plot it is. He has put a great deal of time into it. Each of the smaller bags contained seeds, though of what type I cannot say."

"Probably carrots," said Buck. "Radishes, lettuce, spring vegetables. Them that don't mind a late chill."

Poe nodded. "He soon fetched a cup of tea for himself from inside the house. Then, while I watched, he appeared to take a great deal of pleasure from not only his tea and cakes but from planting his seeds."

"It sounds as if maybe he does live there," I said.

Poe said, "I confirmed this in a conversation with one of his neighbors. Discreetly, of course. In a manner to arouse no suspicions."

"Does he have a wife?" Buck asked. "A family?"

"He lives alone."

"It makes no sense," said Buck. "For a man to have himself two homes."

"And consider the house you saw," said Poe. "It was not a mansion, but neither was it a shack. Would a man of Tevis's position be able to afford such a home?"

Buck screwed up his brow in contemplation, no doubt figuring up all the fourteen-hour days of backbreaking labor he had invested in a home not half as attractive as Tevis's.

Miss Jones answered Poe's question. "I think not," she said.

"Not," said Poe, "unless he was being compensated at a rate somewhat above the norm?"

"Far above," she said.

Poe leaned back in his chair and crossed his arms. He tucked his chin toward his chest and frowned.

"We're getting nowhere," I said.

Poe made no reply, though he raised his eyes to me.

"I'm getting into the house," I said.

"You mustn't!" said Miss Jones.

But Buck asked, "Which house are you talking about?"

"Brunrichter's," I answered.

"We could do it tomorrow," said Buck. "Won't be nobody around but the two of them."

"Better to wait until Sunday, I think. Easter Sunday. That means he'll be at church for a couple of hours. Protestant, that's what he told us—you remember?"

Still Poe said nothing.

Buck said, "On second thought, maybe we'd better go tonight. According to Miss Jones here, Friday night's when he does his dirty business. We go tonight, we maybe stop him from doing it again."

"He's expecting Poe to return on Saturday. He won't do anything tonight. No, I think Sunday morning is best. Mrs. Dalrymple will go to church as well, I know she will. As for Tevis, if he doesn't go to church and doesn't go back to his own house, well, I'll just have to deal with him, I suppose."

"I'm the one to deal with him," said Buck.

Miss Jones said, "You will not. Neither of you. I simply will not permit it."

"Miss Jones," I started, having no idea what I would blurt out next but intent on refuting her somehow. Before I could do so, Poe raised a hand to silence me. I knew by this gesture that he was about to speak. But first we were forced to endure another of his damn pauses.

"While at the good doctor's home this morning," he finally said, "I observed a certain oddness to the building. Have you noticed it, Augie?"

I had not, and shook my head.

"On the right side of the house, the last window on the first floor opens off the library. Directly above it, the last window on the upper floor opens off the doctor's bedroom. And yet . . . ," he stroked his chin. "And yet the building continues beyond those windows for another ten feet or so."

I tried my best to envision it. "But the library wall on that side of the building has no doorway."

"Nor, if I recall correctly from my brief visit there, does the bedroom above it."

"All of which means what?" Buck asked.

Poe drew himself up until he was sitting erect. He placed both hands on his knees. "It means," he said, "that although I hold the utmost respect for the wishes of Miss Jones, I find that I must agree with Augie. The house, you see, is not as it appears. Or rather, it is more than it appears. We must get inside that house."

Buck and I nodded. Miss Jones said nothing but sat there shaking her head.

Nothing more could be accomplished by Poe or me for the rest of the day or the whole of the next, so we busied ourselves with letters, mine to Mrs. Clemm (with no reference to our current complications), Poe's to former colleagues in New York and Philadelphia, in an effort to revive his sagging literary possibilities. Both of us assumed, at least in our public faces, that this mess would soon be over and we would continue with our lives on more or less the same course as before our collision with Pittsburgh.

The next day Miss Jones and Buck put in a long morning of walking so as to determine the hours for Sunday's Easter services. We knew that Brunrichter, like many confirmed atheists, assumed the mask of a believer for professional reasons. That is, though he placed the whole of his faith in the revelations of science, he attended church weekly as an aid to his reputation and standing in the community.

Poe thought he recalled being told by Mrs. Dalrymple that she was Episcopalian—a foggy memory at best. Tevis was the unknown. We suspected, however, that believer or not he would be a churchgoer too, if only at his employer's insistence.

"The biggest scoundrels," said Poe, "will invariably make the biggest show of piety."

Playing the possibilities, then, Miss Jones composed a chart on which she listed the Sunday hours of worship service for any and all of the churches the Brunrichter household might attend. In the end she pronounced the hour between ten and eleven next morning our hour of opportunity.

"One hour only?" said Poe. "It is a very large house, Miss Jones."

"But there will be four of us to search it," she said.

"Three," he corrected.

"Now, Mr. Poe—"

"No, Miss Jones. You will not risk all you have labored to create."

"But if I choose—"

"You will not choose. And that, my dear lady, to whom each of us is forever indebted, is the end of it."

He capped the statement with something like a bow, which culminated with him touching his lips to the back of her brittle hand. I could not help but smile at the way she blushed and very nearly tittered. Had I attempted to placate her with such a gesture, she would have raked her knuckles across my skull.

In any case, the matter was settled. And so followed a restless afternoon. Upon sunset, the restlessness increased. Poe and Miss Jones pretended to read, Buck and I played euchre, then poker, then cribbage. After dinner Poe recited for us, at Miss Jones's request, her favorite poem—a generous gesture on his part but one that did little to ease our restiveness.

Imagine, if you will, the author seated not far from the parlor's fireplace, so that the orange glow from the low flames falls on the side of his face, the other side in shadow, while he declaims, in a tone of melancholy both well-practiced and real, "when each pale and dying ember/wrought its ghost upon the floor," and then later when he reads to his breathless audience of three, sotto voce, "It is the beating of the hideous heart!"

Not long after, Miss Jones fetched blankets for Buck and Poe, and I brought mine up from the basement, and we each claimed a narrow piece of the parlor floor. Miss Jones bade us good night and good rest and left us alone for the remainder of the evening.

One final bit of conversation for the night was this, after the lamp had been extinguished and we each lay on our backs, watching the dance of flame shadows on the white ceiling:

Buck said, "I never been read to by anyone before except for my Susan."

"Whose voice, I am sure," said Poe, "was far more mellifluous than my own."

"I'm not saying I didn't enjoy yours," said Buck. "It's just that I ain't never heard anything like it before."

"Strange how comfortable it was for me," said Poe. "I have never been so at ease with an audience."

"Maybe from now on you will be."

"Thank you, sir. Your good wishes are appreciated."

There was a long pause then. There seemed nothing more to say. But then Buck went ahead and said it, what I, for one, was thinking too.

"I hope Susan got to hear it. I hope it works that way."

I clenched my fists beneath the blanket. I squeezed my eyes.

"Do you figure it does, Mr. Poe?"

Another pause. Then, "I think, sir, that if anything survives this misfortune we call Life, it is the goodness of a soul like your daughter's."

"And may the same hold true for your own. For your own precious wife, I mean."

"Hand in hand," said Poe, the life-long scorner, the cynic formed of misery. "Even now they stand and watch us, Buck. Hand in hand."

Chapter Thirty-three

Easter morning, a clear sky, robin's egg blue. We had been in concealment since before the wispy fog had lifted, the three of us watching the mansion from a stand of birches some sixty yards from the house, watching across a wide expanse of yard, none of us with much to say, more eager than worried, though I imagined I detected, despite the morning's clarity and glimmer, some kind of sadness in the air, so that even as I watched a flock of grackles pecking at the soft ground, even as I smiled to see the white-and-yellow heads of Easter lilies peeking from the grass, I felt a vague, unsettling heaviness in my chest, and spent some time in reverie of those not so distant days made sweeter now in afterthought than they had ever been in fact.

A sound from the rear dooryard, the clap of a door. Marcus Keesling, a dark-haired boy, maybe twelve or so, came leading a roan mare from the stable. Brunrichter kept two horses, this one and its matched mate, identical but for the white blaze on the first mare's chest.

One after another the horses were led to the carriage house. Poe looked to me and nodded; a signal to be ready. I did the same to Buck.

Tevis was the first to emerge from the house. Straight across the yard to the carriage house, whose double door had now been swung open. The snap of reins,

Tevis's gruff, "Haw!" and out came the horses trotting smartly, hitched to a brougham.

Tevis pulled the carriage close to the rear door, from which Mrs. Dalrymple emerged, still tying her bonnet. She climbed up beside Tevis, leaving the interior of the carriage empty. Then around to the front of the house to wait near the veranda. Tevis set the brake and climbed down and stood ready at the carriage door.

Several minutes passed before Brunrichter emerged. Black frockcoat and trousers, wine-colored waistcoat, and one of his fancy glass canes—perhaps the very one he had given me, which I then chose to leave behind when I vacated the house. Before coming down off the porch he turned and locked the door. Locked it, I told myself, because there were secrets inside.

Soon the carriage went out the gate and turned toward town. Buck and I, ready to run, looked to Poe; he stood with his head cocked, listening, one hand slightly raised as a signal that we should wait. I waited until the clop of hooves could no longer be heard, and then, though Poe remained motionless, hand in the air, I ran anyway, zigzagging back through the trees so as to approach the mansion from its front face lest I be spotted by the stable boy in the rear.

Poe's "Wait!" was just a whisper and it did nothing to slow me. Nor did it hold back Buck, who raced close on my heels. He reached the veranda only seconds behind me. I went from window to window along the porch, but none would budge.

Poe soon joined us. "No luck?" he asked.

"We might try the back. But I have my doubts we will find a door unlocked. Plus, the stable boy is back there somewhere. Probably his father as well."

"Can you get onto the roof?" Poe asked. "Or have you lost the knack?"

I knew a challenge when I heard one. Off the porch and around to the far side I went, surveying the possibilities, Poe at my side. I had brought along a small pry bar, both as weapon and tool, and I pulled it from my jacket now and gripped it tightly. I could only assume that Buck remained as we had left him, his huge paw on the glass doorknob, squeezing, eyes hard, as if he intended to tear the door off its hinges.

I asked Poe, "Can you boost me onto the porch roof?"

"You'll never reach it."

"If I stand on your shoulders I might."

"It's sixteen feet at its lowest."

"I'll get a chair off the porch for you to stand on."

"They are wicker, Augie. Slow down and think."

I turned away from the house then, let my gaze travel over the ground. Several yards beyond the rear of the mansion, overturned atop a woodpile, was a handcart. "There!" I said. "We can prop that cart against the house."

Poe eyed it critically. "Precarious at best."

I grinned at him. "Have you lost the knack?"

His eyes narrowed. "Get it," he said.

I sprinted to the corner of the house, peeked toward the outbuildings, saw no one, heard nothing. Raced forward hunkered low. Seized the cart by its handles, hoisted it onto its front wheel and ran.

Safe behind the house again, I slowed and pushed the cart past Poe, who continued to watch the stables. Satisfied that I had not been seen, he finally joined me near the front corner of the house, where I attempted to make the overturned cart as stable as possible. He gave the cart a shake. "It appears solid enough," he said. "All right, climb aboard." And with that he knelt.

I was the larger man and by all rights should have hoisted Poe onto the roof. But I was more adept with a pry bar than he, more experienced as a sneak thief. I straddled his neck.

Poe struggled to stand erect. "Wait until I am in place and stabilized," he said. "Then you can stand."

With that he moved to the overturned cart. I placed both hands against the wall, dug in my fingernails, hoping to take some of the weight off Poe. Still it was no easy task for him to lift even one foot onto the edge of the cart. He struggled mightily, several times lunging upward, shifting his weight, but he could not elevate his other foot off the ground.

He stood there panting, hand to the wall, with me still astride his shoulders. "Let's trade positions," I whispered.

Poe put a foot to the cart again. "One more time."

Again he struggled. But it was hopeless. "This is nonsense," I whispered. "Where's Buck. He can *throw* me onto the roof."

As if in answer, a shattering of glass. I knew without needing to see—I could see it all too clearly in my mind's eye—that we had exhausted Buck's patience. Life had exhausted Buck's patience. He had put a fist through the etched glass door, consequences be damned.

Poe was crabbing sideways, trying to see onto the porch. I heard footsteps racing through the rear yard. "Put me down!" I hissed. "Down!"

Poe sank to his knees. "Stay here," I told him, then hopped off just in time to hear a startled yelp from the opposite side of the porch. By the time I reached the porch, Buck was holding the stable boy by the scruff of the neck.

The boy looked at Buck and then at me. "Are you robbing the place?" he asked, his eyes a bit too wide with eagerness.

Buck said, "You know where things are in there, do you?"

"I ain't never been inside except for the kitchen. Wouldn't mind going in with you, though."

Buck turned his head just slightly and said, loud enough for Poe to hear, "I think a better place for you is back where you came from. Your father out there too?"

"Taking a nap," the boy said.

"Time to rise and shine," said Buck as he hauled the boy off the porch.

Ten seconds later I signaled to Poe. Then he and I stepped onto the porch. The foyer now stood open to us, littered with milky glass. I swept a hand toward the shattered entrance. "Welcome home," I said.

Poe went straight to the far wall of the library. He rapped his knuckles here and there, listening for a hollow sound, a secret panel. "There are only four possibilities," he told me. "The entrance is here, or through the master bedroom, or from the attic or the cellar. You try upstairs."

I was out of the room in an instant, across the foyer and under the massive chandelier, for which I felt an almost overwhelming contempt. Nothing would have pleased me more than to pull the entire glittering thing to the floor.

But it was, after all, just an object. And while the destruction of objects might be useful in the venting of excess animus, the truest satisfaction could come only from destroying the ultimate source of one's hatred. I went straight to Brunrichter's bedroom.

The place reeked to me. It reeked of his unctuous smoothness, it stank of his arrogance. Whatever oils he applied to his hair, whatever scents he employed, those fragrances in my nostrils smelled only of deceit, an odor of charred logs and wet ash.

His bed, the Turkish carpet, the landscapes and pastoral scenes that hung on the walls, even the bookcases and the volumes they contained—all were so neat, so undisturbed. It aggravated me to find no robe tossed carelessly over a chair, no well-worn slipper kicked into a corner. But on the window seat there was a squirrel cage, and I smiled to see it empty. A squirrel in the house is thought to bring good luck, and I was determined that Brunrichter should enjoy no such thing.

To the wall in question. From the center of the room I scrutinized it. I could detect nothing amiss. Then closer, to lift every picture away from the wall, to slide my hand up and down the textured wall covering, over the intaglio of slender vines and delicate flowers against a background of cream. Again, no sign of a secret entrance.

I even looked under the bed. Behind the heavy, carved headboard. Inside the mahogany chifforobe.

Frustrated, I stepped back to the center of the room. Then, beginning in an upper corner, I ran my gaze down to the floor, then slowly up to the ceiling again until I had scrutinized every inch of the wall. My gaze had come up and over the chifforobe when the import of what I had observed just a moment earlier suddenly dawned on me.

Casters. The chifforobe sat atop metal casters. Why

would a piece of furniture so huge, nearly seven feet high and over four feet wide, and filled with a dozen suits of clothes and overcoats, be outfitted for movement?

I seized the wardrobe by its corner and swung it clear of the wall. Nothing behind it. I pushed it farther to the side, so that light from the window was not blocked from falling over the wall. Still, no seams were visible in the wall covering.

All that was visible, all that was out of the ordinary, was but a pale gray shadow, irregular and no larger than my palm, at chest level on the wall. I looked closer. It was an adumbration left by routine touch, the oils and fingerprints accumulated over time from a hand pressed to just that spot. Precisely that spot, and no other on the entire wall.

I pressed my fingertips to the shadow. Pushed inward. The wall gave way just slightly beneath my touch, no more than a quarter of an inch no matter how hard I pushed, and I pushed, finally, with both hands and all my strength. But now, at last, I could see the seam, the cleverly hidden opening.

I still had the pry bar in my belt. I lifted my hands from the door momentarily, reaching for the pry bar. And as my weight came off the wall there was a subtle click, and now the wall sprang open toward me! The door was constructed not to open inward at one's touch, but to spring outward by an inch or so, just wide enough that I could slip my fingers into the opening and pull the doorway fully open.

The interior was pitch-black and the light from the room did not enter very far. The air that rushed out at me was warm and stale and dry.

I started inside, gingerly feeling my way. And then

thought of Poe. Out into the hallway I went, to the railing that overlooked the stairway and foyer. I could see or hear no one below. I hurried halfway down the stairs then, far enough to see into the library, where Poe, standing on a chair, had his eye pressed to a golden gasolier sconce mounted some five feet below the twelve-foot ceiling.

"Sssst—Poe!" I hissed at him.

He turned sharply, saw me hunkered on the stairs, and grinned. "There's a room behind this wall," he said.

"I know. I found the doorway upstairs. Where's Buck?"

"Not back from the stables yet. But look here—you see this? From down below it looks like nothing more than a pearl button inlaid on the sconce—you see it?"

"What of it?" I asked.

"A lens! An eyepiece!"

"Can you see anything through it?"

He shook his head. "The lens is convex. Besides, the room on the other side is dark."

"But there is definitely a room there?"

"I am certain of it. On this wall alone there are four sconces, all identical. Similar ones exist throughout the house. I would not be surprised to find these eyepieces in other rooms as well."

"Let's see what's in there," I told him, and back up the stairs I went, with Poe not far behind me.

He came into the bedroom, saw me waiting by the secret doorway. "Momentarily," he said. He then scrutinized the room just as I had done. But where I had seen nothing, he saw a great deal.

"There," he said, and pointed to the wall on his right. Another sconce, this one only five feet off the floor. He leaned against the wall and put his eye to the lens.

"What can you see?"

"It looks into the bath and the toilet."

"You mean, when I was in there . . ."

He turned from the wall. "You. Me. All of his guests, I daresay."

"The bastard!"

He crossed to a small bed table on which set a candle in its silver holder. He opened the bed-table drawer, found the lucifers, pocketed several of them, then struck another and lit the candle. "Let us proceed," he said, and with that he stepped through the secret doorway.

The corridor walls were bare planking, as was the floor, and the dark grain of the wood seemed to soak up much of the candle's illumination. Twice in the first eight paces Poe had to pause to cup his hand around the flame when a draft threatened to extinguish it.

We were nearly upon another door before we detected it, for no knob protruded to break the plane of the wall, only a short leather cord used for pulling the door shut. But more corridor lay in front of us. "Wait here by this door," Poe told me. "I'll check farther along."

"I should go back for another light."

He handed me the candlestick, removed the candle and broke it in half. He lit the bottom half on the top, stuck one piece in the holder and kept the other for himself. "Wait here for me," he said.

"We need to be quick."

"The room lies farther down."

"We don't know where Buck is or what he's up to."

"Wait here."

With that he strode forward, holding the candle as far ahead of him as he could reach. I watched for only a few seconds before returning my attention to the closed door at hand. I put a palm to it and pushed lightly. It gave way without much effort and spilled a rush of cooler air out at me. Before me lay a narrow staircase leading steeply down.

"Another door!" Poe called out from ten feet down the corridor.

"See what you can find! I'll go this way!"

I was two steps down when some muttered protest from Poe reached my ears, some mumbled epithet I took to be his admonition that I wait for him. But I was in no mood for waiting. We had wasted far too much time already, and there was little way to tell in these narrow, blackened confines, with no timepiece in our pockets, how many minutes had already passed.

With each downward step the coolness deepened. I counted the stairs as I descended—sixteen, seventeen, eighteen—going well past any number that would have brought me to the mansion's ground floor, and continuing on until, after step thirty-three, I was confronted with another blank face, another empty doorway.

Gingerly I pushed it open. But nothing lay beyond it but the cellar, no different from any to be expected in a house so large, its nooks filled with gardening tools and other implements, old chairs, a bin stacked with firewood, cubicles in which barrels of salted meat and hams wrapped in burlap were stored, baskets filled with apples, cabbages, onions, turnips, parsnips and squash, shelves lined with dusty jars of Mrs. Dalrymple's pickled fruits and confitures.

The entire area was much brighter than the stairway and corridor had been; light entered through four narrow windows mounted at ground level. I had a quick peek out each of these windows, just to orient myself, and in one of them spotted Buck coming out of the carriage house, an ax in hand. I shivered to think of what use he would make of it—or already had.

The cellar walls were of limestone, all but the one closest to where I now stood. It was paneled in wide vertical planks. A question occurred to me then: Why have a secret staircase leading to the cellar?

It made no sense, unless the cellar itself was but a way station. Which implied the presence of another secret doorway. And where would such a doorway be, in limestone or wood?

I found it not four feet to my left. The door opened onto another corridor, but this one a tunnel of earthen walls and trampled earth floor. The scent of mildew and soil mold was thick in the tunnel, and the space resonated with a dull kind of hum, more felt than heard. I told myself that it was nothing more than the movement of cool air through the tunnel, for the candle would surely have flickered out had I not kept a hand cupped in front of the flame. Yet I could not shake the notion that the low-pitched hum was the moan of the earth itself.

Every twenty feet or so, a truss of wooden beams shored up the ceiling. Now and then I stepped into a shallow pool of clay-slimed water. As I walked I kept one eye on the ceiling and wondered how much earth waited above me, ready to tumble down. I wondered too about rats and snakes, whether they frequented this place. Had even a mole crossed my path I would surely have jumped out of my boots. But step after step I encountered nothing, only rock and clay and the sticky damp odor of my escalating claustrophobia.

I must have walked at least two hundred yards when my candle blinked out. And I had no lucifer, had not thought to take a few of Poe's. I stood there in the sudden darkness, breathless, tasting my own fear, one hand gripping the pry bar. What now? I had no idea how much farther this tunnel stretched, nor what might lie at the end of it. Furthermore I began to think it a mistake to have abandoned Poe and Buck at the mansion. Neither knew the whereabouts of the other. Poe was no doubt cursing my heedlessness, just as I had begun to do.

Good sense dictated that I retrace my steps. And it is amazing how persistent good sense can be when mixed with a hearty helping of fear. I was afraid to go on, afraid to keep creeping forward into blackness.

The return trip was made at a slower pace, one hand riding along the wall. I moved with the hesitancy of a blind man. Every time I knocked loose a stone or clod of dirt, the sudden soft clattering froze me in my tracks. Fortunately I had left the doorway to the cellar standing open, and after several long minutes was able to detect a feeble glow, toward which I flew like a crippled moth to a flame.

Then, in the basement, I was faced with another choice: To return to the master bedroom via the secret passageway, or to take the more attractive path, up the cellar steps and into the mansion's kitchen. I was halfway up the cellar steps when a mumbling of voices reached me—those of Mrs. Dalrymple and Mr. Tevis!

I had to warn Poe. Perhaps he already knew, but I could not be sure of that. Back to the secret stairway, again into darkness. Creeping quickly upward, keenly aware of every creak of wood as I ascended.

At the top of the stairs, another decision: Into the master bedroom, or to the secret chamber where last I had seen Poe headed? I chose the latter. I had progressed no more than three paces, however, before I sensed that I was not alone.

"Poe?" I whispered, pry bar at the ready, my body poised in a half crouch.

"Shhh," he answered, and I relaxed my fists.

He came closer. Put a hand on my shoulder and leaned toward me, as if to whisper in my ear. Then put a hand to the back of my head, and with the other hand pressed a cloth to my nose and mouth, an action that caused me to gasp and jerk away, but too late, for one breath had filled my lungs with an astringent scent and I felt the darkness shifting out from under me, felt it swirling up from the floor like an eddy sucking me in, the pry bar slipping from my hand to land with a thud, then nothing more.

Chapter Thirty-four

Voices in the distance, coming closer. Eyelids heavy, struggling to lift. I tried to raise a hand to my face but my arm, no matter how I struggled, would not rise. My stomach felt odd, my throat tight. The space around me rocked back and forth and I swallowed hard to suppress the seasickness.

The voices came much closer now. Brunrichter. Poe. One of them mentioned something about "our brotherhood." Another, or perhaps the same one, spoke of "my bitter disappointment."

I forced my eyelids open by a slit. But light, too much light. I closed my eyes again and listened. There was a hissing in my ears.

". . . not the man I had thought you to be," said Brunrichter. "not by half." Poe answered something but I could not follow it. I drifted away.

Minutes later—maybe only seconds—my consciousness swung back toward the voices. They seemed clearer now, and angry.

Poe said, "The boy suspected. But I was seduced by your flattery."

"Your greatest weakness!" Brunrichter cried, shrill, on the verge of hysteria. His voice was a screech in my ears, jarring me awake. I sat motionless.

"You pretend to be a man of logic," he continued. "And you can be—more's the pity! But then that nonsense of yours. The Particle Divine! You call that logic, Edgar? It is feebleness of thought. You succumbed to your despair."

"And you," said Poe, his voice calmer, softly drawling, "you have succumbed to madness."

"You think this madness?"

"How could I gaze upon this room and think otherwise?"

Brunrichter sniffed at this, clicked his tongue. I heard him moving about, pacing. Again I opened my eyes. Again the brightness of the room assailed me so that I would have squeezed my eyes shut tight had I not glimpsed in the glare something too horrific to turn from, there within an arm's reach on the very table at which I sat, a long refectory table in a long narrow room bathed in the light from a half-dozen hissing gas lights. A single oil lamp burned at the far end of the table. Arranged down the center of the table, each in its own separate bell jar, each looking eerily alive in amber liquid, seven severed heads with eyes wide open, mouths formed into smiles, long hair softly floating, as the hair of seven mermaids might.

They did not seem real to me. They could not be real. But the shock of seeing them sent a terrible heat racing through me so that I burned from top to bottom. The sickness bubbled up in me again and I moved just slightly, lifted a hand to lay upon my stomach. Though a heaviness remained I could move my limbs now, saw that I was unrestrained, and for just an instant I thought of leaping to my feet, but then I saw through one of the jars the dark shape behind it, and lifted my gaze higher. Tevis stood against the wall, watching me. His eyes were empty. His face was stone. In his right hand, laid flat against his chest, a pistol.

"I offered you the opportunity to be whole," Brunrichter was saying, his back to me, head thrown back, hand rubbing his neck. "The opportunity to make both of us whole. You as the brilliant theorizer, the creator of possibilities—"

"Fictions!" said Poe. He was seated farther down the table, turned toward Brunrichter. "Tales I composed for money alone. That is all they meant to me."

"Because they were meant for *me*!" said Brunrichter. "One half of the mind creates; the other half applies!"

"What have you applied, Alfred? These girls are not alive."

"There will always be failures. Failures are the path to success."

"You murdered them for no reason."

Brunrichter spun to face him. "Science!" Brunrichter screamed, the spittle flying from his mouth. "In the name of science! How can you not understand?"

"Because I am not you. And I, yes, yes, I too have suffered my madnesses, but none like yours. Like this. This is depravity."

A few moments passed, and a smile came to Brunrichter's face. He closed his eyes and continued to smile. Then he looked again at Poe. "With that, dear Edgar, you have selected your fate."

The sentence hung there in the air, a guillotine's blade about to fall. But before it could, a thunderclap. I thought at first that Tevis had fired his pistol, but no, he was as surprised as the rest of us and had leapt away from the wall, his face now white with fear.

Another explosion. The entire room rattled. One of the white globes on the gaslights fell to the floor and shattered. The liquid in the bell jars rippled, hair swayed like kelp.

A third explosion, and with it the wall on the other side of the table cracked, a jagged rent in the wood. Tevis quickly moved to my side of the table, stood so that he could keep his pistol trained on me and his eye on the crack in the wall. But Brunrichter rushed to the wall even as the thunder continued and put his eye to a small round lens and peered out into the library. There he must have seen what I could only picture in my mind, Buck Kemmer wielding his ax, turning the wall to splinters.

With the next blow the crack in the wall tripled in width, wide enough that I could now see through to the other side. Brunrichter scurried into a far corner and for the first time looked my way. "You've come awake," he said. "Good. Just in time." With a jerk of his hand he signaled to Tevis, who reached into the pocket of his church coat and withdrew a second pistol, which he tossed to the doctor. Both men took aim on Buck.

Another blow of Buck's ax. The wall stood cleaved, the opening nearly a foot wide now. "They've got pistols!" I screamed. "Go for the police!"

Brunrichter's face darkened, and as his hand swung toward me I dove from my chair, sidelong under the table. His shot shattered two of the bell jars, sent a shower of glass and formaldehyde over my head. Poe jerked backward in his chair, knocking it over, twisting as he fell to land on his hands and knees. Tevis slid along the wall to stand with his back to the only exit, putting Poe and me and Brunrichter between himself and Buck's ax.

And Buck, instead of heeding my advice, doubled his efforts. Having seen that the secret room was elevated, its floor perhaps four feet above the library's floor, he had shoved the divan closer to the wall and stood atop it, legs spread wide for balance as he once again attacked the wall. Brunrichter gripped his empty pistol by the barrel now, held it like a bludgeon, and pressed himself into the far corner. His eyes darted from Poe to Tevis to Buck. I came out from under the table on the other side, Buck's side, and inched my way toward Tevis. Now he did not know who to aim at, me or Buck. His pistol jerked from side to side.

Three more blows of the ax, five seconds at the most, and Buck was finished with the wall. With his left hand he seized the edge of broken board, raised a foot to the secret room's floor, and heaved himself up, coming in sideways. He was only halfway through the opening, the ax still dangling on the library side, when he saw the table and the five remaining jars. It was too much for him. He stopped. He squeezed shut his eyes.

Tevis fired.

Buck fell back into the library, crashing down on the divan. Brunrichter began to laugh, a silly, girlish giggle. But his happiness was shortlived. For with a roar Buck came diving back into the room with us, in as far as his waist and then dragging himself up, bellowing bull-like as he wrestled his bulk inside, up onto his knees and jerking the ax in behind him, the right half of his shirt already dark with blood. I went to him and gripped an arm, meaning to help him to his feet, but he shook me off, did not recognize me in his rage, but moved in on Brunrichter, made his way down the length of the table as broken glass crunched underfoot.

Tevis, his pistol useless, fled through the secret door. Brunrichter moved to do the same but Poe stood up and blocked his retreat. To Poe he said, his eyes on Buck, "You've got to stop this!" He put out his hands as if to seize Poe by the lapels, to embrace him, but Poe stepped back, one hand raised.

Poe said to Buck, "He's not the one who killed your Susan."

Buck stopped. He blinked. Waved a hand at the table. "He's the one done this, ain't he?"

"But not Susan."

Buck hesitated for a moment, then shook his head just once and came around the table. Brunrichter dropped to his knees, clutched at Poe's trousers, whimpered for salvation. I heard little that he said, and cared of it even less, but stood there enjoying the roar of rage inside my head. The smell of blood already filled the room but it was not enough for me, I was eager for more.

And Poe, I think, did what he could to stay Buck's ax. I see him protesting, his hands shielding the doctor's head. I remember it as a dream, all bathed in red.

In the end Buck seized Brunrichter by the throat and jerked him to his feet, thrust him hard against the wall and held him there, Buck's huge hand clamped around the doctor's neck while the ax rose in his right hand, level with the doctor's head. Then, with a snap of Buck's wrist, the ax came forward, and the blade cleaved the wall, not two inches from Brunrichter's ear.

The doctor was unconscious on his feet, I think, but no matter. Buck released the ax handle, left it stuck in the wall, and drove his fist into Brunrichter's face. I heard bones shatter, and a moan escaped my lips, and I was only a little embarrassed by the satisfaction I felt.

Now Buck turned to Poe. He nodded toward the open doorway. "It was him then?"

We knew by his tone what he intended to do. "The police will be notified," said Poe. "They will have him by nightfall. As for you—," and he put a hand on Buck's arm, a gesture not of remonstrance but something else, of compassion, affection, of love.

Buck looked down at Poe's hand. Smiled. Patted it twice with the same hand that had laid Brunrichter out. Then Buck turned away. He seized the unconscious doctor by his shirt front, hauled him up and tossed him over a shoulder. With a blood-soaked hand he wrenched the ax from the wall, then pushed past Poe as if he were not there and strode out into the corridor.

Poe turned to me. "We've got to stop him."

"We can try," I said. I grabbed the oil lamp off the table and followed Poe out the door.

* * *

We tracked Buck without difficulty along the corridor and into the cellar and its tunnel, marked as they were now by the trail of blood, which shone oily black in the lamplight. There seemed a great deal of blood, and I voiced my concern that Buck might collapse deep inside the tunnel, leaving Poe and me to somehow haul him out and to the hospital.

"It's not all his," Poe remarked, and pointed to the two recurring patterns in the trail, some of it dripped down the center of the floor (Buck's blood, falling from his wound as he, bent forward, hurried along), some of it flung to one side or the other (Brunrichter's blood, dripping from his shattered mouth as he hung draped over Buck's shoulder).

"Brunrichter won't die from his injury," I said as we walked as briskly as we dared, "but I'm not so sure about Buck."

"He took the pistol ball a few inches below his right shoulder. Too high for the lungs."

"He could bleed to death though."

"That he could."

We caught up with Buck not far from where I had turned back my first time in the tunnel. I held the lamp close to Brunrichter's face. He was unconscious but breathing.

Buck did not so much as turn his head to acknowledge our presence. Head lowered, bent slightly forward at the waist, the heavy ax still clutched by its hosel in his left hand, he moved like a bull in slow charge.

I spoke to him in a hoarse whisper. "You don't even know where this tunnel leads."

He answered without whispering, making no attempt

to conceal his approach from whoever waited ahead. "I figure it's where that other one went."

"And what do you expect to do if you find him?"

"A lot worse than I done to this one."

I glanced back at Poe, my eyebrows raiséd in question. He shook his head. No, his eyes told me, we should not stop him. Not because he shouldn't be stopped but because we were not up to the task. I did not believe that Buck would ever turn the ax on either Poe or me but I had no doubt that he would do whatever else necessary to keep from being hampered in his goal.

And so we stayed with him. I held the light aloft so as to better show the way.

We must have trudged nearly five hundred yards through that damp and musty darkness. By then I think we all knew or at least suspected where the tunnel would terminate, and so were not at all surprised to come finally to a wall of rock and dirt against which a ladder rested.

At the top of the ladder, a rectangle of dim light, an opening not even four feet square, not much bigger than the eye of God through which I had squeezed. And in making that comparison I was reminded suddenly of what Buck had risked to save me from a hanging, of all he had done on my behalf, and I resolved to do as much or more for him.

We stood looking up at the opening. "You'll never make it through," I told him, "it's too small. We'll have to go back."

He said only, "I'll make it," and raised a foot to the ladder.

"Buck, wait. Let me go first. Maybe I can enlarge the opening somehow."

He turned to me, faced me dead-on. His gaze was softer than I expected. "You wouldn't be planning to get in my way here, would you, son?"

Any half-formed thoughts of subterfuge I might have harbored immediately crumbled. I answered with a smile. I put my hand on the ax handle, half atop his own hand. "Better let me have this," I said.

A moment's pause, and then his hand came off the ax.

Poe said, "Blow out the lamp."

I did so, set the lamp out of the way, and moved cautiously up the ladder.

The mausoleum was empty, its granite door standing open. Noon light filled the doorway but came not much farther inside than the threshold, so that the gray walls and floor were only dully illuminated. I pushed the ax up ahead of me, laid it on the floor, slid it out of my way beneath a marble bench, and slithered out.

To the side of the opening lay the slab of flooring that had been removed, a slab of faux marble constructed, in fact, of wood with but a thin layer of marble atop. Mounted on each side of this slab, allegedly as ornament but practicably as handles, was a white marble dove of peace.

Breathlessly I listened for sounds from outside. A bird in the distance, a killdeer shrieking in whistling flight. Then a breeze, so sweetly fresh, washing in through the door, filling me, momentarily, with a debilitating nostalgia, so that for a few aching moments I wanted nothing more but than to lie there undisturbed, breathing in the sweetness of pine and grass and gazing outward at a blue unbroken sky.

But soon Buck's head emerged behind me. He looked

around for a moment, then said, "I'll hand him up to you."

"Send Poe up first."

In the meantime I climbed to my feet, grabbed the ax, held it at the ready across my chest, and crept to the door. Peeked out. And saw no one. Fields of grass, rounded hills. Far ahead and below, the gleaming twist of the Allegheny.

By now Poe had joined me. I nodded to him, then spoke to Buck through the opening in the floor. "All's clear outside. Hand him up."

A moment later, up came Brunrichter's head, lolling forward. I bent to seize him under one arm, Poe the other, and together we dragged him clear of the opening. We laid him between two of the three marble sepulchers aligned vertically against the rear wall. Covering the wall above these sepulchers was an intaglio of an angel seated on a stone, releasing from her hands a dove.

On each of the other walls was a thin rectangular window of thick stained glass. Even those on which the sunlight fell directly allowed little light to enter. Still I could make out the pain on Buck's face as he squirmed and twisted in an attempt to work a shoulder through the opening.

Poe said to Buck, "The floor is laid with marble slabs, each two inches thick. We will have to go back."

Buck said nothing. He continued to ram his shoulder against the floor.

"There is no one here, sir. The scoundrel is gone."

"In that case help me out of here so that I can go find him."

"He is halfway to the waterfront by now. We need to alert the watchmen. And to fetch a carriage to take you and Dr. Brunrichter to a hospital."

But Buck was having none of that. He held out an arm to me. "Try pulling," he said.

I looked at Poe. "It's probably quicker than going the whole way back."

He rubbed his chin, then sighed. Then together we knelt, one on either side of Buck, to pull at him wherever we could lay our hands. But it was no good. His chest alone filled most of the cavity. No matter how much skin he scraped off, he would not pass through.

Then Poe sat suddenly upright, head cocked. "Shhh!" he said.

I listened, heard nothing. And whispered, "What is it?"

He waved me silent. We sat motionless.

And soon I heard it too. A man's voice, the words too distant to be understood.

Poe hurried to the doorway, eased himself around the frame, peeked out. Three seconds later he scurried back to us. "Two men coming!" he whispered. He laid a hand atop Buck's head. "Back down!"

Buck would not budge. "How far?"

"Forty, fifty yards, but coming this way. Back down!"

And Buck's head dipped down below the opening. But only for a moment. Buck Kemmer was not built for retreat. He sank only low enough that he could explode upward again, ramming his injured shoulder into the corner of the slab that blocked his ascent. The slab lifted up by an inch, then fell back into place the moment he drew away from it. Two seconds later he rammed the slab again, and this time when it sprang loose of the earth I seized it by the edge and held it up. Poe, too, slipped his fingers into the crook, and then Buck put both hands against it, and we pulled it up by six inches, and then slid it aside atop the adjoining slab.

Now Buck dug into the earth with his hands, clawing and scrabbling to break it free, pulling it down atop him. "Move aside," I told him, and went after it with the ax, chopping madly.

Ten seconds later Buck said, "That's enough!" and before I had caught a breath he was pushing through the opening, stained head to foot with sweat and dirt and blood.

The moment he was clear we eased the second slab back into place. The voices outside sounded nearly upon us now. Buck went immediately to Brunrichter, seized him by an arm and waistband and all but flung him into the narrow space on the far side of the third sepulcher.

As if by agreement, though not another word was spoken, Poe and I stationed ourselves with our backs against the forward wall, side by side to the right of the door. Buck did the same on the opposite side. The ax, unfortunately, remained where last I had laid it, atop the marble bench.

The men outside were close enough now that we heard not only their voices but their footsteps. They approached at a hurried pace. Tevis was doing most of the talking, his words a tumbled rush of fear. But it was Brother Jarvis who came through the door first, his coarse cassock swishing against his legs. He strode a full yard inside, thumbing back the hammer of the revolver he held in both hands. It was then he saw the ax.

He stopped. A moment passed. He made to turn to the right, meaning, I suppose, to face Tevis, who was stalled directly at his back, but the turn was never completed. For suddenly Jarvis was snapped in the opposite direction, whipped around violently as a man will whip a rattlesnake to break its spine. The revolver, and the monk's hand atop it, were enclosed in the vise of Buck Kemmer's hand.

Tevis turned to flee but both Poe and I slid to the side and blocked the doorway.

Buck tightened the vise now, fingers digging in between Jarvis's knuckles. With his free hand, knees buckling, Jarvis swung at Buck's face, and though first one and then a second blow landed, they had no effect. Buck wrenched the revolver free then, seized the monk by his cassock and with a quick half-spin flung him easily against the sepulchers.

And then Buck turned to Tevis.

"It was him!" Tevis cried, and jammed a finger toward the monk. Jarvis had landed hard against a marble edge and lay curled on the floor, writhing and moaning.

"He's the one killed your girl!" Tevis screamed. "I had nothing to do with it!"

Buck brought the revolver up to the side of Tevis's head.

"Mr. Kemmer," said Poe. His voice was tight and pitched higher than normal, but as hushed as a prayer.

Tevis stood backed hard against me now, my hands pressed to his shoulders to prevent further retreat. I could feel the wild tremblings through my hands.

"I swear it's the truth," Tevis said. "I never touched a one of them. Never even came close to your daughter."

Buck slid the revolver around until its barrel was centered on Tevis's forehead.

"Mr. Kemmer," Poe said again.

Buck never took his eyes off Tevis. His voice sounded dead to me. "You should go for the police now, Mr. Poe."

Poe answered, "You need to come as well. Leave Augie here with the weapon."

Buck shook his head. "I'd better stay."

From where Poe stood he could not see Buck's eyes. But I could. And those eyes, once so deeply green, as clear and green as the river at its source, had now gone black.

I said to Poe, "Go to the railroad depot. Straight across the field and toward the Allegheny. If you can't find a watchman you can at least find a carriage and some men there."

Poe said, "I think it unwise to leave just now."

I told him, "There's nothing else for you to do."

Some moments passed before he finally nodded, squeezed past Tevis and me, and set off on a run.

Buck then put a hand on Tevis's arm, not tightly, casually, a gentlemanly touch. "We have a quarter hour or so," he told him. "You might as well rest." With that he led Tevis to the marble bench and indicated with a wave of the revolver that he should sit. Tevis did so, nervously, his hand poised and trembling not far from the ax blade. More than once he looked down at the ax.

Buck glanced my way then and held out the revolver. I thought he was handing it over to me, and after a moment's hesitation I reached for it. But he pulled it back. "I never seen one like this before," he said. "Have you?"

I squinted for a closer look. The long black barrel and ebony grips. "It's a Patterson," I told him. "Made by Colt."

"How many shots?"

"Five," I said.

Buck nodded, but he did not smile. He turned away

from me then and went to stand over Brother Jarvis. The monk still lay on his side, hand pressed to his back, face contorted and white. "Did you do what he says?" Buck asked.

Brother Jarvis only licked his lips, tongue flicking wildly. His lips made a clicking sound, glutinous and sticky. Brunrichter, behind the sepulcher, groaned. Jarvis jerked his head up at the sound.

"He's here too," said Buck. "So you can stop thinking he'll be along to save you."

Tevis said, vehement with terror, "I'm telling you it's the truth!"

"And you did what?" Buck asked.

"I didn't do nothing. I buried the bodies of those other ones, that's all I did. After he was done with them."

"Which he?"

Tevis jerked his chin at Jarvis.

"Done how?" said Buck.

"How do you think? Same thing he did to that girl of yours."

Buck squeezed shut his eyes. I watched his hand on the revolver. For a moment everything else in my range of vision went black. And I asked, "Is that why he killed her? So she wouldn't tell?"

"The doctor had him do it," Tevis said. "To get at you."

Brunrichter began to whimper now. We could hear him sliding around, trying to upright himself behind the sepulchers. No doubt he wished to speak in his own defense, but could fit no words through his shattered jaw.

When Buck opened his eyes again it was to look at me, a question. Was Tevis to be believed?

I told him, "Jarvis was at the house the night Susan

and I went there. I saw him at the top of the stairs. With Brunrichter."

Buck faced Tevis again. "The doctor paid you well, didn't he?"

"He didn't do what this one did, if that's what you're asking. All he was interested in was the science."

"And he paid you well for your help."

"I took care of the bodies afterward. That's all I ever did."

"That's all," said Buck. He lowered the revolver a bit, a gesture that looked harmless, like the easing of his tension, and shot Tevis through the chest. The man tumbled backward off the bench, his head striking the nearest sepulcher. I flinched at the gunshot, and again at the awful crack of bone. Tevis flopped awkwardly onto his side, and then lay motionless, one leg still draped, almost casually, across the marble bench.

"My god!" cried Jarvis. "My god! Sweet Jesus!"

Buck tossed the revolver down into the hole. I think I must have lurched for it, must have made a sudden move, because Buck thrust out a hand against my chest. When I looked up at him, he smiled. "Time to go now, Augie."

"Good," I said, "that's good. Let's go."

He moved closer. I noticed that he was listing to one side now, that when he raised his arms to lay both hands upon my shoulder, his right arm came up slowly, lagging behind the other.

I told him, "No, Buck. You can't even think about that."

"Can't think about what?"

"What you're up to now."

"You think you know?"

"We think the same way, you and me."

He nodded. There were tears in his eyes. "She was so special, Augie. You know how rare she was."

"I know," I said.

He embraced me then, left arm squeezing hard, rough lips pressed to my cheek. He held me so long and hard that I was nearly breathless, nearly choked by the tears that would not come.

And then, not yet pulling away, he moved his mouth to my ear. "You have to live for her now too."

He gave me no chance to answer, not a second for protest before he spun me away from him and with his one good arm seized me around the waist and lifted me up. He took two long steps and was at the door and flung me outward, out over the marble porch and past the marble columns, onto the border of delicate shells. I barely had time to raise my head off the ground before he stepped back inside and pulled shut the door.

I pounded on the door. I raced from one window to another, hammered on the leaded glass until my knuckles were bloody. I pressed my face to the glass, tried to see inside, but the glass was too thick.

I leaned against the door then, my ear to the seam. The hollow scrape of the ax blade as it scraped across the floor. The muted echo of one man's desperate cries, high pitched and incredulous. Another man's mumbled shrieks. And a third man's voice, peaceful at last.

"You reap what you sow."

Epilogue

A pewter gray morning, heavy with rain. The rain would not fall for a while yet though, not until the weight in the clouds grew insupportable, too heavy to bear. And then it would come in a downpour, a sudden and violent emptying. This is the way with grief as well. Some individuals contain it longer than others can, shoulder the weight until it is double what others might carry. But in the end it crashes down upon us all. You cannot escape this life without being drenched and sometimes drowned by it.

Buck Kemmer once told me that he did not weep when his young wife died. There was Susan to tend to, her living and therefore his own to provide for. But now that burden, blessing though it was, had been lifted from him. All responsibilities had been dispatched. And the last sound I heard from him was the sound of his weeping, the sudden and violent release of a strong man's tears locked away in a house for the dead.

As for Poe and myself, we passed our final moments together in Pittsburgh by gazing toward the rising sun, still but a dull wet glow in the dull metal sky. His bag was at his side. Mine sat between my feet. I had managed to recover it from the police but only through Poe's intervention; the High Constable, despite the fact that we had identified for him the murderer of the seven girls and Susan's murderer as well, was not pleased that I had managed to escape from his jail, and threatened to incarcerate me again as punishment for this indignity. Poe then announced that as my foster father he would be very grateful if this were not to happen, so grateful, in fact, that he might even refrain from employing his pen in a recounting of this whole sad episode, this tawdry tale of depravity in a city that hoped to grow and prosper, and of how the police had been outwitted at every turn, bested by a mere poet and dockworker, their magnificent new jail bested by a mere boy, who, by the way, was himself a fine journalist and more than capable of retelling the tale himself.

In the end my bag was returned to me, empty but for my clothes and the sketch Poe had made. We tried then to recover my money from the police, my life savings, but of course they insisted that no money had been found on my person or in my bag, and no amount of innuendo could convince them to change that story. The High Constable's patience soon wore thin and he suggested that our business in Pittsburgh was complete and perhaps we had better be on our way now, back to wherever it was we called home. Home, he said, was where people would forgive you the trouble you caused. Where they might overlook your peculiar ways and let you live your life in peace. So good luck to us both, and Godspeed.

Next morning, Poe and I stood alone on Ferguson Street, not far from where it was crossed by the railroad tracks on which he would soon travel north to the Pennsylvania Pike, then eastward by coach.

"We rode into this city on a raft of coffins," he said. "We should have taken it for a sign, and turned away without a second glance."

It saddened me to see him leaving Pittsburgh in this manner, without fanfare, no throng of well-wishers to see him off. He was on his way back to New York City, there to try to pick up the pieces, if any remained, of his career. He looked little stronger, hardly more fit for the battle than when I had found him in Philadelphia. I might have suggested, I suppose, that I accompany him for a while. But I did not. Nor did he. He knew, we both knew, that we were on our own from this point on.

He asked, "Have you decided yet where you will go?"

I pondered that for a moment, a gutter rat once again, my pockets home to but a sheet of folded paper, blank, a stub of pencil, a tiny black feather, and the five dollars Poe had insisted I borrow from him. "Not yet," I answered.

"Will you promise me this, at least? That you will not choose Mexico?"

I failed to respond quickly enough to reassure him. He said, "The walls of Vera Cruz fell seven days ago. Mexico City is next. The fighting is all but finished."

"Just as well," I finally said. "I believe I've had enough of carnage for a while."

He nodded. And offered me a father's hand. Some

forty yards behind us, a steam whistle blew. Yet still he did not release me.

"I cannot help but think . . . ," he said, but let the sentence die unfinished. His gaze slowly slid from horizon to ground.

Then, "I am a weak man, Augie. I'm sorry for that. Were it not for my behavior at the reception . . . were it not for my gullibility . . ."

He waited, I suppose, to be absolved by me. But how could I absolve another when so rife with guilt myself?

The whistle blew a second time, a short blast and a longer one. He lifted his eyes to mine. "Write to Muddy when you can."

I nodded. We stood like that awhile longer, each seeing his own reflection in the other's eyes. His hand tightened around mine. "There is no end to the misery of this world, is there, son?"

Was I falling away from him, beginning to swoon? Is that why his hand gripped so tightly?

"No end," he said. "No end."

Then suddenly, abruptly, he pulled his hand free. He snatched up his bag, made a quarter turn, squared his shoulders, and marched away.

I remained where I stood a good while longer, watched the train heading north, looked for him in the windows of the cars, but saw only strangers.

Afterward I faced east again. The sun was brighter now, fully half above the horizon. But not bright enough to draw me into it, to pull me east.

Then north. The Great Lakes. The frozen land beyond. They did not call me either.

The west? Back through the buckeyes? No. The child in me was buried there.

And so I slept that night on the wide Ohio, on a sidewheeler called the *Brilliance*. And as I slept to the churning wheel's thrum I dreamed that I stood at the steamboat's stern, gazing upriver into the trembling yellow light of a late afternoon. Buck came walking quietly across the deck to join me there.

Several minutes passed before he spoke. "Do you think ill of me?" he asked.

I told him that I was weary of bitterness, too tired for anger, too empty for remorse. "Besides," I said, "I would have done the same."

He clapped a hand against my back, but it carried no weight. "I was thinking I might ride along with you now. Could they use a man like me down there?"

"You're used to the docks. It's mostly desert, from what I hear."

"They can't use a man with a weak mind and a strong back? A mule's a handy thing to have no matter where you are."

I shrugged. "War will probably be over before I get that far."

"In that case we'll just have to start another one!"

He laughed, but when the laughter faded out, he too was gone.

I clutched the rail and leaned against it. In my hands and in my feet I could feel the hum and movement of the water, the slow tumble through gravity of every drop of river on its relentless migration to the sea. And I was reminded then of Poe's heretical notion, now not so strange at all, that gravity is the call of the Particle Divine, the summons home to every drop and dim small wink of life.

And whether it was the faint vibration of this movement of river and flesh and stars that finally loosened my heart, or whether it was only the surging flood of sorrow in a dream, whatever it was, I took from my pocket a small black feather, and touched it to my lips. And then, with arm outstretched beyond the rail, I opened my palm up to the fading yellow light, tight fist unfurled, and I set the feather free.